By Mary Norton

THE BORROWERS
THE BORROWERS AFIELD
THE BORROWERS AFLOAT
THE BORROWERS ALOFT
THE BORROWERS AVENGED
BED-KNOB AND BROOMSTICK
POOR STAINLESS
ARE ALL THE GIANTS DEAD?

THE
BORROWERS AFLOAT

Mary Norton

ILLUSTRATED BY BETH AND JOE KRUSH

sandpiper

Houghton Mifflin Harcourt

BOSTON NEW YORK

www.hmhbooks.com

The Library of Congress has cataloged the hardcover edition as follows:
Norton, Mary.
The Borrowers afloat /Mary Norton; illustrated by Beth and Joe Krush.
p. cm.
Sequel to: The Borrowers afield.
Summary: The Borrowers, a family of miniature people, journey down a drain,
live briefly in a teakettle, and are swept away in a flood before finding a new home.
[1. Fantasy.] I. Krush, Beth, ill. II. Krush, Joe, ill. III. Title
PZ7.N8248Bl   1986
[Fic]   86-4613

ISBN: 978-0-15-210345-3 hardcover
ISBN: 978-0-15-204733-7 paperback

Printed in the United States of America
DOC 20 19 18 17 16 15 14 13
4500404114

For Peter and Caroline

THE BORROWERS AFLOAT

Chapter One

"But what do they talk about?" asked Mr. Beguid, the lawyer. He spoke almost irritably, as of foolish goings-on.

"They talk about the borrowers," said Mrs. May.

They stood beneath the shelter of the hedge among wet, treelike cabbages, which tumbled in the wind. Below them on this dark, dank afternoon, a lamp glowed warmly through the cottage window. "We could have an orchard here," she added lightly, as though to change the subject.

"At our time of life," remarked Mr. Beguid, gazing still at the lighted window below them in the hollow, "yours and mine—it's wiser to plant flowers than fruit . . ."

"You think so?" said Mrs. May. She drew her ulster cape about her against the eddying wind. "But I'll leave her the cottage, you see, in my will."

"Leave whom the cottage?"

"Kate, my niece."

"I see," said Mr. Beguid, and he glanced again toward the lighted window behind which he knew Kate was sitting: a strange child, he thought; disconcerting—the way she gazed through one with wide unseeing eyes and yet would chatter by the hour with old Tom Goodenough, a rascally one-time gamekeeper. What could they have in common, he asked himself, this sly old man and eager, listening child? There they had been now (he glanced at his watch) for a good hour and a quarter, hunched by the window, talking, talking . . .

"Borrowers . . ." he repeated, as though troubled by the word. "What kind of borrowers?"

"Oh, it's just a story," said Mrs. May lightly, picking her way amongst the rain-drenched cabbages toward the raised brick path, "something we used to tell each other, my brother and I, when we stayed down here as children."

"At Firbank Hall, you mean?"

"Yes, with Great-Aunt Sophy. Kate loves this story."

"But why," asked Mr. Beguid, "should she want to tell it to him?"

"To old Tom? Why not? As a matter of fact, I believe it's the other way round: I believe he tells it to her."

As he followed Mrs. May along the worn brick path, Mr. Beguid became silent. He had known this family most of his life, and a strange lot (he had begun to think lately) they were.

"But a story made up by you?"

"Not by me, no—" Mrs. May laughed as though embarrassed. "It was my brother, I think, who made it up. If it was made up," she added suddenly, just above her breath.

Mr. Beguid pounced on the words. "I don't quite follow you. This story you speak of, is it something that actually happened?"

Mrs. May laughed. "Oh no, it couldn't have actually happened. Not possibly." She began to walk on again, adding over her shoulder, "It's just that this old man, this old Tom Goodenough, seems to know about these people."

"What people? These cadgers?"

"Not cadgers—borrowers . . ."

"I see," said Mr. Beguid, who didn't see at all.

"We called them that," and turning on the path, she waited for him to catch up with her. "Or rather they called themselves that—because they had nothing of their own at all. Even their names were borrowed. The family we knew—father, mother, and child—were called Pod, Homily and little Arrietty." As he came beside her, she smiled. "I think their names are rather charming."

"Very," he said, a little too drily. And then, in spite of himself, he smiled back at her. Always, he remembered, there had been in her manner this air of gentle mockery; even as a young man, though attracted by her prettiness, he had found her disconcerting. "You haven't changed," he said.

She at once became more serious. "But you can't deny that it was a strange old house?"

"Old, yes. But no more strange than"—he looked down the slope—"than this cottage, say."

Mrs. May laughed. "Ah, there Kate would agree with you! She finds this cottage quite as strange as we found Firbank, neither more nor less. You know, at Firbank, my brother and I—right from the very first—had this feeling that there were other people living in the house besides the human beings."

"But—" exclaimed Mr. Beguid, exasperated, "there can be no such thing as 'people' other than human beings. The terms are synonymous."

"Other personalities, then. Something far smaller than a human being but like them in essentials—a little larger-seeming in the head, perhaps, a little longer in the hands and feet. But very small and hidden. We imagined that they lived like mice—in the wainscots, or behind the skirtings, or under the floorboards—and were entirely dependent on what they could filch from the great house above. Yet you couldn't call it stealing: it was more a kind of garnering. On the whole, they only took things that could well be spared."

"What sort of things?" asked Mr. Beguid. Suddenly feeling foolish, he sprang ahead of her to clear a trail of bramble from her path.

"Oh, all sorts of things. Any kind of food, of course, and any other small movable objects which might be useful—matchboxes, pencil ends, needles, bits of stuff—anything they could turn into tools or clothes or furniture. It

14

was rather sad for them, we thought, because they had a sort of longing for beauty and for making their dark little holes as charming and comfortable as the homes of human beings. My brother used to help them"—Mrs. May hesitated suddenly as though embarrassed—"or so he said," she concluded lamely, and she gave a little laugh.

"I see," said Mr. Beguid again. He became silent as they skirted the side of the cottage to avoid the dripping thatch. "And where does Tom Goodenough come in?" he asked at last as she paused beside the water butt.

She turned to face him. "Well, it's extraordinary, isn't it? At my age—nearly seventy—to inherit this cottage and find him still here in possession?"

"Not in possession, exactly—he's the outgoing tenant."

"I mean," said Mrs. May, "to find him here at all. In the old days, when they were boys, he and my brother used to go rabbiting—in a way they were great companions. But that all ended—after the rumpus."

"Oh," said Mr. Beguid, "so there was a rumpus?" They stood together by the weatherworn front door, and intrigued against his wish, he withdrew his hand from the latch.

"There most certainly was," exclaimed Mrs. May. "I should have thought you might have heard about it. Even the policeman was implicated—you remember Ernie Runacre? It must have gone all over the village. The cook and the gardener got wind of these creatures and determined to smoke them out. They got in the local ratcatcher and sent up here for Tom to bring his ferret. He was a boy then, the gamekeeper's grandson—a little older than we were, but still quite young. But"—Mrs. May turned suddenly toward him—"you *must* have heard something of this?"

Mr. Beguid frowned. Past rumors stirred vaguely in his memory . . . some nonsense or other at Firbank Hall; a cook with a name like Diver or Driver; things missing from the cabinet in the drawing room . . .

"Wasn't there"—he said at last—"some trouble about an emerald watch?"

"Yes, that's why they sent for the police."

"But"—Mr. Beguid's frown deepened—"this woman, Diver or—"

"Driver! Yes, that was the name."

"And this gardener—you mean to say they believed in these creatures?"

"Obviously," said Mrs. May, "or they would not have made all this fuss."

"What happened?" asked Mr. Beguid. "Did they catch them? No, no—I don't mean that! What I meant to say is—what did they turn out to be? Mice, I suppose?"

"I wasn't there myself at the time—so I can't say 'what they turned out to be.' But according to my brother, they escaped out of doors through a grating just in the nick of time: one of those ventilator things set low down in the brickwork outside. They ran away across the orchard and"—she looked around her in the half light—"up into these fields."

"Were they seen to go?"

"No," said Mrs. May.

Mr. Beguid glanced swiftly down the mist-enshrouded slopes. Against the pallid fields the woods beyond looked dark—already wrapped in twilight.

"Squirrels," he said, "that's what they were, most likely."

"Possibly," said Mrs. May. She moved away from him to where, beside the washhouse, the workmen that morning had opened up a drain. "Wouldn't this be wide enough to take sewage?"

"Wide enough, yes," said Mr. Beguid, "but the sanitary inspector would never allow it: all these drains flow into the stream. No, you'll have to have a septic tank, I'm afraid."

"Then what was this used for?"

He nodded toward the washhouse. "The overflow from the sink." He glanced at his watch. "Could I give you a lift anywhere? It's getting rather late . . ."

"That's very kind of you," said Mrs. May as they moved toward the front door.

"An odd story," remarked Mr. Beguid, putting his hand to the latch.

"Yes, very odd."

"I mean—to go to the lengths of sending for the police. Extraordinary."

"Yes," agreed Mrs. May, and paused to wipe her feet on a piece of torn sacking that lay beside the step.

Mr. Beguid glanced at his own shoes and followed her example. "Your brother must have been very convincing."

"Yes, he was."

"And very inventive."

"Yes, according to my brother there was quite a colony of these people. He talked about another lot, cousins of the ones at Firbank, who were supposed to live in a badger's set—up here on the edge of these woods. Uncle Hendreary and Aunt Lupy . . ." She looked at him sideways. "This lot had four children."

"According to your brother," remarked Mr. Beguid, as he reached again for the latch.

"And according to old Tom—" She laughed and lowered her voice. "Old Tom swears that the story is true. But *he* contends that they did not live in the badger's set at all; or that, if they did, it could not have been for long. He insists that for years and years they lived up here, in the lath and plaster beside the fireplace."

"Which fireplace?" asked Mr. Beguid uneasily.

"This fireplace," said Mrs. May. As the door swung open, she dropped her voice to a whisper. "Here in this very cottage."

"Here in this very cottage . . ." repeated Mr. Beguid

in a startled voice, and standing aside for Mrs. May to pass, he craned his neck forward to peer within, without advancing across the threshold.

The quiet room seemed empty: all they could see at first was yellow lamplight spilling across the flagstones and dying embers in the grate. By the window stood a stack of hazel wands, split and trimmed for thatching, beyond them a wooden armchair. Then Kate emerged rather suddenly from the shadows beside the fireplace. "Hullo," she said.

She seemed about to say more, but her gaze slid past Mrs. May to where Mr. Beguid hovered in the doorway. "I was looking up the chimney," she explained.

"So I see—your face is black!"

"Is it?" said Kate, without interest. Her eyes looked very bright and she seemed to be waiting—either, thought Mrs. May, for Mr. Beguid to shut the door and come in or for Mr. Beguid to shut the door and depart.

Mrs. May glanced at the empty armchair and then past Kate toward the door of the washhouse. "Where's Tom?"

"Gone out to feed the pig," said Kate. Again she hesitated, then, in a burst, she added, "Need we go yet? It's only a step across the fields, and there's something I terribly want to show you—"

Mr. Beguid glanced at his watch. "Well, in that case—" he began.

"Yes, please don't wait for us," interrupted Mrs. May

impulsively. "As Kate says, it's only a step . . ."

"I was only going to say," continued Mr. Beguid stolidly from his neutral position on the threshold, "that as this lane's so narrow and the ditches so full of mud, I propose to drive on ahead and turn the car at the crossroads." He began to button up his overcoat. "Perhaps you would listen for the horn?"

"Yes, yes, indeed. Thank you . . . of course. We'll be listening . . ."

When the front door had closed and Mr. Beguid had gone, Kate took Mrs. May by the hand and drew her urgently toward the fireplace. "And I've heaps to tell you. Heaps and heaps . . ."

"We weren't rude, were we?" asked Mrs. May. "I mean to Mr. Beguid? We didn't shoo him off?"

"No, no, of course not. You thanked him beautifully. But look—" Kate went on. "Please look!" Loosing Mrs. May's hand, she ran forward and—with much tugging and panting—dragged out the log box from where it was jammed against the wall beside the hearth. A rat hole was revealed in the skirting—slightly Gothic in shape. "That's where they lived—" cried Kate.

Mrs. May, in spite of herself, felt a curious sense of shock; staring down at it, she said uneasily, "We mustn't be too credulous, Kate. I mean, we can't believe *quite* everything we hear. And you know what they say about old Tom?"

"In the village? Yes, I know what they say—'the big-

gest liar in five counties.' But all that started *because* of the
borrowers. At first, you see, he used to talk about them.
And that was his mistake. He thought people would be
interested. But they weren't interested—not at all: they
just didn't believe him." Kate knelt down on the hearth,
and breathing rather heavily, she peered into the darkness of the hole. "There was only one other human being, I think, who really believed in the borrowers. . . ."

"Mrs. Driver, you mean, the cook at Firbank?"

Kate frowned, sitting back on her heels. "No, I don't
really think that Mrs. Driver *did* believe in them. She saw
them, I know, but I don't think she trusted her eyes. No,
the one I was thinking of was Mild Eye, the gypsy. I
mean, he actually shook them out of his boot onto the
floor of his caravan. And there they were—right under

his nose—and no two ways about it. He tried to grab them, Tom says, but they got away. He wanted to put them in a cage and show them for pennies at the fair. It was Tom who rescued them. With the help of Spiller, of course."

"Who was Spiller?" asked Mrs. May—she still stared, as though spellbound, at the rat hole. Kate seemed amazed. "You haven't heard of Spiller?"

"No," said Mrs. May.

"Oh," cried Kate, throwing her head back and half closing her eyes, "Spiller was wonderful!"

"I am sure he was," said Mrs. May. She pulled forward a rush-seated chair and rather stiffly sat down on it. "But you and Tom have been talking for days, remember. . . . I'm a little out of touch. What was Spiller supposed to be —a borrower?"

"He *was* a borrower," corrected Kate, "but rather on the wild side—he lived in the hedgerows, and wore old moleskins, and didn't really wash. . . ."

"He doesn't sound so *tremendously* wonderful."

"Oh, but he was: Spiller ran for Tom and Tom rushed down and rescued them; he snatched them up from under the gypsies' noses and pushed them into his pockets; he brought them up here—all four of them—Spiller, Pod, Homily, and Arrietty. And he set them down very carefully, one by one"—Kate patted the warm flagstones— "here, on this very spot. And then, poor things, they ran away into the wall through that rat hole in the skirting"

—Kate lowered her head again, trying to peer in—"and up a tiny ladder just inside to where the cousins were living. . . ." She scrambled up suddenly and, stretching one arm as far as it would go, she tapped on the plaster beside the chimney. "The cousins' house was somewhere up here. Quite high. Two floors they had—between the lath and plaster of the washhouse wall and the lath and plaster of this one. They used the chimney, Tom says, and they tapped the washhouse pipes for water. Arrietty didn't like it up there: she used to creep down in the evenings and talk to young Tom. But our lot did not stay there long. Something happened, you see—"

"Tell me," said Mrs. May.

"Well, there isn't really time now. Mr. Beguid will start hooting. . . . And old Tom's the one to tell it: he seems to know everything—even what they said and did when no one else was there. . . ."

"He's a born storyteller, that's why," said Mrs. May, laughing. "And he knows people. Given a struggle for life, people react very much alike—according to type, of course—whatever their size or station." Mrs. May leaned forward as though to examine the skirting. "Even I," she said, "can imagine what Homily felt, homeless and destitute, faced with that dusty hole. . . . And strange relations living up above who didn't know she was coming and whom she hadn't seen for years . . ."

Chapter Two

But Mrs. May was not quite right: she had underestimated their sudden sense of security—the natural joy a borrower feels when safely under cover. It is true that, as they filed in through the Gothic-shaped hole in the skirting, they had felt a little nervous, a little forlorn; this was because, at first glance, the cavelike space about them seemed disappointingly uninhabited: empty, dark and echoing, it smelled of dust and mice. . . .

"Oh, dear," Homily had muttered incredulously, "they can't live here!" But as her eyes became used to the dimness, she had stooped suddenly to pick up some object from the floor. "My goodness," she whispered excitedly to Pod, "do you know what this is?"

"Yes," Pod had told her. "It's a bit of quill pipe-cleaner. Put it down, Homily, and come on, do. Spiller's waiting."

"It's the spout of our old oak-apple teapot," Homily had persisted. "I'd know it anywhere and it's no good telling me any different. So they *are* here . . ." she mused wonderingly as she followed Pod into the shadows, ". . .

and from somewhere, somehow, they've got hold of some of our things."

"We go up here," said Spiller, and Homily saw that he stood with his hand on a ladder. Glancing up to where the rungs soared away above them into dimness, she gave a slight shudder. The ladder was made of matchsticks, neatly glued and spliced to two lengths of split cane such as florists use to support potted plants.

"I'll go first," said Pod. "We better take it one at a time."

Homily watched fearfully until she heard his voice from above.

"It's all right," he whispered from some invisible eyrie. "Come on up."

Homily followed, her knees trembling, and emerged at last onto the dim-lit platform beside Pod—an aerial landing stage, that was what it seemed like—which creaked a little when she stepped on it and almost seemed to sway. Below lay hollow darkness, ahead an open door. "Oh, my goodness," she muttered, "I do hope it's safe. . . . Don't look down," she advised Arrietty, who came up next.

But Arrietty had no temptation to look down: her eyes were on the lighted doorway and the moving shadows within; she heard the faint sound of voices and a sudden high-pitched laugh.

"Come on," said Spiller, slipping past and making toward the door.

Arrietty never forgot her first sight of that upstairs room: the warmth, the sudden cleanliness, the winking candlelight, and the smell of home-cooked food.

And so many voices . . . so many people . . .

Gradually, in a dazed way, she began to sort them out. That must be Aunt Lupy embracing her mother—Aunt Lupy so round and glowing, her mother so smudged and lean. Why did they cling and weep, she wondered, and squeeze each other's hands? They had never liked each other—all the world knew that. Homily had thought Lupy stuck-up because, back in the big house, Lupy had lived in the drawing room and (she had heard it rumored) changed for dinner at night. And Lupy despised Homily for living under the kitchen and for pronouncing parquet "parkett."

And here was Uncle Hendreary, his beard grown thinner, telling her father that this could not be Arrietty, and her father, with pride, telling Uncle Hendreary it could. Those must be the three boy cousins—whose names she had not caught—graduated in size but as like as peas in a pod. And this thin, tall, fairylike creature, neither old nor young, who hovered shyly in the background with a faint uneasy smile, who was she? Could it be Eggletina? Yes, she supposed it could.

And there was something strangely unreal about the room—furnished with dollhouse furniture of every shape and size, none of it matching or in proportion. There were chairs upholstered in rep or velvet, some of them too

26

small to sit in and some too steep and large; there were chiffoniers that were too tall and occasional tables far too low; and a toy fireplace with colored plaster coals and its fire irons stuck down all-of-a-piece with the fender; there were two make-believe windows with curved pelmets and red satin curtains, each hand-painted with an imitation view—one looked out on a Swiss mountain scene, the other on a Highland glen ("Eggletina did them," Aunt Lupy boasted in her rich society voice. "We're going to have a third when we get the curtains—a view of Lake Como from Monte S. Primo"); there were table lamps and standard lamps, flounced, festooned, and tasseled, but the light in the room, Arrietty noticed, came from humble dips like those they had made at home.

Everybody looked extraordinarily clean, and Arrietty became even shier. She threw a quick glance at her father and mother and was not reassured: none of their clothes had been washed for weeks nor, for some days, had their hands and faces. Pod's trousers had a tear in one knee and Homily's hair hung down in snakes. And here was Aunt Lupy, plump and polite, begging Homily please to take off her things in the kind of voice, Arrietty imagined, usually reserved for feather boas, opera cloaks, and freshly cleaned kid gloves.

"Poor dear Lupy," Homily was saying, glancing wearily about, "what a lot of furniture! Whoever helps you with the dusting?" And swaying a little, she sank on a chair.

They rushed to support her, as she hoped they might. Water was brought and they bathed her face and hands. Hendreary stood with the tears in his brotherly eyes. "Poor valiant soul," he muttered, shaking his head. "Your mind kind of reels when you think of what she's been through. . . ."

Then, after a quick wash and brush up all round and a brisk bit of eye-wiping, they all sat down to supper. This they ate in the kitchen, which was rather a comedown except that, in here, the fire was real: a splendid cooking-range made of a large, black door-lock; they poked the fire through the keyhole, which glowed handsomely, and the smoke, they were told, went out through a series of pipes to the cottage chimney behind.

The long, white table was richly spread: it was an eighteenth-century finger-plate off some old drawing-room door—white-enameled and painted with forget-me-nots—supported firmly on four stout pencil stubs where once the screws had been; the points of the pencils emerged slightly through the top of the table; one was copying ink, and they were warned not to touch it in case it stained their hands.

There was every kind of dish and preserve—both real and false; pies, puddings, and bottled fruits out of season —all cooked by Lupy, and an imitation leg of mutton and a dish of plaster tarts borrowed from the dollhouse. There were three real tumblers as well as acorn cups and a couple of green glass decanters.

Talk, talk, talk. . . . Arrietty, listening, felt dazed. "Where is Spiller?" she asked suddenly.

"Oh, he's gone off," said Hendreary vaguely. He seemed a little embarrassed and sat there frowning and tapping the table with a pewter spoon (one of a set of six, Homily remembered angrily; she wondered how many were left).

"Gone off where?" asked Arrietty.

"Home, I reckon," Hendreary told her.

"But we haven't thanked him," cried Arrietty. "Spiller saved our lives!"

Hendreary threw off his gloom. "Have a drop of blackberry cordial," he suggested suddenly to Pod. "Lupy's own make. Cheer us all up. . . ."

"Not for me," said Homily firmly, before Pod could speak. "No good never comes of it, as we've found out to our cost."

"We haven't even thanked him," persisted Arrietty, and there were tears in her eyes.

Hendreary looked at her, surprised. "Spiller? He don't hold with thanks. He's all right . . ." and he patted Arrietty's arm.

"Why didn't he stay for supper?"

"He don't ever," Hendreary told her. "Doesn't like company. He'll cook something on his own."

"Where?"

"In his stove."

"But that's miles away!"

"Not for Spiller—he's used to it. Goes part way by water."

"And it must be getting dark," Arrietty went on unhappily.

"Now don't you fret about Spiller," her uncle told her. "You eat up your pie. . . ."

Arrietty looked down at her plate (pink celluloid, it was, part of a tea service that she seemed to remember); somehow she had no appetite. She raised her eyes. "And when will he be back?" she asked anxiously.

"He don't come back much. Once a year for his new clothes. Or if young Tom sends 'im special."

Arrietty looked thoughtful. "He must be lonely," she ventured at last.

"Spiller? No, I wouldn't say he was lonely. Some borrowers is made like that. Solitary. You get 'em now and again." He glanced across the room to where his daughter, having left the table, was sitting alone by the fire. "Eggletina's a bit like that. . . . Pity, but you can't do nothing about it. Them's the ones as gets this craze for humans—kind of man-eaters, they turns out to be. . . ."

Very dark it was, this strange new home, almost as dark as under the floorboards at Firbank, and lit by wax dips fixed to upturned drawing pins (how many human dwellings must be burned down, Arrietty realized suddenly, through the carelessness of borrowers running about with lighted candles). In spite of Lupy's polishings, the compartments smelled of soot and always in the background a pervading odor of cheese.

The cousins all slept in the kitchen—for warmth, Lupy explained. The ornate drawing room was only rarely used. Outside the drawing room was the shadowed platform with its perilous matchstick ladder leading down below.

Above this landing, high among the shadows, were the two small rooms allotted them by Lupy. There was no way up to them as yet, except by climbing hand over hand from lath to lath and scrabbling blindly for footholds, to emerge at length on a rough piece of flooring made by Hendreary from the lid of a cardboard shoe box.

"Do those rooms good to be used," Lupy had said (she knew Pod was a handyman), "and we'll lend you furniture to start with."

"To start with," muttered Homily that first morning as, foot after hand, she followed Pod up the laths. Unlike most borrowers, she was not very fond of climbing. "What are we meant to do after?"

She dared not look down. Beneath her, she knew, was the rickety platform below which again were further depths and the matchstick ladder gleaming like a fishbone. "Anyway," she comforted herself, feeling clumsily for footholds, "steep it may be, but at least it's a separate entrance. . . . What's it like, Pod?" she asked as her head emerged suddenly at floor level through the circular trap door—very startling it looked, as though decapitated.

"It's dry," said Pod, noncommittally; he stamped about a bit on the floor as though to test it.

"Don't stamp so, Pod," Homily complained, seeking a foothold on the quivering surface. "It's only cardboard."

"I know," said Pod. "Mustn't grumble," he added as Homily came toward him.

"At least," said Homily, looking about her, "back home under the kitchen, we was on solid ground. . . ."

"You've lived in a boot since," Pod reminded her, "and you've lived in a hole in a bank. And nearly starved. And nearly frozen. And nearly been captured by the gypsies. Mustn't grumble," he said again.

Homily looked about her. Two rooms? They were barely that: a sheet of cardboard between two sets of laths, divided by a cloth-covered book cover, on which the words "Pig Breeders' Annual, 1896" were stamped in tarnished gold. In this dark purple wall, Hendreary had cut a door. Ceilings there were none, and an eerie light came down from somewhere far above—a crack, Homily supposed, between the floorboards and the whitewashed walls of the gamekeeper's bedroom.

"Who sleeps up there," she asked Pod. "That boy's father?"

"Grandfather," said Pod.

"He'll be after us, I shouldn't wonder," said Homily, "with traps and what-not."

"Yes, you've got to be quiet," said Pod, "especially

with gamekeepers. Out most of the day, though, and the young boy with him. Yes, it's dry," he repeated, looking about him, "and warm."

"Not very," said Homily. As she followed him through the doorway, she saw that the door was hung by the canvas binding that Hendreary had not cut through. "Soon fray, that will," she remarked, swinging the panel to and fro, "and then what?"

"I can stitch it," said Pod, "with me cobbler's thread. Easy." He laid his hands on the great stones of the farther wall. " 'Tis the chimney casing," he explained. "Warm, eh?"

"Um," said Homily, "if you lean against it."

"What about if we sleep here—right against the chimney?"

"What in?" asked Homily.

"They're going to lend us beds."

"No, better keep the chimney for cooking." Homily ran her hands across the stones and from a vertical crevice began to pick out the plaster. "Soon get through here to the main flue. . . ."

"But we're going to eat downstairs with them," Pod explained. "That's what's been arranged—so that it's all one cooking."

"All one cooking and all one borrowing," said Homily. "There won't be no borrowing for you, Pod."

"Rubbish," said Pod. "Whatever makes you say a thing like that?"

"Because," explained Homily, "in a cottage like this with only two human beings, a man and a boy, there aren't the pickings there were back at Firbank. You mark my words: I been talking to Lupy. Hendreary and the two elder boys can manage the lot. They won't be wanting competition."

"Then what'll I do?" said Pod. A borrower deprived of borrowing—especially a borrower of Pod's standing? His eyes became round and blank.

"Get on with the furniture, I suppose."

"But they're going to lend us that."

"Lend us!" hissed Homily. "Everything they've got was ours!"

"Now, Homily—" began Pod.

Homily dropped her voice, speaking in a breathless whisper. "Every single blessed thing. That red velvet chair, the dresser with the painted plates, all that stuff the boy brought us from the dollhouse . . ."

"Not the keyhole stove," put in Pod, "not that dining table they've made from a doorplate. Not the—"

"The imitation leg of mutton, that was ours," interrupted Homily, "and the dish of plaster tarts. All the beds were ours, and the sofa. And the palm in a pot. . . . *And* they got your hatpin, over behind the stove. Been poking the fire with it most likely. I wouldn't put it past them. . . ."

"Now listen, Homily," pleaded Pod, "we've been into all that, remember. I'll take back the hatpin—that I will

35

take—but findings keepings, as they say. Far as they knew we was dead and gone—like as we might be lost at sea. The things all came to them in a plain white pillowcase delivered to the door. See what I mean? It's like as if they was left them in a will."

"I would never have left anything to Lupy," remarked Homily.

"Now, Homily, you've got to say they've been kind."

"Yes," agreed Homily, "you've got to say it."

Unhappily she gazed about her. The cardboard floor was scattered with lumps of fallen plaster. Absent-mindedly she began to push these toward the gaps where the floor, being straight-edged, did not fit against the rough plaster. They clattered hollowly down the hidden shaft into Lupy's kitchen.

"Now you've done it," said Pod. "And that's the kind of noise we mustn't make, not if we value our lives. To human beings," he went on, "droppings and rollings means rats or squirrels. You know that as well as I do."

"Sorry," said Homily.

"Wait a minute," said Pod. He had been gazing upwards toward the crack of light, and now in a flash he was on the laths and climbing up toward it.

"Careful, Pod," whispered Homily. He seemed to be pulling at some object that was hidden from Homily by the line of his body. She heard him grunting with the effort.

"It's all right," said Pod in his normal voice, beginning

36

to climb down again. "There isn't no one up there. Here you are," he went on as he landed on the floor and handed her an old bone toothbrush, slightly taller than herself. "The first borrowing," he announced modestly, and she saw that he was pleased. "Someone must have dropped it up there in the bedroom, and it wedged itself in this crack between the floorboards and the wall. We can borrow from up there," he went on, "easy; the wall's fallen away like or the floorboards have shrunk. Farther along it gets even wider. . . . And here you are again," he said and handed her a fair-sized cockleshell he had pulled out from the rough plaster. "You go on sweeping," he told her, "and I'll pop up again, might as well, while it's free of human beings. . . ."

"Now, Pod, go careful . . ." Homily urged him, with a mixture of pride and anxiety. She watched him climb the laths and watched him disappear before, using the cockleshell as a dustpan, she began to sweep the floor. When Arrietty arrived to tell them a meal was ready, a fair-sized haul was laid out on the floor; the bottom of a china soap dish for baths, a crocheted table mat in red and yellow that would do as a carpet, a worn sliver of pale green soap with gray veins in it, a large darning needle—slightly rusted—three aspirin tablets, a packet of pipe cleaners, and a fair length of tarred string.

"I'm kind of hungry," said Pod.

Chapter Three

They climbed down the laths onto the platform, keeping well away from the edge, through Lupy's drawing room, into the kitchen.

"Ah, here you are," cried Lupy, in her loud, rich, aunt-like voice—very plump she looked in her dress of purple silk, and flushed from the heat of the stove. Homily, beside her, looked as thin and angular as a clothes peg. "We were just going to start without you."

The doorplate table was lit by a single lamp; it was made from a silver salt shaker with a hole in the top, out of which protruded a wick. The flame burned stilly in that airless room, and the porcelain table top, icily white, swam in a sea of shadow.

Eggletina, by the stove, was ladling out soup, which Timmus, the younger boy, unsteadily carried round in yellow snail shells—very pretty they looked, scoured and polished. They were rather alike—Eggletina and Timmus—Arrietty thought, quiet and pale and watchful-seeming.

Hendreary and the two elder boys were already seated, tucking into their food.

"Get up, get up," cried Lupy archly, "when your aunt comes in," and her two elder sons rose reluctantly and quickly sat down again. "Harpsichord manners . . ." their expressions seemed to say. They were too young to remember those gracious days in the drawing room of the big house—the Madeira cake, little sips of China tea, and music of an evening. Churlish and shy, they hardly ever spoke. "They don't much like us," Arrietty decided as she took her place at the table. Little Timmus, his hands in a cloth, brought her a shell of soup. The thin shell was piping hot, and she found it hard to hold.

It was a plain meal, but wholesome: soup, and boiled butter beans with a trace of dripping—one bean each. There was none of that first evening's lavishness when Lupy had raided her store cupboards. It was as though she and Hendreary had talked things over, setting more modest standards. "We must begin," she had imagined Lupy saying to Hendreary in a firm, self-righteous voice, "as we mean to go on."

There was, however, a sparrow's egg omelette, fried in a tin lid, for Hendreary and the two boys. Lupy saw to it herself. Seasoned with thyme and a trace of wild garlic, it smelled very savory and sizzled on the plate. "They've been borrowing, you see," Lupy explained, "out of doors all morning. They can only get out when the front door's

open, and on some days they can't get back. Three nights Hendreary spent once in the woodshed before he got his chance."

Homily glanced at Pod, who had finished his bean and whose eyes had become strangely round. "Pod's done a bit, too, this morning," she remarked carelessly, "more high than far; but it does give you an appetite. . . ."

"Borrowing?" asked Uncle Hendreary. He seemed amazed, and his thin beard had ceased the up-and-down movement that went with his eating.

"One or two things," said Pod modestly.

"From where?" asked Hendreary, staring.

"The old man's bedroom. It's just above us. . . ."

Hendreary was silent a moment and then he said, "That's all right, Pod," but as though it wasn't all right at all. "But we've got to go steady. There isn't much in this house, not to spare like. We can't all go at it like bulls at gates." He took another mouthful of omelette and consumed it slowly while Arrietty, fascinated, watched his beard and the shadow it threw on the wall. When he had swallowed, he said, "I'd take it as a favor, Pod, if you'd just leave borrowing for a while. We know the territory, as you might say, and we work to our own methods. Better we lend you things, for the time being. And there's food for all, if you don't mind it plain."

There was a long silence. The two elder boys, Arrietty noticed, shoveling up their food, kept their eyes on their plates. Lupy clattered about at the stove. Eggletina sat looking at her hands, and little Timmus stared wonderingly from one to another, eyes wide in his small pale face.

"As you wish," said Pod slowly, as Lupy bustled back to the table.

"Homily," said Lupy brightly, breaking the awkward silence, "this afternoon, if you've got a moment to spare, I'd be much obliged if you'd give me a hand with Spiller's summer clothes. . . ."

Homily thought of the comfortless rooms upstairs and of all she longed to do to them. "But of course," she told Lupy, trying to smile.

"I always get them finished," Lupy explained, "by early spring. Time's getting on now: the hawthorn's out—or so they tell me." And she began to clear the table; they all jumped up to help her.

"Where *is* Spiller?" asked Homily, trying to stack the snail shells.

"Goodness knows," said Lupy, "off on some wild goose chase. No one knows where Spiller is. Nor what he does for that matter. All I know is," she went on, taking the plug out of the pipe (as they used to do at home Arrietty remembered) to release a trickle of water, "that I make his moleskin suits each autumn and his white kid ones each spring and that he always comes to fetch them."

"It's very kind of you to make his suits," said Arrietty, watching Lupy rinse the snail shells in a small crystal salt cellar and standing by to dry them.

"It's only human," said Lupy.

"Human!" exclaimed Homily, startled by the choice of word.

"Human—just short like that—means kind," explained Lupy, remembering that Homily, poor dear, had had no education, being dragged up as you might say under a kitchen floor. "It's got nothing at all to do with human beings. How could it have?"

"That's what I was wondering . . ." said Homily.

"Besides," Lupy went on, "he brings us things in exchange."

"Oh, I see," said Homily.

"He goes hunting, you see, and I smoke his meat for him—there in the chimney. Some we keep and some he takes away. What's over I make into paste with butter on the top—keeps for months that way. Birds' eggs, he brings, and berries and nuts . . . fish from the stream. I smoke the fish, too, or pickle it. Some things I put down in salt. . . . And if you want anything special, you tell Spiller—ahead of time, of course—and he borrows it from the gypsies. That old stove he lives in is just by their camping site. Give him time and he can get almost anything you want from the gypsies. We have a whole arm of a waterproof raincoat, got by Spiller, and very useful it was when the bees swarmed one summer—we all crawled inside it."

"What bees?" asked Homily.

"Haven't I told you about the bees in the thatch?

43

They've gone now. But that's how we got the honey, all we'd ever want, and a good, lasting wax for the candles. . . ."

Homily was silent a moment—enviously silent, dazzled by Lupy's riches. Then she said, as she stacked up the last snail shell, "Where do these go, Lupy?"

"Into that wickerwork hair-tidy in the corner. They won't break—just take them on the tin lid and drop them in. . . ."

"I must say, Lupy," Homily remarked wonderingly as she dropped the shells one by one into the hair-tidy (it was horn-shaped with a loop to hang it on and a faded blue bow on the top), "that you've become what I'd call a very good manager. . . ."

"For one," agreed Lupy, laughing, "who was brought up in a drawing room and never raised a hand."

"You weren't *brought up* in a drawing room," Homily reminded her.

"Oh, I don't remember those Rain-pipe days," said Lupy blithely. "I married so young. Just a child . . ." and she turned suddenly to Arrietty. "Now, what are you dreaming about, Miss-butter-wouldn't-melt-in-her-mouth?"

"I was thinking of Spiller," said Arrietty.

"A-ha!" cried Aunt Lupy. "She was thinking of Spiller!" And she laughed again. "You don't want to waste precious thoughts on a ragamuffin like Spiller. You'll meet lots of nice borrowers, all in good time. Maybe, one day, you'll meet one brought up in a library: they're the best, so they say, gentlemen all, and a good cultural background."

"I was thinking," continued Arrietty evenly, trying to keep her temper, "that I couldn't imagine Spiller dressed up in white kid."

"It doesn't stay white long," cried Lupy. "Of that I can assure you! It has to be white to start with because it's made from an evening glove. A ball glove, shoulder length—it's one of the few things I salvaged from the drawing room. But he will have kid, says it's hard-wearing. It stiffens up, of course, directly he gets it wet, but he soon wears it soft again. And by that time," she added, "it's all colors of the rainbow."

Arrietty could imagine the colors; they would not be "all colors of the rainbow"; they would be colors without real color, the shades that made Spiller invisible—soft fawns, pale browns, dull greens, and a kind of shadowy gun-metal. Spiller took care about "seasoning" his clothes: he brought them to a stage where he could melt into the landscape, where one could stand beside him, almost within touching distance, and yet not see him. Spiller deceived animals as well as gypsies. Spiller deceived hawks, and stoats, and foxes. . . . Spiller might not wash but he had no Spiller scent: he smelled of hedgerows, and bark, and grasses, and of wet sun-warmed earth; he smelled of buttercups, dried cow dung, and early morning dew. . . .

"When will he come?" Arrietty asked, but ran away upstairs before anyone could tell her. She wept a little in the upstairs room, crouched beside the soap dish.

To talk of Spiller reminded her of out-of-doors and of a wild, free life she might never know again. This new-found haven among the lath and plaster had all too soon become another prison. . . .

Chapter Four

It was Hendreary and the boys who carried the furniture up the laths with Pod standing by to receive it. In this way, Lupy lent them just what she wished to lend and nothing they would have chosen. Homily did not grumble, however. She had become very quiet lately as slowly she realized their position.

Sometimes they stayed downstairs after meals, helping generally or talking to Lupy. But they gauged the length of these visits according to Lupy's mood: when she became flustered, blaming them for some small mishap brought on by herself, they knew it was time to go. "We couldn't do right today," they would say, sitting empty-handed upstairs on Homily's old champagne corks that Lupy had unearthed for stools. They would sit by the chimney casing in the inner room to get the heat from the stones. Here Pod and Homily had a double bed, one of those from the dollhouse. Arrietty slept in the outer room, close beside the entrance hole. She slept on a thickish piece of wadding, borrowed in the old days from a box of artist's pastels, and they had given her most of the bedclothes.

"We shouldn't have come, Pod," Homily said one evening as they sat alone upstairs.

"We had no choice," said Pod.

"And we got to go," she added and sat there watching him as he stitched the sole of a boot.

"To where?" asked Pod.

Things had become a little better for Pod lately: he had filed down the rusted needle and was back at his cobbling. Hendreary had brought him the skin of a weasel, one of those nailed up by the gamekeeper to dry on the outhouse door, and he was making them all new shoes. This pleased Lupy very much, and she had become a little less bossy.

"Where's Arrietty?" asked Homily one evening.

"Downstairs, I shouldn't wonder," said Pod.

"What does she do downstairs?"

"Tells Timmus a story and puts him to bed."

"I know that," said Homily, "but why does she stay so long? I'd nearly dropped off last night when we heard her come up the laths. . . ."

"I suppose they get talking," said Pod.

Homily was silent a moment and then she said, "I don't feel easy. I've got my feeling. . . ." This was the feeling borrowers get when human beings are near; with Homily it started at the knees.

Pod glanced up toward the floorboards above them

from whence came a haze of candlelight. "It's the old man going to bed."

"No," said Homily, getting up. "I'm used to that. We hear that every night." She began to walk about. "I think," she said at last, "that I'll just pop downstairs. . . ."

"What for?" asked Pod.

"To see if she's there."

"It's late," said Pod.

"All the more reason," said Homily.

"Where else would she be?" asked Pod.

"I don't know, Pod. I've got my feeling and I've had it once or twice lately," she said.

Homily had grown more used to the laths: she had become more agile, even in the dark. But tonight it was very dark indeed. When she reached the landing below, she felt a sense of yawning space and a kind of draft from the depth, which eddied hollowly around her: feeling her way to the drawing-room door, she kept well back from the edge of the platform.

The drawing room, too, was strangely dark and so was the kitchen beyond: there was a faint glow from the keyhole fire and a rhythmic sound of breathing.

"Arrietty?" she called softly from the doorway, just above a whisper.

Hendreary gave a snort and mumbled in his sleep: she heard him turning over.

"Arrietty . . ." whispered Homily again.

"What's that?" cried Lupy, suddenly and sharply.

"It's me . . . Homily."

"What do you want? We were all asleep. Hendreary's had a hard day. . . ."

"Nothing," faltered Homily, "it's all right. I was looking for Arrietty. . . ."

"Arrietty went upstairs hours ago," said Lupy.

"Oh," said Homily, and was silent a moment: the air was full of breathing. "All right," she said at last, "thank you . . . I'm sorry . . ."

"And shut the drawing-room door onto the landing as you go out. There's a howling draft," said Lupy.

As she felt her way back across the cluttered room, Homily saw a faint light ahead, a dim reflection from the landing. Could it come from above, she wondered, where Pod, two rooms away, was stitching? Yet it had not been there before. . . .

Fearfully she stepped out on the platform. The glow, she realized, did not come from above but from somewhere far below. The matchstick ladder was still in place, and she saw the top rungs quiver. After a moment's pause she summoned up the courage to peer over. Her startled eyes met those of Arrietty, who was climbing up the ladder and had nearly reached the top. Far below Homily could see the Gothic shape of the hole in the skirting: it seemed a blaze of light.

"Arrietty!" she gasped.

Arrietty did not speak. She climbed off the last rung of

the ladder, put her finger to her lips, and whispered. "I've got to draw it up. Move back." And Homily, as though in a trance, moved out of the way as Arrietty drew the ladder up rung over rung until it teetered above her into the darkness, and then, trembling a little with the effort, she eased it along and laid it against the laths.

"Well—" began Homily in a sort of gasp. In the half-light from below they could see each other's faces: Homily's aghast with her mouth hanging open; Arrietty's grave, her finger to her lips. "One minute," she whispered and went back to the edge. "All right," she called out softly into the space beneath; Homily heard a muffled thud, a scraping sound, the clap of wood on wood, and light below went out.

"He's pushed back the log box," Arrietty whispered across the sudden darkness. "Here, give me your hand. . . . Don't worry," she beseeched in a whisper, "and don't take on! I was going to tell you anyway." And supporting her shaking mother by the elbow, she helped her up the laths.

Pod looked up startled. "What's the matter?" he said as Homily sank down on the bed.

"Let me get her feet up first," said Arrietty. She did so gently and covered her mother's legs with a folded silk handkerchief, yellowed with washing and stained with marking ink, which Lupy had given them for a bedcover.

Homily lay with her eyes closed and spoke through pale lips. "She's been at it again," she said.

"At what?" asked Pod. He had laid down his boot and had risen to his feet.

"Talking to humans," said Homily.

Pod moved across and sat on the end of the bed. Homily opened her eyes. They both stared at Arrietty.

"Which ones?" asked Pod.

"Young Tom, of course," said Homily. "I caught her in the act. That's where she's been most evenings, I shouldn't wonder. Downstairs, they think she's up, and upstairs, we think she's down."

"Well, you know where that gets us," said Pod. He became very grave. "That, my girl, back at Firbank was the start of all our troubles."

"Talking to humans . . ." moaned Homily, and a quiver passed over her face. Suddenly she sat up on one elbow and glared at Arrietty. "You wicked, thoughtless girl, how *could* you do it again!"

Arrietty stared back at them, not defiantly exactly, but as though she were unimpressed. "But with this one downstairs," she protested, "I can't see why it matters. He knows we're here anyway, because he put us here himself! He could get at us any minute if he really wanted to. . . ."

"How could he get at us," said Homily, "right up here?"

"By breaking down the wall; it's only plaster."

"Don't say such things, Arrietty," shuddered Homily.

"But they're true," said Arrietty. "Anyway," she added, "he's going."

"Going?" said Pod sharply.

"They're both going," said Arrietty, "he and his grandfather; the grandfather's going to a place called Hospital, and the boy is going to a place called Leighton Buzzard to stay with his uncle who is an ostler. What's an ostler?" she asked.

But neither of her parents replied: they were staring blankly, struck dumb by a sudden thought.

"We've got to tell Hendreary," said Pod at last, "and quickly."

Homily nodded. She had swung her legs down from the bed.

"No good waking them now," said Pod. "I'll go down first thing in the morning."

"Oh, my goodness," breathed Homily, "all those poor children . . ."

"What's the matter?" asked Arrietty. "What have I said?" She felt scared suddenly and gazed uncertainly from one parent to the other.

"Arrietty," said Pod, turning toward her. His face had become very grave. "All we've told you about human beings is true; but what we haven't told you, or haven't stressed enough, is that we, the borrowers, cannot survive without them." He drew a long deep breath. "When they close up a house and go away, it usually means we're done for. . . ."

"No food, no fire, no clothes, no heat, no water . . ." chanted Homily, almost as though she were quoting.

"Famine . . ." said Pod.

Chapter Five

Next morning, when Hendreary heard the news, a conference was called around the doorplate. They all filed in, nervous and grave, and places were allotted them by Lupy. Arrietty was questioned again.

"Are you sure of your dates, Arrietty?"

Yes, Arrietty was sure.

"And of your facts?" Quite sure. Young Tom and his grandfather would leave in three days' time in a gig drawn by a gray pony called Duchess and driven by Tom's uncle, the ostler, whose name was Fred Tarabody and who lived in Leighton Buzzard and worked at the Swan Hotel— what was an ostler she wondered again—and young Tom was worried because he had lost his ferret although it had a bell round its neck and a collar with his name on. He had lost it two days ago down a rabbit hole and was afraid he might have to leave without it, and even if he found it, he wasn't sure they would let him take it with him.

"That's neither there nor here," said Hendreary, drumming his fingers on the table.

They all seemed very anxious and at the same time curiously calm.

Hendreary glanced round the table. "One, two, three, four, five, six, seven, eight, nine," he said gloomily and began to stroke his beard.

"Pod, here," said Homily, "can help borrow."

"And I could, too," put in Arrietty.

"And I could," echoed Timmus in a sudden squeaky voice. They all turned round to look at him, except Hendreary, and Lupy stroked his hair.

"Borrow *what?*" asked Hendreary. "No, it isn't borrowers we want; on the contrary"—he glanced across the table, and Homily, meeting his eye, suddenly turned pink—"it's something left to borrow. They won't leave a crumb behind, those two, not if I know 'em. We'll have to live, from now on, on just what we've saved. . . ."

"For as long as it lasts," said Lupy grimly.

"For as long as it lasts," repeated Hendreary, "and such as it is." All their eyes grew wider.

"Which it won't do forever," said Lupy. She glanced up at her store shelves and quickly away again. She too had become rather red.

"About borrowing . . ." ventured Homily. "I was meaning out-of-doors . . . the vegetable patch . . . beans and peas . . . and suchlike."

"The birds will have them," said Hendreary, "with this house closed and the human beings gone. The birds always know in a trice. . . . And what's more," he went on, "there's more wild things and vermin in these woods than in all the rest of the county put together . . . weasels, stoats, foxes, badgers, shrikes, magpies, sparrow hawks, crows. . . ."

"That's enough, Hendreary," Pod put in quickly. "Homily's feeling faint. . . ."

"It's all right . . ." murmured Homily. She took a sip of water out of the acorn cup, and staring down at the table, she rested her head on her hand.

Hendreary, carried away by the length of his list, seemed not to notice. ". . . owls and buzzards," he concluded in a satisfied voice. "You've seen the skins for yourselves nailed up on the outhouse door, and the birds strung up on a thornbush, gamekeeper's gibbet they call it. He keeps them down all right, when he's well and about. And the boy, too, takes a hand. But with them two gone—!" Hendreary raised his gaunt arms and cast his eyes toward the ceiling.

No one spoke. Arrietty stoke a look at Timmus, whose face had become very pale.

"And when the house is closed and shuttered," Hendreary went on again suddenly, "how do you propose to get out?" He looked round the table triumphantly as one who had made a point. Homily, her head on her hand, was silent. She had begun to regret having spoken.

"There's always ways," murmured Pod.

Hendreary pounced on him. "Such as?" When Pod did not reply at once, Hendreary thundered on, "The last

time they went away we had a plague of field mice . . . the whole house awash with them, upstairs and down. Now when they lock up, they lock up proper. Not so much as a spider could get in!"

"Nor out," said Lupy, nodding.

"Nor out," agreed Hendreary, and as though exhausted by his own eloquence, he took a sip from the cup.

For a moment or two no one spoke. Then Pod cleared his throat. "They won't be gone forever," he said.

Hendreary shrugged his shoulders. "Who knows?"

"Looks to me," said Pod, "that they'll always need a

gamekeeper. Say this one goes, another moves in like. Won't be empty long—a good house like this on the edge of the coverts, with water laid on in the washhouse. . . ."

"Who knows?" said Hendreary again.

"Your problem, as I see it," went on Pod, "is to hold out over a period."

"That's it," agreed Hendreary.

"But you don't know for how long; that's your problem."

"That's it," agreed Hendreary.

"The farther you can stretch your food," Pod elaborated, "the longer you'll be able to wait. . . ."

"Stands to reason," said Lupy.

"And," Pod went on, "the fewer mouths you have to feed, the farther the food will stretch."

"That's right," agreed Hendreary.

"Now," went on Pod, "say there are six of you . . ."

"Nine," said Hendreary, looking round the table, "to be exact."

"You don't count us," said Pod. "Homily, Arrietty, and me—we're moving out." There was a stunned silence round the table as Pod, very calm, turned to Homily. "That's right, isn't it?" he asked her.

Homily stared back at him as though he were crazy, and, in despair, he nudged her with his foot. At that she swallowed hastily and began to nod her head. "That's right . . ." she managed to stammer, blinking her eyelids.

Then pandemonium broke out: questions, suggestions, protestations, and arguments. . . . "You don't know what you're saying, Pod," Hendreary kept repeating, and Lupy kept on asking, "Moving out where to?"

"No good being hasty, Pod," Hendreary said at last. "The choice of course is yours. But we're all in this together, and for as long as it lasts"—he glanced around the table as though putting the words on record—"and such as it is, what is ours is yours."

"That's very kind of you, Hendreary," said Pod.

"Not at all," said Hendreary, speaking rather too smoothly, "it stands to reason."

"It's only human," put in Lupy: she was very fond of this word.

"But," went on Hendreary, as Pod remained silent, "I see you've made up your mind."

"That's right," said Pod.

"In which case," said Hendreary, "there's nothing we can do but adjourn the meeting and wish you all good luck!"

"That's right," said Pod.

"Good luck, Pod," said Hendreary.

"Thanks, Hendreary," said Pod.

"And to all three valiant souls—Pod, Homily, and little Arrietty—good luck and good borrowing!"

Homily murmured something and then there was silence: an awkward silence while eyes avoided eyes. "Come on, me old girl," said Pod at last, and turning to Homily, he helped her to her feet. "If you'll excuse us," he said to Lupy, who had become rather red in the face again, "we got one or two plans to discuss."

They all rose, and Hendreary, looking worried, followed Pod to the door. "When do you think of leaving, Pod?"

"In a day or two's time," said Pod, "when the coast's clear down below."

"No hurry, you know," said Hendreary. "And any tackle you want—"

"Thanks," said Pod.

". . . just say the word."

"I will," said Pod. He gave a half-smile, rather shy, and went on through the door.

Chapter Six

Homily went up the laths without speaking; she went straight to the inner room and sat down on the bed. She sat there shivering slightly and staring at her hands.

"I had to say it," said Pod, "and we have to do it, what's more."

Homily nodded.

"You see how we're placed?" said Pod.

Homily nodded again.

"Any suggestions?" said Pod. "Anything else we could do?"

"No," said Homily, "we've got to go. And what's more," she added, "we'd have had to anyway."

"How do you make that out?" said Pod.

"I wouldn't stay here with Lupy," declared Homily, "not if she bribed me with molten gold, which she isn't likely to. I kept quiet, Pod, for the child's sake. A bit of young company, I thought, and a family background. I even kept quiet about the furniture. . . ."

"Yes, you did," said Pod.

"It's only—" said Homily, and again she began to shiver, "that he went on so about the vermin. . . ."

"Yes, he did go on," said Pod.

"Better a place of our own," said Homily.

"Yes," agreed Pod, "better a place of our own. . . ." But he gazed round the room in a hunted kind of way, and his flat round face looked blank.

When Arrietty arrived upstairs with Timmus, she looked both scared and elated.

"Oh," said Homily, "here you are." And she stared rather blankly at Timmus.

"He would come," Arrietty told her, holding him tight by the hand.

"Well, take him along to your room. And tell him a story or something. . . ."

"All right. I will in a minute. But, first, I just wanted to ask you—"

"Later," said Pod, "there'll be plenty of time: we'll talk about everything later."

"That's right," said Homily. "You tell Timmus a story."

"Not about owls?" pleaded Timmus; he still looked rather wide-eyed.

"No," agreed Homily, "not about owls. You ask her to tell you about the dollhouse"—she glanced at Arrietty —"or that other place—what's it called now?—that place with the plaster borrowers?"

But Arrietty seemed not to be listening. "You did mean it, didn't you?" she burst out suddenly.

Homily and Pod stared back at her, startled by her tone. "Of course, we meant it," said Pod.

"Oh," cried Arrietty, "thank goodness . . . thank goodness," and her eyes filled suddenly with tears. "To be out of doors again . . . to see the sun, to . . ." Running forward, she embraced them each in turn. "It will be all right—I know it will!" Aglow with relief and joy, she turned back to Timmus. "Come, Timmus, I know a lovely story—better than the dollhouse—about a whole town of houses: a place called Little Fordham. . . ."

This place, of recent years, had become a kind of legend to borrowers. How they got to know it no one could remember—perhaps a conversation overheard in some kitchen and corroborated later through dining room or nursery—but know of it they did. Little Fordham, it appeared, was a complete model village. Solidly built, it stood out of doors in all weather in the garden of the man who had designed it, and it covered half an acre. It had a church, with organ music laid on, a school, a row of shops, and—because it lay by a stream—its own port, shipping and custom houses. It was inhabited—or so they had heard—by a race of plaster figures, borrower-size, who stood about in frozen positions, or who, wooden-faced and hopeless, traveled interminably in trains. They also knew that from early morning until dusk troops of human beings wound around and about it, removed on asphalt paths and safely enclosed by chains. They knew—as the birds knew—that these human beings would drop litter —sandwich crusts, nuts, buns, half-eaten apples, ("Not that you can live on that sort of stuff," Homily would remark. "I mean, you'd want a change. . . .") But what fascinated them most about the place was the number of empty houses—houses to suit every taste and every size of family: detached, semidetached, stuck together in a row, or standing comfortably each in its separate garden —houses that were solidly built and solidly roofed, set firmly in the ground, and that no human being, however curious, could carelessly wrench open—as they could with dollhouses—and poke about inside. In fact, as Arrietty had heard, doors and windows were one with the structure—there were no kinds of openings at all. But this was a drawback easily remedied. "Not that they'd open up the front doors—" she explained in whispers to Timmus as they lay curled up on Arrietty's bed. "Borrowers wouldn't be so silly: they'd burrow through the soft earth and get in underneath . . . and no human being would know they were there."

"Go on about the trains," whispered Timmus.

And Arrietty went on, and on—explaining and inventing, creating another kind of life. Deep in this world she forgot the present crisis, her parents' worries and her un-

cle's fears, she forgot the dusty drabness of the rooms between the laths, the hidden dangers of the woods outside
and that already she was feeling rather hungry.

Chapter Seven

"But where are we going to?" asked Homily for about the twentieth time. It was two days later, and they were up in Arrietty's room sorting things for the journey, discarding and selecting from oddments spread round on the floor. They could only take—Pod had been very firm about this—what Lupy described as hand luggage. She had given them for this purpose the rubberized sleeve of the waterproof raincoat, which they had neatly cut up into squares.

"I thought," said Pod, "we'd try first to make for that hole in the bank. . . ."

"I don't think I'd relish that hole in the bank," said Homily. "Not without the boot."

"Now, Homily, we've got to go somewhere . . . and it's getting on for spring."

Homily turned and looked at him. "Do you know the way?"

"No," said Pod and went on folding the length of tarred string. "We've got to ask."

"What's the weather like now?" asked Homily.

"That's one of the things," said Pod, "I've told Arrietty to find out."

With some misgivings, but in a spirit of "needs must," they had sent her down the matchstick ladder to interview young Tom. "You've got to ask him to leave us some loophole," Pod had instructed her, "no matter how small, so long as we can get out of doors. If need be, we can undo the luggage and pass the pieces through one by one. If the worst came to the worst, I wouldn't say no to a ground-floor window and something below to break the drop. But like as not, they'll latch those tight and shutter them across. And tell him to leave the wood box well pulled out from the skirting. None of us can move it, not even when it's empty. A nice pickle we'd be in, and all the Hendrearys too, if he trundles off to Leighton Buzzard and leaves us shut in the wall. And tell him where we're making for—that field called Perkin's Beck—but don't tell him nothing about the hole in the bank—and get him to give you a few landmarks, something to put us on our way. It's been a bit chilly indoors lately, for March: ask him if there's snow. If there's snow, we're done: we've got to wait. . . ."

But could they wait, he wondered now as he hung the coil of tarred string on a nail in the lath and thoughtfully took up his hatpin. Hendreary had said in a burst of generosity, "We're all in this together." But Lupy had remarked afterwards, discussing their departure with Homily, "I don't want to seem hard, Homily, but in times like these, it's each one for his own. And in our place you'd say the same." She had been very kind about giving them things —the mackintosh sleeve was a case in point—but the store shelves, they noticed, were suddenly bare: all the food had been whisked away and hidden out of sight, and Lupy had doled out fifteen dried peas that she had said she hoped would "last them." These they kept upstairs, soaking in the soap dish, and Homily would take them down three at a time to boil them on Lupy's stove.

To "last them" for how long, Pod wondered now, as he rubbed a speck of rust off his hatpin. Good as new, he thought, as he tested the point, pure steel and longer than he was. No, they would have to get off, he realized, the minute the coast was clear, snow or no snow. . . .

"Here's someone now," exclaimed Homily. "It must be Arrietty." They went to the hole and helped her onto the floor. The child looked pleased, they noticed, and flushed with the heat of the fire. In one hand she carried a long steel nail, in the other a sliver of cheese. "We can eat this now," she said excitedly. "There's a lot more downstairs: he pushed it through the hole behind the log box. There's a slice of dry bread, some more cheese, six roasted chestnuts, and an egg."

"Not a hen's egg?" said Pod.

"Yes."

"Oh, my," exclaimed Homily, "how are we going to get it up the laths?"

"And how are we going to cook it?" asked Pod.

Homily tossed her head. "I'll boil it with the peas on Lupy's stove. It's our egg; no one can say a word."

"It's boiled already," Arrietty told them, "hard boiled."

"Thank goodness for that," exclaimed Pod. "I'll take down the razor blade—we can bring it up in slices. What's the news?" he asked Arrietty.

"Well, the weather's not bad at all," she said. "Spring-like, he says, when the sun's out, and pretty warm."

"Never mind that," said Pod. "What about the loop-hole?"

"That's all right too. There's a worn-out place at the bottom of the door—the front door—where feet have been kicking it open, like Tom does when his arms are full of sticks. It's shaped like an arch. But they've nailed a piece of wood across it now to keep the field mice out. Two nails it's got, one on either side. This is one of them;

young Tom pulled it out," and she showed them the nail she had brought. "Now all we've got to do, he says, is to swing the bit of wood up on the other nail and prop it safely, and we can all go through—underneath. After we've gone, Hendreary and the cousins can knock it in again, that is if they want to."

"Good," said Pod. "Good." He seemed very pleased. "They'll want to all right, because of the field mice. And when did he say they were leaving, him and his grandpa, I mean?"

"What he said before: the day after tomorrow. But he hasn't found his ferret."

"Good," said Pod again. He wasn't interested in ferrets. "And now we'd better nip down quick and get that food up the laths, or someone might see it first."

Homily and Arrietty climbed down with him to lend a hand. They brought up the bread and cheese and the roasted chestnuts, but the egg they decided to leave. "There's a lot of good food in a hen's egg," Pod pointed out, "and it's all wrapped up already, as you might say, clean and neat in its shell. We'll take that egg along with us and we'll take it just as it is." So, they rolled the egg along inside the wainscot to a shadowy corner in which they had seen shavings. "It can wait for us there," said Pod.

Chapter Eight

On the day the human beings moved out, the borrowers kept very quiet. Sitting round the doorplate table, they listened to the bangings, the bumpings, the runnings up and downstairs with interest and anxiety. They heard voices they had not heard before and sounds that they could not put a name to. They went on keeping quiet . . . long after the final bang of the front door had echoed into silence.

"You never know," Hendreary whispered to Pod. "They might come back for something." But after a while the emptiness of the house below seemed to steal in upon them, seeping mysteriously through the lath and plaster— and it seemed to Pod a final kind of emptiness. "I think it's all right now," he ventured at last. "Suppose one of us went down to reconnoitre?"

"I'll go," said Hendreary, rising to his feet. "None of you move until I give the word. I want the air clear for sound. . . ."

They sat in silence while he was gone. Homily stared

at their three modest bundles lying by the door, strapped by Pod to his hatpin. Lupy had lent Homily a little moleskin jacket—for which Lupy had grown too stout. Arrietty wore a scarf of Eggletina's; the tall, willowy creature had placed it round her neck, wound it three times about, but had said not a word. "Doesn't she ever speak?" Homily had asked once, on a day when she and Lupy had been more friendly. "Hardly ever," Lupy had admitted, "and never smiles. She's been like that for years, ever since that time when as a child she ran away from home. . . ."

After a while Hendreary returned and confirmed that the coast was clear. "But better light your dips; it's later than I thought. . . ."

One after another they scrambled down the matchstick ladder, careless now of noise. The wood box had been pulled well back from the hole, and they flowed out into the room—cathedral-high, it seemed to them, vast and still and echoing, but suddenly all their own. They could do anything, go anywhere. The main window was shuttered as Pod had foreseen, but a smaller, cell-like window, sunk low and deep in the wall, let in a last pale reflection of the sunset. The younger cousins and Arrietty went quite wild, running in and out of the shadows among the chair legs, exploring the cavern below the table top, the underside of which, cobweb hung, danced in the light of their dips. Discoveries were made and treasures found —under rugs, down cracks in the floor, between loose hearth stones—here a pin, there a matchstick, a button, an old collar-stud, a blackened farthing, a coral bead, a hook without its eye, and a broken piece of lead from a lead pencil. (Arrietty pounced on this last and pushed it into her pocket; she had had to leave her diary behind, with other nonessentials, but one never knew. . . .) Then dips were set down and everybody started climbing—except Lupy, who was too stout; and Pod and Homily who watched silently, standing beside the door. Hendreary tried an overcoat on a nail for the sake of what he might find in the pockets, but he had not Pod's gift for climbing fabric and had to be rescued by one of his sons from where he hung, perspiring and breathing hard, clinging to a sleeve button.

"He should have gone up by the front buttonholes," Pod whispered to Homily. "You can get your toes in and pull the pocket toward you like by folding in the stuff. You never want to make direct for a pocket. . . ."

"I wish," Homily whispered back, "they'd stop this until we're gone." It was the kind of occasion she would have enjoyed in an ordinary way—a glorious bargain hunt—findings keepings with no holds barred; but the shadow of their ordeal hung over her and made such antics seem foolish.

"Now," exclaimed Hendreary suddenly, straightening his clothes and coming toward them as though he had guessed her thought, "we'd better test out this escape route."

He called up his two elder sons, and together the three

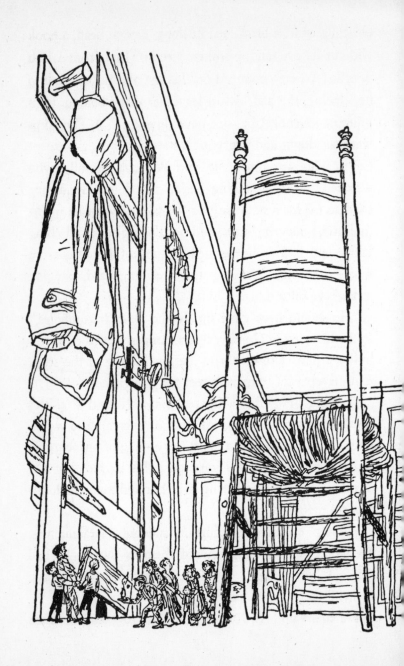

of them, after spitting on their hands, laid hold of the piece of wood that covered the hole in the door.

"One, two, three—hup!" intoned Hendreary, ending on a grunt. They gave a mighty heave and the slab of wood pivoted slowly, squeaking on its one nail, revealing the arch below.

Pod took his dip and peered through. Grass and stones he saw for a moment and some kind of shadowy movement before a draft caught the flame and nearly blew it out. He sheltered the flame with his hand and tried again.

"Quick, Pod," gasped Hendreary, "this wood's heavy. . . ."

Pod peered through again. No grass now, no stones— a rippling blackness, the faintest snuffle of breath, and

two sudden pin points of fire, unblinking and deadly still.

"Drop the wood," breathed Pod—he spoke without moving his lips. "Quick," he added under his breath as Hendreary seemed to hesitate, "can't you hear the bell?" And he stood there as though frozen, holding his dip steadily before him.

Down came the wood with a clap, and Homily screamed. "You saw it?" said Pod, turning. He set down his dip and wiped his brow on his sleeve; he was breathing rather heavily.

"Saw it?" cried Homily. "In another second it would have been in here amongst us."

Timmus began to cry and Arrietty ran to him. "It's all right, Timmus, it's gone now. It was only an old ferret, an old tame ferret. Come, I'll tell you a story." She took him under a rough wooden desk where she had seen an old account book; setting it up on its outer leaves, she made it into a tent. They crept inside, just the two of them, and between the sheltering pages they soon felt very cozy.

"Whatever was it?" cried Lupy, who had missed the whole occurrence.

"Like she said—a ferret," announced Pod. "That boy's ferret I shouldn't wonder. If so, it'll be all round the house from now on seeking a way to get in. . . ." He turned to Homily. "There'll be no leaving here tonight."

Lupy, standing in the hearth where the ashes were still warm, sat down suddenly on an empty matchbox that gave an ominous crack. ". . . nearly in amongst us," she repeated faintly, closing her eyes against the ghastly vision. A faint cloud of wood ash rose slowly around her, which she fanned away with her hand.

"Well, Pod," said Hendreary after a pause, "that's that."

"How do you mean?" said Pod.

"You can't go that way. That ferret'll be round the house for weeks. . . ."

"Yes . . ." said Pod, and was silent a moment. "We'll have to think again." He gazed in a worried way at the shuttered window; the smaller one was a wall aperture, glazed to give light but with the glass built in—no possibility there.

"Let's have a look at the washhouse," he said. This door luckily had been left ajar, and, dip in hand, he slid through the crack. Hendreary and Homily slid through after him, and after a while Arrietty followed. Filled with curiosity, she longed to see the washhouse, as she longed to see every corner of this vast human edifice now that they had it to themselves. The chimney she saw, in the flickering light of the dip, stood back to back with the one in the living room; in it there stood a dingy cooking stove. Flagstones covered the floor. An old mangle stood in one corner, in the other a copper for boiling clothes. Against the wall, below the window, towered a stone sink. The window above the sink was heavily shuttered and rather high. The door, which led outside, was bolted in two places and had a zinc panel across the bottom, reinforcing the wood.

"Nothing doing here," said Hendreary.

"No," agreed Pod.

They went back to the living room. Lupy had recovered somewhat and had risen from the matchbox, leaving it slightly askew. She had brushed herself down and was packing up the borrowings preparatory to going upstairs. "Come along, chicks," she called to her children. "It's nearly midnight and we'll have all day tomorrow. . . ." When she saw Hendreary, she said, "I thought we might go up now and have a bite of supper." She gave a little laugh. "I'm a wee bit tired—what with ferrets and so on and so forth."

Hendreary looked at Pod. "What about you?" he said, and as Pod hesitated, Hendreary turned to Lupy. "They've had a hard day too—what with ferrets and so on and so forth—and they can't leave here tonight. . . ."

"Oh?" said Lupy, and stared. She seemed slightly taken aback.

"What have we got for supper?" Hendreary asked her.

"Six boiled chestnuts"—she hesitated—"and a smoked minnow each for you and the boys."

"Well, perhaps we could open something," suggested Hendreary after a moment. Again Lupy hesitated, and the pause became too long. "Why, of course—" she began in a flustered voice, but Homily interrupted.

"Thank you very much. It's very kind of you, but

we've got three roast chestnuts ourselves . . . and an egg."

"An egg," echoed Lupy, amazed. "What kind of an egg?"

"A hen's egg . . ."

"A *hen's* egg," echoed Lupy again, as though a hen were a pterodactyl or a fabulous bird like the phoenix. "Wherever did you get it?"

"Oh," said Homily, "it's just an egg we had."

"And we'd like to stay down here a bit," put in Pod, "if that's all right with you."

"Quite all right," said Lupy stiffly. She still looked amazed about the egg. "Come, Timmus."

It took some minutes to round them all up. There was a lot of running back for things, chatter at the foot of the ladder, callings, scoldings, giggles, and "take-cares." "One at a time," Lupy kept saying, "one at a time, my lambs." But at last they were all up and their voices became more muffled as they left the echoing landing for the inner rooms beyond. Light running sounds were heard, small rollings, and the faintest of distant squeakings.

"How like mice we must sound to humans," Arrietty realized as she listened from below. But after a while even these small patterings ceased and all became quiet and still. Arrietty turned and looked at her parents: at last they were alone.

Chapter Nine

"Between the devil and the deep blue sea, that's us," said Pod with a wan smile. He was quoting from Arrietty's diary and proverb book.

They sat grouped on the hearth where the stones were warm. The iron shovel, still too hot to sit on, lay sprawled across the ashes. Homily had pulled up the crushed matchbox lid on which, with her lighter weight, she could sit comfortably. Pod and Arrietty perched on a charred stick; the three lighted dips were set between them on the ash. Shadows lay about them in the vast confines of the room, and now that the Hendrearys were out of earshot (sitting down to supper most likely), they felt drowned in the spreading silence.

After a while this was broken by the faint tinkle of a bell—quite close it seemed suddenly. There was a slight scratching sound and the lightest, most delicate of snuffles. They all glanced wide-eyed at the door, which, from where they sat, was deeply sunk in shadow.

"It can't get in, can it?" whispered Homily.

"Not a hope," said Pod. "Let it scratch . . . we're all right here."

All the same Arrietty threw a searching glance up the wide chimney; the stones, she thought, if the worst came to the worst, looked uneven enough to climb. Then suddenly, far, far above her, she saw a square of violet sky and in it a single star, and, for some reason, felt reassured.

"As I see it," said Pod, "we can't go and we can't stay."

"And that's how I see it," said Homily.

"Suppose," suggested Arrietty, "we climbed up the chimney onto the thatch?"

"And then what?" said Pod.

"I don't know," said Arrietty.

"There we'd be," said Pod.

"Yes, there we'd be," agreed Homily unhappily, "even supposing we could climb a chimney, which I doubt."

There was a few moments' silence, then Pod said solemnly, "Homily, there's nothing else for it . . ."

". . . but what?" asked Homily, raising a startled face. Lit from below, it looked curiously bony and was streaked here and there with ash. And Arrietty, who guessed what was coming, gripped her two hands beneath her knees and stared fixedly down at the shovel, which lay sideways across the hearth.

"But to bury our pride, that's what," said Pod.

"How do you mean?" asked Homily weakly, but she knew quite well what he meant.

"We got to go, quite open-like, to Lupy and Hendreary and ask them to let us stay. . . ."

Homily put her thin hands on either side of her thin face and stared at him dumbly.

"For the child's sake . . ." Pod pointed out gently.

The tragic eyes swiveled round to Arrietty and back again.

"A few dried peas, that's all we'd ask for," went on Pod very gently, "just water to drink and a few dried peas. . . ."

Still Homily did not speak.

"And we'd say they could keep the furniture in trust like," suggested Pod.

Homily stirred at last. "They'd keep the furniture anyway," she said huskily.

"Well, what about it?" asked Pod after a moment, watching her face.

Homily looked round the room in a hunted kind of way, up at the chimney then down at the ashes at their feet. At last she nodded her head. "Should we go up now," she suggested after a moment in a dispirited kind of voice, "while they're all at supper and get it over with?"

"Might as well," said Pod. He stood up and put out a hand to Homily. "Come on, me old girl," he coaxed her. Homily rose slowly and Pod turned to Arrietty, Homily's hand pulled under his arm. Standing beside his wife, he drew himself up to his full six inches. "There's two kinds of courage I know of," he said, "and your mother's got both of 'em; you make a note of that, my girl, when you're writing in your diary. . . ."

But Arrietty was gazing past him into the room; she was staring white-faced into the shadows beyond the log box toward the scullery door.

"Something moved," she whispered.

Pod turned, following the direction of her eyes. "What like?" he asked sharply.

"Something furry . . ."

They all froze. Then Homily, with a cry, ran out from between them. Amazed and aghast, they watched her scramble off the hearth and run with outstretched arms toward the shadows beyond the log box. She seemed to be laughing—or crying—her breath coming in little gasps. ". . . the dear boy, the good boy . . . the blessed creature!"

"It's Spiller!" cried Arrietty on a shout of joy.

She ran forward too, and they dragged him out of the shadows, pulled him onto the hearth and beside the dips, where the light shone warmly on his suit of moleskins, worn now, slightly tattered, and shorter in the leg. His feet were bare and gleaming with black mud. He seemed to have grown heavier and taller. His hair was still as ragged and his pointed face as brown. They did not think to ask him where he had come from; it was enough that he was there. Spiller, it seemed to Arrietty, always materialized out of air and dissolved again as swiftly.

"Oh, Spiller!" gasped Homily, who was not supposed

to like him. "In the nick of time, the very nick of time!" And she sat down on the charred stick, which flew up, the farther end scattering a cloud of ash, and burst into happy tears.

"Nice to see you, Spiller," said Pod, smiling and looking him up and down. "Come for your summer clothes?" Spiller nodded; bright-eyed, he gazed about the room, taking in the bundles strapped to the hatpin, the pulled-out position of the log box, the odd barenesses and rearrangements that signify human departure. But he made no comment. Countrymen, such as Spiller and Pod were, do not rush into explanations; faced with whatever strange evidence, they mind their manners and bide their time. "Well, I happen to know they're not ready," Pod went on. "She's sewn the vest, mind, but she hasn't joined up the trousers. . . ."

Spiller nodded again. His eyes sought out Arrietty who, ashamed of her first outburst, had become suddenly shy and had withdrawn behind the shovel.

"Well," said Pod at last, looking about as though aware suddenly of strangeness in their surroundings, "you find us in a nice sort of pickle. . . ."

"Moving house?" asked Spiller casually.

"In a manner of speaking," said Pod. And as Homily dried her eyes on her apron and began to pin up her hair, he outlined the story to Spiller in a few rather fumbling words. Spiller listened with one eyebrow raised and his mocking v-shaped mouth twisted up at the corners. This was Spiller's famous expression, Arrietty remembered, no matter what you were telling him.

". . . and so," said Pod, shrugging his shoulders, "you see how we're placed?"

Spiller nodded, looking thoughtful.

"Must be pretty hungry now, that ferret," Pod went on, "poor creature. Can't hunt with a bell: the rabbits hear him coming. Gone in a flash the rabbits are. But with our short legs he'd be on us in a trice—bell or no bell. But how did you manage?" Pod asked suddenly.

"The usual," said Spiller.

"What usual?"

Spiller jerked his head toward the washhouse. "The drain, of course," he said.

Chapter Ten

"What drain?" asked Homily, staring.

"The one in the floor," said Spiller, as though she ought to have known. "The sink's no good—got an 's' bend. And they keep the lid on the copper."

"I didn't see any drain in the floor . . ." said Pod.

"It's under the mangle," explained Spiller.

"But—" went on Homily. "I mean, do you always come by the drain?"

"And go," said Spiller.

"Undercover, like," Pod pointed out to Homily. "Doesn't have to bother with the weather."

"Or the woods," said Homily.

"That's right," agreed Spiller. "You don't want to bother with the woods. Not the woods," he repeated thoughtfully.

"Where does the drain come out?" asked Pod.

"Down by the kettle," said Spiller.

"What kettle?"

"His kettle," put in Arrietty excitedly. "That kettle he's got by the stream. . . ."

"That's right," said Spiller.

Pod looked thoughtful. "Do the Hendrearys know this?"

Spiller shook his head. "Never thought to tell them," he said.

Pod was silent a moment and then he said, "Could anyone use this drain?"

"No reason why not," said Spiller. "Where you making for?"

"We don't know yet," said Pod.

Spiller frowned and scratched his knee where the black mud, drying in the warmth of the ash, had turned to a powdery gray. "Ever thought of the town?" he asked.

"Leighton Buzzard?"

"No," exclaimed Spiller scornfully. "Little Fordham."

Had Spiller suggested a trip to the moon, they could not have looked more astonished. Homily's face was a study in disbelief, as though she thought Spiller was romancing. Arrietty became very still; she seemed to be holding her breath. Pod looked ponderously startled.

"So there is such a place?" he said slowly.

"Of course there is such a place," snapped Homily. "Everyone knows that; what they don't know exactly is —*where?* And I doubt if Spiller does either. . . ."

"Two days down the river," said Spiller, "if the stream's running good."

"Oh," said Pod.

"You mean we have to swim for it?" snapped Homily.

"I got a boat," said Spiller.

"Oh, my goodness . . ." murmured Homily, suddenly deflated.

"Big?" asked Pod.

"Fair," said Spiller.

"Could she take passengers?" asked Pod.

"Could do," said Spiller.

"Oh, my goodness . . ." murmured Homily again.

"What's the matter, Homily?" asked Pod.

"Can't see myself in a boat," said Homily. "Not on the water, I can't."

"Well, a boat's not much good on dry land," said Pod. "To get something, you got to risk something—that's how it goes. We got to find somewhere to live."

"There might be something, say, in walking distance," faltered Homily.

"Such as?"

"Well," said Homily unhappily, throwing a quick glance at Spiller, "say, for instance . . . Spiller's kettle."

"Not much accommodation in a kettle," said Pod.

"More than there was in a boot," retorted Homily.

"Now, Homily," said Pod, suddenly firm, "you wouldn't be happy, not for twenty-four hours, in a kettle; and inside a week you'd be on at me night and day to find some kind of craft to get you downstream to Little Fordham. Here you are with the chance of a good home, fresh start, and a free passage, and all you do is go on like a maniac about a drop of clean running water. Now, if it was the drain you objected to—"

Homily turned to Spiller. "What sort of boat?" she asked nervously. "I mean, if I could picture it like . . ."

Spiller thought a moment. "Well," he said, "it's wooden."

"Yes?" said Homily.

Spiller tried again. "Well, it's like . . . you might say it was something like a knife box."

"How much like?" asked Pod.

"Very like," said Spiller.

"In fact," declared Homily triumphantly, "it *is* a knife box?"

Spiller nodded. "That's right," he admitted.

"Flat-bottomed?" asked Pod.

"With divisions, like, for spoons, forks, and so on?" put in Homily.

"That's right," agreed Spiller, replying to both.

"Tarred and waxed at the seams?"

"Waxed," said Spiller.

"Sounds all right to me," said Pod. "What do you say, Homily?" It sounded better to her too, Pod realized, but he saw she was not quite ready to commit herself. He turned again to Spiller. "What do you do for power?"

"Power?"

"Got some kind of sail?"

Spiller shook his head. "Take her downstream, loaded —with a paddle; pole her back upstream in ballast. . . ."

"I see," said Pod. He sounded rather impressed. "You go often to Little Fordham?"

"Pretty regular," said Spiller.

"I see," said Pod again. "Sure you could give us a lift?"

"Call back for you," said Spiller, "at the kettle, say. Got to go upstream to load."

"Load what?" asked Homily bluntly.

"The boat," said Spiller.

"I know that," said Homily, "but with what?"

"Now, Homily," put in Pod, "that's Spiller's business. No concern of ours. Does a bit of trading up and down the river I shouldn't wonder. Mixed cargo, eh, Spiller? Nuts, birds' eggs, meat, minnows . . . that sort of tackle —more or less what he brings Lupy."

"Depends what they're short of," said Spiller.

"They?" exclaimed Homily.

"Now, Homily," Pod admonished her, "Spiller's got his customers. Stands to reason. We're not the only borrowers in the world, remember. Not by a long chalk. . . ."

"But these ones at Little Fordham," Homily pointed out, "they say they're made of plaster?"

"That's right," said Spiller, "painted over. All of a piece . . . except one," he added.

"One live one?" asked Pod.

"That's right," said Spiller.

"Oh, I wouldn't like that," exclaimed Homily, "I wouldn't like that at all: not to be the one live borrower among a lot of dummy waxworks or whatever they call themselves. Get on my nerves that would. . . ."

"They don't bother him," said Spiller. "Leastways not as much, he says, as a whole lot of live ones might."

"Well, that's a nice friendly attitude, I must say," snapped Homily. "Nice kind of welcome we'll get, I can see, when we turn up there unexpected. . . ."

"Plenty of houses," said Spiller, "no sort of need to live close. . . ."

"And he doesn't own the places," Pod reminded her.

"That's true," said Homily.

"What about it, Homily?" said Pod.

"I don't mind," said Homily, "providing we live near the shops . . ."

"There's nothing in the shops," explained Pod in a patient voice, "or so I've heard tell, but bananas and suchlike made of plaster and all stuck down in a lump."

"No, but it sounds nice," said Homily. "Say you were talking to Lupy—"

"But you won't be talking to Lupy," said Pod. "Lupy won't even know we're gone until she wakes up tomorrow morning thinking that she's got to get us breakfast. No, Homily," he went on earnestly, "you don't want to make for shopping centers and all that sort of caper; better some quiet little place down by the water's edge. You won't want to be everlastingly carting water. And, say Spiller comes down pretty regular with a nice bit of cargo, you want somewhere he can tie up and unload. . . . Plenty of time, once we get there, to have a look round and take our pick."

"Take our pick . . ." Suddenly Homily felt the magic of these words: they began to work inside her—champagne bubbles of excitement welling up and up—until, at last, she flung her hands together in a sudden joyful clap. "Oh Pod," she breathed, her eyes brimming, as, startled by the noise, he turned sharply toward her. "Think of it —all those houses . . . We could try them *all* out if we wanted, one after another. What's to prevent us?"

"Common sense," said Pod; he smiled at Arrietty. "What do you say, lass? Shops or water?"

Arrietty cleared her throat. "Down by water," she whispered huskily, her eyes shining and her face tremulous in the dancing light of the dip, "at least to start with. . . ."

There was a short pause. Pod glanced down at his tackle strapped to the hatpin and up at the clock on the wall. "Getting on for half-past one," he said. "Time we had a look at this drain. What do you say, Spiller? Could you spare us a minute? And show us the ropes like?"

"Oh," exclaimed Homily, dismayed, "I thought Spiller was coming with us."

"Now, Homily," explained Pod, "it's a long trek and he's only just arrived; he won't want to go back right away."

"I don't see why not if his clothes aren't ready—that's what you came for, isn't it, Spiller?"

"That and other things," said Pod. "Daresay he's brought a few oddments for Lupy."

"That's all right," said Spiller. "I can tip 'em out on the floor."

"And you will come?" cried Homily.

Spiller nodded. "Might as well."

Even Pod seemed slightly relieved. "That's very civil of you, Spiller," he said, "very civil indeed." He turned to Arrietty. "Now, Arrietty, take a dip and go and fetch the egg."

"Oh, don't let's bother with the egg," said Homily.

Pod gave her a look. "You go and get that egg, Arrietty. Just roll it along in front of you into the washhouse, but be careful with the light near those shavings. Homily, you bring the other two dips and I'll get the tackle. . . ."

Chapter Eleven

As they filed through the crack of the door onto the stone flags of the washhouse, they heard the ferret again. But Homily now felt brave. "Scratch away," she dared it happily, secure in their prospect of escape. But when they stood at last, grouped beneath the mangle and staring down at the drain, her new-found courage ebbed a little and she murmured, "Oh, my goodness. . . ." Very deep and dark and well-like it seemed, sunk below the level of the floor. The square grating that usually covered it lay beside it at an angle, and in the yawning blackness she could see the reflections of their dips. A dank draft quivered round the candle flames, and there was a sour smell of yellow soap, stale disinfectant, and tea leaves.

"What's that at the bottom?" she asked, peering down. "Water?"

"Slime," said Spiller.

"Jellied soap," put in Pod quickly.

"And we've got to wade through that?"

"It isn't deep," said Spiller.

"Not as though this drain was a sewer," said Pod, trying to sound comforting and hearty. "Beats me though," he went on to Spiller, "how you manage to move this grating."

Spiller showed him. Lowering the dip, he pointed out a short length of what looked like brass curtain rod, strong but hollow, perched on a stone at the bottom of the well and leaning against the side. The top of this rod protruded slightly above the mouth of the drain. The grating, when in place, lay loosely on its worn rim of cement. Spiller explained how, by exerting all his strength on the rod from below, he could raise one corner of the grating—as a washerwoman with a prop can raise up a clothesline. He would then slide the base of the prop onto the raised stone in the base of the shaft, thus holding the contraption in place. Spiller would then swing himself up to the mouth of the drain on a piece of twine tied to a rung of the grating. "Only about twice my height," he explained. The twine, Pod gathered, was a fixture. The double twist round the light iron rung was hardly noticeable from above, and the length of the twine, when not in use, hung downwards into the drain. Should Spiller want to remove the grating entirely, as was the case today, after scrambling through the aperture raised by the rod, he would pull the twine after him, fling it around one of the stays of the mangle above his head, and would drag and pull on the end. Sometimes, Spiller explained, the grating slid easily; at other times it stuck on an angle. In which event, Spiller would produce a small but heavy bolt, kept specially for the purpose, which he would wind into the free end of his halyard and, climbing into the girder-like structure at the base of the mangle, would swing himself out on the bolt, which, sinking under his weight, exerted a pull on the grating.

"Very ingenious," said Pod. Dip in hand he went deeper under the mangle, examined the wet twine, pulled on the knots, and finally, as though to test its weight, gave the grating a shove. It slid smoothly on the worn flagstones. "Easier to shove than to lift," he remarked. Arrietty, glancing upwards, saw vast shadows on the washhouse ceiling—moving and melting, advancing and receding—in the flickering light from their dips: great wheels, handles, rollers, shifting spokes . . . as though, she thought, the mangle under which they stood was silently and magically turning. . . .

On the ground, beside the drain, she saw an object she recognized: the lid of an aluminum soapbox, the one in which the summer before last Spiller had spun her down the river, and from which he used to fish. It was packed now with some kind of cargo and covered with a piece of worn hide—possibly a rat skin—strapped over lid and all with lengths of knotted twine. From a hole bored in one end of the rim a second piece of twine protruded. "I pull her up by that," explained Spiller, following the direction of her eyes.

"I see how you get up," said Homily unhappily, peering into the slime, "but it's how you get down that worries me."

"Oh, you just drop," said Spiller. He took hold of the twine as he spoke and began to drag the tin lid away toward the door.

"It's all right, Homily," Pod promised hurriedly, "we'll let you down on the bolt," and he turned quickly to Spiller. "Where you going with that?" he asked.

Spiller, it seemed, not wishing to draw attention to the drain, was going to unpack next door. The house being free of humans and the log box pulled out, there was no need to go upstairs. He could dump what he'd brought beside the hole in the skirting.

While he was gone, Pod outlined a method of procedure. ". . . if Spiller agrees," he kept saying, courteously conceding the leadership.

Spiller did agree, or rather he raised no objections. The empty soapbox lid, lightly dangling, was lowered onto the mud; into this they dropped the egg—rolling it to the edge of the drain as though it were a giant rugby football, with a final kick from Pod to send it spinning and keep it clear of the sides. It plopped into the soapbox lid with an ominous crack. This did not matter, however, the egg being hard-boiled.

Homily, with not a few nervous exclamations, was lowered next, seated astride the bolt; with one hand she clung to the twine, in the other she carried a lighted dip. When she climbed off the bolt into the lid of the soapbox, the latter slid swiftly away on the slime, and Homily, for an anxious moment, disappeared along the drain. Spiller drew her back, however, hand over hand. And there she sat behind the egg, grumbling a little, but with her candle still alight. "Two can go in the lid," Spiller had announced, and Arrietty (who secretly had longed to try the drop) was lowered considerately, dip in hand, in the same respectful way. She settled herself opposite her mother with the egg wobbling between them.

"You two are the light-bearers," said Pod. "All you've got to do is to sit quite still and steady the egg—move the lights as we say . . ."

There was a little shuffling about in the lid and some slightly perilous balancing as Homily, who had never liked traveling—as human beings would say—back to the engine, stood up to change seats with Arrietty. "Keep a good hold on that string," she kept imploring Spiller as she completed this maneuver, but soon she and Arrietty were seated again face to face, each with their candle and the egg between their knees. Arrietty was laughing.

"Now I'm going to let you go a little ways," warned Spiller and paid out a few inches of twine. Arrietty and Homily slid smoothly under the roof of their arched tunnel, which gleamed wetly in the candlelight. Arrietty put out a finger and touched the gleaming surface: it seemed to be made of baked clay.

"Don't touch *anything*," hissed Homily, shudderingly, "and don't breathe either—not unless you have to."

Arrietty, lowering her dip, peered over the side at the mud. "There's a fishbone," she remarked, "and a tin bottle top. And a hairpin . . ." she added on a pleased note.

"Don't even *look*," shuddered Homily.

"A hairpin would be useful," Arrietty pointed out.

Homily closed her eyes. "All right," she said, her face drawn with the effort not to mind. "Pick it out quickly and drop it, sharp, in the bottom of the boat. And wipe your hands on my apron."

"We can wash it in the river," Arrietty pointed out.

Homily nodded; she was trying not to breathe.

Over Homily's shoulder Arrietty could see into the well of the drain; a bulky object was coming down the shaft: it was Pod's tackle, waterproof-wrapped and strapped securely to his hatpin. It wobbled on the mud with a slight squelch. Pod, after a while, came after it. Then came Spiller. For a moment the surface seemed to bear their weight then, knee-deep, they sank in slime.

Spiller removed the length of curtain rod from the stone and set it up inconspicuously in the corner of the shaft. Before their descent he and Pod must have placed the grating above more conveniently in position: a deft pull by Spiller on the twine and they heard it clamp down into place—a dull metallic sound that echoed hollowly along the length of their tunnel. Homily gazed into the blackness ahead as though following its flight. "Oh, my goodness," she breathed as the sound died; she felt suddenly shut in.

"Well," announced Pod in a cheerful voice, coming up behind them, and he placed a hand on the rim of their lid, "we're off!"

Chapter Twelve

Spiller they saw, to control them on a shorter length, was rolling up the towline. Not that towline was quite the right expression under the circumstances; the drain ran ahead on a slight downwards incline and Spiller functioned more as a sea anchor and used the twine as a brake.

"Here we go," said Pod, and gave the lid a slight push. They slid ahead on the slippery scum, to be lightly checked by Spiller. The candlelight danced and shivered on the arched roof and about the dripping walls. So thick and soapy was the scum on which they rode that Pod, behind them, seemed more to be leading his bundle than dragging it behind him. Sometimes, even, it seemed to be leading him.

"Whoa, there!" he would cry on such occasions. He was in very good spirits, and had been, Arrietty noticed, from the moment he set foot in the drain. She, too, felt strangely happy. Here they were, the two she held most dear, with Spiller added, making their way toward the dawn. The drain held no fears for Arrietty, leading as it did toward a life to be lived away from dust and candle-light and confining shadows—a life on which the sun would shine by day and the moon by night.

She twisted round in her seat in order to see ahead, and as she did so, a great aperture opened to her left and a dank draft flattened the flame of her candle. She shielded it quickly with her hand and Homily did the same.

"That's where the pipe from the sink comes in," said Spiller, "and the overflow from the copper. . . ."

There were other openings as they went along, drains that branched into darkness and ran away uphill. Where these joined the main drain a curious collection of flot-sam and jetsam piled up over which they had to drag the soap lid. Arrietty and Homily got out for this to make less weight for the men. Spiller knew all these branch drains by name and the exact position of each cottage or house concerned. Arrietty began, at last, to understand the vast resources of Spiller's trading. "Not that you get up into all of 'em," he explained. "I don't mind an 's' bend, but where you get an 's' bend, you're apt to get a brass grille or suchlike in the plug hole."

Once he said, jerking his head toward the mouth of a circular cavern, "Holmcroft, that is. . . . Nothing but bath water from now on. . . ." And, indeed, this cavern, as they slid past it, had looked cleaner than most—a shin-ing cream-colored porcelain—and the air from that point onwards, Arrietty noticed, smelled far less strongly of tea leaves.

Every now and again they came across small branches —of ash or holly—rammed so securely into place that they would have difficulty maneuvering round them. They were set, Arrietty noticed, at almost regular intervals. "I can't think how these tree things get down drains, anyway," Homily exclaimed irritably when, for about the fifth time, the soapbox lid was turned up sideways and eased past and she and Arrietty stood ankle-deep in jetsam, shielding their dips with their hands.

"I put them there," said Spiller, holding the boat for them to get in again. The drain at this point dropped more steeply. As Homily stepped in opposite Arrietty, the soapbox lid suddenly slid away, dragging Spiller after. He slipped and skidded on the surface of the mud, but miraculously he kept his balance. They fetched up in a tangle against the trunk of one of Spiller's treelike erections and Arrietty's dip went overboard. "So that's what they're for," exclaimed Homily as she coaxed her own flattened wick back to brightness to give Arrietty a light.

But Spiller did not answer straight away. He pushed past the obstruction, and as they waited for Pod to catch up, he said suddenly, "Could be . . ."

Pod looked weary when he came up to them. He was panting a little and had stripped off his jacket and slung it round his shoulders. "The last lap's always the longest," he pointed out.

"Would you care for a ride in the lid?" asked Homily. "Do, Pod!"

"No, I'm better walking," said Pod.

"Then give me your jacket," said Homily. She folded it gently across her knees and patted it soberly as though (thought Arrietty, watching) it were tired, like Pod.

And then they were off again—an endless, monotonous vista of circular walls. Arrietty after a while began to doze; she slid forward against the egg, her head caught up on one knee. Just before she fell asleep, she felt Homily slide the dip from her drooping fingers and wrap her round with Pod's coat.

When she awoke, the scene was much the same: shadows sliding and flickering on the wet ceiling, Spiller's narrow face palely lit as he trudged along, and the bulky shape beyond that was Pod. Her mother, across the egg, smiled at her bewilderment. "Forgotten where you were?" asked Homily.

Arrietty nodded. Her mother held a dip in either hand, and the wax, Arrietty noticed, had burned very low. "Must be nearly morning," Arrietty remarked. She still felt very sleepy.

"Shouldn't wonder . . ." said Homily.

The walls slid by, unbroken except for archlike thickenings at regular intervals where one length of pipe joined another. And when they spoke, their voices echoed hollowly back and forth along the tunnel.

"Aren't there any more branch drains?" Arrietty asked after a moment.

Spiller shook his head. "No more now. Holmcroft was the last. . . ."

"But that was ages ago . . . we must be nearly there."

"Getting on," said Spiller.

Arrietty shivered and drew Pod's coat more tightly around her shoulders; the air seemed fresher suddenly and curiously free from smell. "Or perhaps," she thought, "we've grown more used to it. . . ." There was no sound except for the whispering slide of the soapbox lid and the regular plop and suction of Pod's and Spiller's footsteps. But the silt seemed rather thinner: there was an occasional grating sound below the base of the tin lid as though it rode on grit. Spiller stood still. "Listen!" he said.

They were all quiet but could hear nothing except Pod's breathing and a faint musical drip somewhere just ahead of them. "Better push on," said Homily suddenly, break-

ing the tension. "These dips aren't going to last for ever."

"Quiet!" cried Spiller again. Then they heard a faint drumming sound, hardly more than a vibration.

"Whatever is it?" asked Homily.

"Can only be Holmcroft," said Spiller. He stood rigid, with one hand raised, listening intently. "But," he said, turning to Pod, "who ever'd be having a bath at this time o' night?"

Pod shook his head. "It's morning by now," he said, "must be getting on for six."

The drumming sound grew louder, less regular, more like a leaping and a banging. . . .

"We've got to run for it—" cried Spiller. Towline in hand, he swung the tin lid round and, taking the lead, flew ahead into the tunnel. Arrietty and Homily banged and rattled behind him. Dragged on the short line, they swung

shatteringly, thrown from wall to wall. But, panic-stricken at the thought of total darkness, each shielded the flame of her candle. Homily stretched out a free hand to Pod who caught hold of it just as his bundle bore down on him, knocking him over. He fell across it, still gripping Homily's hand, and was carried swiftly along.

"Out and up," cried Spiller from the shadows ahead, and they saw the glistening twigs wedged tautly against the roof. "Let the traps go," he was shouting. "Come on —climb!"

They each seized a branch and swung themselves up and wedged themselves tight against the ceiling. The over-turned dips lay guttering in the tin lid and the air was filled with the sound of galloping water. In the jerking light from the dips they saw the first pearly bubbles and the racing, dancing, silvery bulk behind. And then all was choking, swirling, scented darkness. . . .

After the first few panic-stricken seconds, Arrietty found she could breathe and that the sticks still held. A millrace of hot scented water swilled through her clothes, piling against her at one moment, falling away the next. Sometimes it bounced above her shoulders, drenching her face and hair; at others it swirled steadily about her waist and tugged at her legs and feet. "Hold on," shouted Pod above the turmoil.

"Die down soon," shouted Spiller.

"You there, Arrietty?" gasped Homily. They were all

there and all breathing, and, even as they realized this, the water began to drop in level and run less swiftly. Without the brightness of the dips, the darkness about them seemed less opaque, as though a silvery haze rose from the water itself, which seemed now to be running well below them, and from the sound of it, as innocent and steady as a brook.

After a while they climbed down into it and felt a smoothly running warmth about their ankles. At this level they could see a faint translucence where the surface of the water met the blackness of the walls. "Seems lighter," said Pod wonderingly. He seemed to perceive some shifting in the darkness where Spiller splashed and probed. "Anything there?" he asked.

"Not a thing," said Spiller.

Their baggage had disappeared—egg, soapbox lid and all—swept away on the flood.

"And now what?" asked Pod dismally.

But Spiller seemed quite unworried. "Pick it up later," he said. ". . . nothing to hurt. And saves carting."

Homily was sniffing the air. "Sandalwood!" she exclaimed suddenly to Arrietty. "Your father's favorite soap."

But Arrietty, her hand on a twig to steady herself against the warm flow eddying past her ankles, did not reply; she was staring straight ahead down the incline of the drain. A bead of light hung in the darkness. For a moment she thought that, by some miraculous chance, it might be one of the dips—then she saw it was completely round and curiously steady. And mingled with the scent of sandalwood she smelled another smell—minty, grassy, mildly earthy . . .

"It's dawn," she announced in a wondering voice. "And what's more," she went on, staring spellbound at the distant pearl of light, "that's the end of the drain."

Chapter Thirteen

The warmth from the bath water soon wore off and the rest of the walk was chilly. The circle of light grew larger and brighter as they advanced toward it until, at last, its radiance dazzled their eyes.

"The sun's out," Arrietty decided. It was a pleasant thought, soaked to the skin as they were, and they slightly quickened their steps. The bath-water flow had sunk to the merest trickle and the drain felt gloriously clean.

Arrietty, too, felt somehow purged as though all traces of the old dark, dusty life had been washed away—even from their clothes. Homily had a similar thought.

"Nothing like a good, strong stream of soapy water running clean through the fabric . . . no rubbing or squeezing; all we've got to do now is lay them out to dry."

They emerged at last, Arrietty running ahead onto a small sandy beach that fanned out sideways and down to the water in front. The mouth of the drain was set well back under the bank of the stream, which overhung it, crowned with rushes and grasses: a sheltered, windless corner on which the sun beat down, rich with the golden promise of an early summer.

"But you can never tell," said Homily gazing around at the weatherworn flotsam and jetsam spewed out by the drain, "not in March . . ."

They had found Pod's bundle just within the mouth of the drain where the hatpin had stuck in the sand. The soapbox lid had fetched up, upside down, against a protruding root, and the egg, Arrietty discovered, had rolled right into the water; it lay in the shallows below a fishboning of silver ripples and seemed to have flattened out. But when they hooked it onto the dry sand, they saw it was due to refraction of the water: the egg was still its old familiar shape but covered with tiny cracks. Arrietty and Spiller rolled it up the slope to where Pod was unpacking the water-soaked bundles, anxious to see if the mackintosh covering had worked. Triumphantly he laid out the contents one by one on the warm sand. "Dry as a bone . . ." he kept saying.

Homily picked out a change of clothes for each. The jerseys, though clean, were rather worn and stretched: they were the ones she had knitted—so long ago it seemed now—on blunted darning needles when they had lived under the kitchen at Firbank. Arrietty and Homily undressed in the mouth of the drain, but Spiller—although offered a garment of Pod's—would not bother to change. He slid off round the corner of the beach to take a look at his kettle.

When they were dressed and the wet clothes spread out to dry, Homily shelled off the top of the egg. Pod wiped down his precious piece of razor blade, oiled to preserve it against rust, and cut them each a slice. They sat in the sunshine, eating contentedly, watching the ripples of the stream. After a while Spiller joined them. He sat just below them, steaming in the warmth and thoughtfully eating his egg.

"Where is the kettle exactly, Spiller?" asked Arrietty. Spiller jerked his head. "Just round the corner."

Pod had packed the Christmas pudding thimble, and they each had a drink of fresh water. Then they packed up the bundles again, and leaving the clothes to dry, they followed Spiller round the bend.

It was a second beach, rather more open, and the kettle lay against the bank at the far end. It lay slightly inclined, as Spiller had found it, wedged in by the twigs and branches washed by the river downstream. It was a corner on which floating things caught up and anchored themselves against a projection of the bank; the river twisted inwards at this point, running quite swiftly just below the kettle where, Arrietty noticed, the water looked suddenly deep.

Beyond the kettle a cluster of brambles growing under the bank hung out over the water—with new leaves growing among the tawny dead ones; some of these older shoots were trailing in the water, and in the tunnel beneath them, Spiller kept his boat.

Arrietty wanted to see the boat first, but Pod was examining the kettle, in the side of which, where it met the base, was a fair-sized circular rust hole.

"That the way in?" asked Pod.

Spiller nodded.

Pod looked up at the top of the kettle. The lid, he noticed, was not quite in, and Spiller had fixed a piece of twine to the knob in the middle of the lid and had slung it over the arched handle above.

"Come inside," he said to Pod. "I'll show you . . ."

They went inside while Arrietty and Homily waited in the sunshine. Spiller appeared again almost immediately at the rust-hole entrance, exclaiming irritably, "Go on, get out. . . ." And, aided by a shove from Spiller's bare foot, a mottled yellow frog leapt through the air and slithered swiftly into the stream. It was followed by two wood lice, which, as they rolled themselves up in balls, Spiller stooped down and picked up from the floor and threw lightly onto the bank above. "Nothing else," he remarked to Homily, grinning, and disappeared again.

Homily was silent a moment and then she whispered to Arrietty, "Don't fancy sleeping in there tonight. . . ."

"We can clean it out," Arrietty whispered back. "Remember the boot," she added.

Homily nodded, rather unhappily. "When do you think he'll get us down to Little Fordham?"

"Soon as he's been upstream to load. He likes the moon full. . . ." Arrietty whispered.

"Why?" whispered Homily.

"He travels mostly at night."

"Oh," said Homily, her expression bewildered and slightly wild.

A metallic sound attracted their attention to the top of the kettle. The lid, they saw, was wobbling on and off, raised and lowered from inside. "According to how you want it . . ." said a voice. "Very ingenious," they heard a second voice reply in curiously hollow tones.

"Doesn't sound like Pod," whispered Homily, looking startled.

"It's because they're in a kettle," explained Arrietty.

"Oh?" said Homily again. "I wish they'd come out."

They came out then, even as she spoke. As Pod stepped down on the flat stone that was used as a doorstep, he looked very pleased. "See that?" he said to Homily.

Homily nodded.

"Ingenious, eh?"

Homily nodded again.

"Now," Pod went on happily, "we're going to take a look at Spiller's boat. What sort of shoes you got on?"

They were old ones Pod had made. "Why?" asked Homily. "Is it muddy?"

"Not that I know of. But if you're going aboard, you don't want to slip. Better go barefoot like Arrietty. . . ."

Chapter Fourteen

Although she seemed nearly aground, a runnel of ice-cold water ran between the boat and the shore; through this they waded, and Spiller, at the prow, helped them to climb aboard. Roomy but clumsy (Arrietty thought as she scrambled in under the legging) but, with her flat bottom, practically impossible to capsize. She was, in fact, as Homily had guessed, a knife box: very long and narrow, with symmetrical compartments for varying sizes of cutlery.

"More what you'd call a barge," remarked Pod, looking about him. A wooden handle rose up inside, to which, he noticed, the legging had been nailed. "Holds her firm," explained Spiller, tapping the roof of the canopy, "say you want to lift up the sides."

The holds were empty at the moment, except for the narrowest. In this Pod saw an amber-colored knitting needle that ran the length of the vessel, a folded square of frayed red blanket, a wafer-thin butter knife of tarnished Georgian silver, and the handle and blade of his old nail scissor.

"So you've still got that?" he said.

"Comes in useful," said Spiller. "Careful," he said as Pod took it up, "I've sharpened it up a bit."

"Wouldn't mind this back," said Pod, a trifle enviously, "say, one day, you got another like it."

"Not so easy to come by," said Spiller, and as though to change the subject, he took up the butter knife. "Found this wedged down a crack in the side . . . does me all right for a paddle."

"Just the thing," said Pod. All the cracks and joins were filled in now, he noticed, as regretfully he put back the nail scissor. "Where did you pick up this knife box in the first place?"

"Lying on the bottom upstream. Full of mud when I spotted her. Bit of a job to salvage. Up by the caravans, that's where she was. Like as not, someone pinched the silver and didn't want the box."

"Like as not," said Pod. "So you sharpened her up?" he went on, staring again at the nail scissor.

"That's right," said Spiller, and stooping swiftly, he snatched up the piece of blanket, "You take this," he said. "Might be chilly in the kettle."

"What about you?" said Pod.

"That's all right," said Spiller. "You take it!"

"Oh," exclaimed Homily, "it's the bit we had in the boot . . ." and then she colored slightly. "I think," she added.

"That's right," said Spiller, "better you take it."

"Well, thanks," said Pod and threw it over his shoulder. He looked around again; the legging, he realized, was both camouflage and shelter. "You done a good job, Spiller. I mean . . . you could live in a boat like this—come wind, say, and wet weather."

"That's right," agreed Spiller, and he began to ease the knitting needle out from under the legging, the knob emerging forward at an angle. "Don't want to hurry you," he said.

Homily seemed taken aback. "You going already?" she faltered.

"Sooner he's gone, sooner he's back," said Pod. "Come on, Homily, all ashore now."

"But how long does he reckon he'll be?"

"What would you put it at, Spiller?" asked Pod. "A couple of days? Three? Four? A week?"

"May be less, may be more," said Spiller. "Depends on the weather. Three nights from now, say, if it's moon-light. . . ."

"But what if we're asleep in the kettle?" said Homily.

"That's all right, Homily; Spiller will *knock*." Pod took her firmly by the elbow. "Come on now, all ashore . . . you too, Arrietty."

As Homily, with Pod's help, was lowered into the water, Arrietty jumped from the side; the wet mud, she noticed, was spangled all over with tiny footprints. They linked arms and stood well back to watch Spiller depart. He unloosed the painter, and paddle in hand, let the boat slide stern foremost from under the brambles. As it glided out into open water, it became unnoticeable suddenly and somehow part of the landscape; it might have been a curl of bark or a piece of floating wood.

It was only when Spiller laid down the paddle and stood up to punt with the knitting needle that he became at all conspicuous. They watched through the brambles as, slowly and painstakingly, leaning at each plunge on his pole, he began to come back upstream. As he came abreast of them, they ran out from the brambles to see better. Shoes in hand, they crossed the beach of the kettle and, to keep up with him, climbed round the bluff at the corner and onto the beach of the drain. There, by a tree root,

which came sharply into deepish water, they waved him a last good-by.

"Wish he hadn't had to go," said Homily, as they made their way back across the sand toward the mouth of the drain.

There lay their clothes, drying in the sun, and as they approached, an iridescent cloud like a flock of birds flew off the top of the egg. "Bluebottles!" cried Homily, running forward; then, relieved, she slackened her steps. They were not bluebottles after all but cleanly burnished river flies, striped gaily with blue and gold. The egg appeared untouched, but Homily blew on it hard and dusted it up with her apron because, she explained, "You never know where they may have put their feet. . . ."

Pod, poking about among the flotsam and jetsam, salvaged the circular cork that Homily had used as a seat. "This'll just about do it . . ." he murmured reflectively.

"Do what?" asked Arrietty idly. A beetle had run out from where the cork had been resting, and stooping, she held it by its shell. She liked beetles: their shiny, clear-cut armor, their mechanical joints and joins. And she liked just a little to tease them: they were so easy to hold by the sharp edge of their wing casings and so anxious to get away.

"One day you'll get bitten . . ." Homily warned her as she folded up the clothes, which still, though dry, smelled faintly and pleasantly of sandalwood, "or stung, or nipped, or whatever they do, and serve you right."

Arrietty let the beetle go. "They don't mind, really," she remarked, watching the horned legs scuttle up the slope and the fine grains of dislodged sand tumbling down behind them.

"And here's a hairpin," exclaimed Pod. It was the one Arrietty had found in the drain, clean-washed now and gleaming. "You know what we should do," he went on, "while we're here, that is?"

"What?" asked Homily.

"Come along here regular like, every morning, and see what the drain's brought down."

"There wouldn't be anything I'd fancy," said Homily, folding the last garment.

"What about a gold ring? Many a gold ring, or so I've heard, gets lost down a drain . . . and you wouldn't say no to a safety pin."

"I'd sooner a safety pin," said Homily, "living as we do now."

They carried the bundles round the bluff onto the beach by the kettle. Homily climbed on the smooth stone that wedged the kettle at an angle and peered in through the rust hole. A cold light shone down from above where the lid was raised by its string: the interior smelled of rust and looked very uninviting.

"What we want now, before sundown," said Pod, "is some good clean dried grass to sleep on. We've got the piece of blanket . . ."

He looked about for some way of climbing the bank. There was a perfect place, as though invented for borrowers, where a cluster of tangled roots hung down from the lip of the cliff that curved deeply in behind them. At some time the stream had risen and washed the roots clean of earth, and they hung in festoons and clusters, elastic but safely anchored. Pod and Arrietty went up, hand over hand; there were handholds and footholds, seats, swings, ladders, ropes. . . . It was a borrowers' gymnasium and almost a disappointment to Arrietty when—so soon—they reached the top.

Here among the jadelike spears of new spring growth were pale clumps of hairlike grasses bleached to the color of tow. . . . Pod reaped these down with his razor blade and Arrietty tied them into sheaves. Homily, below, collected these bundles as they pushed them over the cliff edge and carried them up to the kettle.

When the floor of the kettle was well and truly lined, Pod and Arrietty climbed down. Arrietty peered in through the rust hole: the kettle now smelled of hay. The sun was sinking and the air felt slightly colder. "What we all need now," remarked Homily, "is a good hot drink before bed. . . ." But there was no means of making one, so they got out the egg instead. There was plenty left: they each had a thickish slice, topped up by a leaf of sorrel.

Pod unpacked his length of tarred string, knotted one end securely, and passed the other through the center of the cork. He pulled it tight.

"What's that for?" asked Homily, coming beside him, wiping her hands on her apron (. . . no washing up, thank goodness: she had carried the egg shells down to the water's edge and had thrown them into the stream).

"Can't you guess?" asked Pod. He was trimming the cork now, breathing hard, and beveling the edges.

"To block up the rust hole?"

"That's right," said Pod. "We can pull it tight like some kind of stopper once we're all safely inside. . . ."

Arrietty had climbed up the roots again. They could see her on top of the bank. It was breezier up there and her hair was stirring slightly in the wind. Around her the great grass blades, in gentle motion, crossed and recrossed against the darkening sky.

"She likes it out of doors . . ." said Homily fondly.

"What about you?" asked Pod.

"Well," said Homily after a moment, "I'm not one for insects, Pod, never was. Nor for the simple life—if there is such a thing. But tonight"—she gazed about her at the peaceful scene—"tonight, I feel kind of all right."

"That's the way to talk," said Pod, scraping away with his razor blade.

"Or, it might," said Homily, watching him, "be partly due to that cork."

An owl hooted somewhere in the distance, on a hollow, wobbling note . . . a liquid note, it seemed, falling musically on the dusk. But Homily's eyes widened. "Arrietty—" she called shrilly. "Quickly! Come on down."

They felt snug enough in the kettle—snug and secure, with the cork pulled in and the lid let down. Homily had insisted on the latter precaution. "We won't need to *see*," she explained to Pod and Arrietty, "and we get enough air down the spout."

When they woke in the morning, the sun was up and the kettle felt rather hot. But it was exciting to lift off the lid, hand over hand on the twine, and to see a cloudless sky. Pod kicked out the cork, and they crawled through the rust hole and there again was the beach. . . .

They breakfasted out-of-doors. The egg was wearing down, but there was two-thirds left to go. "And sunshine feeds," said Pod. After breakfast Pod went off with his hatpin to see what had come down the drain; Homily busied herself about the kettle and laid out the blanket to air; Arrietty climbed the roots again to explore the top of the bank. "Keep within earshot," Pod had warned them, "and call out now and again. We don't want accidents at this stage—not before Spiller arrives."

"And we don't want them then," retorted Homily. But she seemed curiously relaxed: there was nothing to do but wait—no housework, no cooking, no borrowing, no planning. "Might as well enjoy ourselves," she reflected and settled herself in the sun on the piece of red blanket. To Pod and Arrietty she seemed to be dozing, but this was not the case at all. Homily was busy daydreaming about a house with front door and windows—a home of their very own. Sometimes it was small and compact, sometimes four stories high. And what about the castle she wondered?

For some reason the thought of the castle reminded her of Lupy. What would they be thinking now—back there in that shuttered house? That we've vanished into thin air—that's what it will seem like to them. Homily imagined Lupy's surprise, the excitement, the conjectures. . . . And, smiling to herself, she half closed her eyes: never would they think of the drain. And never, in their wildest dreams, would they think of Little Fordham. . . .

Two halcyon days went by, but on the third day it rained. Clouds gathered in the morning and by afternoon there was a downpour. At first, Arrietty—avid to stay outdoors—took shelter among the roots under the overhanging bank, but soon the rain drove in on the wind and leaked down from the bank above. The roots became slippery and greasy with mud—so all three of them fled to the drain. "I mean," said Homily as they crouched in the entrance, "at least from here we can see out, which is more than you can say for the kettle."

They moved from the drain, however, when Pod heard a drumming in the distance. "Holmcroft," he exclaimed after listening a moment. "Come on, get moving. . . ." Homily, staring at the gray veil of rain outside, protested that, if they were in for a soaking, they might just as well have it hot as cold.

Chapter Fifteen

It was a good thing they moved, however: the stream had risen almost to the base of the bluff round which they must pass to get to the kettle. Even as it was, they had to wade. The water looked thick and brownish. The delicate ripples had become muscular and fierce, and as they hurried across the second beach, they saw great branches borne on the flood, sinking and rising as the water galloped past.

"Spiller can't travel in this . . ." moaned Homily as they changed their clothes in the kettle. She had to raise her voice against the drumming of the raindrops on the lid. Below them, almost as it might be in their cellar, they heard the thunder of the stream. But the kettle perched on its stone and wedged against the bank felt steady as a citadel. The spout was turned away from the wind and no drop got in through the lid. "Double rim," explained Pod. "Well made, these old fashioned kettles. . . ."

Banking on Spiller's arrival, they had eaten the last of the egg. They felt very hungry and stared with tragic eyes through the rust hole when, just below them, a half loaf went by on the flood.

At last it grew dark and they pulled in the cork and prepared to go to sleep. "Anyway," said Pod, "we're warm and dry. And it's bound to clear up soon. . . ."

But it rained all the next day. And the next. "He'll never come in this," moaned Homily.

"I wouldn't put it past him," said Pod. "That's a good solid craft that knife box, and well covered in. The current flows in close here under those brambles. That's why he chose this corner. You mark my words, Homily, he might fetch up here any moment. Spiller's not one to be frightened by a drop of rain. . . ."

That was the day of the banana. Pod had gone out to reconnoiter, climbing gingerly along the slippery shelf of mud beneath the brambles. The current, twisting in, was pouring steadily through Spiller's boathouse, pulling the trailing brambles in its wake. Caught up in the branches where they touched the water, Pod had found half a packet of sodden cigarettes, a strip of water-logged sacking, and a whole, rather overripe banana.

Homily had screamed when he pushed it in inch by inch through the rust hole. She did not recognize it at first, and later, as she saw what it was, she began to laugh and cry at the same time.

"Steady, Homily," said Pod, after the final push, as he peered in, grave-faced, through the rust hole. "Get a hold on yourself."

Homily did—almost at once. "You should have warned us," she protested, still gasping a little and wiping her eyes on her apron.

"I did call out," said Pod, "but what with the noise of the rain . . ."

They ate their fill of the banana—it was overripe already and would not last for long. Pod sliced it across, skin and all; he thus kept it decently covered. The sound of the rain made talking difficult. "Coming down faster," said Pod. Homily leaned forward, mouthing the words. "Do you think he's met with an accident?"

Pod shook his head. "He'll come when it stops. We got to have patience," he added.

"Have what?" shouted Homily above the downpour.

"Patience," repeated Pod.

"I can't hear you. . . ."

"Patience!" roared Pod.

Rain began to come in down the spout. There was nothing for it but to sacrifice the blanket. Homily stuffed it in as tightly as she could, and the kettle became very airless. "Might go on for a month," she grumbled.

"What?" shouted Pod.

"For a month," repeated Homily.

"What about it?"

"The rain," shouted Homily.

After that they gave up talking: the effort seemed hardly worthwhile. Instead, they lay down in the layers of dried grasses and tried to go to sleep. Full-fed and in that airless warmth, it did not take them long. Arrietty dreamed she was at sea in Spiller's boat: there was a gentle rocking motion, which at first seemed rather pleasant, and then in her dream the boat began to spin. The spinning increased and the boat became a wheel, turning . . . turning. . . . She clung to the spokes, which became like straw and broke away in her grasp. She clung to the rim, which opened outwards and seemed to fling her off, and a voice was calling again and again, "Wake up, Arrietty, wake up. . . ."

Dizzily she opened her eyes, and the kettle seemed full of a whirling half-light. It was morning, she realized, and someone had pulled the blanket from the spout. Close behind her she made out the outline of Pod; he seemed in some strange way to be glued to the side of the kettle. Opposite her she perceived the form of her mother, spread-eagled likewise in the same fixed, curious manner. She herself, half sitting, half lying, felt gripped by some dreamlike force.

"We're afloat," cried Pod, "and spinning." And Arrietty, besides the kettle's spin, was aware of a dipping and swaying. "We've come adrift. We're in the current," he went on, "and going downstream fast. . . ."

"Oh, my . . ." moaned Homily, casting up her eyes. It was the only gesture she could make, stuck as she was like a fly to flypaper. But even as she spoke, the speed slackened and the spinning turns slowed down, and Arrietty watched her mother slide slowly down to a sitting position on the squelching, waterlogged floor. "Oh, my goodness . . ." Homily muttered again.

Her voice, Arrietty noticed, sounded strangely audible: the rain had stopped at last.

"I'm going to get the lid off," said Pod. He, too, as the kettle ceased twisting, had fallen forward to his knees and now rose slowly, steadying himself by a hand on the wall, against the swaying half-turns. "Give me a hand with the twine, Arrietty."

They pulled together. Water had seeped in past the cork in the rust hole and the floor was awash with sodden grass. As they pulled, they slid and slithered, but gradually the lid rose and above them they saw, at last, a circle of bright sky.

"Oh, my goodness," Homily kept saying, and sometimes she changed it to, "Oh, my goodness me. . . ." But she helped them stack up Pod's bundles. "We got to get out on deck like," Pod had insisted. "We don't stand a chance down below."

It was a scramble: they used the twine, they used the hatpin, they used the banana, they used the bundles, and somehow—the kettle listing steeply—they climbed out on the rim to hot sunshine and a cloudless sky. Homily sat crouched, her arms gripped tightly round the stem of the arched handle, her legs dangling below. Arrietty sat beside her holding onto the rim. To lighten the weight, Pod cut the lid free and cast it overboard: they watched it float away.

". . . seems a waste," said Homily.

Chapter Sixteen

The kettle turned slowly as it drifted—more gently now—downstream. The sun stood high in a brilliant sky: it was later than they had thought. The water looked muddy and yellowish after the recent storm, and in some places had overflowed the banks. To the right of them lay open fields and to the left a scrub of stunted willows and taller hazels. Above their heads golden lamb's tails trembled against the sky and armies of rushes marched down into the water.

"Fetch up against the bank any minute now," said Pod hopefully, watching the flow of the stream. "One side or another," he added, "a kettle like this don't drift on forever. . . ."

"I should sincerely hope not," said Homily. She had slightly relaxed her grip on the handle and, interested in spite of herself, was gazing about her.

Once they heard a bicycle bell, and some seconds later a policeman's helmet sailed past just above the level of the bushes. "Oh, my goodness," muttered Homily, "that means a footpath. . . ."

"Don't worry," said Pod. But Arrietty, glancing quickly at her father's face, saw he seemed perturbed.

"He'd only have to glance sideways," Homily pointed out.

"It's all right," said Pod, "he's gone now. And he didn't."

"What about Spiller?" Homily went on.

"What about him?"

"He'll never find us now."

"Why not?" said Pod. "He'll see the kettle's gone. As far as Spiller's concerned, all we've got to do is bide our time, wait quietly—wherever we happen to fetch up."

"Suppose we don't fetch up and go on past Little Fordham?"

"Spiller'll come on past looking for us."

"Suppose we fetch up amongst all those people . . . ?"

"What people?" asked Pod a trifle wearily. "The plaster ones?"

"No, those human beings who swarm about on the paths . . ."

"Now, Homily," said Pod, "no good meeting trouble halfway."

"Trouble?" exclaimed Homily. "What are we in now, I'd like to know?" She glanced down past her knees at the sodden straw below. "And I suppose this kettle'll fill up in no time . . ."

"Not with the cork swollen up like it is," said Pod. "The wetter it gets, the tighter it holds. All you got to do,

Homily, is to sit there and hold on tight; and, say, we come near land, get yourself ready to jump." As he spoke, he was busy making a grappling hook out of his hatpin, twisting and knotting a length of twine about the head of the pin.

Arrietty, meanwhile, lay flat on her stomach gazing into the water below. She was perfectly happy: the cracked enamel was warm from the sun and with one elbow crooked round the base of the handle she felt curiously safe. Once in the turgid water she saw the ghostly outline of a large fish, fanning its shadowy fins and standing backwards against the current. Sometimes there were little forests of water weeds, where blackish minnows flicked and darted. Once a water rat swam swiftly past the kettle, almost under her nose: she called out then excitedly—as though she had seen a whale. Even Homily craned over to watch it pass, admiring the tiny air bubbles that clung like moonstones among the misted fur. They all stood up to watch it climb out on the bank and shake itself hurriedly into a cloud of spray before it scampered away into the grasses. "Well I never," remarked Homily. ". . . natural history," she added reflectively.

Then, raising her eyes, she saw the cow. It stood quite motionless above its own vast shadow, hock deep and silent in the fragrant mud. Homily stared aghast and even Arrietty felt grateful for a smoothly floating kettle and a stretch of water between. Almost impertinently safe

she felt—so near and yet so far—until a sudden eddy in the current swung them in toward the bank.

"It's all right," called Pod as Arrietty started back. "It won't hurt you. . . ."

"Oh, my goodness . . ." exclaimed Homily, making as though to climb down inside the rim. The kettle lurched.

"Steady," cried Pod, alarmed, "keep her trimmed!" And, as the kettle slid swiftly shoreward, he flung his weight sideways, leaning out from the handle. "Stand by . . ." he shouted as with a vicious twist they veered round sharply, gliding against the mud. "Hold fast!" The great cow backed two paces as they careered up under her nose. She lowered her head and swayed slightly as though embarrassed, and then, sniffing the air, she clumsily backed again.

The kettle teetered against the walls and craters of the cow tracks, pressed by the current's flow; a faint vibration of drumming water quivered through the iron. Then Pod, leaning outwards, clinging with one hand to the rim, shoved his hatpin against a stone; the kettle bounced slightly, turning into the current, and, in a series of bumps and quivers, began to turn away.

"Thank goodness for that, Pod . . ." cried Homily, "thank goodness . . . thank goodness . . . oh my, oh my, oh my!" She sat clinging to the base of the handle, white-faced and shaking.

"It would never hurt you," said Pod as they glided out to midstream, "not a cow wouldn't . . ."

"Might tread on us," gasped Homily.

"Not once it's seen you, it wouldn't."

"And it did see us," cried Arrietty gazing backward. "It's looking at us still . . ."

Watching the cow, relaxed and relieved, they were none of them prepared for the bump. Homily, thrown off balance, slid forward with a cry—down through the lid hole onto the straw below. Pod just in time caught hold of the handle rail, and Arrietty caught hold of Pod. Steadying Arrietty, Pod turned his head; the kettle, he saw, had fetched up against an island of sticks and branches, plumb in the middle of the stream. Again the kettle thrummed, banging and trembling against the obstructing sticks; little ripples rose up and broke like waves among and around the weed-strewn, trembling mass.

"Now, we are stuck," remarked Pod, "good and proper."

"Get me up, Pod—do . . ." they heard Homily calling from below.

They got her up and showed her what had happened. Pod, peering down, saw part of a gatepost and coils of rusted wire: on this projection a mass of rubbish was entangled, brought down by the flood, a kind of floating island, knitted up by the current and hopelessly intertwined.

No good shoving with his pin: the current held them head on and, with each successive bump, wedged them more securely.

"It could be worse," remarked Homily surprisingly, when she had got her breath. She took stock of the nest-like structure: some of the sticks, forced above water, had already dried in the sun; the whole contraption, to Homily, looked pleasantly like dry land. "I mean," she went on, "we could walk about on this. I wouldn't say, really, but what I don't prefer it to the kettle . . . better than floating on and on and on, and ending up, as might well be, in the Indian Ocean. Spiller could find us here easy enough . . . plumb in the middle of the view."

"There's something in that," agreed Pod. He glanced up at the banks: the stream here was wider, he noticed. On the left bank, among the stunted willows that shrouded the towpath, a tall hazel leaned over the water; on the right bank, the meadows came sloping down to the stream and, beside the muddy cow tracks, stood a sturdy clump of ash. The tall boles, ash and hazel, stood like sentinels, one each side of the river. Yes, it was the kind of spot Spiller would know well; the kind of place, Pod thought to himself, to which humans might give a name. The water on either side of the midstream obstruction flowed dark and deep, scooped out by the current into pools. Yes, it was the kind of place he decided—with a slight inward tremor of his "feeling"—where in the summer human beings might come to bathe. Then, glancing downstream, he saw the bridge.

Chapter Seventeen

It was not much of a bridge—wooden, moss-grown, with a single handrail—but, in their predicament, even a modest bridge was still a bridge too many: bridges are highways, built for humans, and command long views of the river . . .

Homily, when he pointed it out, seemed strangely unperturbed: shading her eyes against the sunlight, she gazed intently down river. "No human being that distance away," she decided at last, "could make out what's on these sticks. . . ."

"You'd be surprised," said Pod. "They spot the movement like . . ."

"Not before we've spotted them. Come on, Pod; let's unload the kettle and get some stuff dried out."

They went below, and by shifting the ballast, they got the kettle well heeled over. When they had achieved sufficient list, Pod took his twine and made the handle fast to the sunken wire netting. In this way, with the kettle held firm, they could crawl in and out through the lid hole.

Soon all the gear was spread out in the warmth, and sitting in a row on a baked branch of alder, they each fell to on a slice of banana.

"This could be a lot worse," said Homily, munching and looking about her. She was thankful for the silence and the sudden lack of motion. Down between the tangled sticks were well-like glintings of dark water, but it was quiet water and, from her high perch, far enough away to be ignored.

Arrietty, on the contrary, had taken off her shoes and stockings and was trailing her feet in the delicate ripples that played about the outer edges.

The river seemed full of voices, endless, mysterious murmurs like half-heard conversations. But conversations without pauses—breathless, steady recountings. . . . "She said to me, I said to her. And then . . . and then . . . and then. . . ." After a while Arrietty ceased to listen as, so often, she ceased to listen to her mother when Homily, in the vein, went on and on and on. But she was aware of the sound and the deadening effect it would have on sounds made farther afield. Against this noise, she thought, something could creep up on you and, without hint or warning, suddenly be there. And then she realized that nothing could creep up on an island unless it were afloat or could swim. But, even as she thought this thought, a blue tit flew down from above and perched beside her on a twig. It cocked its head sideways at the pale ring of banana skin that had enclosed her luncheon slice.

She picked it up and threw it sideways toward him—like
a quoit—and the blue tit flew away.

Then she crept back into the nest of flotsam. Sometimes
she climbed under the dry twigs onto the wet ones below.
In these curious hollows, cut with sunlight and shadow,

there was a vast choice of handholds and notches on which to tread. Above her a network of branches crisscrossed against the sun. Once she went right down to the shadowed water and, hanging perilously above it, saw in its blackness her pale reflected face. She found a water snail

clinging to the underside of a leaf, and once, with a foot, she touched some frogs' spawn, disturbing a nest of tadpoles. She tried to pull up a water weed by the roots but, slimily, it resisted her efforts—stretching part way like a piece of elasticized rubber, then suddenly springing free.

"Where are you, Arrietty?" Homily called from above. "Come up here where it's dry. . . ."

But Arrietty seemed not to hear: she had found a hen's feather, a tuft of sheep's wool, and half a ping-pong ball, which still smelled strongly of celluloid. Pleased with these borrowings, she finally emerged. Her parents were suitably impressed, and Homily made a cushion of the sheep's wool, wedged it neatly in the half-ball, and used it as a seat. "And very comfortable too," she assured them warmly, wobbling slightly on the curved base.

Once two small humans crossed the bridge, country boys of nine or ten. They dawdled and laughed and climbed about and threw sticks into the water. The borrowers froze, staring intently as, with backs turned, the two boys hung on the railings, watching their sticks drift downstream.

"Good thing we're upstream," murmured Pod from between still lips.

The sun was sinking and the river had turned to molten gold. Arrietty screwed up her eyelids against the glitter. "Even if they saw us," she whispered, her eyes on the bridge, "they couldn't get at us—out here in deep water."

"Maybe not," said Pod, "but the word would get around. . . ."

The boys at length disappeared. But the borrowers remained still, staring at the bushes and trying to hear above the bubble of the river any sound of human beings passing along the footpath.

"I think they must have gone across the fields," said Pod at last. "Come on, Arrietty, give me a hand with this waterproof. . . ."

Pod had been preparing a hammock bed for the night where four stout sticks lay lengthwise in a hollow: a mackintosh ground sheet, their dry clothes laid out on top, the piece of lamb's wool for a pillow and, to cover them, another ground sheet above the piece of red blanket. Snug, they would be, in a deep cocoon—protected from rain and dew and invisible from the bank.

As the flood water began to subside, their island seemed to rise higher; slimy depths were revealed among the structure, and gazing down between the sticks at the rusted wire, they discovered a waterlogged shoe.

"Nothing to salvage there," remarked Pod after a moment's thoughtful silence, "except maybe the laces. . . ."

Homily, who had followed them downwards, gazed wonderingly about her. It had taken courage to climb down into the depths. She had tested every foothold: some of the branches were rotten and broke away at a touch; others less securely wedged were apt to become detached, and quivers and slidings took place elsewhere—like a distant disturbance in a vast erection of spilikins. Their curious island was only held together, she realized, by the interrelation of every leaf, stick, and floating strand of weed. All the same, on the way up, she snapped off a living twig of hawthorn for the sake of the green leaf buds. "A bit of salad like, to eat with our supper," she explained to Arrietty. "You can't go on forever just on egg and banana. . . ."

Chapter Eighteen

They ate their supper on the upstream side of the island, where the ripples broke at their feet and where the kettle, tied on its side, had risen clear of the water. The level of the stream was sinking fast and the water seemed far less muddy.

It was not much of a supper—the tail end of the banana that had become rather sticky. They still felt hungry, even after they had finished off the hawthorn shoots, washing them down with draughts of cold water. They spoke wistfully of Spiller and a boat chock-full of borrowings.

"Suppose we miss him?" said Homily. "Suppose he comes in the night?"

"I'll keep watch for Spiller," said Pod.

"Oh, Pod," exclaimed Homily, "you've got to have your eight hours!"

"Not tonight," said Pod, "nor tomorrow night. Nor any night while there's a full moon."

"We could take it in turns," suggested Homily.

"I'll watch tonight," said Pod, "and we'll see how we go."

Homily was silent, staring down at the water. It was a dreamlike evening: as the moon rose, the warmth of the day still lingered on the landscape in a glow of tranquil light. Colors seemed enriched from within, vivid but softly muted.

"What's that?" said Homily suddenly, gazing down at the ripples. "Something pink . . ."

They followed the direction of her eyes. Just below the surface something wriggled, held up against the current.

"It's a worm," said Arrietty after a moment.

Homily stared at it thoughtfully. "You said right, Pod," she admitted after a moment. "I have changed. . . ."

"In what way?" asked Pod.

"Looking at that worm," said Homily, "all scoured and scrubbed like—clean as a whistle—I was thinking"—she hesitated—"well, I was thinking . . . I could eat a worm like that. . . ."

"What, raw?" exclaimed Pod, amazed.

"No, stewed of course," retorted Homily crossly, "with a bit of wild garlic." She stared again at the water. "What's it caught up on?"

Pod craned forward. "I can't quite see . . ." Suddenly his face became startled and his gaze, sharply intent, slid away on a rising curve toward the bushes.

"What's the matter, Pod?" asked Homily.

He looked at her aghast—a slow stare. "Someone's fishing," he breathed, scarcely above his breath.

"Where?" whispered Homily.

Pod jerked his head toward the stunted willows. "There —behind those bushes . . ."

Then Homily, raising her eyes at last, made out the fishing line. Arrietty saw it too. Only in glimpses was it visible: not at all under water but against the surface here and there they perceived the hair-thin shadow. As it rose, it became invisible again, lost against the dimness of the willows, but they could follow its direction.

"Can't see nobody," whispered Homily.

"Course you can't," snapped Pod. "A trout's got eyes, remember, just like you and me. . . ."

"Not *just* like—" protested Homily.

"You don't want to show yourself," Pod went on, "not when you're fishing."

"Especially if you're poaching," put in Arrietty. Why are we whispering, she wondered—our voices can't be heard above the voices of the river?

"That's right, lass," said Pod, "especially if you're poaching. And that's just what he is, I shouldn't wonder —a poacher."

"What's a poacher?" whispered Homily.

Pod hushed her, raising his hand. "Quiet, Homily." And then he added aside, "a kind of human borrower."

"A human borrower . . ." repeated Homily in a bewildered whisper: it seemed a contradiction in terms.

"Quiet, Homily," pleaded Pod.

"He can't hear us," said Arrietty, "not from the bank. Look—" she exclaimed. "The worm's gone."

So it had, and the line had gone too.

"Wait a minute," said Pod. "You'll see—he sends **it** down on the current."

Straining their eyes, they made out the curves of floating line and, just below the surface, the pinkness of the worm sailing before them. The worm fetched up in the same spot, just below their feet, where again it was held against the current.

Something flicked out from under the sticks below them; there was a flurry of shadow, a swift half-turn, and most of the worm had gone.

"A fish?" whispered Arrietty.

Pod nodded.

Homily craned forward: she was becoming quite excited. "Look, Arrietty—now you can see the hook!"

Arrietty caught just a glimpse of it and then the hook was gone.

"He felt that," said Pod, referring to the fisherman. "Thinks he got a bite."

"But he did get a bite," said Arrietty.

"He got a bite but he didn't get a fish. Here it comes again. . . ."

It was a new worm this time, darker in color.

Homily shuddered. "I wouldn't fancy that one, whichever way you cooked it."

"Quiet, Homily," said Pod as the worm whisked away.

"You know," exclaimed Homily excitedly, "what **we** could do—say we had some kind of fire. We could **take** the fish off the hook and cook and eat it ourselves. . . ."

"Say there was a fish *on* the hook—" remarked Pod, gazing soberly toward the bushes. Suddenly he gave a cry and ducked sideways, his hands across his face. "Look out!" he yelled in a frantic voice.

It was too late: there was the hook in Homily's skirt, worm and all. They ran to her, holding her against the pull of the line while her wild shrieks echoed down the river.

"Unbutton it, Homily! Take the skirt off! Quick . . ."
But Homily couldn't or wouldn't. It might have had something to do with the fact that underneath she was wearing a very short red flannel petticoat that once had belonged to Arrietty and did not think it would look seemly, or she might quite simply just have lost her head. She clung to Pod, and dragged out of his grasp, she clung to Arrietty. Then she clung to the twigs and sticks as she was dragged past them toward the ripples.

They got her out of the water as the line for a moment went slack, and Arrietty fumbled with the small jet bead that served Homily's skirt as a button. Then the line went taut again. As Pod grabbed hold of Homily, he saw out of the corner of his eye that the fisherman was standing up.

From this position, on the very edge of the bank, he could play his rod more freely. A sudden upward jerk, and Homily, caught by her skirt and shrieking loudly, flew upside down into the air with Pod and Arrietty fiercely clinging each to an arm. Then the jet button burst off, the skirt sailed away with the worm, and the borrowers, in a huddle, fell back on the sticks. The sticks

sank slightly beneath the impact and rose again as gently, breaking the force of their fall.

"That was a near one," gasped Pod, pulling his leg out of a cleft between the branches. Arrietty, who had come down on her seat, remained sitting: she seemed shaken but unhurt. Homily, crossing her arms, tenderly massaged

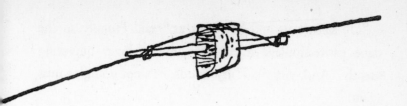

her shoulders: she had a long graze on one cheek and a jagged tear in the red flannel petticoat. "You all right, Homily?"

Homily nodded, and her bun unrolled slowly. White-faced and shaking, she felt mechanically for hairpins: she was staring fixedly at the bank.

"And the sticks held," said Pod, examining his grazed shin: he swung the leg slightly. "Nothing broken," he said. Homily took no notice: she sat, as though mesmerized, staring at the fisherman.

"It's Mild Eye," she announced grimly after a moment.

Pod swung round, narrowing his eyes. Arrietty stood up to see better: Mild Eye, the gypsy . . . there was no mistaking the apelike build, the heavy eyebrows, the thatch of graying hair.

"Now we'll be for it," said Homily.

Pod was silent a moment. "He can't get at us here," he decided at last, "right out in midstream; the water's goo and deep out here, on both sides of us like."

"He could stand in the shallows and reach," said Homily.

"Doubt if he'd make it," said Pod.

"He knows us and he's seen us," said Homily in the same expressionless voice. She drew a long, quivering breath. "And, you mark my words, he's not going to miss again!"

There was silence except for the voices of the river. The babbling murmur, unperturbed and even, seemed suddenly alien and heartless.

"Why doesn't he move?" asked Arrietty.

"He's thinking," said Homily.

After a moment Arrietty ventured timidly, "Of what he's going to charge for us, and that, when he's got us in a cage?"

"Of what he's going to do next," said Homily.

They were silent a moment, watching Mild Eye.

"Look," said Arrietty.

"What's he up to now?" asked Pod.

"He's taking the skirt off the hook!"

"And the worm too," said Pod. "Look out!" he cried as the fisherman's arm flew up. There was a sudden jerk among the sticks, a shuddering series of elastic quivers. "He's casting for us," shouted Pod. "Better we get under cover."

"No," said Homily, as their island became still again; she watched the caught branch, hooked loose, bobbing away down river. "Say he drags this obstruction to bits, we're safer on top than below. Better we take to the kettle—"

But even as she spoke, the next throw caught the cork in the rust hole. The kettle, hooked by its stopper and tied to the sticks, resisted the drag of the rod: they clung together in silent panic as just below them branches began to slide. Then the cork bounced free and leapt away, dancing on the end of the line. Their island subsided again, and unclasping each other, they moved apart listening wide-eyed to the rhythmic gurgle of water filling the kettle.

The next throw caught a key branch, one on which they stood. They could see the hook well and truly in, and the trembling strain on the twine. Pod clambered alongside and, leaning back, tugged downwards against the pull. But strain as he might, the line stayed taut and the hook as deeply embedded.

"Cut it," cried someone above the creaking and groaning. "Cut it . . ." the voice cried again, tremulously faint, like the rippling voice of the river.

"Then give me the razor blade," gasped Pod. Arrietty brought it in a breathless scramble. There was a gentle twang, and they all ducked down as the severed line flew free. "Now why," exclaimed Pod, "didn't I think of that in the first place?"

He glanced toward the shore. Mild Eye was reeling in; the line, too light now, trailed softly on the breeze.

"He's not very pleased," said Homily.

"No," agreed Pod, sitting down beside her, "he wouldn't be."

"Don't think he's got another hook," said Homily.

They watched Mild Eye examine the end of his line, and they met his baleful gaze as, throwing the rod aside, he angrily stared across at them.

"Round one to us," said Pod.

Chapter Nineteen

They settled themselves more comfortably, preparing for a vigil. Homily reached behind her into the bedding and pulled out the piece of red blanket. "Look, Pod," she said in an interested voice as she tucked it around her knees, "what's he up to now?" They watched intently as Mild Eye, taking up his rod again, turned toward the bushes. "You don't think he's given it up?" she added as Mild Eye, making for the towpath, disappeared from view.

"Not a hope," said Pod, "not Mild Eye. Not once he's seen us and knows we're here for the taking."

"He can't get at us here," said Homily again, "and it'll be dark soon." She seemed strangely calm.

"Maybe," said Pod, "but look at that moon rising. And we'll still be here in the morning." He took up his razor blade. "Might as well free that kettle: it's only a weight on the sticks. . . ."

Homily watched him slice through the twine, and, a little sadly, they watched the kettle sink.

"Poor Spiller," said Arrietty, "he was kind of fond of that kettle. . . ."

"Well, it served its purpose," said Pod.

"What if we made a raft?" suggested Homily suddenly. Pod looked about at the sticks and down at the twine in his hand. "We could do," he said, "but it would take a bit of time. And with him about"—he jerked his head toward the bushes—"I reckon we're as safe here as anywhere."

"And it's better here," said Arrietty, "for being seen."

Homily, startled, turned and looked at her. "Whatever do you want to be seen for?"

"I was thinking of Spiller," said Arrietty. "With this kind of moon and this sort of weather, he'll come tonight most likely."

"Pretty well bound to," agreed Pod.

"Oh dear," said Homily, pulling the blanket around her, "whatever will he think? I mean, finding me like this —in Arrietty's petticoat?"

"Nice and bright," said Pod, "catch his eye nicely, that petticoat would."

"Not short and shrunk up like it is," complained Homily unhappily, "and a great tear in the side like."

"It's still bright," said Pod, "a kind of landmark. And I'm sorry now we sunk the kettle. He'd have seen that too. Well, can't be helped. . . ."

"Look—" whispered Arrietty, gazing at the bank.

There stood Mild Eye. Just beside them he seemed now:

he had walked down the towpath behind the bushes and had emerged on the bank beside the leaning hazel. In the clear shadowless light he seemed extraordinarily close: they could even see the pallor of his one blue eye in contrast to the fiercely shadowed black one; they could see the joints in his fishing rod and the clothes pegs and coils of clothesline in his basket, which he carried half slung on his forearm and tilted toward them. Had it been dry land between them, four good strides would have brought him across.

"Oh dear," muttered Homily, "now what?"

Mild Eye, leaning his rod against the hazel, set down the basket from which he took two fair-sized fish strung together by the gills. These he wrapped carefully in several layers of dock leaves.

"Rainbow trout," said Arrietty.

"How do you know?" asked Homily.

Arrietty blinked her eyelids. "I just know," she said.

"Young Tom," said Pod, "that's how she knows, I reckon—seeing his granddad's the gamekeeper. And that's how she knew about poachers, eh, Arrietty?"

Arrietty did not reply: she was watching Mild Eye as he returned the fish to the basket. Very carefully he seemed to be placing them, deep among the clothes pegs. He then took up two coils of clothesline and laid these carelessly on top.

Arrietty laughed. "As if," she whispered scornfully, "they wouldn't search his basket!"

"Quiet, Arrietty," said Homily, watching intently as Mild Eye, staring across at them, advanced to the edge of the bank. "It's early yet to laugh. . . ."

On the edge of the bank Mild Eye sat down and, his eyes still fixed on the borrowers, began to unlace his boots.

"Oh, Pod," moaned Homily suddenly, "you see those boots? They are the same, aren't they? I mean—to think we lived in one of them! Which was it, Pod, left or right?"

"The one with the patch," said Pod, alert and watching. "He won't make it," he added throughtfully, "not by paddling."

"Think of him wearing a boot patched up by you, Pod."

"Quiet, Homily—" pleaded Pod as Mild Eye, barefoot by now, began to roll up his trousers. "Get ready to move back."

"And me getting *fond* of that boot!" exclaimed Homily just above her breath. She seemed fascinated by the pair of them, set neatly together now, on the grassy verge of the stream.

They watched as Mild Eye, a hand on the leaning hazel, lowered himself into the water. It came to just above his ankles. "Oh, my," muttered Homily, "it's shallow. Better we move back. . . ."

"Wait a minute," said Pod. "You watch!"

The next step took Mild Eye in to well above the knee,

wetting the turnup of his trousers. He stood, a little non-plussed, holding tight to the leaning branch of the hazel.

"Bet it's cold," whispered Arrietty.

Mild Eye stared as though measuring the distance between them, and then he glanced back at the bank. Sliding his hand farther out along the branch, he took a second step. This brought him in almost to the thigh. They saw him start as the coldness of the water seeped through his trousers to his skin. He glanced at the branch above. It was already bending; he could not with safety move farther. Then, his free arm outstretched toward them, he began to lean. . . .

"Oh, my—" moaned Homily, as the swarthy face came nearer. The outstretched fingers had a greedy steadiness about them. Reaching, reaching . . .

"It's quite all right," said Pod.

It was as though Mild Eye heard him. The black eye widened slightly while the blue one smoothly stared. The stream moved gently past the soaking corduroys. They could hear the gypsy's breathing.

Pod cleared his throat. "You can't do it," he said. Again the black eye widened and Mild Eye opened his mouth. He did not speak, but his breathing became even deeper and he glanced again at the shore. Then clumsily he began to retreat, clinging to his branch, and feeling backwards with his feet for rising ground on the slimy bottom. The branch creaked ominously under his weight and, once in

shallower water, he quickly let it go and splashed back unaided to the bank. He stood there dripping and gasping and staring at them heavily. There was still no expression on his face. After a while he sat down; and rather unsteadily, still staring, he rolled himself a cigarette.

Chapter Twenty

"I told you he couldn't make it," said Pod. "Needed a good half yard or another couple of feet. . . ." He patted Homily on the arm. "All we've got to do now is to hold out till dark, and Spiller will come for sure."

They sat in a row on the same stick, facing upstream. To watch Mild Eye, they had to turn slightly sideways to the left.

"Look at him now," whispered Homily. "He's still thinking."

"Let him think," said Pod.

"Supposing Spiller came now?" suggested Arrietty, gazing hopefully along the water.

"He couldn't do anything," said Pod, "not under Mild Eye's nose. Say he did come now, he'd see we were all right like and he'd take cover near until dark. Then he'd bring his boat alongside on the far side of the island and take us all aboard. That's what I reckon he'd do."

"But it won't ever get dark," Arrietty protested, "not with a full moon."

"Moon or no moon," said Pod, "Mild Eye won't sit there all night. He'll be getting peckish soon. And as far as he calculates, he's got us all tied up like and safe to leave for morning. He'll come along then, soon as it's light, with all the proper tackle."

"What is the proper tackle?" asked Homily uneasily.

"I hope," said Pod, "that not being here, we won't never need to know."

"How does he know we can't swim?" asked Arrietty.

"For the same reason as we know he can't: if he could've swum, he'd have swum. And the same applies to us."

"Look," said Arrietty, "he's standing up again . . . he's getting something out of the basket!"

They watched intently as Mild Eye, cigarette dangling out of the corner of his mouth, fumbled among the clothes pegs.

"Oh my," said Homily, "see what's he doing? He's got a coil of clothesline. Oh, I don't like this, Pod. This looks to me"—she caught her breath—"a bit like the proper tackle."

"Stay quiet and watch," said Pod.

Mild Eye, cigarette in mouth, was deliberately unfolding several lengths of line, which, new and stiff, hung in curious angles. Then, an end of rope in his hand, he stared at the trunk of the hazel. "I see what he's going to do," breathed Homily.

"Quiet, Homily—we all see. But"—Pod narrowed his

eyes, watching intently as Mild Eye attached the length of rope above a branch high on the trunk of the hazel—"I can't quite figure where it gets him. . . ."

Climbing down off a curve of root, Mild Eye pulled on the rope, testing the strength of the knot. Then, turning toward them, he gazed across the river. They all turned round, following the direction of his eyes. Homily gasped. "He's going to tie the other end to that ash tree. . . ." Instinctively she ducked as the coil of rope came sailing above their heads and landed on the opposite bank. The slack of rope, missing their island by inches, trailed on the surface of the water. "Wish we could get at it," muttered Homily, but, even as she spoke, the current widened the loop and carried it farther away. The main coil seemed caught in the brambles below the alder. Mild Eye had disappeared again. He emerged, at last, a long way farther down the towpath almost beside the bridge.

"Can't make out what he's up to," said Homily, as Mild Eye, barefoot still, hurried across the bridge, "throwing that rope across. What's he going to do—walk the tightrope or something?"

"Not exactly," said Pod. "The other way round like: it's a kind of overhead bridge as you might say, and you get across by handholds. Done it myself once, from a chair back to lamp table."

"Well, you need both hands for that," exclaimed Homily. "I mean, he couldn't pick us up on the way. Unless he does it with his feet . . ."

"He doesn't need to get right across," explained Pod. He sounded rather worried. "He just needs something to hang onto that's a bit longer than that hazel branch, something he knows won't give way. He just wants a bit more reach, a bit more safe lean-over. . . . He was pretty close to us that time he waded, remember?"

"Yes . . ." said Homily uneasily, watching as Mild Eye picked his way rather painfully along the left bank and made toward the ash tree. "That field's full of stubble," she remarked after a moment.

The rope flew up, scattering them with drops, as Mild Eye pulled it level and made it fast. It quivered above them, still dripping slightly—taut, straight, and very strong-looking. "Bear a couple of men his weight," said Pod.

"Oh, my goodness . . ." whispered Homily.

They stared at the ash tree: a cut end of clothesline hung the length of the bole, still swinging slightly from Mild Eye's efforts. "Knows how to tie a knot . . ." remarked Homily.

"Yes," agreed Pod, looking even more glum. "You wouldn't undo that in a hurry."

Mild Eye took his time walking back. He paused on the bridge and stared awhile up the river as though to admire his handiwork; confident, he seemed suddenly, and in no particular hurry.

"Can he see us from there?" asked Homily, narrowing her eyes.

"I doubt it," said Pod, "not if we're still. Might get a glimpse of the petticoat . . ."

"Not that it matters either way," said Homily.

"No, it don't matter now," said Pod. "Come on now," he added as Mild Eye left the bridge and behind the bushes was starting along the towpath. "What we better do, I reckon, is get over to the far side of the island and each of us straddle a good thick twig: something to hold onto. He may make it and he may not, but we got to keep steady now, all three of us, and take our chance. There ain't nothing else we can do."

They each chose a thickish twig, picking the ones that seemed light enough to float and sufficiently furnished with handholds. Pod helped Homily, who was trembling so violently that she could hardly keep her balance. "Oh, Pod," she moaned, "I don't know what I feel like—perched up here on my own. Wish we could all be together."

"We'll be close enough," said Pod. "And maybe he won't even get within touching distance. Now you hold tight and, no matter what happens, don't you let go. Not even if you end up in the water."

Arrietty sat on her twig as though it were a bicycle: there were two footholds and places for both hands. She felt curiously confident: if the twig broke loose, she felt, she could hold on with her hands and use her feet as paddles. "You know," she explained to her mother, "like a water beetle. . . ." But Homily who, in shape, was more like a water beetle than any of them, did not seem comforted.

Pod took his seat on a knobbly branch of elder. "And make for this far bank," he said, jerking his head toward the ash tree, "if you find you can make for anywhere. See that piece of rope he's left dangling? Well, we might make a grab at that. Or some of those brambles where they trail down into the water . . . get a hold on one of them. Depends where you fetch up . . ."

They were high enough to see across the sticks of their island, and Homily, from her perch, had been watching Mild Eye. "He's coming now," she said grimly. In her dead, expressionless voice there was a dreadful kind of calm.

They saw that this time he laid both hands on the rope and lowered himself more easily into the water. Two careful steps brought him thigh-deep on his foremost leg; here he seemed to hesitate. "Only wants that other couple of feet," said Pod.

Mild Eye moved his foremost hand from the rope and, leaning carefully, stretched out his arm toward them. He waggled his fingers slightly, calculating distance. The rope, which had been so taut, sagged a little under his weight and the leaves of the hazel rustled. He glanced behind him, as he had done before, and seemed reassured by the lissome strength of the tree; but the light was fading, and from across where they waited, they could not see his expression. Somewhere in the dusk a cow lowed sadly and they heard a bicycle bell. If only Spiller would come . . .

Mild Eye, sliding his grasp forward, steadied himself a moment and took another step. He seemed to go in deep, but he was so close now that the height of their floating island hid him from the waistline down. They could no longer see the stretching fingers, but they heard the sticks creak and felt the movement: he was drawing their island toward him.

"Oh, Pod," cried Homily, as she felt the merciless pull of that unseen hand and the squeakings and scrapings below her, "you've been so good to me. All your life you've been so good. I never thought to tell you, Pod—never once—how good you've always been . . ."

She broke off sharply as the island lurched, caught on the barbed-wire obstruction, and, terror-stricken, clutched at her twig. There was a dull crack and two outside branches dislodged themselves slowly and bobbed away downstream.

"You all right, Homily?" called Pod.

"So far," she gasped.

Then everything seemed to happen at once. She saw Mild Eye's expression turn to utter surprise as, lurching forward to grab their island, he pitched face downwards into the water. They went down with him in one resounding splash—or rather, as it seemed to Homily, the water rushed up to them. She had opened her mouth to scream but closed it just in time. Bubbles streamed past her face and tendrils of clinging weed. The water was icily cold but alive with noise and movement. No sooner had she let go her twig, which seemed to be dragging her down, than the hold on the sticks was released and the island rushed up again. Gasping and coughing, Homily broke surface; she saw the trees again, the rising moon, and the dim, rich evening sky. Loudly she called out for Pod.

"I'm here," cried a choked voice from somewhere behind her. There was a sound of coughing. "And Arrietty too. Hold tight, like I said! The island's moving . . ."

The island swung, as though on a pivot, caught by one end on the wire. They were circling round in a graceful curve toward the bank of the ash tree. Homily realized, as she grabbed for a handhold, that Mild Eye in falling had pushed on their floating sticks.

They stopped a little short of the bank, and Homily could see the trailing brambles and the trunk of the ash tree with its piece of hanging cord. She saw Pod and Arrietty had clambered down to the sticks that were nearest the shore, at which, with their backs to Homily, they seemed to be staring intently. As she made her way toward them, slipping and sliding on the wet branches, she heard Arrietty talking excitedly, clutching her father by the arm. "It is . . ." she kept saying, "it is . . ."

Pod turned as Homily approached to help her across the sticks. He seemed preoccupied and rather dazed. A long piece of weed hung down his back in a slimy kind of pigtail. "What's the matter, Pod? You all right?"

Behind them they heard bellows of fright as Mild Eye, emerging from the depths, struggled to find a foothold. Homily, alarmed, gripped Pod by the arm. "It's all right," he told her. "He won't bother with us. Not again tonight at any rate . . ."

"What happened, Pod? The rope broke—or what? Or was it the tree?"

"Seemingly," said Pod, "it were the rope. But I can't see how. Hark at Arrietty." He nodded toward the bank. "She says it's Spiller's boat . . ."

"Where?"

"There under the brambles."

Homily, steadying herself by clinging to Pod, peered forward. The bank was very close now—barely a foot away.

"It is, I know it is," cried Arrietty again, "that thing under there like a log."

"It's like a log," said Pod, "because it is a log."

"Spiller!" called Homily on a gentle rising note, peering into the brambles.

"No good," said Pod, "we've been calling. And, say it was his boat, he'd answer. Spiller—" he called again in a vehement whisper. "You there?"

There was no reply.

"What's that?" cried Pod, turning. A light had flashed on the opposite bank somewhere near the towpath. "Someone's coming," he whispered. Homily heard the sudden jangle of a bicycle and the squeak of brakes as it skidded to a stop. Mild Eye had ceased his swearing and his spitting and, though still in the water, it seemed he had ceased to move. The silence was absolute, except for the running of the river. Homily, about to speak, felt a warning grip on her arm. "Quiet," whispered Pod. A human being on the opposite bank was crashing through the bushes. The light flashed on again and circled about: this time it seemed more blinding, turning the dusk into darkness.

"Hallo . . . hallo . . . hallo . . . 'allo . . ." said a voice. It was a young voice, both stern and gay. It was a voice that seemed familiar to Homily, though, for the moment, she could not put a name to it. Then she remembered that last day at Firbank, under the kitchen floor: the goings on above and the ordeal down below. It was the voice, she realized, of Mrs. Driver's old enemy—Ernie Runacre, the policeman.

She turned to Pod. "Quiet!" he warned her again as the circle of light trembled across the water. On the sticks—if none of them moved—he knew they would not be seen. Homily, in spite of this, gave a sudden loud gasp. "Oh, Pod—" she exclaimed.

"Hush," urged Pod, tightening his grip on her arm.

"It's our nail scissor," persisted Homily, dropping her voice to a breathy kind of whisper. "You must look, Pod. Halfway down the ash tree . . ."

Pod swiveled his eyes round: there it hung, glittering against the bark. It seemed attached in some way to the spare end of rope that Mild Eye had left dangling.

"Then it was Spiller's boat," Arrietty whispered excitedly.

"Keep quiet, can't you—" begged Pod through barely opened lips, "till he shifts the beam of the light!"

But Ernie Runacre, on the opposite bank, seemed taken up with Mild Eye. "Now then," they heard him say in the same brisk policeman's voice, "what's going on here?" And the light beam flicked away to concentrate on the gypsy.

Pod drew a sigh of relief. "That's better," he said, relaxing slightly and using his normal voice.

"But where is Spiller?" fussed Homily, her teeth chattering with cold. "Maybe he's met with an accident."

"But that was Spiller," put in Arrietty eagerly, "coming down the tree with the nail scissor. He'd have it slung by the handle on his shoulder."

"You mean you saw him?"

"No, you don't see Spiller. Not when he doesn't want you to."

"He'd kind of match up with the bark," explained Pod.

"Then if you didn't see him," said Homily after a moment, "how can you be certain?"

"Well, you can't be certain," agreed Pod.

Homily seemed perturbed. "You think it was Spiller cut the rope?"

"Seemingly," said Pod. "Shinned up the tree by that loose bit of leftover. Like I used to with my name tape, remember?"

Homily peered at the brambles. "Say that is his boat under there, which I doubt—why didn't he just come and fetch us?"

"Like I told you," said Pod wearily, "he was laying up till dark. Use your head, Homily. Spiller needs this river—it's his livelihood, like. True, he might have got us off. But—say he was spotted by Mild Eye: he'd be marked down by the gypsies from then on—boat and all. See what I mean? They'd be on the watch for him. Sometimes," Pod went on, "you don't talk like a borrower. You and Arrietty both—you go on at times as though you never heard about cover and such-like, let alone about being seen. You go on, the both of you, like a couple of human beings. . . ."

"Now, Pod," protested Homily, "no need to get insulting."

"But I mean it," said Pod. "And as far as Spiller knew, we was all right here till dark. Once the hook had gone."

They were quiet a moment, listening to the splashes across the water. Homily, caught by the sound of that brisk, familiar voice, moved away from Pod in order to hear what was happening. "Come on, now," Ernie Runacre was saying, "get your foot on that root. That's right. Give us your hand. . . . Bit early, I'd say, for a dip. Wouldn't choose it myself. Sooner try me hand at a bit of fishing . . . providing, of course, I weren't too particular about the bylaws. Come on now"—he caught his breath as though to heave—"one, two, three—hup! Well, there you are! Now, let's take a look at this basket. . . ."

Homily, to get a glimpse of them, had hauled herself up on a twig when she felt Pod's hand on her arm. "Watch," she exclaimed excitedly, gripping his fingers with hers, "he'll find that borrowed fish! That rainbow trout or whatever it's called. . . ."

"Come on, now," whispered Pod.

"Just a minute, Pod—"

"But he's waiting," insisted Pod. "Better we go now, he says, while they're taken up with that basket. . . . And that light on the bank, he says, will make the river seem darker."

Homily turned slowly: there was Spiller's boat, bobbing alongside, with Spiller and Arrietty in the stern. She saw their faces, pale against the shadows, lit by the rising moon. All was quiet, except for the running of the ripples.

Dazedly she began to climb down. "Spiller . . ." she breathed. And, missing a foothold, she stumbled and clung to Pod.

He supported and gently guided her down to the water. As he helped her aboard, he said, "You and Arrietty better get in under the canopy. Bit of a squeeze now because of the cargo, but it can't be helped. . . ."

Homily hesitated, gazing dumbly at Spiller, as they met face to face in the stern. She could not, at that moment, find words to thank him, nor dare she take his hand. He seemed aloof, suddenly, and very much the captain: she just stood and looked at him until, embarrassed, he frowned and looked away. "Come, Arrietty," said Homily huskily and, feeling rather humbled, they crept in under the legging.

Chapter Twenty-one

Perched on top of the cargo, which felt very nubbly, Homily and Arrietty clung together to share their last traces of warmth. As Pod let go the painter and Spiller pushed off with his butter knife, Homily let out a cry. "It's all right," Arrietty soothed her. "See, we're in the current. It was just that one last lurch."

The knife box now rode smoothly on the ripples, gracefully veering with the river's twists and turns. Beyond the canopy and framed in its arch, they could see Pod and Spiller in the stern. What were they talking about, Arrietty wondered, and wished very much she could hear.

"Pod'll catch his death," muttered Homily unhappily, "and so will we all."

As the moon gained in brilliance, the figures in the stern became silvered over. Nothing moved except Spiller's hand on the paddle as deftly, almost carelessly, he held the boat in the current. Once Pod laughed, and once they heard him exclaim, "Well, I'm danged . . ."

"We won't have any furniture or anything," said Homily after a while, "only the clothes we stand up in—say we were standing up, I mean. Four walls, that's all we'll have: just four walls!"

"And windows," said Arrietty. "And a roof," she added gently.

Homily sneezed loudly. "Say we survive," she sniffed, fumbling about for a handkerchief.

"Take mine," said Arrietty, producing a sodden ball. "Yours went away with the skirt."

Homily blew her nose and pinned up her dripping hair; then, clinging together, they were silent awhile, watching the figures in the stern. Homily, very tense, seemed to be thinking. "And your father's lost his hacksaw," she said at last.

"Here's Papa now," Arrietty remarked as a figure darkened the archway. She squeezed her mother's arm. "It will be all right. I know it will. Look, he's smiling. . . ."

Pod, climbing onto the cargo, approached them on hands and knees. "Just thought I'd tell you," he said to Homily, slightly lowering his voice, "that he's got enough stuff in the holds he says to start us off housekeeping."

"What sort of stuff?" asked Homily.

"Food mostly. And one or two tools and such to make up for the nail scissor."

"It's clothes we're short of . . ."

"Plenty of stuff for clothes, Spiller says, down at Little Fordham. Any amount of it, dropped gloves, handker-

chiefs, scarves, jerseys, pullovers—the lot. Never a day passes, he says, without there isn't something."

Homily was silent. "Pod," she said at last, "I never even thanked him."

"That's all right. He don't hold with thanks."

"But, Pod, we got to do something. . . ."

"I been into that," said Pod. "There's no end to the stuff we could collect up for him once we get settled like, in a place of our own. Say every night we whipped round quick after closing time. See what I mean?"

"Yes," said Homily uncertainly: she could never quite visualize Little Fordham.

"Now," said Pod, squeezing past them, "he's got a

whole lot of sheep's wool, he says, up for'ard. Better you both undress and tuck down into it. Might get a bit of sleep. We won't be there, he says, not much before dawn. . . ."

"But what about you, Pod?" asked Homily.

"That's all right," said Pod, poking about for'ard. "He's lending me a suit. Here's the sheep's wool," he said and began to pass it back.

"A suit?" echoed Homily amazed. "What kind of a suit?" Mechanically she stacked up the sheep's wool. It smelled a little oily, but there seemed to be plenty of it.

"Well," said Pod, "his summer clothes." He sounded rather self-conscious.

"So Lupy finished them?"

"Yes, he went back for them."

"Oh," exclaimed Homily, "did he tell them anything about us?"

"Not a word. You know Spiller. They did the telling. Very upset Lupy was, he says. Went on about you being the best friend she ever had. More like a sister to her, she says. Seems she's gone into mourning."

"Mourning! Whatever for?"

"For us, I reckon," said Pod. He smiled wanly and began to unbutton his waistcoat.

Homily was silent a moment. Then she, too, smiled—a little puffed up, it seemed, by the thought of Lupy in black. "Fancy!" she said at last and, suddenly cheerful, began to unbutton her blouse.

Arrietty, already undressed, had rolled herself into the sheep's wool. "When did Spiller first spot us?" she asked sleepily.

"Saw us in the air," said Pod, "when we were on the hook."

"Goodness . . ." murmured Arrietty. Drowsily she seemed trying to think back. "And that's why we didn't see him."

"And why Mild Eye didn't either. Too much going on. Spiller took his chance like a flash: slid on quick, close as he could get, and drove in under those brambles."

"Wonder he didn't call out to us," said Homily.

"He did," exclaimed Pod, "but he wasn't all that close. And what with the noise of the river . . ."

"Hush—" whispered Homily. "She's dropping off . . ."

"Yes," went on Pod, lowering his voice, "he called all right; it was just that we didn't seem to hear him. Excepting, of course, that once."

"When was that?" asked Homily. "I never heard nothing."

"That fourth throw," whispered Pod, "when the hook caught in our stick, remember? And I was down there pulling? Well, he yelled out then at the top of his lungs. Remember a voice calling, 'cut it'? Thought it was you at the time. . . ."

"Me?" said Homily. In the wool-filled dimness there were faint, clicking, mysterious unbuttonings. . . .

"But it was Spiller," said Pod.

"Well, I never . . ." said Homily. Her voice sounded

muffled: in her modest way she was undressing under the sheep's wool and had disappeared from view. Her head emerged at last, and one thin arm with a sodden bundle of clothes. "Anywhere we can hang these out, do you think?"

"Leave them there," said Pod as, grunting a little, he struggled with Spiller's tunic, "and Arrietty's too. I'll ask Spiller . . . dare say we'll manage. As I see it," he went on, having got the tunic down past his waist and the trousers dragged up to meet it, "in life as we live it—come this thing or that thing—there's always some way to manage. Always has been and, like as not, always will be. That's how I reckon. Maybe we could fly the clothes, like, strung out on the knitting needle . . ."

Homily watched him in silence as he gathered the garments together. "Maybe . . ." she said, after a moment.

"Lash the point, say, and fly the knob?"

"I meant," said Homily softly, "what you said before: that maybe there is always some way to manage. The trouble comes, like—or so it seems to me—in whether or not you hit on it."

"Yes, that's the trouble," said Pod.

"See what I mean?"

"Yes," said Pod. He was silent a moment, thinking this out. "Oh, well . . ." he said at last, and turned as if to go.

"Just a minute, Pod," pleaded Homily, raising herself on an elbow, "let's have a look at you. No, come a bit closer. Turn round a bit . . . that's right. I wish the light was better. . . ." Sitting up in her nest of fleece, she gave him a long look—it was a very gentle look for Homily. "Yes . . ." she decided at last, "white kind of suits you, Pod."

In the large kitchen at Firbank Hall, Crampfurl, the gardener, pushed his chair back from the table. Picking his teeth with a whittled matchstick, he stared at the embers of the stove. "Funny . . ." he said.

Mrs. Driver, the cook, who was clearing the dishes paused in her stacking of the plates; her suspicious eyes slid sideways. "What is?"

"Something I saw . . ."

"At market?"

"No—tonight, on the way home. . . ." Crampfurl was silent a moment, staring toward the grate. "Remember that time—last March, wasn't it—when we had the floor up?"

Mrs. Driver's swarthy face seemed to darken. Tightening her lips, she clattered the plates together and, almost angrily, threw the spoons into a dish. "Well, what about it?"

"Kind of nest—you said it was. Mice dressed up, you said . . ."

"Oh, I never—"

"Well, you ask Ernie Runacre; he was there—nearly split his sides laughing. Mice dressed up, you said. Those were the very words. Saw them running, you said . . ."

"I swear I never."

Crampfurl looked thoughtful. "You've a right to deny it. But couldn't help laughing meself. I mean, there you was, perched up on that chair and—"

"That'll do." Mrs. Driver drew up a stool and sat down on it heavily. Leaning forward, elbows on knees, she stared into Crampfurl's face. "Suppose I did see them— what then? What's so funny? Squeaking and squawking and running every which way. . . ." Her voice rose. "And what's more . . . now I *will* tell you something, Crampfurl—" She paused to draw a deep breath. "They were more like *people* than mice. Why, one of 'em even—"

Crampfurl stared back at her. "Go on. Even what?"

"One of 'em even had its hair in curlers . . ."

She glared as she spoke, as though daring him to smile. But Crampfurl did not smile. He nodded slowly. He broke his matchstick in half and threw it into the fire. "And yet," he said, rising to his feet, "if there'd been anything, we'd have found it at the time. Stands to reason— with the floor up and that hole blocked under the clock." He yawned noisily, stretching his forearms. "Well, I'll be getting on. Thanks for the pie . . ."

Mrs. Driver did not stir. "For all we know," she persisted, "they may be still about. Half the rooms being closed, like."

"No, I wouldn't say that was likely; we been more on the watch-out and there'd be some kind of traces. No, I got an idea they escaped—say, there *was* something here in the first place."

"There was something here all right! But what's the good of talking . . . with that Ernie Runacre splitting his sides. And"—she glanced at him sharply—"what's changed you all of a sudden?"

"I don't say I have changed. It's just that I got thinking. Remember that scarf you was knitting—that gray one? Remember the color of the needles?"

"Needles . . . kind of coral, wasn't they? Pinkish like . . ."

"Coral?"

"Soon tell; I've got them here." She crossed to the dresser, pulled out a drawer, and took out a bundle of knitting needles tied about with wool. "These are them, these two here. More pinkish than coral. Why do you ask?"

Crampfurl took up the bundle. Curiously, he turned it about. "Had an idea they was yellow . . ."

"That's right, too—fancy you remembering! I did start with yellow, but I lost one—that day my niece came, remember, and we brought up tea to the hayfield?"

Crampfurl, turning the bundle, selected and drew out a needle; it was amber-colored and slightly translucent. He measured it thoughtfully between his fingers. "One like this, weren't it?"

"That's right. Why? You found one?"

Crampfurl shook his head. "Not exactly." He stared

at the needle, turning it about: the same thickness, that other one, and—allowing for the part that was hidden— about the same length. . . . Fragile as glass it had looked in the moonlight, with the darkened water behind. Staring, staring, he had leaned down over the bridge. . . . The paddle, doubly silvered, had flashed like a fish in the stern. As the strange craft came nearer, he had caught a glimpse of the butter knife, observed the shape of the canopy and the bargelike depth of the hull. The set of signals flying from the masthead seemed less like flags than miniature garments strung like washing in the breeze —a descending scale of trousers, pants and drawers, topped gallantly (or so it had seemed) by a fluttering red-flannel petticoat—and tiny shreds of knitted stocking whipped eel-like about the mast. Some child's toy, he had thought . . . some discarded invention, abandoned and left to drift . . . until, as the craft approached the shadow of the bridge, a face had looked up from the stern, bird's-egg pale and featureless in the moonlight, and with a mocking flick of the paddle—a fishtail flash that broke the surface to spangles—the boat had vanished beneath him.

No, he decided—as he stood there twisting the needle —he would not tell Driver of this. Nor how, from the farther parapet, he had watched the boat emerge and had followed its course downstream. How blackly visible it had looked against the glittering water, the masthead garments now in fluttering silhouette. . . . How it had dwindled in size until a tree shadow, flung like a shawl across the moonlit river, had absorbed it into darkness.

No, he wouldn't tell Driver this. Leastways, not to-night, he wouldn't.

THE BORROWERS AFLOAT

Praise for Alexandra Potter

'Nobody does it quite like Alexandra Potter'   *Daily Mail*

'*Me and Mr Darcy* is sure to score points with all you hopeless romantics out there'   *Heat*

'Feel-good fiction full of unexpected twists and turns'   *OK!*

'Great fun'   *Closer*

'Funny, romantic . . . tale about what might happen if all your wishes suddenly came true'   *Daily Mirror*

'Fantastically funny'   *Elle*

'A winning formula of chaotic heroine meeting eccentric hero, and, after misunderstandings, finding love. Sharply written, pacey and funny . . . pure self-indulgence'   *The Times*

'I loved it – it's fun, fast and feel-good – the perfect three! Positively dripping with humour and heart'   Helen Lederer

'Essential reading for anyone who thinks the grass is greener on the other side'   *Company*

'The perfect reading romcom'   *Daily Mail*

ALEXANDRA POTTER

Who's That Girl?

HODDER

First published in Great Britain in 2009 by Hodder & Stoughton
An Hachette Livre UK company

First published in paperback in 2009

6

A CIP catalogue record for this title
is available from the British Library

B format Paperback ISBN 978 0 340 95411 9
A format Paperback ISBN 978 0 340 95412 6

Typeset in Plantin Light by Hewer Text UK Ltd, Edinburgh
Printed and bound by Clays Ltd, St Ives plc

Hodder & Stoughton policy is to use papers that are natural, renewable
and recyclable products and made from wood grown in sustainable
forests. The logging and manufacturing processes are expected to
conform to the environmental regulations of the country of origin.

Hodder & Stoughton Ltd
338 Euston Road
London NW1 3BH

For Beatrice

ACKNOWLEDGEMENTS

Big, big thank-yous as always to my wonderful agent Stephanie Cabot and everyone at The Gernert Agency in New York; to my fantastic editor Sara Kinsella and the equally fantastic Isobel Akenhead and to everyone who's worked so hard behind the scenes at Hodder.

To my parents – I won't go into a teary Oscar-speech, but I can't say thank you enough for your continued love and support over the years. I honestly couldn't do this without you. And to my sister, I'll just say thanks Kel, for everything. (I had to keep that simple, otherwise it's going to run into pages . . .)

I also want to use this opportunity to mention my dear friend Mishky who I don't see as often as I'd like, but who's always there on the other end of the phone with kind words and encouragement.

Huge thanks also go to Dana, fellow writer and dear friend, who managed to keep me just about sane while I zipped back and forth between 1997 and 2007 and being 21 and 31 – trust me, time travel ain't easy – if wormholes do exist there were several moments when I wanted to throw myself down one . . .

Thanks also to Saar for all those hours spent brainstorming, cups of tea when I had writer's block, and never once complaining about having a dining-room table covered in calendars, index cards, and post-it notes for the best part of a year . . . And of course a big hug for my muse Barney.

I spent part of the time in England working on this book, and I want to say an extra special thank you to Tricia and Matthew – two amazing friends – for their generous hospitality in allowing me to be a writer in residence in their lovely house in Wimble-don, which came complete with the adorable Mr George. Thanks guys!

And finally, if I could meet my twenty-one year old self, I'd tell her that she will make some wonderful friends in her life: one of whom will be called Beatrice. Thanks Bea for your continuing friendship, boundless enthusiasm, and insider knowledge about the world of PR. And for making me laugh. A lot. This book is dedicated to you.

20 August 1997

Dear Diary,

Woke up with a terrible hangover. Last night Nessy and I
went to that new pub called the Wellington. It was such a
laugh! We drank a bottle of cava before we went out, as
we could only afford to buy one drink each. I saw Billy
Romani, the musician. God, he's so gorgeous, but he
doesn't even know I exist . . .

   Still loving my new job on the magazine – the people
are really cool and I'm learning a lot. Next stop "Vogue"!
Well, we can dream . . . Rang Dad from work and wished
him happy birthday – he loved his card and pressie!!!
Arranged to go home to visit him and Mum next
weekend. I miss them!

   Super-hot again. At lunchtime Nessie and I sunbathed
in the park and topped up our tans. She couldn't stop
talking about Julian, her new boyfriend. They've only
been on a few dates but she's already madly in love!

   Well, anyway, must get ready. I'm going to a party
tonight and am wearing my new miniskirt from Miss
Selfridge. Can't wait – it's going to be so much fun!!!

iCal

20 August 2007

06.00	Wake up.
06.15	Personal trainer.
07.30	Check emails.
08.00	Leave for office. En route make and return calls.
09.00	Arrive at office. Track news stories.
10.00	Write emails and touch-base with Bea.
11.00	Work on tomorrow's meeting for Larry Goldstein.
12.30	Lunch meeting with journalists from *Daily Standard* et al.
15.00	Write press release.
16.00	Connect Johnny Bird, West End hairstylist, with new editor of *Cuts* magazine for a quote and interview about his new shampoo range.
17.00	Write that press release!
18.00	Work on the award application for Cloud Nine account.
19.00	Dinner with Miles.
22.00	Review schedule for next day and prepare.
23.00	Read chapter in *Finding Yourself Made Easy*.
24.00	Go to sleep.

Chapter One

Woosh-woooosshhh-woosh-wooooshhhh.

Ah, what total bliss. Listening to the waves gently rolling in on the deserted beach – *wooosh* – their white, frothy peaks caressing the empty stretch of sand, before rolling back out again. *Woooossshhhh.* In and out they go. It's like the most wonderful lullaby. Relaxing. Soothing. Calming. My mind is drifting. My body is floating. I'm in a deeply peaceful place of serenity—

BEEP-BEEP-BEEP-BEEP!

Argh. No, I'm not. I'm in my flat in London, it's Monday morning, and I'm being jolted awake by the piercing sound of my alarm clock.

Heart thumping, mind racing, I roll over in bed, lift up my aromatherapy eye mask and peer anxiously at the time: 06.00. My stomach lurches. God, is that the time already? I have a personal-training session booked before work – I have to get up.

BEEEEEPPPPP!!!!

Like now.

I hit the 'off' button and throw back my sheets. I just bought these sheets. They're made from pure organic, unbleached cotton, which the saleswoman in John Lewis assured me would help my allergies. I have tons of allergies, which is a bit embarrassing, as that makes me sound like one of those trendy, annoying types who wear Crocs and think it's cool to have a wheat intolerance, but I *genuinely* do have allergies. Really, I do. Anyway, I thought I'd give the sheets a try. I'm not sure if they're helping, though, as I only have to think about how much I paid for them and my eyes start watering.

The alarm is now silent, but for a moment I can't rouse the energy to move. Arms and legs outstretched, I lie starfish-wide on my mattress, my eye mask still on my head, the humidifier puffing out little clouds of steam. My sound machine continues playing in the corner. It's set to 'Relaxing Ocean Lullaby' to help aid restful sleep. That's because not only do I have a ton of allergies, but I'm also a bad sleeper. Just terrible. I find it so hard to switch off. As soon as I close my eyes, all these niggling worries begin running around in my head like millions of ants.

I tried counting them once, like they tell you to do with sheep, but it had the opposite effect. Instead of making me fall asleep, it made me wide awake with fear and I ended up staying up that whole night watching cosmetic-surgery-gone-wrong programmes on TV. Not only was I exhausted the next day, but I now have these weird nightmares about vaginal rejuvenation. (Trust me, there is such a thing as too much information.) So that's the last time I'm ever going to try *that*.

Saying that, it might help if I gave myself more than five hours' sleep a night. It was nearly 1 a.m. when I finished reading the chapter in my new book, *Finding Yourself Made Easy*, and turned out the light. But then all successful women survive on hardly any sleep, don't they? Margaret Thatcher used to run the country on four hours, and I'm always reading articles about Madonna getting up at 4 a.m. to do Ashtanga yoga.

A yawn rips through me. Maybe just this once I'll treat myself to another five minutes in bed. I mean, another five minutes aren't going to hurt, are they?

I am just curling back into the foetal position when I feel a twinge of doubt. Actually, on second thoughts, better make it two minutes. I've got a busy week ahead of me. Tomorrow I'm meeting with a potential new client – Larry Goldstein, a high-profile cosmetic dentist from LA who does all the big Hollywood stars, is opening a flagship store here in London. He's looking for a public-relations firm to help launch it. *Mine*, I hope.

I feel a flutter of pride. I still can't quite believe I have my own company – Merryweather PR – which, according to a recent mention in the business section of the *Telegraph*, is 'a London-based boutique public-relations company. Specialising in health and beauty, it was formed three years ago by Charlotte Merry-weather [that's me!], PR expert and experienced journalist, who prides herself on giving each client the individual and personal touch.'

Which reminds me – I must check to see if Mr Goldstein has any personal dietary requirements. Only last week I made a reservation for some clients at this trendy new sushi restaurant that has a month-long waiting list (in order to get a table, I had to beg, plead and bribe the restaurant with the promise of a dazzling mention in all forthcoming press releases) only to discover when we arrived that the MD of the company was pregnant and couldn't eat raw fish.

My flutter of pride is quickly swamped by a familiar pang of worry.

OK, sod the extra two minutes in bed. Make it one.

Oh, and I mustn't forget to reply to those emails from my personal financial adviser. Now I'm in my thirties, I have to think about savings and retirement funds. Apparently, my shares in South-East Asia are looking healthy, but my pension isn't performing well. All fascinating stuff . . . if I had the faintest clue what he was talking about.

Fifty-five seconds.

Which is why I need to order a couple of those books off Amazon called things like *Investing for People Who Thought Dow Jones Was a Welsh Tenor Until Very Recently* or whatever.

Fifty seconds.

Miles, my boyfriend, says it's really important to plan for the future. He's a property developer and he's always talking security and investments. In fact last week when we were in bed, I zoned out in the middle of a conversation about buy-to-let mortgages and imagined myself snogging Jake Gyllenhal.

Actually, I've been doing that a lot lately . . .

Forty-five seconds.

But that's normal. Everyone fantasises in relationships. I know, because I read that in one of my self-help books too. We've been together for eighteen months and we have a great relationship. OK, so the sex isn't always mind-blowing, but that isn't everything, is it? When I was younger, it was really important, but nowadays there's so much more to think about.

Forty seconds.

Like my dry-cleaning. I must remember to pick up my dry-cleaning.

Thirty-five seconds.

And go food shopping. I shop at this really cool organic supermarket where I once spotted Gwyneth Paltrow by the King Edward potatoes. Unfortunately it's very expensive – a banana's like £2.50 or something – but I really try to eat a healthy, well-balanced, organic diet. This week, though, I was too busy and so there's nothing in the fridge.

Actually, that's a fib. There's lots of manky rotting vegetables. That's the only problem with buying organic. It goes off really quickly as it's not stuffed full of preservatives and E-numbers. In fact, to tell the truth, I usually end up throwing it away and going out to eat.

Thirty seconds.

Which reminds me. I promised to cook dinner tonight for Miles. Well, 'cook' is a slight euphemism. It's generally more a case of me emptying pre-washed organic rocket out of a bag and pricking the sleeve of some porcini risotto from the supermarket's 'restaurant range'. I'm a huge fan of those ranges. All right, they're a bit pricey, but they're *so* worth it. I mean, have you ever made risotto? It takes *ages*. Literally hours. All that faffing about stirring in vegetable stock every five minutes, until your carpel tunnel is killing you and you're drunk from polishing off the white wine that was meant for the risotto. (Well, you have to do *something* while you're stirring – it's so goddamn boring.) Then, to add insult to injury, it still turns out lumpy and tasteless, and you have to spend weeks eating it because it's like magic porridge and what started out as just two cupfuls of Arborio is now enough to feed an army.

My mind is racing at its usual hundred miles an hour, and I roll over and hug my pillow to my chest.

Twenty-five seconds.

On second thoughts I don't have time to go food shopping. We'll have to eat out instead. But that's OK. It's a good excuse to try that new gastropub in my neighbourhood. It opened a few weeks ago and I've been dying to go.

Twenty seconds.

Oh God, and now I've just remembered: it's Dad's birthday today.

My heart sinks. Mum left three messages on my machine last week to remind me and I *still* forgot. I haven't even sent him a card. Dad will be so upset if he doesn't get a card through the post. Last year I sent him an e-card as work was manic as usual, but when I called him, his voice was all small and Mum had to get on the phone and make cheery conversation about next-door's new extension.

Fifteen seconds.

My stomach clenches. OK, Charlotte, don't stress. You'll end up with that funny bumpy rash on your chest and you'll have to wear polo necks all week and look like Diane Keaton in *Something's Gotta Give*. I'll call Interflora and get an express delivery. So what if he's a man? Everyone likes flowers, right? I'll just ask for manly colours or something.

Ten seconds.

Do they *do* flowers in navy blue?

Five seconds.

Right, that's it. Time's up.

I pull myself up on to my elbows and take out my mouth-guards. According to my dentist, I grind. He says if I don't wear them, I'm going to end up with teeth ground down to little stumps and I'll look like Shane MacGowan from the Pogues!

Well, he didn't *exactly* say I'd look like Shane MacGowan, but that's only because he doesn't know who Shane MacGowan or the Pogues are. Anyway, that's beside the point. I still had to have them made and they cost over a thousand pounds. Vanessa, my best friend, thought I was crazy. She says I should have spent the money on a holiday as I just need to relax.

Honestly, I love Vanessa, but she's the one who's crazy. *A holiday?* Like I have *time* for a holiday. Besides, I do lots of things to relax. For example, I do Pilates. Actually, perhaps *do* is a little bit of an exaggeration – I did it once and fell asleep during the mat exercises – but I've every *intention* of doing it regularly. And I take baths with scented candles and lavender oil and a glass of chilled Sauvignon Blanc. Admittedly, I haven't taken one recently – in fact these days it's more a case of dashing in and out of the shower with a Bic razor – but still. *Plus* I even have Paul McKenna's relaxation CD, which my mum sent me. Somewhere. Tucked away in a drawer probably.

But I'm definitely going to listen to it when I have a minute . . .

OK, so I wouldn't go as far as to say I'm *relaxed* as such, but who is these days? I run a company. I have a mortgage, and responsibilities, and lines round my eyes to take care of. I mean, it's not like I'm twenty-one any more.

And thank goodness.

Back then I was renting a room, working in a dead-end job and always broke. Now I have my own successful PR company, a lovely flat in a leafy part of West London and one of those new convertible Beetles. I eat out at restaurants and can afford to shop for designer clothes and take luxury holidays.

Not that I do of course, as I never have the time, but I'm just saying.

I even have my own personal trainer.

Speaking of whom . . . Dragging myself out of bed, I swap my warm, fleecy pyjamas for my gym kit and hurry across to the window. I open the blind and pull back the curtains. It's still pitch black outside and for a moment I pause to stare into the silent, sleeping street.

I'm thirty-one years old and I've got the life I always dreamed of.

The doorbell rings, interrupting my thoughts, and I turn away from the window.

'Coming,' I yell loudly, and rubbing the sleep from my puffy eyes, I dash for the door.

Chapter Two

An hour later, after running around the park and doing about a million star jumps, Richard, my personal trainer, is jogging me back to my flat. Richard used to be in the Territorial Army and likes to push me really hard.

Unfortunately I don't mean 'push me' as in I'm on a swing wearing a floaty dress and going, 'Weeeee,' but as in me face down on the tarmac gasping for breath while he barks at me to do another fifty press-ups.

'OK, Charlotte, why don't we sprint the last hundred metres, huh?'

Trust me, I have *dozens* of reasons why we shouldn't, but Richard has already zoomed ahead of me, all six foot three of solid muscle in racer-back vest and tiny black shorts. I grip on to my hand-weights and lurch after his receding figure, which is springing buoyantly along the pavement on powerful calves.

'C'mon, no slacking. Fill those lungs. Lift those knees. *Hup, hup, hup, hup.*'

I swear Richard has the biggest calf muscles I've ever seen. Apparently, when he was in the TA, he would run hundreds of miles with a backpack that weighed more than me. Which I always find a comforting thought – just in case I should collapse and need to be carried home one day, or something.

I finally catch him up outside my flat.

'See you same time Wednesday.' Still running on the spot, Richard slaps me heartily on the back and I nearly keel over.

'Same time Wednesday,' I reply cheerfully, smiling brightly and opening my front door.

'Now, don't forget to stretch out those muscles,' he yells, grabbing his elbows and effortlessly throwing in a little bit of over-arm stretching.

'I won't.' I beam, giving a jaunty wave before disappearing inside. Where I collapse on the hall carpet.

I do this three times a week. When I was younger, I used to be such a slob, but now I'm older and wiser and know it's really important to keep fit. Although right now 'fit' isn't *exactly* the word I'd choose to describe how I'm feeling. I'd go for something slightly different. Like *exhausted* or *in agony*.

With sweat pouring down my face I lie spread-eagled on the floor like a chalk drawing at a murder scene and concentrate on catching my breath.

Of course, there are some mornings when I'd love a lie-in, but I also love being able to fit into my jeans. Plus, like Richard says, cardio is essential to maintain a healthy heart. I rest my hand on my heart protectively. It's hammering so hard in my chest it feels as if it's going to explode.

Not that it's going to. I mean, hearts don't *just* explode, do they?

I take off my heart monitor and look at the digital display. Gosh, that's quite a lot of heartbeats per minute, isn't it? I feel a prickle of anxiety. And I am really breathless.

Scenes from *ER* come rushing back – you know, the ones with a patient on a trolley and a handsome doctor yelling, 'Clear!' as he grabs the defibrillator and slams two massive electric shocks into their chest.

My anxiety cranks up a notch. Oh my God, I'm not *really* having a heart attack, am I? And on my dad's birthday! I clutch my chest in horror. If I die, he'll never be able to celebrate it again. Instead of spending it at the pub with his friends, he'll have to spend it kneeling at my graveside, grieving the loss of his only daughter.

Charlotte, stop it! I grab hold of myself. Don't be so ridiculous. You're *supposed* to get your heartrate up, that's the *whole* idea. You've just been exercising. And exercise is good for you. Hoisting myself up from the hall carpet, I catch my reflection in the mirror. My face is covered in bright purple blotches, I have bloodshot eyes, and my hair is plastered to my head in a sort of sweat helmet.

Oh.

Well, anyway, I can't stand around here all day – I need to get ready for work. Automatically I check the time on the clock on the hall table. I have lots of clocks. Vanessa's always teasing me by calling my flat Switzerland, but however hard I try, I always seem to be running late. That's because I'm on a really tight schedule. I don't have time to just 'chill out' as she puts it.

Tugging off my sweaty gym gear en route to the bathroom, I dash into the shower. That's not to say I don't ever chill out. Of course I do. For example, if there's ever a free window in my diary, I *always* schedule in something relaxing. The problem is, I never seem to have any free windows . . .

OK. Make-up? Perfect yet 'natural'. *Check.*

Hair? Dead straight yet flippy at the ends. *Check.*

Outfit? Standing in front of the full-length mirrors in my walk-in wardrobe, I check out my black pencil skirt and pussybow blouse. It has to be professional yet funky. Street yet chic. Cool yet – what's the word? – polished. I frown at my feet and slip on a different pair of designer heels. Much better. *Check.*

Running through my usual checklist before I go to work, I dash out of the bedroom and start racing around the flat collecting my things.

Laptop? I don't go anywhere without my iBook. Not even to the loo. Well, you never know when you might need to Google something. I snap it shut, sweep it up from the table and tuck it under my arm. *Check.*

Briefcase? My eyes fall upon it. Perched on the sofa, bursting with tons of documents that I need to read and sign. Asap. *Check.*

Yoga mat in case I get a free window later? (Yeah, right.) *Check.*

BlackBerry? Shit, where is it? Oh, right, yes, in my hand. Of course. *Check.*

My heart has recovered, by the way. I knew it would of course. I was just having a little panic. I do that sometimes, especially if it's anything health-related, but I'm just being careful. Better to be safe than sorry, that's what I always say.

Unfortunately my GP doesn't share my attitude. He seems to think I'm a hypochondriac or something. Only last week I had this funny-looking rash on my chest and when I Googled my symptoms, they were exactly the same as this flesh-eating bug from the Amazon. OK, so I haven't 'recently travelled to the Amazon' as my GP put it, but there was no need for him to get so grumpy. He didn't send me to the hospital for tropical diseases or anything! Just told me it was probably my eczema flaring up and to rub on some E45 cream.

Which I did, and it went away, but still, it *could* have been a flesh-eating bug.

With a gaggle of bags hanging off each shoulder, I leave money for the cleaner and dash out of the door. Then dash right back in as I'm blinded by the bright sunshine.

Sunglasses? My eyes sweep across the hall table on which stands a lamp, a white orchid and several framed photographs, and fall on one taken at my graduation. Mum and Dad are standing next to me, very much the proud parents. They looked pretty much the same then as they do now, although Dad had more hair and Mum was going through her pearly lipstick stage, but I'm barely recognisable. I'm wearing the traditional black gown and my mortar board is balanced precariously on top of my hair, which is long, dark and scrunch-dried to within an inch of its life. Unlike being blow-dried straight into a bob and coloured honey-blonde every six weeks like it is now.

The photo was also taken before I discovered tweezers and I have two thick black caterpillars where I now have perfectly arched eyebrows. And that smile! I peer at my crooked front teeth, which are now straightened, thanks to braces in my late twenties. God, I looked so different back then.

I'm distracted by my sunglasses, which I spot behind the photo and sunnies in place, I hurry out the door, down the front steps and beep the lock on my new Beetle. The lights flash and I tug open the door. Dammit, I've got another parking ticket. I curse, snatching it from under my windscreen wiper and throwing myself into the plush, cream leather interior. I stuff it in a side pocket along with all the other tickets, turn the ignition and shift the gearstick. The engine roars into life.

Gosh, I love my car. It's really powerful and has all these little extras, like heated seats, and satellite navigation, and a dashboard that lights up at night like a cockpit. The day I got it I was so excited. I remember just looking at it, parked outside my flat, all shiny and gleaming and brand new. I couldn't believe it was mine.

Though to tell you the truth, it's not as much fun as I thought it would be, since you can't drive faster than twenty miles an hour in London, I reflect as I pull out of my parking space and immediately hit rush-hour traffic.

In fact you're probably quicker on the Tube.

My BlackBerry suddenly springs to life and starts ringing shrilly. I glance at the clock on the dashboard: it's not even 8 a.m.

'Hello, Merryweather PR . . . Ah, yes, wonderful to hear from you. Now, about that contract . . .' Clipping on my earpiece, I quickly switch into work mode and start fielding calls.

Twenty minutes later and I'm running late. The traffic is terrible, worse than usual. It's all to do with the Olympics. There's a huge urban development programme going on in London at the moment and they've started demolishing all these old buildings in preparation for 2012. I read in the paper something about how it's one of the biggest and most complex visions ever in sheer size and scope: 'Dig, Demolition, Design' they've named it. But it's not just limited to the East End. Apparently, the whole city's being regenerated. There's even plans to build this amazing, state-of-the-art design centre not that far from my office and they're digging up all these thousands of tons of earth for the foundations. 'A feat of engineering' the *Evening Standard* called it.

A great stonking big hole in the ground that's making me late is what I call it, I fume, still edging along at a snail's pace. Frustrated, I drum my fingers on the steering wheel, feeling the ever-present knot in my stomach tighten as I glance at the time. Shit. I start running through my diary in my head. I've got a big week ahead of me and masses to do this morning. I don't want to be late.

Then I see a sign that makes my heart sink: ROADWORKS AHEAD: FOLLOW DIVERSION. This is all I need. Now I really *am* going to be late.

Exasperated, I follow the cars as they merge into one lane and begin crawling through the bright orange traffic cones. I mean, seriously, can we go any slower? I glance at the speedometer. I'm going less than *five* miles an hour! At this rate I'll get to the office by . . . I try doing the calculations in my head. Oh, God, I don't know, but it's going to take for ever. And I still won't have got there.

Painstakingly slowly we take a left and start weaving down various side streets until finally I see what looks like a main road ahead. Hopefully we're nearing the end of the diversion. I spot a set of lights. And they're green. *Come on, come on, come on.* Cars in front of me are filtering through.

I edge forwards, bumper to bumper. And now the lights are turning to amber. I try to squeeze through.

They change to red.

Argh.

Thwarted, I stop dead. Feeling the pressure building, I sit hunched over the steering wheel. OK, come on now, Charlotte, just relax, I instruct myself sternly. Getting all stressed out isn't going to make you go any faster, is it? Let's just do some relaxing breathing. Like we do in yoga. Closing my eyes, I flare my nostrils and take a deep breath. *In and out. In and out. In and—*

Oh, sod it. I snap open my eyes. Well, I'm sorry, Shivanyandra or whatever your name is, but this is useless. I'm going to have to ring Bea and see if she can rearrange my diary. I'm supposed to be on a conference call in fifteen minutes. Desperately, I snatch up my BlackBerry. But just when I thought it couldn't get any worse.

It has.

I've got no reception.

Great. Just great. What am I going to do now?

Chucking it down in exasperation, I glance back at the lights: they're still red. Jesus. These must be the longest lights in history. Distractedly, I let my eyes drift along the road, taking in my surroundings. There's a newsagent's on the corner, people waiting at the bus-stop, a tatty tanning salon that looks like it's been there for years. Actually, now I think of it, it has been there for years.

I haven't been paying attention, but now I realise where I am. I used to drive down this road to work every morning when I first moved to London. Only back then I used to drive in the opposite direction. I wonder how long it is since I last came down here. My memory flicks back. It was my first job and I was only twenty-one. God, it seems like another lifetime. Like another person.

Thinking back, my gaze floats across the intersection. Opposite, a line of cars are waiting and my eyes fall on the one at the front. It's an old Beetle, just like I used to drive back then, I notice. Gosh, how funny. It's almost identical. Same funny tangerine colour with the boxy little grille and rust around the headlights. It's even got a WWF sticker like I used to have, peeling off on the windscreen. I glance at the driver.

Oh my God, she looks just like me!

Me when I was twenty-one.

She's singing along to the radio, scrunching her dark, curly hair in the rear-view mirror just like I used to. She's even wearing a red-and-white T-shirt a bit like the one I always used to wear . . .

I stare in amazement as the lights change and the Beetle drives towards me.

Beeeeeeeeeeeeep.

The honking of a horn snaps me out of my daze and I slam my foot on the accelerator. The engine promptly stalls. Bollocks. Flustered, I quickly turn the ignition. Only I'm all fingers and thumbs and I can't get it to start and now several cars are honking their horns and – Suddenly the engine fires into life.

With an embarrassing screech of tyres I speed away from the lights, my mind whirring. I can't believe how much that girl looked like me when I was younger. The resemblance was uncanny. If it wasn't impossible, I'd almost think it *was* me. Goosebumps prickle on my arms and I give a little shiver. God, that was the weirdest thing . . .

Ahead, I see a sign looming – END OF DIVERSION – and feel a rush of relief. Thank God. My BlackBerry beeps from the passenger seat and I scramble for it. Hallelujah! I've got a signal. Plus five missed calls. OK, back to the real world. And slamming my foot on the accelerator, I speed-dial the office.

Chapter Three

B y the time I arrive at the office I've taken nine calls, replied to two emails (surreptitiously while stuck in yet more traffic) and put in a rush order at Interflora. Unfortunately they didn't do navy blue flowers – in fact the woman sounded quite puzzled when I asked – but they had purple, which is practically the same as navy blue.

Sort of.

As I charge through the door, my assistant, Beatrice, is waiting for me with a cup in her outstretched hand. This is how she greets me every morning: double espresso with a splash of soya milk. I'm on the phone with a journalist and I throw her a grateful smile and sweep it up like a relay runner. After two years we've perfected the pass. We don't spill a drop.

I continue across the office, my stiletto heels clicking on the floor. (Polished cement, very *de rigueur*. In fact the whole office is totally cutting-edge; in the PR world appearances are everything.) 'So I'll send over the new product for you to try. I'm sure you'll want to feature it in the magazine . . . Oh, right, you want the *whole range*?' Gosh, journalists can be so greedy. 'Absolutely. I'll get it biked over straight away!' I say cheerfully.

Reaching my desk, I end the call, sink down into my chair and drain my double espresso in one desperate gulp. I'm so fuzzy-headed before my morning coffee I can't think straight, let alone *see* straight. Which of course totally explains that weird incident at the lights.

'Morning,' chirps Beatrice, hugging a file to her chest and beaming.

Beatrice is always to be found hugging files to her chest. Not because she's actually working on anything in the files, but because it's an attempt to hide her impressively large chest (or 'bosoms', as she likes to call them), which she inherited from her grandmother, the Duchess of something or other. Along with a double string of pearls, a substantial trust fund and a little 'bolt-hole' in town. The little bolt-hole being a ginormous penthouse flat in Devonshire Square, W1.

Honestly, Bea is so jammy I should hate her, but she makes it impossible by being one of the nicest people I've ever met.

'Hi, Bea. Thanks for the coffee.' I smile gratefully.

'Good weekend?' she says brightly, striding over to me and unlooping my bags, which I'd forgotten were still hanging from my shoulders. Deftly, she puts each in their place.

'It was OK. I had quite a lot of work to catch up on.' I shrug, thinking back to yesterday. I spent it at the dining-room table surrounded by paperwork while Miles played squash, which seems to be pretty much how I spend my weekends these days.

Plonking my elbows on a pile of papers, I rub my forehead. I can already feel the beginnings of a tension headache. 'Any messages?'

'Larry Goldstein's assistant called to confirm your lunch tomorrow at the Electric in Notting Hill.' She begins peeling off Post-it notes. 'Sally Pitt, the editor of the lifestyle section of the *Daily Standard*, called. They want to interview you for an article they're doing on women who have it all.' She throws me an excited look. 'Oh, and Melody called. Several times in fact.'

Melody is a famous TV presenter who recently had a baby, shed a truckload of weight and is now making a fortune sharing her 'secret' through her DVD, books, TV series and her new range of pre-packaged healthy meals, Easy Without the E-Numbers, for which we do the PR.

'She's a little upset about the Sunday papers.' Beatrice produces a copy of one of the tabloids. On the front page is a photograph of Melody stuffing her face with a large Big Mac and fries. The headline 'SECRETS AND FRIES' screams across the front.

'Ah, yes.' I pull a face. 'I saw them.'

'Actually, I think her exact words were . . .' Beatrice peels off a Post-it note and begins reading earnestly ' "Fucking furious. I want to fucking kill the fucking *News of the Screws*." '

Despite my anxiety, I can't help smiling. With Bea's cut-glass accent, it's like hearing the Queen blaspheming. Honestly, posh people shouldn't swear. It just doesn't sound right.

'I can imagine.' I nod, spreading the paper across my desk and feeling the knot in my stomach tightening.

Melody might be the nation's darling: all sweetness and light and toothpaste-ad smiles – but away from the cameras she's got a worse temper than . . . well, I don't want to mention any names as I don't want to get sued, but think of someone with a terrible temper and it's worse. Much, *much* worse.

'Do you think she supersized it?' says Beatrice, peering over my shoulder at the photograph. Beatrice just watched the docu-film about the man who lived on McDonald's for a month and she can't stop going on about it. Bea's like that. She watches movies about five years after they come out. It's the same with everything, music, fashion . . .

I take in Bea's outfit. She's wearing her faithful twinset, a knee-length skirt in grey tweed, opaque tights and the black court shoes from M&S she's had for ever. Oh, and don't forget the pearls.

Actually, on second thoughts, I'm not sure what she's wearing was even in fashion five years ago.

'Does it matter?' I shrug, rubbing my temples. My head is really starting to throb. 'Supersized or not, she's launching her latest diet book, *Just Say No to Junk*, next month,' I remind her. 'And we're currently doing the promotion on her new range of Easy Without the E-Numbers soups.'

Beatrice frowns. 'Hmm, yes, that is slightly unfortunate.'

Beatrice has a knack for understatement. Being a small boutique agency, we only have a few accounts – I take care of the large ones, while Beatrice deals with the smaller ones – and Melody's range of products is one of our biggest and most profitable. The last thing I need is for a paparazzi photograph to jeopardise that by discrediting her as a health and fitness guru.

'It's potentially a disaster,' I murmur, shaking out two paracetamol from the family-sized bottle I keep on my desk and flicking on my computer. The screen comes awake and I quickly start typing into Google.

Beatrice tightens her grip on her pearls. 'Golly,' she says in a hushed voice. '*A disaster?*'

A bunch of articles pop up on my screen and I click one of them. '*Potentially*,' I correct her, quickly scanning through the article. After a moment's pause I look up at Bea. 'Call her agent and tell him we're going to put together a press release saying she's hypoglycaemic.'

Beatrice throws me a puzzled look.

'In other words she has low blood sugar.'

Her face floods with recognition. 'Oh, what a coincidence!' she whoops, galvanised by this piece of information. 'So does Mummy! She can't go anywhere without her Ritz crackers! Once she forgot them and her level dropped and she fainted. Right at the feet of Prince Philip.' She pauses as she sees my expression. 'We were in the Royal Enclosure at Ascot at the time,' she explains.

'Beatrice, she's not really hypoglycaemic.'

She looks at me blankly. Then it registers. 'Oh . . . I see . . . Gosh, you mean it's all a *ruse*,' she says, her voice lowered.

I nod.

'Gosh, Charlotte, you're so clever. That's why I love working for you!'

People are often fooled by Bea. They dismiss her as a ditzy Sloane, rather like I did when she first came for an interview, out of breath from running from the Tube, with her hair all over the place and a ladder in her tights. But in fact she's super-brainy and behind that dumb-blonde persona lies an academic genius. This is a woman who got a first in applied mathematics and double physics at Cambridge University and in her spare time solves geometric equations, 'just for fun'.

To be honest, she's totally overqualified for the job. We're the same age and she should be working in some lab somewhere, doing something mind-bogglingly scientific. But she insisted she really wanted to work in PR and was incredibly enthusiastic. Plus she has the poshest voice I've ever heard, which in the world of PR is invaluable.

Traditionally the girls who work in public relations are middle-class girls from the Home Counties, not girls from Yorkshire with an accent that's pure Pennines. Actually, mine isn't so much pure Pennines any more. Ten years of London have mellowed it to the point where I take *barths* not baths and tea is something I drink, not something I eat at 5 p.m.

Nevertheless, Bea's cut-glass accent opens doors that mine never could. We work as a team. A sort of bait and switch. I make the deals, get the contracts and take care of our clients, but Bea is the first point of contact for the press and media. And for that, her knack for sounding like the Queen is priceless.

The phone starts ringing and Bea rushes to answer it. 'Good morning, Merryweather PR,' she trills. 'Which publication are you calling from? The *Telegraph*? Oh, how thrilling! My grandfather was the editor for many years.'

See what I mean?

After rescuing the Melody account from imploding, the rest of the morning slips away in the usual hive of activity: making calls to journalists, writing press releases, taking conference calls with clients. One minute it's 9 a.m. and I'm trying to think of something sexy and fabulous to say about a dandruff shampoo, which is part of the new range by Johnny Bird, a West End hairstylist, and the next minute it's nearly one and I'm being tossed about in the back of a cab on my way to a lunch meeting at the Wolseley, a fashionable restaurant in Piccadilly. Usually I drive, but today I thought a cab might be quicker. More importantly, it means I can catch up with some work on the way.

I hang on to a strap to steady myself while reading an email that's just popped in on my BlackBerry. Scrolling down with my thumb, I'm about to start typing a reply when my mobile starts ringing. I have a BlackBerry and a mobile. The BlackBerry's for business; the mobile's for personal calls. Normally I switch it to silent during day, but I must have forgotten. I dig it out and glance at the screen. It's my parents.

Oh, shoot. Dad's birthday. I was going to call as soon as I had a free minute.

The thing is, I'm still waiting for that free minute.

'Hello, Charlotte Merryweather speaking,' I say out of habit before I can stop myself.

'Oh, so you *are* alive!' laughs a voice dryly.

'Oh, hi, Mum,' I say innocently, trying not to think of all the voicemail messages she's left over the past week. 'How are you?'

'Didn't you get my messages?' she demands, refusing to be sidetracked by pleasantries.

'Um . . . yes, but I—'

She doesn't let me finish. 'Well, let's just hope your father and I never have an emergency,' she continues tetchily. 'We'll be dead and buried before they can get hold of you.'

I roll my eyes. My mother loves melodrama. It's all the soaps she watches.

'I mean, what's the point of having a phone if you never answer it?'

'I was probably in meetings,' I proffer weakly.

'I called you at home this morning. You still didn't answer.'

Honestly, you'd think my mother was a prosecution lawyer, not a school secretary.

'I must have been out. I had my trainer at six.'

'Six *in the morning*?' she says, sounding shocked.

'Yeah, I ran five miles.'

'*You ran five miles?*' Her voice has gone all high-pitched. 'Oh, Charlotte,' she gasps anxiously, 'are you sure you're not over-doing it? You should give yourself a lie-in sometimes.'

A lie-in? God, I can't remember the last time I had a lie-in.

Oh, actually, I do – it was the morning after my big twenty-fifth birthday party. Which wasn't that long ago.

It was nearly seven years ago.

'And are you eating properly? You can't exercise on an empty stomach.'

Suddenly Mum's switched from prosecution lawyer into concerned-mother mode.

'Yes. I know,' I lie.

My empty stomach gives an angry growl and I silence it by gulping down the Starbucks that I grabbed before I jumped in the cab.

'Because there was an article in the *Daily Mail* yesterday and it said vegetarians lack . . . Hang on a minute . . .' There's the sound of rustling papers. 'Here it is. "Vegetarians lack essential minerals and vitamins."'

'Rubbish!' I exclaim, rootling around in my handbag and unearthing various vitamins and packets of health supplements. I'm forever buying different types. Only last week I read an article about ground apricot kernels. Apparently, you can live to be a hundred if you eat them in the right quantities. Unscrewing the lids, I swallow a handful. Unfortunately the quantities are so large you'd have to live to be a hundred just to have enough time to eat all the bloody things.

'A cooked breakfast, that's what you need.'

'I don't have time to be eating a cooked breakfast,' I reply a little impatiently.

'Well, you know what they say, "All work and no play makes Jack a dull boy."' She clucks disapprovingly.

I roll my eyes again. 'I bet Jack was successful, though,' I can't resist muttering.

My mum is always telling me I work too hard. Which is true. I *do* work too hard, but that's just part of running a successful business. Mum doesn't understand. She never wanted a career. All she wanted was to get married and have a family. For her, a job was just a job. A way to earn a bit of 'pocket money' as she puts it. But then she's always had Dad to look after her financially. It's different for my generation. *Better.*

At least I like to think so.

'Did I tell you, Marion just had a third grandchild?' replies Mum, ignoring me pointedly.

Yes, three times, I think, as I drain the last of my Starbucks.

'That's great. Send her my congratulations.'

'Her daughter's your age, you know,' she persists. 'Remember Caroline Godfrey? You were both angels in the school nativity.'

And that's another thing my mum does. Tells me all about her friends' daughters and how they're giving birth at a rate of knots. Populating the village with lots of bouncy, rosy-cheeked grandchildren, while her mean, selfish daughter lives over two hundred miles away in London, has personal-training sessions and is a vegetarian. Worse still, she *isn't even married.*

Talking of which.

'How's Miles?'

Oh-oh.

Let me translate. In mother-tongue 'How's Miles?' means 'Has he proposed yet?'

To be fair, it's not just Mum who does this. Miles and I have been together for eighteen months and everyone assumes he's going to propose. Everyone also assumes I'm going to say yes. After all, why wouldn't I? He ticks all those boxes that they go on about in women's magazines: he's handsome, successful, loyal, reliable *and* we never argue. In fact in the whole time we've been together we've never once had a row. Which is great, isn't it?

Only sometimes there's a part of me that wouldn't *mind* the odd argument. Like I say to Miles, we're allowed to have different opinions. It might even help add a teensy-weensy bit more excitement to the relationship, a bit more *va-va-voom*.

Anyway, like I was saying, I can't think of a single reason to say no.

Not that I'm trying to, of course.

'He's great. Is Dad there?' I say brightly, swiftly sidestepping the subject. 'I want to wish him happy birthday.'

'Oh, yes, hang on, he's just getting the post.'

I wince.

'David luv, it's our Lottie,' she calls loudly, then lowers her voice conspiratorially. 'You did send him a card, didn't you?' she hisses.

'Um . . . actually, I've sent flowers instead,' I say brightly.

'Flowers?' she repeats blankly, taken aback. 'For your *father*?'

'Why not? Dad loves flowers,' I say defensively. 'He's always gardening.'

'Well, I suppose so . . .' She trails off and I can tell she's wishing I'd just sent a Hallmark card and a pair of socks from M&S like a normal daughter. Huge bouquets being delivered to Mr Merryweather will no doubt cause a stir in their tiny village. I can practically hear Mum now, explaining to the locals: 'They're from his daughter. She lives in *Lundon*, you know.' Which, in tiny villages in the Yorkshire Dales, is explanation enough.

'Y'all right, poppet?' Dad's hearty voice sounds down the line and I feel a warm glow.

Ours has never been an easy relationship as we're both very stubborn. My teenage years were spent engaged in a perpetual battle over how loud I could play The Smiths. (Me: very loud. Dad: 'Bloody turn it off – it's music to slit your wrists to!') Yet despite our differences (or should that be similarities?) we're still incredibly close – in fact our birthdays are just four days apart.

'Hi, Dad, happy birthday,' I say, smiling and wedging the phone under my chin. We're coming up to the Wolseley and I want to touch up my make-up quickly before my meeting.

'Thanks, luv. I haven't opened my cards yet,' he replies cheerfully.

Guilt stabs. Dad will love his flowers, I just know it, but still. 'So what are you going to do today?' I ask, changing the subject. I open my compact and tilt it to the light. The dark shadows under my eyes loom into view.

'Oh, you know, a bit of this and that. What about you? When are you going to come visit?'

'Soon,' I reply, dabbing furiously with my Touche Éclat concealer. I don't like to look as if I'm wearing too much make-up, so this morning I just went for primer, light-diffusing foundation, concealer, powder, bronzer, a slight blush on the apples of my cheeks, mascara, a slick of lip balm . . . You know, the irony is, you have to wear an awful lot of make-up to look natural.

'You say "soon" every time,' he grumbles. 'We haven't seen you since Christmas.' Mid-dab I pause. Gosh, is it really that long? I think back to my mad dash up the M1 on Christmas Eve. I hadn't been able to get away before. Melody was launching a new range of diet shakes in the new year and Beatrice had been off with the flu, so I'd been working round the clock, doing everything myself. Most of Christmas Day was spent at my laptop trying to finish a press release, and then I was back in the office on Boxing Day.

'I know. I'm sorry, Dad. Things are just a bit hectic, that's all. I had to work over the weekend on a big deadline, and this week I'm pitching for a new account.' I give up on my dark circles, click my compact shut and stick on my sunglasses instead. 'I promise the first free weekend I have I'll drive up with Miles. You can see my new car. You'll love it, Dad. You can take it for a spin.'

'Hmm, yes, I read an article about one of those new VW Beetles in that magazine you got me . . .'

I can feel Dad softening. He adores tinkering around with cars, lifting up the bonnet, admiring the engineering.

'Whereabouts, luv?' the cabbie interrupts over the speaker.

'Hang on a minute, Dad.' I look up to see the restaurant looming before me. 'Anywhere here's fine,' I reply, leaning forward so the driver can hear me, before being suddenly thrown back as the cab swerves into the kerbside and comes to a shuddering halt. I quickly gather together my things, which have been flung across the back seat.

'Sorry about that,' I gasp into my phone as I clamber out on to the pavement. 'Thanks. If I could just get a receipt . . .' Passing the driver a tenner, I catch sight of myself in the cab window and immediately set about smoothing my hair. 'You were saying,' I continue, switching back to Dad.

I've become quite an expert at having two conversations at once. At first it used to freak me out and I'd get all muddled, but now I've grown used to it.

'Well, as long as you're all right,' he says, placated. 'We just miss our little girl, that's all.'

I feel a wave of affection. *Little girl?* In four days I'll be turning thirty-two. In eight years I'll be forty!

OK, I really shouldn't have had that thought.

'I miss you too, Dad,' I reply, hurrying up the front steps. 'But you don't have to worry about me, honestly.' Pushing through the glass doors, my heels clatter into the marbled lobby.

'And you're happy, aren't you?'

I spot a couple of large mirrors on the wall next to me and immediately begin checking out my reflection. 'Of course I am,' I say distractedly.

Out of the corner of my eye I see a couple of the journalists I'm meeting pulling up outside in a cab. My nerves jangle. I always feel like this before one of these lunches. I have to do a little presentation of a new product we represent and it's my opportunity to get press and promotion. As much as it's dressed up as lunch and wine and chit-chat, there's a lot of pressure on me.

'Look, Dad, I'm going to have to go . . .'

'Oh, right, well, off you go, then. It was nice speaking to you.'

I feel a stab of regret. We've barely spoken. But it's like that nowadays. When I was younger, I would sit on the phone for hours, talking about anything and everything, but now I'm lucky if I can snatch five minutes.

'I'll call you tonight,' I say hastily.

'Well, ta-ra, luv. Have a good day.'

'I will. You too, Dad.'

I snap my mobile closed, but for a moment I can't bring myself to move. My mind returns to my conversation with Dad, and for a moment I think about what he just said. Am I happy? I mean, *am I?*

'Charlotte!' I come to and turn round to see a woman in her early fifties. It's Katie Proctor, a journalist I've known since my days as a freelance writer. Grinning widely, she gives me a big perfumed hug. 'Ooh, are those new shoes?' she gasps, pointing at my feet. 'They're adorable.'

I feel a beat of pleasure. 'I didn't think you were coming.' I smile, kissing her on both blushered cheeks. 'You never RSVPed!' I throw her a mock look of disapproval.

'I know, I'm terrible.' She rolls her eyes guiltily. 'Do you forgive me?'

If it was anyone else, I'd be thrown into a panic, but Katie is more a friend than a work contact. 'Of course. How are you?'

'Parched! C'mon, let's go have a drink and catch up.'

We link arms, and as we enter the bar, I compose myself. Honestly, I don't know what's got into me today. The other journalists start arriving, and plunged into a cacophony of air-kissing, introductions and ice-cold Sauvignon Blanc, I pin on a bright smile and set to work.

Of course I'm happy. Why on earth wouldn't I be?

Chapter Four

L unch is a success.

The journalists leave tipsy, clutching goody bags and promising lots of press. I put the huge bill on my expenses, wave them off in their cabs and collapse on to the back seat of mine.

At least, I hope it was a success. I feel the familiar pangs of worry as my cab starts weaving through the traffic on the way back to the office.

My face aches from smiling. That's the thing about my job. It might look easy, sipping wine and nibbling on a marinated vegetable and watercress salad, but schmoozing is hard work. You're on full alert the whole time. Trying to mix business with pleasure, trying to find the right balance between discussing your clients and discussing so-and-so's recent break-up: 'He did what? No! That's terrible! You poor thing. You should get away for a few days. Treat yourself to a spa weekend. Talking of which, I know an amazing one in Scotland that we just happen to do the PR for . . .'

I make it back to my desk by around three and spend the rest of the afternoon chained to my keyboard. Beatrice leaves at six on the dot. She has salsa on Mondays and is in love with Pablo, the Brazilian instructor. Whenever she talks about him, she puts on this really over-the-top South American accent, all very dramatic with lots of lisping and rolling of Rs, and starts tossing her hair around, which is quite hard as it's a short bob. The transformation is incredible. It's like she goes from this no-nonsense English rose with sturdy calves to this tempestuous

Latino seductress. In fact I could have *sworn* I saw a pair of fishnets in her handbag when she left. Bea in fishnets! The mind boggles.

Anyhow, as usual Beatrice (or should I say *Be-a-treeth*?) tries to 'encourage' me, as she puts it, to leave the office with her by starting to turn off the lights while I'm still sitting here typing. Bea is not one to give subtle hints. Trust me, she would have pulled out the plug on my computer if I hadn't managed to fob her off by saying I was just finishing up some paperwork for tomorrow's meeting and I'd be following her in five.

Of course I'm fibbing, and of course she knows I'm fibbing, but whereas normally she would have called me up on it and waited next to me like a sentry, tonight the lure of Pablo and salsa is too strong and she's out of the door faster than you can say, 'Salida Cubana.'

Which means it's nearly eight by the time I finally put my computer to sleep, gather up my bags and leave the office. And then that's only because Miles has called twice from that new gastropub wondering where I am. I lie and say I'm just five minutes away.

It's really ten.

Oh, all right, then, twenty.

'Sorry I'm late.'

As I walk into the pub, I spot Miles sitting up at the bar. He's already ordered a bottle of wine for us and is reading the *Evening Standard* property supplement. He looks up and smiles, and I feel a warm glow.

'They've run out of the *moules*,' he says pleasantly as I bend across to give him a kiss. He smells of aftershave, and his face is tickly with the soft blond fuzz that's sprouted since he last shaved, which in Miles's case was probably a few days ago. Miles has such baby-fine hair. He's in his thirties and is still trying to grow his sideburns.

'Aw, damn,' I sympathise, sliding on to the bar stool next to him.

You see, this is what I love about Miles. No getting pissed off that I'm late. No big row. Just his usual, calm, composed self.

'So what else looks good on the menu?' Shrugging off my coat, I reach for the bowl of olives and nibble off the salty flesh. 'Mmm, these are delicious.'

Finally I can try to relax a bit. Have a drink. Some food. I rub my stomach. The knot that's been there all day feels as if it might be starting to subside.

'Well, the fish special sounds interesting . . .' He squints myopically at the blackboard, his brow creased in concentration, trying to decipher the chalk handwriting. He looks so cute when he does that. Like a little schoolboy, not a successful thirtysomething property developer.

'Good choice.'

A male voice next to me makes me turn round. Further along from me, sitting up at the bar, is a man eating alone. He's got short, dark, curly hair and has little round glasses balanced on the end of his nose, which I can't help noticing are all bent out of shape.

'I'd recommend the fish.' He gestures to his plate and smiles, revealing a faint Joaquin Phoenix-type scar running from nostril to lip, half hidden beneath his five-o'clock shadow.

'Hmm, no, I'm afraid I can't eat fish.' I shake my head.

'Oh, right. I didn't realise you were a vegetarian.' He nods and looks a bit embarrassed that he's said anything.

And now I feel bad. After all, he was only trying to be friendly.

'Well, I am, but I eat fish,' I confess. 'Only the thing is, I had fish the other day, so I can't have it twice,' I explain, and smile. 'All that mercury.'

We both look down at his plate again. The half-eaten salmon looks back at us. There's an awkward pause.

'Well, I guess in that case there's always the macaroni cheese,' he suggests, reading off the blackboard.

I shrug and wrinkle up my nose. 'Dairy.'

'Is that bad?' He looks puzzled.

'I have to avoid it.'

He eyes me suspiciously. 'Right . . .' he says slowly, and suddenly I discern the corners of his mouth twitching slightly.

I feel my guilt at being dismissive dispersing. Hang on a minute, is he finding my food allergies amusing or something? Is he – I feel a prickle of indignation – *laughing at me*?

'I was told to by a nutrionist,' I protest defensively, remembering the conversation I had with Dr Bruce, Melody's nutritionist, when I was doing a press release for one of her books. I'd complained of being tired and she'd drawn up a long list of things for me to avoid.

Saying that, I've been avoiding them for six months and I still feel exhausted.

'I'm not supposed to eat wheat or refined sugars either,' I add defensively. 'I'm intolerant.'

'You don't say?' he replies, clicking his tongue sympathetically, but his eyes give him away. Yup, he's definitely laughing at me.

Riled, I return my attention to Miles. 'What are you getting, darling?' I say pointedly, turning my back to the man at the bar. Honestly, it's not like I *asked* him to talk to me. He talked to me first!

'Well, actually, I think I'm going to go for the Thai green vegetable curry,' he muses.

'Ooh, yes, that sounds delicious,' I agree, a little louder than necessary. 'I'll have that too.'

Huh, that'll show him. Feeling a beat of satisfaction that I'm choosing something entirely different to his suggestions, I try attracting the attention of one of the bar staff so we can order.

'Gosh, it's really busy, isn't it?' I tut, waving futilely at someone pulling a pint while Miles sits next to me, waiting patiently. 'It's going to take for ever to get served.'

'Well, lucky you for I've finished my break,' says a now-familiar voice. I turn sideways to see the man next to me getting up from his stool, empty plate in hand, and lifting up the hatch to access the bar. At the same time I notice he's wearing an apron. 'Go ahead,' he says, picking up a pad and pen.

Oh, no. I feel a mixture of dismay and relief. He works here.

'Well, I'd like the Thai curry,' Miles is saying pleasantly.

'Righty-ho.' He smiles, scribbling it down. 'And for you?' He looks up at me and I could swear he's still got that amused expression in his eye.

'I'll have the same. Please,' I say decisively.

'You sure?' He cocks his head, eyes twinkling, pen poised.

'Absolutely,' I say firmly.

'OK.' He sucks air in through his teeth and writes it down.

I watch him, feeling a tweak of irritation, but as he turns to ring it up at the cash register, I suddenly have a thought. 'Hang on a minute, does that have nuts in it?'

He pauses from punching in the total and looks up. 'You're allergic to nuts too?'

My earlier twinge of irritation now goes up a notch to full-blown annoyance.

'Yes, very,' I snap, looking at him tight-faced. 'I could go into anaphylactic shock.'

'She has to carry an EpiPen,' adds Miles, sliding his arm round my waist protectively. 'A single nut could be lethal.' He looks at me, his face suffused with concern. 'Couldn't it, darling?'

I meet his unwavering gaze and for a moment I forget my annoyance and feel a rush of love towards him. Gosh, I am so lucky to have Miles as a boyfriend. He is so supportive and understanding.

'Wow.'

Unlike some men, I think, flicking my eyes back to the barman, who's just standing there, barely keeping a straight face.

'Yeah, I know. Pretty scary, huh? It's life-threatening on a daily basis,' nods Miles, thinking he's being genuine and not hearing the sarcasm in the barman's voice.

Blatantly ignoring the barman, I pick up the *Evening Standard* and pretend to be engrossed in an article about house prices. Hopefully he'll get the message.

He doesn't.

'That's terrible. Every meal must be terrifying.'

'I manage,' I snap from behind the paper.

'Yes, but we have to be extra vigilant,' confides Miles. 'Remember that time when we were having drinks at the Oxo Tower, darling? And you ate the pretzel that had been contaminated by salted peanuts . . .'

I feel a clench of irritation. And now it's directed at Miles. Honestly! Does he have to tell this guy everything? Can't he just ignore him like I'm doing?

'. . . and it was pretty scary there for a moment, I can tell you. Poor Charlotte's throat swelled up, her lips went all puffy, and she got this horrible rash.'

Oh, God. Please. Shut up, Miles. I shoot him a sideways look to silence him, but he's so absorbed in telling his story and defending my honour that he doesn't notice.

'Really? A horrible rash?' repeats the barman, pulling a face. 'Ouch.'

And you can shut up too, I think, looking daggers at him.

'I mean, can you imagine? Using the same bowl for pretzels that you earlier used for salted peanuts? Without washing it first?' Miles looks aghast. 'I wrote a pretty stern letter to the management afterwards, didn't I, Charlotte? Obviously they refunded our bar bill, but that wasn't the point.'

'Oh, look, there's a table free over there,' I pipe up, suddenly seeing a couple standing up to leave in the far corner of the pub. 'Let's grab it before it's taken!'

Jumping up from my bar stool, I scoop up my bags and coat

and hurry over to it. Anything to get away from that annoying barman. Honestly. Interfering like that.

I look over at Miles and wave. Abandoned at the bar, he seems a bit confused as to where I've suddenly disappeared to. As he spots me, he starts politely saying goodbye to the barman. That's the thing about Miles – he's so well mannered. It's like when we have sex. He always asks permission and afterwards he says thank you, which I think is taking your pleases and thank-yous to the extreme, but that's a public-school education for you.

Tucking the newspaper under his arm, he picks up our bottle of wine and glasses, and makes his way over.

'Don't worry, I've sorted it all out,' he says, sitting down. 'It doesn't contain nuts and the barman says he'll be sure to warn the kitchen of your allergies.'

'Great, thanks.' I smile, taking the glasses from him and pouring the wine. 'So how's work?' I ask, swiftly changing the subject. Despite our false start, I'm determined to have a nice evening with Miles. We barely saw each other last week because we were both so busy. *And* the weekend before that, come to think of it.

'Oh, you know, the usual.' He shrugs, settling back into his seat and taking a glug of wine.

Miles develops and invests in property – both here and abroad – and has what he calls 'quite a portfolio'. He's a real expert when it comes to house prices, and up-and-coming areas, and mortgage rates. That's one of the reasons we don't live together. He says we should be sensible and wait till the market levels off before we . . . How did he put it? Ah, yes, that was it: *consolidate.*

I remember because he got this meaningful look in his eye and reached for my hand, which is really unlike Miles as he never wants to hold hands. He gets all self-conscious at what he calls PDA or 'public displays of affection'.

'I signed the Aquarius deal. They start building next month.'
'Brilliant!'

'And it looks like I might be able to get investors for my other idea, so I think I'm going to fly up there tomorrow for a couple of days.'

'Which idea is that?'

'The project in Leeds?' He raises his eyebrows as if to remind me.

'Oh, to convert that old warehouse into luxury flats?'

'No, that was Manchester,' he corrects, frowning slightly. 'Anyway, I don't want to bore you with all this, darling.' Smiling, he rubs my hand lightly with his finger. 'Let's talk about something else.'

'No, please continue,' I say encouragingly. 'It's fascinating.'

Well, all right, perhaps 'fascinating' is a *bit* of an exaggeration, but it's important to show an interest in your partner's career. That's what a loving, caring, mature relationship is all about, according to a book I read recently called *Good Listener, Great Lover*. I read a lot of those kind of books. They used to call them self-help, but that's so nineties. Now they're called self-awareness. In which case I should be super-aware as I've got stacks of them. A whole bookcase in fact. And I'm always buying more.

'Maybe later,' he says, taking a sip of his wine and idly reaching for a section of the newspaper. But I can tell he's glad I said that. I feel pleased with myself and pick up another section. Honestly, it's such a relief finally to be in a proper, grown-up, mature relationship. Two professionals, sharing a bottle of good red wine, eating a bowl of mixed olives, reading different sections of the same newspaper.

Flicking absently through the pages, I feel a glow of contentment. When I was younger, I used to be so clueless about men. I was attracted to all the wrong guys and spent most of my twenties lurching from one disappointment to the next. So when I turned thirty, I decided that was it. No more players. No more bad boys. No more disastrous flings and stormy relationships.

Six months later I met Miles. We were introduced at a dinner party, and when he loosened his tie and stumbled over a polite hello, I knew I'd never have to spend another evening listening to Nirvana's 'Smells Like Teen Spirit' being picked out on a Fender guitar, talking about commitment issues or worrying about a roving eye. Here was a man whom I could trust. Who was a grown-up. Who had a successful career, his own flat on Hampstead Heath and not a single T-shirt with a skull and crossbones on the front. I glance across at him now. Instead he's wearing a lovely cashmere jumper that I bought him for his birthday last year. Gosh, he looks so adorable in it.

Taking a mouthful of wine, Miles catches me looking at him.

A man with whom I have shared interests and can have a proper civilised conversation.

'So?' he says, putting down his section of the paper.

'So?' I repeat, putting down mine.

Only, the thing is, for a tiny moment I can't think what to say. It's like my mind's gone blank. How weird. Obviously my lack of sleep is really catching up with me. I must be totally overtired.

'I'm thinking of investing in another buy-to-let property abroad,' he says casually.

Property! Of course. That's what we were talking about. How could I forget?

'Oh, where?' I ask interestedly.

'Well, I'm not sure yet,' he confesses, 'but I was thinking about Dubai.'

'Wow. Fab!'

If I'm honest, I find all this talk about security and investments a bit boring, and have a tendency to zone out, but now I'm getting older, I have to think about this stuff. As Miles always says, your property is your pension.

'Apparently, there's a couple of off-plan developments that could bring in a very good yield.'

'Really? That sounds . . . um . . . interesting.'

It's just sometimes I don't always want to be thinking about pensions and retirement. I mean, OK, so I'm turning thirty-two in four days, but it's not like I'm a hundred. Occasionally it would be nice to stop thinking about the future and just think about now for a change. Something spontaneous. Something fun.

'Two Thai green curries and a mixed-leaf salad?'

I look up to see the barman hovering with three large plates.

'Organic, in case you should ask,' he adds pointedly, shooting me a look.

'Yes, here, please,' says Miles, gesturing at the middle of the table. 'We're splitting the salad. Is that OK, darling?'

'Of course.' I smile brightly, ignoring the barman. 'It looks delicious!'

Honestly, what am I moaning about? This is great. Miles is great. Everything is great.

Miles passes me a napkin and impulsively I lean over to give him a kiss.

See, we can be fun and spontaneous.

Except my aim is off and I knock over his wine glass instead.

'Oh, shit. Sorry.'

'Whoops, nearly,' gasps Miles, catching it before red wine goes everywhere. 'Phew, that was lucky.' Placing it back upright on the table, he gives a little laugh. 'That could have been a bit embarrassing, couldn't it?'

'Yeah.' I nod, catching the barman's eye and quickly looking away.

And now I feel like a total clumsy idiot.

There's a tiny pause, and I think about attempting that kiss again, but somehow the moment has passed.

'Mmm, this looks delicious, doesn't it?' says Miles, picking up his fork.

'Um . . . yes . . . delicious,' I reply, doing the same.

And turning our attention to the food, we both fall silent and start eating.

Chapter Five

Laptop? *Check.*
Briefcase? *Check.*
BlackBerry? *Check.*

It's the next morning and as usual I'm rushing around my flat, going through my itinerary to make sure I haven't forgotten anything.

OK, I think that's everything.

Grabbing my keys, I let the front door slam shut behind me as I race down the front steps. Scrambling into my car, I reverse out of my space and right into rush-hour. Ahead, I can see the signs for the diversion and as traffic starts merging into one lane, I resign myself to another long journey into work.

My stomach gurgles. Yet again I haven't had time for any breakfast. Flicking open my glove compartment, I rummage around. I keep a stash of energy bars in here, just for emergencies.

OK, so they're not *just* for emergencies – they're usually my breakfast these days, when I *get* to eat breakfast, that is. I buy them in bulk from the health-food store. Finishing a call, I tear open the wrapper and take a bite. These are full of oaty goodness and are super-delicious.

Well, actually, they're not *that* delicious. In fact, they remind me a bit of the food I used to feed my pet gerbil, but they're a lot healthier than a Twix, which is what I used to eat in my twenties.

I chew quickly as we crawl along the high street, taking advantage of the few moments of silence before my phone starts ringing.

It's that Beetle again.

As I pull up at the lights, I feel a jolt of surprise. *Gosh, what a coincidence.* My eyes flick automatically towards the driver and I catch the briefest of glimpses. A split second. Barely long enough to see more than a flash of that same long, dark, curly hair before I'm blinded by the morning sunlight bouncing off the windscreen. Then she's gone. Disappeared behind a sunvisor. And I'm left staring at the car, feeling vaguely unsettled.

And slightly bewildered.

I peer closer. I didn't imagine it. That really *does* look like my old car, I determine, my chest resting against the steering wheel, my brow furrowed as I squint in the sunlight. In fact, it's exactly the same, complete with animal-rights sticker and rusting headlights. And bashed on the left-hand side from when I forgot to put on the handbrake and it rolled down the hill into the village and the farmer's tractor . . .

As the lights change and the Beetle drives past me, I gaze at it in stunned disbelief.

There's nothing else for it, it *has* to be my old car. It failed its MOT years ago on about a hundred different points . . . A vague memory stirs: the mechanic calling it a death trap and telling me that the next time I put my foot on the brake pedal, my foot would go through the bottom as it was so rusty. Dad very sweetly bought it off me as he loves fixing up old cars. He gave it to Mum as a runaround, something to use for taking the dogs on long muddy walks in the Dales, until eventually they ended up selling it to someone.

Someone who must now be living in London. Someone who must look a lot like I used to when I was twenty-one, I decide, feeling a flash of jubilant triumph. *See.* I knew there had to be a rational explanation.

As I drive off, I glance in my rear-view mirror, but the Beetle has already disappeared. It must have turned off somewhere, I muse idly, sailing across the intersection. And there was me beginning to think—

I catch myself. Well, let's just say I was beginning to think all kinds of silly nonsense.

As usual Beatrice is waiting for me with an outstretched cup of coffee. 'Morning,' she trills chirpily.

'Morning.' Scooping up my coffee, I march over to my desk, turn on my computer and start checking my emails. 'Any messages?'

'Larry Goldstein's people called to apologise that he's running late for lunch – I've changed the reservation to two p.m. – but he's very excited about meeting you.' She beams and crosses her fingers.

'Anything else?'

'Oh, and Miles called.'

I look up, surprised. Miles never calls me at the office – he knows how busy I am. Plus he was supposed to be flying up to Leeds this morning. I feel a flicker of worry.

'Is he OK?' I ask, going from zero to panic in less time than it takes to say 'accident and emergency'.

'Yes, fine,' breezes Beatrice. 'He'd just landed.'

Immediately I relax.

'He said he tried calling you this morning but couldn't get through to you on your mobile.'

'Oh, God, I probably forgot to turn it on,' I groan, digging it out of my pocket. 'I was in a bit of a rush this morning.' I glance at the screen. That's funny – it *is* on. I mustn't have been able to get any reception. Like yesterday, I remember. 'He should have tried me on my BlackBerry,' I think out loud.

'He did. He couldn't get through on that either.'

'Really? How odd.' Puzzled, I now look at my BlackBerry. But no, that's on too, and there are five bars of reception.

'They're called dropped calls,' says Beatrice knowledgeably. 'Apparently, they are a growing problem because of the sheer volume of people using mobile devices. In fact, I read in the *New Scientist* that the number continues to grow at an exceptional rate and it's been predicted that by 2010 there will be more than one and a half billion wireless-device users worldwide —'

'What did Miles say?' I interrupt hastily, before I'm quoted the entire *New Scientist* report.

But she's mid-flow. 'Although technically for it to be a dropped call I think you have to be actually cut off in the middle of a call, rather than not be able to get through at all, but essentially it's the same thing – too much phone traffic . . .' She trails off as she catches my eyes, and blushes. 'Oh, right, yes, sorry, Miles . . .' Scrambling for her jotter pad, she solemnly reads, ' "Has just had word from a contact that an amazing house is about to come on the market and wants to make sure you'll be free to go and look at it with him when he gets back." ' She looks up, her eyes shining. 'Are you two moving in together?'

'Well, we've talked about it,' I say, suddenly feeling a bit awkward.

'Golly, how exciting.'

'Er, yes, isn't it?'

To be honest, I'm feeling slightly taken aback. It's one thing talking about it, but it's another actually going to look at houses. It suddenly all feels very real, and not some far-off plan we talk about every now and again over a bottle of red wine and some mixed olives.

'Apparently, they can't get the keys until Thursday, but fortunately I've already checked the diary and managed to move a meeting with the beauty editor of *Elle*, so now there's nothing in the diary for that lunchtime,' Beatrice is chuntering away. 'I called him back to confirm that you'll meet him there at one o'clock.'

'Wow. Ms Efficiency.' I laugh lightly.

'Well, I do try.' She beams, handing me a Post-it note. 'This is the address.'

I look at it feeling slightly dazed. Beatrice has the neatest handwriting and yet the address seems to swim in front of my eyes. I take a much-needed gulp of coffee.

'You and Miles are like the most perfect couple. That's the kind of relationship I aspire to.'

'You do?' I look back at Beatrice, clutching her jotter pad to her chest, her face all wistful.

'Absolutely,' she exclaims, nodding vigorously. 'You're both so successful and attractive, and you have these exciting designer lives.'

Hearing her talking about us like that, I feel a beat of pride. I suppose we do really, I muse, imagining Miles and me in one of those glossy at-home shoots in *OK!*: 'Property baron Miles and partner Charlotte, owner of Merryweather PR, relax in their stylish new home and talk to us about property, pension plans and—'

Actually, that doesn't sound very exciting, does it? I try to think of something else. I mean, come on. We must do *something* exciting.

But my mind remains blank. It's too early – my brain's not working properly yet, I decide. Plus I've got other things on my mind. Speaking of which.

'Would you get me the Goldstein file, please?'

'Oh, of course. Coming right up.' Snapping out of her romantic daydream about me and Miles, Beatrice dashes over to her beloved filing cabinets.

Draining the rest of my coffee, I make a start on my inbox – I've got thirty-three unread emails.

As for me and Miles, I'll think of something exciting later.

'Another macchiato?' asks the waitress politely.

I glance at my empty cup. I've been mainlining caffeine all morning to make sure I'm totally clear-headed and focused for this meeting, but I think I might have overdone it. I feel more jittery and anxious than ever. 'Er, no, thanks, I'll just have some water instead.'

It's nearly two o'clock and I'm sitting at a table at the Electric, a trendy private members' club in Notting Hill, waiting to meet

Larry Goldstein, the Hollywood cosmetic dentist, famous for the whiter-than-white smiles of all the big-name celebrities, and owner of a hugely successful chain of Star Smile clinics in the US. He's over from LA to meet with PR companies to discuss launching the first Star Smile clinic here in the UK.

My body tenses and I realise I've begun shredding my business card. Despite my shiny, suited veneer, I'm really nervous. I'm up against some stiff competition, but if I can win this launch, it will give Merryweather PR a huge amount of international publicity and put us firmly on the map.

'Still or sparkling?'

'Definitely still,' says a voice with an American accent before I can answer.

I look up to see an older man. Attractive in that square-jawed, classic kind of way, he's wearing a pale blue Ralph Lauren shirt and his steel-grey hair is swept back from his tanned temples, as if he just ran his fingers effortlessly through it while stepping off a yacht in St Tropez. And not, as is more likely, a result of half an hour with a hairdryer and lots of product. He reminds me of Blake Carrington from *Dynasty*. In fact, for a moment there I almost think it *is* Blake Carrington from *Dynasty*.

'Dr Goldstein?' I ask, hurriedly sweeping the little scraps of business-card confetti off the tablecloth into the palm of my hand. I stuff them into my tote bag under the table as I stand up.

'Well, I was the last time I looked,' he says, laughing confidently.

'Charlotte Merryweather from Merryweather PR,' I reply, giving him one of my professional smiles as I go to shake his hand. 'A pleasure to meet you finally.'

'Please, call me Larry.' He grins. 'And I assure you the pleasure's all mine.' Taking my hand in both of his, he squeezes his fingers around my own.

'OK, Larry it is,' I say cheerfully, doing my best to appear like this super-confident career woman with her own successful PR company. And not how I really feel, which is so anxious I can feel damp patches forming under my armpits despite wearing a ton of anti-perspirant.

'Excellent!' He beams.

He's still holding my hand and I'm beginning to feel a little self-conscious. But that's probably because he's American, I tell myself, as he finally lets go. They're all very touchy-feely, aren't they? Unlike us reserved Brits with our brisk handshakes.

We break apart and sit down facing each other. As first impressions go, he's much older than I thought he was going to be. When I Googled him, his age came up as a vague late forties, but sitting here in the flesh, it's obvious those photographs on his website are airbrushed as he looks at least a decade older. Saying that, he's incredibly well preserved. Evidently no stranger to Botox, his forehead is unnaturally smooth and his eyes are a little stretched, but apart from that, he looks normal.

Except for his smile, that is.

As the waitress reappears with a bottle of still water and starts pouring, I gaze at his smile, transfixed. We're just not used to these kind of smiles in the UK. These perfect white-picket-fence smiles are the preserve of the Hollywood A-list and British reality-TV stars who *think* they're Hollywood A-listers. It's slightly bizarre to see teeth like this in real life. I mean, they're so *white*. And so, well, *big*.

'Carbonated drinks erode the tooth enamel,' he's saying now, flashing me his blindingly white smile, which has nothing to do with tooth enamel and everything to do with porcelain veneers the size of dinner plates. 'Just a little tip.'

'Oh, right . . . um, thank you.' I nod, mentally striking another thing off my list. God, what next? Soon I won't be able to eat or drink *anything*. In fact, at this rate I'll be on a drip. 'So have you visited London before?' I ask brightly, quickly brushing away the worrying image of me being fed saline solution intravenously.

'Many times. London is one of my favourite cities. I always feel so at home here,' he enthuses, taking a sip of water.

I suppress a smile of amusement. With his California tan and perfect smile, Larry Goldstein couldn't look *less* at home among grey-faced, wonky-toothed Londoners.

'Well, you certainly brought the good weather with you,' I say, launching into my well-rehearsed patter for visiting overseas clients. 'So tell me, is this just a business trip, or do you have any fun things planned while you're here?'

'Oh, I'm hoping I'm going to have some time for pleasure.' He smiles, resting his elbows on the table and leaning towards me.

For a split second I feel a little prickle of something, but I'm too busy focusing on making relaxed small talk to give it much thought.

'Well, there's a Frida Kahlo exhibition on at the Tate Modern that's amazing,' I continue. 'You should check it out.' I only know this because Beatrice went last weekend and told me about it.

'Oh, really? That sounds fascinating. I love Frida Kahlo. Tell me, what's your favourite painting of hers?'

Bollocks. All I know about Frida Kahlo is that she had a monobrow and Salma Hayek played her in the movie.

'All of them.' I smile brightly. 'They're all amazing.'

'Spoken like a true PR person.' He laughs smoothly and fixes me with his gaze. For the first time I notice how blue his eyes are. They almost don't look real. In fact, everything about Larry Goldstein is so perfect it seems fake. 'Which is why I'm really excited about this lunch,' he continues. 'I've heard great things about you and your company.'

'Why, thank you.' I smile, relieved to be off the topic of Frida and on to something I know a lot more about: *work*. Taking this as my cue, I pull out my portfolio from my briefcase and open it up on the table. 'As you can see from this portfolio of media coverage I've achieved for my other clients, this is the sort of thing you could expect from Merryweather PR . . .' I turn it round so he can see it and start leafing through the pages.

'Mmm, yes, very impressive.' He nods, looking at a full-colour spread from *The Times*.

I feel a beat of pride. 'Obviously it's impossible to guarantee anything,' I continue, 'but with such a strong brand as yours combined with my journalistic experience and intimate knowledge of how the business works, I think ours would be an incredibly successful and mutually beneficial partnership.'

'Mutually beneficial?' he says, glancing up from my portfolio and raising his eyebrows, which, now I'm up close, I notice are plucked into two perfect arches.

'Yes. With the right media coverage in the right places, we could raise your profile here in the UK. Let the public know who you are. What Star Smile stands for. And Merryweather PR has the expertise to do this and would be delighted to do so.' I'm in my stride now, and I have to say, I'm feeling pretty confident.

But then I should be. I've spent weeks working towards this meeting, researching information, putting together ideas, making sure I've thought of everything. I'm one hundred per cent prepared for this.

'And you say you have an *intimate* knowledge of how the business works?'

He's looking at me intently and for some reason I get this brief niggle of disquiet. The same feeling I had when he shook my hand earlier.

'Um . . . yes,' I reply, quickly brushing it aside and swinging back into full professional mode. 'That's something we pride ourselves on at Merryweather PR.'

'How intimate?' Still holding my gaze, he leans his body further across the table. Not a lot. Maybe only an inch, if that, but it's enough to make that niggle that I just brushed away come racing back again. And this time it's twice as big.

'Would you care to hear the specials?' The waitress is back and interrupts our conversation.

'Oh, yes, please,' I reply, glad of the distraction.

'Well, for appetisers, we have an heirloom tomato salad . . .'

Focusing my attention on the waitress, I listen to her going through the list, until after a few moments it feels safe to sneak a peek across at Larry Goldstein. Only his gaze is no longer on me, but on the pretty young waitress. And now he's throwing her that great big shiny smile of his.

And I'm totally overreacting, I realise, feeling both relieved and a bit silly. It's no biggie. He's obviously a bit of a flirt, that's all. Just humour him. And looking back at the waitress, I concentrate on what I'm going to have for lunch.

Chapter Six

Underneath the perfect tan, I discover Larry Goldstein is actually a very smart businessman. He asks lots of pertinent questions and seems genuinely impressed by both myself and the company.

'So tell me, how did you get started in the business?' As our entrées arrive, he looks at me, eyebrows raised with interest.

'Well, my background is actually in journalism. I studied English literature at university. Originally I wanted to be a writer.'

'A bit of a wordsmith, huh?' He smiles, pausing from eating to study me with interest.

'Well, I try,' I reply lightly, flicking back my hair under his gaze. 'In fact, my first job was for British Worldwide Press, a big London publishing company, as the editor of one of their magazines.'

'Wow.' Larry Goldstein widens his eyes and looks suitably impressed. 'That's amazing.'

I feel myself blush slightly. 'Well, yes,' I admit, trying to appear nonchalant at this compliment, while the little voice in my head whispers, *'Keep it up, Charlotte, keep it up.'* 'It was a wonderful experience and brilliant hands-on training, but after a few years I decided I wanted a new challenge and turned freelance.'

'Brave girl.' He nods approvingly.

'Fortunately my risk paid off and I wrote for all the big-name glossy magazines and newspapers, which of course is invaluable in terms of contacts now,' I say, waggling my fork emphatically.

'Absolutely,' he agrees just as emphatically, and I feel a slight thrill. I don't like to get my hopes up, but things are looking very good. Very good indeed.

'But after a couple of years I just wasn't feeling stimulated or challenged enough, so when I was presented with an opportunity to move into the exciting world of PR, I jumped at the chance.'

'And you don't regret giving up your writing career?'

'I've never looked back,' I say with conviction.

'That's awesome,' nods Larry Goldstein.

I smile modestly. Though I say it myself, it does all sound pretty awesome, doesn't it?

Except the thing is, it didn't happen *exactly* like that. Not word for word. The *real* truth is this: I left university with big dreams of being a writer and applied for every job in the 'Media' section of the *Guardian* I could find. Nearly a hundred rejection letters later, I finally got an interview with British Worldwide Press. That bit's true. So is the fact it was to be an editor of one of their magazines.

The bit I leave out is that the job was for an editor for their crossword magazine. So, all right, it wasn't exactly *Vanity Fair*, but it was a start. And everyone has to start somewhere, right?

Except there was just one problem: *I'm totally crap at crosswords*.

But I was desperate. And broke. And living at home with my parents.

Thankfully, I got the job and moved to London, and for the next three years I made up crossword clues by day and partied in the bars and clubs of West London by night.

And in my lunch hours? I updated my CV and sent it out to every magazine and newspaper I could think of. Until one day it landed on the right desk at the right time. A new lifestyle magazine was looking for a features writer. It was a dream come true.

Unfortunately the dream only lasted six months before the magazine folded and I found myself unemployed, on the dole and looking for another job. Only I couldn't find one, so I turned freelance.

Freelance. It sounds so exciting and glamorous, doesn't it? Images of me rushing around with a laptop under my arm, writing in coffeeshops, staying up till 3 a.m. smoking cigarettes in order to meet that deadline. How fabulous! I was going to be Carrie in *Sex and the City*.

But life isn't a TV show, and this Carrie wasn't wearing designer heels and being paid a fortune to write a witty sex column. Nope, this Carrie was pitching feature ideas to belligerent editors who never returned her calls. She was watching daytime TV in her pyjamas and worrying how she was going to pay the rent. Trust me, there is nothing sexy about *Richard and Judy* 24/7. And there wasn't even a *sniff* of a cosmopolitan.

This went on for months until a friend of a friend took pity on me and told me about a vacancy at a PR agency. The job involved writing press releases. So you'd still be writing, she reasoned. Well, if you can call a thousand words on shampoo writing. But it paid the bills. And it was only temporary. Just until I finished that novel of mine that I'd been working on in my spare time and had sold it to a publisher in a furious bidding war . . .

I wish.

Because I never did finish it. I got sidetracked. Became too busy. Gave up. I'm not exactly sure why I didn't go back to it, but the truth is that bit by bit my dream of being a writer receded and the reality set in. I got promoted, became more successful, earned more money and then set up my company. And it's true, I never have looked back.

Well, maybe sometimes. When I walk into a bookshop and pick up some author's first novel. Or read a fascinating article in a magazine and think maybe, just maybe, that could have been me. If I'd stuck it out longer. Tried harder. Been a better writer. And for the briefest second the longing is almost palpable.

But then I put it out of mind. I totally made the right decision. I mean, if I'd followed that route, I wouldn't be where I am today: having lunch in a chi-chi private members' club in Notting Hill, on the brink of winning an important account that will take the company to a whole new international level, I think, glancing at Larry Goldstein, who's looking at me thoughtfully.

'You know, I see a lot of myself in you.'

'You do?' I reply, not quite sure whether or not to take that as a compliment.

'Very much so.' He nods. 'And after meeting you and hearing all about your company, I feel very strongly that Merryweather PR might be just what I'm looking for.'

Sitting across the table from him, I smile modestly, the picture of professional poise, but on the inside I want to punch the air with delight. I hardly dare think it, but it's looking very possible that all my hard work and evenings spent suffering through his US TV show, *Celebrity Smile Clinic*, might just pay off.

'Well, as I said before, we'd be more than delighted to represent you here in the UK, Dr Goldstein.' Gosh, I don't know how I'm keeping my voice so calm.

He holds up his hand in modesty.

'I mean Larry,' I say, smiling.

'In fact, the more I think about it, I really don't think there's any point in seeing the other PR companies,' he continues evenly, raising an eyebrow. 'Do you?'

The contract is mine! flashes through my mind as if in neon.

'No . . . I don't think there is,' I reply, just as evenly. I feel a burst of giddy excitement and do my utmost to contain it. Like I said, poised and professional.

'Excellent. So we're agreed.' He smiles, reaching underneath the table to smooth down his napkin.

Oh, my God, I can't wait to call Beatrice and tell her how well the meeting went.

I feel someone's fingers sweep across my inner thigh.

What the . . . ?

I jump and look sharply across at Larry Goldstein, but he's innocently winding spaghetti on to his fork. I stare at him with a mixture of doubt and disbelief. Did I just imagine that? Did that not just happen? My heart thudding, I fidget self-consciously in my chair, pulling down my skirt and crossing my legs.

'Is everything OK?' Larry Goldstein looks over at me, his brow creased with concern.

'Um . . . yes, fine,' I reply politely, taking a gulp of water.

Well, what else am I supposed to say? Did you just stick your hand up my skirt?

Although, that's what I *would* have said when I was younger. I never stopped to think before I opened my mouth in those days – I would say exactly what was on my mind.

But now things are different. *I'm* different. I'm not some impulsive, headstrong twentysomething with nothing to lose. I'm a thirtysomething professional woman with everything to lose. Like my reputation, and a really important contract, I remind myself. I can't just start hurling accusations and causing a scene. Just think of all the possible repercussions.

Sitting bolt upright, I take a couple of slow breaths and concentrate on composing myself. Plus I could have easily made a mistake. Things aren't always what they seem, I tell myself, my mind flicking back to that incident at the lights. It was probably just the tablecloth brushing against my leg or something. In fact, the more I think about it, the more I'm positive that's what happened.

'Wow, the food is delicious, isn't it?'

I snap back to see Larry Goldstein smiling amiably at me.

'Oh . . . um . . . yes, delicious,' I reply.

Disconcerted, I turn back to my main course and continue eating. Only my appetite has disappeared and I'm relieved when a few minutes later the waitress comes to take our plates away.

'Coffee? Dessert?' she asks.

'No, I'm fine, thanks,' I reply, shaking my head. My earlier shiny delight at having won the account seems to have lost its sheen somehow. I know I should be over the moon, but I can't get that bugging feeling out of my head about what just happened. Or what I *thought* just happened, I correct myself quickly.

'Not for me either.' He beams, leaning back in his chair and fixing me with a satisfied smile. 'Coffee is the number-one cause of tooth discolouration.'

'Really?' I say faintly.

'So, now that's sorted, we need to get down to business.' Laying his manicured hands on the tablecloth, he looks at me intently. 'Figure out a game plan.'

'Definitely.' I perk up, relieved to be focusing back on business. I start running through the many lists in my head. 'When were you wanting to make an announcement to the press? Obviously the sooner we get the word out there, the more time we will have to start generating press, building momentum . . .'

'Totally.' He nods. 'Well, let's see . . .' He glances at his iPhone. 'I leave for the States next Wednesday, so how about Tuesday?'

I look at him in disbelief. '*A week today?*'

'Is that a problem?' He throws me a look that leaves me in no doubt that if it is a problem, he'll find a PR company for whom it isn't.

'No, of course not,' I quickly reassure him, while thinking of all the work I'm going to have to do, all the extra hours I'm going to have to put in to get things ready. I can already feel the pressure piling on top of my shoulders.

'Excellent.' He smiles with the confidence of a man who doesn't have problems. He has shiny white teeth, a perfect tan and a prime-time show on American TV. And he plays golf with Jack Nicholson, according to one of his press cuttings. 'So you're up for the challenge?'

'Absolutely.' I sit more upright and throw back my shoulders. Honestly, what's wrong with me? I love challenges. And I want this contract. This is my big opportunity. 'As I said before, Merryweather PR might be a smaller agency, but that works in our favour because we can give you a lot more personal attention,' I say with renewed enthusiasm.

'I like the sound of that,' he replies, a smile playing on his lips.

'So have you secured a location for the clinic?' I say briskly, ignoring a feeling of discomfort and forging ahead through my list.

'Almost,' he replies, and leans back in his chair. 'I've had a location guy scouting for the right space for a while now and we're down to two. Usually I go with my gut on things.' He gestures towards me. 'But in this case I'm not really feeling it.'

'Maybe I could offer some input?' I suggest.

'That would be awesome,' he enthuses. 'I'm flying to Brussels tomorrow for an international conference on the latest breakthroughs in cosmetic dentistry, but I'm back the next day.'

'Great.' I nod, pulling out my BlackBerry and scrolling through my diary. 'What time were you thinking?'

'Well, I'm pretty busy all day with designers.' Suddenly I get a horrible feeling where this is going. 'How about in the evening? Dinner maybe?'

I was *so* hoping he wasn't going to say that.

'It will give us a chance to get to know each other a bit more.'

I'm nodding and smiling as he's talking, but I'm flashing back to a few moments ago. Did I imagine it? *Did I?*

'It's important to make sure we're on the same page. Don't you think?'

He is smiling smoothly at me and automatically I switch on my professional smile, but my mind's all over the place. I wanted this contract more than anything, but now . . .

Larry Goldstein is still looking at me expectantly, waiting for an answer.

'Absolutely. Thursday evening it is, then!' I suddenly hear myself saying.

He breaks into a wide smile. 'Excellent!' Picking up his glass of water, he clinks it against mine. 'That's a date!'

I smile brightly. I've done it! The contract's mine.

Oh God.

Chapter Seven

I wave Larry Goldstein off in a cab and cross the street to where my car's parked. I check the time. Lunch went on for a lot longer than I expected and it's late. I need to get back to the office, tell Bea the good news and —

'Lottie!'

A familiar voice behind me interrupts my train of thought and I swing round. No one ever calls me that any more except . . . Squinting in the bright summer sunshine, I peer down the busy street, past cafés spilling out on to the pavement, people drinking cappuccinos and eating pastries, shoppers laden down with designer bags, a mother with a double buggy and an ageing cocker spaniel . . .

'*Nessy!*' I break into a grin. 'What are you doing here?'

'I live here, you idiot,' she counters jovially. 'What are you doing here?'

Vanessa is my oldest friend. I met her the day I went to London to interview for my first job on the puzzle magazine. She was sitting on a wall, outside the office, smoking a cigarette and looking utterly cool. To a nervous girl just off the National Express coach from Yorkshire and wearing her mother's suit, Vanessa epitomised everything about London. Six foot tall and a platinum blonde, she was twenty-five years old and shared a flat with some friends in Kensington. I was in awe of her.

I still am a bit. Happily married to Julian, her handsome lawyer husband, she's mum to two adorable children and lives in a big, rambling house in Notting Hill, with a fridge covered in finger paintings and thousands of family photographs cluttering the walls. We lead completely different lives and don't get to see each other as much as we'd like, but we're still incredibly close.

'I had a business lunch,' I say, gesturing to the restaurant. 'I was just going back to the office.'

'Bollocks to that.' She frowns, looping her arm through mine. 'Aunty Charlotte is coming back to ours for a cup of tea, isn't she?' She peers into the double buggy, where Ruby, aged three, and Sam, who's just turned one, giggle and gurgle respectively. 'See, that's a yes – in case you needed me to translate,' she says, and I can't help laughing.

'OK,' I surrender. I know better than to argue with Vanessa. 'But just one cup.'

'One cup,' she repeats innocently, and grasping the handle of the double buggy and the dog lead with one hand and me with the other, she propels us all down the high street.

'God, I wish someone would stick their hand up my skirt.'

I've just spent the last ten minutes telling her all about my weird 'incident' with Larry Goldstein, and to be honest, this wasn't the reaction I was expecting.

'Vanessa!' I gasp, horrified.

'Sorry, honey, only joking,' she apologises breezily. 'Well, sort of,' she mutters, furiously blitzing something unidentifiable in the blender until it resembles orange gloop. 'Though I must say, I've seen that Larry Goldstein being interviewed on *Oprah* and he's bloody handsome.'

'So what if he is? In a plastic sort of a way,' I can't help adding. 'That doesn't mean he can make a pass at me in a restaurant. It was a business meeting.'

She pauses from feeding Sam, a spoonful of orange gloop held suspended in the air. '*And?*' she teases. Distractedly she puts the spoon in her own mouth. There's a loud squawk. 'Oops, sorry, darling,' she coos, remembering herself. 'Silly Mummy is hungry too.' Hastily she shovels up another spoonful.

'*And* that's not acceptable!' I admonish. 'It's sexual harassment. Have you never heard of equality in the workplace?'

She screws up her forehead and pretends to think. 'Vaguely. I'm a stay-at-home mother who lives in a world of bathtimes, tantrums and dirty nappies. I gave up my job and my life to breed. Need I say more?' A spoon in each hand, she smiles wryly, then continues alternating orange gloop and pasta between two hungry mouths.

'Yeah, but you love being a mum,' I counter.

'True.' She smiles, turning to me, her face lit up. 'My kids are the best thing, I can't imagine life without them . . .' She breaks off uncomfortably as she catches my eye, and the smile slips from her face. For the briefest moment, a look passes between us. 'But I'm glad I waited until my thirties to have them,' she adds quickly.

She glances away and there's an awkward pause.

I fill it by changing the subject. 'Anyway, you hated your job,' I point out. Vanessa used to work in the solicitors' firm next to my office. That's how she met Julian, her husband. 'You said you couldn't wait to leave.'

'True.' She nods, breaking into a huge smile at Ruby, who's laughing hysterically as she smears orange gloop over her brother.

'You threw a resignation party,' I continue.

'And you couldn't come,' she remarks, shooting me a look.

'I was on a deadline.'

'When aren't you on a deadline?' she counters.

I open my mouth to protest, then close it again. Actually, come to think of it, I can't remember a life before deadlines.

'Gosh, that was a great party.'

I look back at Vanessa, who's gone all dreamy-eyed. 'We had over a hundred people squeezed into the old house. I was pregnant and couldn't drink and so Julian made me Virgin Marys and we played UB40 all night to celebrate my unemployment – you know, UB40: unemployed.' She smiles wistfully, her mind wandering back to that night over three years ago. 'Anyway, it's not as if you're certain this Goldstein chap even *made* a pass. It seems very unlikely. Like you said, you probably made a mistake.'

'True,' I admit. In fact, the more I think about it, I'm almost certain I made a mistake.

'And you got the contract, which is what you wanted, isn't it?'

'True.' I nod.

'So don't look so worried,' she reprimands.

'I'm not,' I reply, quickly uncreasing my forehead.

Well, OK, I am a bit, but I'm not going to admit it.

'Really?' Vanessa looks surprised. 'That's not like you. Usually you worry about everything.'

'I wouldn't say *everything*,' I say, a little miffed.

'You worry about being worried,' she points out, smiling.

'That's not true!' I say defensively.

'What about when we were celebrating your birthday and we bought all that champagne? And as we were about to open it, you got worried the cork was going to pop out and blind someone . . . ?'

'Well, it could have,' I protest. 'I was just being careful.'

'Yelling, "Duck!" and diving for cover?'

I blush. 'OK, so maybe I was a little overcautious, but those corks can be dangerous. They can take an eye out,' I argue, but I don't think Vanessa is listening.

'And what about the time we went to that spa hotel for my hen weekend and we are all having fun by the pool and you lay in the shade and refused to join in because you were worried you were going to slip and bang your head and be paralysed?'

'It happens a lot!' I admonish. 'Haven't you seen *The Sea Inside*?'

'We weren't diving off rocks into the sea, Charlotte. We were messing around on inflatable lilos.'

'Accidents can still happen,' I warn her.

'On a lilo?' she gasps incredulously.

The kettle boils and flicks off and she starts pulling out cups and looking for teabags.

'Do you have any chamomile?' I ask.

'Only Earl Grey,' she replies. 'Go on, live dangerously,' she teases, seeing my expression. 'I remember the days when you didn't even know what herbal tea was, and you certainly wouldn't have drunk it. In fact, you wouldn't drink anything back then unless it was alcoholic.'

I frown and ignore her.

'So how's Miles?' she asks, throwing me a look as she reaches for the kettle.

Vanessa is not what you'd call Miles's biggest fan. She's never actually said anything, but she doesn't have to. Those looks say it all.

'Great,' I enthuse. 'We had dinner last night at this really nice new gastropub.'

'So when are you two going to *consolidate*?' she teases, reaching for the wet-wipes and cleaning Ruby and Sam's faces.

I told Vanessa the story. Now I so wish I hadn't. She's never stopped joking about it.

'We're waiting for the property market to . . . er . . .' Shit. I have no clue what we're supposed to be waiting for the property market to do. I think I probably zoned out at that bit. '. . . do something,' I finish vaguely.

'Right,' says Vanessa, raising an eyebrow. I fidget uncomfortably. 'And when will that be?' She passes me a cup of tea.

I wrack my brains for some recollection of what Miles and I have talked about. We've talked about this for hours. Hours and hours and hours in fact. Which is weird, as I'm sort of having difficulty remembering any of the key points.

'Well, it's impossible to predict,' I say finally, and feel a beat of pleasure at how wise this sounds. 'But we are going to look at a house this week. Apparently, it's just come on the market and it's amazing.' I'm quoting Beatrice, who quoted Miles, so that has to be right.

Vanessa looks impressed. 'Where is it?'

'Um . . .' I pause. I remember looking at the Post-it note with the address, but for some reason I didn't take it in. 'London,' I reply brightly, then before she can fire any more questions at me, continue quickly, 'But we're not in any hurry to move in together. After all, this way we get to catch up on our sleep during the week, so at the weekends we can have lots of sex. It's the perfect arrangement really,' I add, though I'm not quite sure whether it's to convince Vanessa or myself.

'Sleep? Sex?' Vanessa wrinkles her brow as she passes Ruby and Sam a couple of strawberries. 'What are those again?'

I know she's joking, kind of, as she says this kind of stuff all the time, but I detect an edge to her voice that I've never heard before.

'Well, that's the *idea*,' I say, quickly backtracking.

There's a whole chapter in one of my self-help books about how a couple's sex life can suffer after the birth of a child. Apparently, you can become highly sensitive about the subject of sex, so I should probably be sensitive around Vanessa. Just in case.

'Though if you want to know the truth, usually one of us ends up falling asleep in front of *Location, Location, Location*,' I admit. Well, I don't want her feeling bad or anything.

'Before Julian and I had the kids, we were at it like rabbits,' she replies matter-of-factly.

'You were?' I ask, my voice coming out all high-pitched. I look at her, feeling slightly shocked. Vanessa and I don't really talk about sex. We did a bit when we were younger and having flings, but not once we got into proper relationships.

'Oh, absolutely. We couldn't keep our hands off each other,' she sighs, sinking down on to a kitchen stool and looking wistful. 'We were always at it.'

I feel a stab of both alarm and curiosity. 'Like how often?' I ask casually.

'Ooh, I don't know . . .'

If she says three times a week, that's OK. Miles and I have been known to have sex three times a week.

Maybe once.

'. . . every day. Sometimes twice. We used to like to get in a quickie before work,' she confesses, and then blushes like a naughty schoolgirl.

Every day? *Sometimes twice?*

I'm sitting here in the kitchen, sipping my tea and trying to remain very cool, but my jaw is nearly on the floor. For the last year I've been reassuring myself that all couples in their thirties are like Miles and me, having grown-up, comfortable sex in bed on a Saturday night, with the odd scented candle and some massage oil if I remember.

But now this discovery that my best friend – i.e. other people my age – were 'getting in quickies' on a daily basis before their kids came along is a bit worrying. Especially as recently I've been consoling myself that it doesn't matter if me and Miles don't have this incredibly passionate sex life, because once you're married, you stop having sex anyway.

'Well, you know, it's like they say, "It's quality, not quantity," ' I say hurriedly. 'And Miles and I have really good-quality sex.' As I say that, I realise I'm sounding a tad defensive.

'I'm glad someone is,' she quips, pulling out a stash of colouring books and felt-tip pens for Ruby, while jigging Sam on her hip.

'Do you want me to do anything?'

'No, no, I'm fine.' She smiles, stuffing loose strands of hair into her ponytail. For the first time I notice she's got roots, which is so not Vanessa. She's the kind of person who was getting them touched up the day before she gave birth to Sam, despite all those warnings about dyeing your hair when you're pregnant. 'Nonsense,' she pooh-poohed. 'I didn't see Gwen Stefani with regrowth.' Which I was kind of impressed by, as I didn't think Vanessa even knew who Gwen Stefani was.

'What about another cup of tea?' I offer.

'Actually, I might have a glass of Pinot Grigio and sit in the garden,' she says conspiratorially. 'Fancy one?'

About to say yes, I suddenly remember I have to go back to the office before I can go home and change my mind. Maybe alcohol isn't a good idea. Plus I'm driving. 'Better not.' I shake my head. 'I've been drinking a bit too much wine lately. In fact, I might go on this detox my client Melody keeps recommending.'

'Another one?' Vanessa looks at me, agog. 'But you just did one.'

'That was ages ago,' I refute hotly.

'It was last month. I remember because you came over for dinner but refused to eat anything.'

'Oh, right, yes. That was the Lemonade Diet,' I say, remembering.

'Is there a Coca-Cola Diet?' she quips dryly.

'It's not that kind of lemonade,' I retort, but I can't help smiling. 'It's this special liquid made of maple syrup and freshly squeezed lemons. Melody kept raving about it, and it's in her new book, so I thought I should try it. And anyway,' I add, 'that was a cleanse.'

Vanessa pulls a face. 'And there's a *difference*?' Glancing at the empty wine rack, she pads over to the fridge.

'A big difference.' I nod. 'I interviewed this nutritionist when I was writing Melody's press release and she told me that a detox is cutting all the things that are bad for you out of your diet. Like, for example, wine and coffee and sugar.'

Tugging open the door of her huge stainless-steel fridge, Vanessa pulls a face.

'And a cleanse means not eating at all. Though usually you supplement with juices,' I add, as an afterthought. 'Though not orange juice obviously, as that's full of sugar, but you can do all green vegetables, such as celery, and maybe some broccoli, and aubergine. Actually, no, that's purple.'

'Sounds yummy,' she says sarcastically. Tugging out an opened bottle of white, she pulls out the cork. 'Though I think I'll stick with grapes for now. They're green.' A few drops trickle out into her wine glass and she tuts. 'Damn. That was the last bottle.'

'I can pop out for you if you'd like,' I offer.

The door bangs and I hear footsteps approaching in the hallway. George, the cocker spaniel, who's spent the whole time asleep in his basket, suddenly starts wagging his tail.

'I have a better idea. Why don't we both pop out?' she suggests.

'But what about the —'

I'm about to say 'children', but there's screams of 'Daddy' and Julian walks into the kitchen. Tall and handsome with thick, light brown hair and carrying a briefcase, he walks straight over to their chair and high chair and scoops them both up, much to their delight. 'Why hello, you terrible twosome!' he whoops, smothering them in kisses and blowing raspberries into their necks.

I watch fondly. Julian is so good with them, I think, and then I catch Vanessa's face and instead of a glowing smile at this contented picture of a happy family, she's got a pinched expression.

'You're home early.'

Julian stops blowing raspberries to look up at Vanessa. It's almost like he's just noticed she's there. 'I'm afraid I'm not staying. I just popped back for a fresh shirt. I've got to have dinner with a client. Totally last minute.' He pulls an apologetic face.

'Well, in that case I'm going out for a few minutes,' replies Vanessa.

'Out?' He frowns.

'Yes, Charlotte and I are going for a drink.'

'We are?' I say in surprise.

Still holding a child in each arm, he turns round and sees me sitting on a kitchen stool. I wave weakly, suddenly feeling like I'm in the middle of a domestic and wishing I wasn't.

'Oh, hi, Charlotte,' he says, a little awkwardly. 'I didn't see you there.'

'Hi, Julian.' I smile. 'How's work?'

Julian is a big-shot lawyer and is always working on some case involving millions of pounds and high-profile clients. In fact, a couple of weeks ago I was on the elliptical machine at the gym and I saw him on one of the TV screens, being interviewed outside the Old Bailey for the evening news.

'Pretty hectic. We're in court at the moment and the jury—'

Before he can finish, he's interrupted by Vanessa. 'Ready, Charlotte?' She throws me a look. I have the feeling it's more a command than a question.

'Vee, please, I've only just walked in,' he says tersely. 'I've got to leave again in half an hour.'

'I won't be long,' she says, grabbing her handbag from the countertop.

'Can't I just have a few minutes to unwind a little?'

That's it. She pounces on him. '*You* want to unwind a little? What about me? Do you never think I want to unwind a little?'

Sliding off my kitchen stool, I start to back out of the kitchen.

'What am I? An unpaid babysitter?'

Julian's face sets hard. He looks as if he's about to say something, but then reconsiders. 'OK, fine, go ahead.' He sighs and turns back to jiggling Sam and Ruby on each arm. 'Right, who wants to watch *Sponge Bob*?'

There's squeals of excitement. Vanessa throws him a scowl before marching ahead of me out of the kitchen and through the front door.

Chapter Eight

'*Sponge Bob* bloody *Square Pants!*' she grumbles under her breath. 'Can you believe it?' Outside, she turns to me for support and I grapple around for the correct reaction, which isn't easy considering I have no idea what she's talking about. 'Can you bloody believe it!' she insists, her face tight with annoyance. Vanessa can look quite scary when she gets mad. She gets this big crease down the middle of her forehead, and her nostrils flare.

On second thoughts, perhaps I don't actually need to know what she's talking about. I just need to agree with her.

'Um, no . . . definitely not,' I say loyally, and then for good measure throw in a '*Square Bob* indeed!' Complete with a loud tut. See, I can do the loyal best-friend bit.

'You mean *Sponge Bob*,' she corrects, glancing sharply across at me.

Shit.

'Er, yes . . . of course . . . that's exactly what I mean,' I say hastily, trying to brazen it out, but I needn't have worried as she's not listening.

'He knows I don't like them watching too much TV. The odd half an hour is fine. I mean, I'm not one of those women who won't let their children near a television till they're going to university . . .'

She continues ranting as she marches ahead down the street, bag bouncing on her shoulder, arms swinging by her sides. I scurry alongside her. Vanessa is six foot in bare feet and she takes giant strides. I can barely keep up.

'. . . But it's not fair. I never get any time to myself. OK, I know I agreed to stop working and be a stay-at-home mum, but it would be nice if he could take both of them to the park sometime. Give me a bit of me-time. You know he's never looked after the two of them together? Sam is nearly thirteen months old—'

'So is there a place to get a drink nearby?' I interject brightly.

Vanessa stops ranting momentarily and pulls a face. 'You see, that's the thing. He knows we're not really going for a drink.'

'We're not?' I look at her, confused.

'No. I'm not going to leave him to cope with both Ruby *and* Sam. It'll kill him. Well, maybe for ten minutes.' She smiles wanly. 'There's a Tesco Metro on the corner. I'll get a bottle of wine and take it back home.'

As we enter the chilly, air-conditioned, neon-lit frontage of Tesco Metro, Vanessa makes a beeline for the wine cabinet and swiftly picks out a bottle of Pinot Grigio. I get the feeling this is not the first time she's made one of these wine runs. There's no meandering up and down aisles looking for the wine section, minutes spent looking at all the different varieties before making a choice. It's a professional, quick-in-and-out job, and now we're at the cash register and she's pulling out her credit card.

'Oh, and I'll take a couple of these.' She plucks two family-size bags of Maltesers and throws them down on the counter.

Oh-oh. This is really not good. Vanessa started Weight-Watchers last month and has been doing really well. The last few times I've seen her she's been all about points, points, points. I look at the bottle of wine and the Maltesers. She must have a whole week's quota there.

'And a packet of twenty Marlboro Lights.'

'I thought you'd given up,' I say, trying not to sound like the disapproving, health-conscious, anti-smoking friend and sounding exactly like the disapproving, health-conscious, anti-smoking friend.

'So did I,' she says grimly, tapping in her PIN and snatching her carrier bag from the checkout girl, who looks rather terrified at the sight of the angry, six-foot, wild-eyed woman who's already lighting up a cigarette despite the large 'no-smoking' signs.

OK. Perhaps this is not the time to give her a lecture on the dangers of smoking. Instead as we're walking through the automatic doors and on to the pavement, I'm wracking my brains for something to say. Something light. Something to distract her, like for example, 'Look at that lovely painting.' I pause in front of an antique shop. In the window is a large oil-covered canvas.

Vanessa puffs agitatedly on her cigarette. 'What, the one of the bull-fighter goring the bull to death?' she says, puzzled. 'You think that's lovely?'

Oh, shit. I hadn't even looked to see what it was.

Now I look closer, I see his large red cape flung wide, the swords in the bull's back, blood gushing from its neck. Ugh. It's horrible.

'But you're a vegetarian. I thought you'd hate it.'

'I do hate it,' I say hastily, shuddering with disgust. 'But it's got some . . . um . . . interesting use of brushstroke . . .'

'It has?' she asks doubtfully. 'Where?'

Me and my big mouth.

'Um . . . yes, look here . . .' I step right up to the window and peer through the glass. Vanessa joins me. I gesture vaguely. 'See? OK, let's go now.' I link my arm through hers and turn to lead her away, but she holds firm.

'Where? I can't see,' she grumbles.

You know when you've started something you wish you hadn't?

'Over there,' I say breezily, and then tug a little harder, but she's unbudgeable.

'I really can't see what you're talking about,' she snaps, being all passive-aggressive.

See. That's one of the phrases I learned from my self-help books.

'Oh, well, never mind, let's go,' I cajole, noticing a couple of figures inside, standing in the shadows. One of them is an old man with white hair and a tweed jacket. Probably the owner, I think distractedly, as he picks up something and shows it to the *barman from the pub*.

'Oh God, not him,' I groan out loud.

'Who?' pounces Vanessa. I swear she has the reflexes of a cat.

'No one,' I mutter, putting my head down and quickly turning away from the window.

'Where? Inside the shop?'

Vanessa is one of those people who if you say, 'Don't look now,' will look. And she'll make it obvious she's looking.

'Ooh, him?' she exclaims, practically pressing her nose against the glass.

Shit, he's going to see me. He's going to turn round at any moment and see my friend pressed up against the glass like one of those stuffed Garfields you see suckered to car windows. And me standing next to her like a right lemon.

He looks over. And sees me standing there like a right lemon. Fuck. As our eyes lock, I feel a jolt of embarrassment.

'Ooh, he's nice-looking,' she's now cooing approvingly. And loudly.

'*Nessy!*' I hiss. Hastily pulling my eyes away, I scoot a few shops down along the pavement, out of his view. My heart is thumping. God, what's got into me?

'What?' she says innocently. Reluctantly she gives one last look before following me. 'So come on, who is he?' she asks, catching up.

'Oh, no one. Just some barman I met the other night who was really annoying.'

'Are you sure? He looked kind of familiar. Actually, I think he's the husband of one of the women at Ruby's playschool.'

'Really?' Unexpectedly, I feel a beat of dismay. Which is ridiculous. Like I care if he's married.

'Um, maybe not.' She shrugs. 'Oh, I don't know. I don't know anything any more.'

She looks really down and I give her arm a squeeze. 'Vanessa, are you OK?'

'Not really.' She shakes her head. 'I think Julian is having an affair with his secretary.'

Boom. Out of the blue. Just like that. I glance across at her sharply, almost expecting it to be one of her black-humoured jokes, but she's totally straight-faced. So *that's* what this is all about.

'No way,' I say, leaping to his defence. 'Julian would never do that.'

'He's been working late at the office for months, and then one day I just happened to pop in to see him and I saw them together.'

'Together doing what?' I demand.

'Nothing that would incriminate them in a court of law, but . . .' Her voice trails off and she sucks hard on her cigarette. 'It was their body language. I could just tell.'

'You're imagining it,' I say, shaking my head resolutely. 'You're tired with the kids. He's working late. Your mind runs away with itself.'

She looks at me doubtfully. 'You think so?'

'Absolutely.' I nod vigorously.

Reaching her house, we walk down the driveway and she plonks herself on the wall. Hidden from the house behind Julian's Range Rover, she stubs out her cigarette and immediately lights up another. 'I don't know . . . I'm sure I saw something . . .'

'I promise you, you're imagining it,' I say, sitting down next to her. 'Look, if it's any consolation, I was at the traffic lights yesterday morning and for a moment I thought I saw myself in another car,' I confess.

'God, at least I'm not that bad,' she says, pulling a face.

'Well, obviously I didn't *really* think it was me,' I add quickly. 'I'm not *that* crazy, but even so it was very freaky. She looked just like I did when I was twenty-one.'

'Twenty-one,' sighs Vanessa wistfully. She stares into the middle distance. 'If only I knew then what I know now.'

'Like what?' I ask curiously.

'Like smoking isn't cool, so don't start.' She smiles ruefully. 'Because in ten years' time you're going to find it hell to give up.' She exhales smoke through her nostrils. 'And have as many lie-ins as you can manage because once you have kids, you'll never have another one. Oh, and wear miniskirts.'

She says this totally seriously and I look at her in surprise. In my whole life I have only ever seen Vanessa in black trousers.

'But you've never worn miniskirts,' I say.

'Exactly,' she replies. 'I should have. I always thought my legs were too fat, but I look at old photos of me and I was so skinny.'

'So wear a miniskirt now.'

'Are you kidding?' she tuts, staring dolefully down at her legs. 'I'm too old and fat.'

'Don't be silly, you look great.'

'I need to lose at least two stone.' Finishing the cigarette, she opens a packet of Maltesers and cracks one open on her back molars. 'I've got my weigh-in tomorrow and I haven't lost a single pound.'

She looks so miserable there's absolutely no way I can tell her to put down the Maltesers and back away.

'Maybe I should go on that Lemonade Diet you were talking about.' She prods at her stomach as if it's a strange object that really shouldn't be there. 'What can you eat on it?'

'You don't eat.'

She looks at me agog, her hand moving on autopilot from Malteser packet to mouth without taking her eyes off me.

'You just drink the lemonade.'

'For how long?'

'Um, I think I did it for five days.'

'Jesus, Charlotte!' she gasps.

'But I was rubbish and gave up halfway through. You're supposed to do it for ten.'

'Ten days,' she squawks. 'Ten days!'

'According to Melody, my client, you can lose ten pounds.'

She stops squawking. 'Right, that's it,' she declares, galvanised. 'Sod counting points. Where do I sign up?'

I look at her uncertainly. Vanessa? *On a cleanse*? 'Are you sure . . . ?' I say doubtfully. 'You won't be able to drink alcohol . . .'

'I know, I know,' she snaps impatiently. 'Is that it?'

'Well . . .' I hesitate, wondering how I can put it. 'There are a few side effects.'

'You mean, apart from being thin?' she dismisses.

'Yes.' I look at Vanessa, wondering how I can tell her. Even though we're old friends, I'm not sure how to put it. '*Unpleasant* side effects.'

'Such as?' she demands.

I pause. Oh, what the hell, it's best she knows.

'Sharting.'

There, I've said it.

'Excuse me?' Vanessa crinkles up her brow.

'It's the saltwater enema, you see, that you do as well as drinking the lemonade —' I begin quickly explaining, but she interrupts.

'Charlotte, what on earth's "sharting"?'

'It's when you think you're going to . . . fart,' I whisper tentatively.

'That's it?' She rolls her eyes.

'Well, no, instead you actually . . .' I trail off. 'You know.'

'No, I don't know. You're not making any sense,' she snaps impatiently.

'It's the two words joined together . . .' I wince. Oh God, this is hard. 'Farting and—'

'Shit!' she says in horror, suddenly getting it. Her jaw drops open and she clamps her hand over her mouth, and just when I think she's going to launch into a disapproving diatribe, she explodes into hysterical laughter. 'That is *so* funny!' she gasps between giggles. '*Sharting!*' Shoulders shaking, she's rocking backwards and forwards on the garden wall, letting out loud snorts, and I can't help but laugh too. 'That's the old Lottie I know and love! Coming out with something like that! It's the funniest thing I've ever heard!'

My laughter subsides. 'What do you mean, the old Lottie?'

'Well, you know, you're a lot more sensible now – you don't say things like that any more. Unfortunately,' she adds, cracking up again.

I feel a twinge of discomfort. I'm not sure I like that.

'Vanessa? Is that you?' Julian's voice calls from inside.

Immediately she stifles her giggles. 'I should go,' she says reluctantly, standing up and hiding her contraband goods in her large tote.

'Yeah, me too.' I nod, glancing at my watch. 'I need to pop back to the office before I go home.'

'We should do this more often.'

'Definitely.' I love Vanessa, but we just never get to see each other enough these days. 'How about two weeks on Thursday?' I say, checking my BlackBerry.

Vanessa rolls her eyes. 'Are you serious?'

'It's my first free night,' I say defensively.

'What about your birthday?' she gasps.

Suddenly I remember. 'God, I'd totally forgotten about that,' I confess.

'Well, it's this Friday,' reminds Vanessa, shaking her head. 'Don't tell me you were planning to work?'

'No, of course not!' I try to look affronted, but it's a bit hard, considering I spent my last birthday at a conference in Milton Keynes. 'I haven't planned anything.'

'Honestly, Charlotte!' she exclaims. 'What happened to the girl who used to love to party?'

I feel a stab of nostalgia, but I quickly dismiss it. 'She grew up,' I reply touchily.

'Well, the four of us will go out for dinner, then,' she announces, ignoring me. 'You and Miles, and Julian and me.

I'll get a babysitter. We can go to that gastropub you were telling me about.' Smiling triumphantly, she gives me a hug. 'Sorted.'

'You make me laugh.' I grin, hugging her back. In the whole time I've known her, I don't think Vanessa has ever taken no for an answer.

'You make *me* laugh,' she retorts, as if I've just insulted her. 'I haven't laughed that hard in ages. I nearly peed myself!'

I laugh and, waving goodbye, cross the street to walk back to the high street, where my car's still parked.

'Oh, and that's another thing I wish I'd known when I was twenty-one —' Standing on her front steps, she calls after me.

'What?' I ask, turning round.

She grins ruefully. 'Start doing your pelvic-floor exercises *now*!'

Chapter Nine

S queeze and hold. Squeeze and —
     Damn, they're really quite tricky, aren't they?

Forty-five minutes later, after popping back to the office to pick up some files, I'm sitting in traffic on the way home, busily practising my pelvic-floor exercises. To tell the truth, I've never done them before. Of course I've *heard* of them, but sort of vaguely, like when I was flicking through one of the 'older women's' magazines in the doctor's waiting room – you know, the ones that have adverts for StairMaster and articles about how to reupholster furniture – and saw an advert for the KegelMaster 2000. I remember because I thought it sounded a bit like the broomstick in Harry Potter but instead it was a sort of dumb-bell for *down there*.

Anyhow, I always assumed they were something you didn't have to worry about until you were of the age when you start shopping in M&S for Footgloves. In fact, to tell the truth, I'm not even sure how to *do* one.

But after Vanessa's earlier near-miss I need to learn, I tell myself, feeling a little panicked at the thought of myself in adult nappies. I squeeze hard and hold in a rictus of terror.

Holding my squeeze, I shift into first gear as the line of cars in front of me starts moving again. The traffic is still bad because of the diversion. It's going to be like this until next week, I muse, glancing at the large yellow signs. It's going to take ages to get home. Still, it means I've got plenty of time to do my Kegels. In fact, I've done a hundred already, I think proudly.

Though I can't really tell if I'm getting the right muscles. To be honest, I feel as if I'm just clenching my buttocks. I fidget in my seat as I approach the lights. OK, let's try again. This time I'll count to five. Concentrating hard, I try to focus in on *those bits* and squeeze hard.

One, two, three, four —

I'm interrupted by the shrill burble of my phone. I slip on my earpiece and answer.

'Hello, poppet,' says a voice with an unmistakable burr. It's my dad.

'Oh . . . um hi,' I gasp, feeling a flash of embarrassment at being caught doing pelvic-floor exercises by my father. Which is ridiculous. I mean, it's not as if he just caught me having sex.

OK, scrub that image. That does not make me feel any better.

'I'm just ringing to say thanks for the lovely flowers. They came yesterday afternoon.'

'Oh, good.' I smile.

'But you shouldn't have gone to any trouble.'

'Don't be silly, it wasn't any trouble,' I reply. And it's true, it wasn't. I just called up and gave them my credit-card details, I reflect, feeling a twinge of guilt as I think of all the time Dad's spent on me over the years. 'I'm just glad you liked them.'

In my peripheral vision I see a flash of orange and I'm suddenly reminded. 'Hey, Dad, do you remember that old Beetle I used to drive?' I say, glancing quickly sideways. Only now I can't see it. It must have already driven past, I decide, looking at the line of traffic streaming through the traffic lights.

'God, we're going back years now . . .'

'To 1997,' I say automatically.

'Aye, that's right. Bloody hell, you've got a good memory,' he chuckles, sounding impressed. 'Mine's like a sieve these days.'

'Well, can you remember who you sold it to?'

'Now that I do remember . . .'

I wait expectantly, my mind running through people I know in the village to whom he might have sold my old car. Not that I've spent much time there in years, but for the life of me I can't remember anyone else having long, dark, curly hair. Actually, what about the girl who works in the fish and chip shop? No, that was more of a shoulder-length perm. Plus if she's working behind the counter battering cod, what on earth is she doing driving around West London?

'. . . We had it scrapped.'

Startled by his reply, I'm momentarily blown off course.

'But I've seen it in London,' I reply, quickly recovering.

'You can't have done, luv. It failed its MOT so I sold it to a scrap merchant. I remember.'

'I thought your memory was like a sieve,' I remind him teasingly.

'I might have a bad memory, but I'm not bloody senile,' he grumbles. 'I towed it there myself.'

'Well someone must have fixed it up,' I reply stubbornly.

'I saw it being scrapped with my own eyes.'

He's so adamant that for a moment I almost wobble.

'That's impossible,' I argue.

'What's impossible is you seeing it around London.'

This has turned into another one of our arguments. Dad's wrong, and as usual he won't admit it.

'Dad, you're *wrong*.'

'No, I'm not. *You're* wrong.'

Argh. I feel a familiar burst of impatience. This always happens. We go back and forth for hours and nobody ever wins, unless—

Suddenly I get a flash of inspiration. This time I'm going to prove I'm right. Slamming my foot on the accelerator, I pull down sharply on the steering wheel and do a U-turn in the middle of the road.

I'm going to follow it.

'It's probably been made into tin cans by now,' my dad is chuckling down the phone.

Damn. Where did it go? My vision is blocked by a large truck in front of me. Then I glimpse it. Just ahead of me. A flash of orange turning down a side street. Trapped behind the truck, I edge slowly forwards until finally . . .

Indicating left, I pull off the diversion and shoot down a narrow, leafy street in hot pursuit. Just in time to see the tail-lights disappearing round a corner. Cursing under my breath, I race after it. It's a blind corner and as I zoom under a railway bridge, I pop out on to a main road.

And there's the Beetle, waiting at the pedestrian crossing. I pull out and up behind it. Now I can see the number plate as clear as day.

'See, Dad, you're wrong,' I say jubilantly. 'MUG 403P. That's my old number plate!'

Ha-ha! Dad is going to have to eat his words!

Only there's silence on the other end of the line.

'*Dad?*' Frowning, I glance at the screen on my phone; there's no reception. How annoying! That keeps happening to me.

Making a mental note to call the phone company and complain, I stuff it in the centre console and switch my attentions back to the Beetle, which has pulled away from the crossing. For a moment I entertain turning round, going back the way I came. After all, I've seen the number plate now. It has to be my old car. There's no other explanation.

Then again, I have come this far. And now I am kind of curious to find out who's driving . . . Plus if I'm to win this argument with Dad, I'm going to need hard evidence and I've got a camera on my mobile.

A few minutes later and we're zipping down leafy streets in Camden, North London. Now an expensive area, it used to be my neighbourhood when I first moved to London. Way back when you could rent a room for £50 a week, I shared a rambling terrace house with six others on a little dead-end street, tucked away behind the back of a church.

In fact, this is exactly the same route I used to drive home, I realise as the Beetle suddenly hangs a left at a mini-roundabout without indicating. Gosh, whoever she is, she's a terrible driver.

She doesn't indicate. Or slow down over speed-bumps, I curse silently, as she shoots off ahead of me. Honestly! If she's not careful, she's going to ruin the suspension on that car.

Come to think of it, that was how I ruined it.

No sooner has the thought popped into my head than we turn a corner and I suddenly see the turning for my old street up ahead. It's like a blast from the past: *Kilmaine Terrace*. Gosh, it's been years since I've been down there. Well, there's never been a reason to. It's a dead-end street, I muse, my attention switching back to the Beetle, which is still zipping ahead, until without warning the driver slams on the brakes.

God, wouldn't it be funny if—

She swerves right into Kilmaine Terrace.

My stomach spasms.

You have got to be kidding.

As I watch the car disappearing down the street, I feel a bit stunned. Talk about a coincidence. Indicating, I follow. The street looks exactly the same. Large white terrace houses, cherry trees . . . My eyes flick forwards. I used to live at number thirty-nine, overlooking the little square right at the end. I hang back as the Beetle zips towards it, the noise of its exhaust reverberating off the houses. It doesn't show any sign of slowing down.

Don't stop outside number thirty-nine.

A voice suddenly pops into my head and I jump. I realise I'm silently praying the Beetle is going to stop outside a different house. Any house. Just not number thirty-nine. That would be too freaky. Too weird. *Too much* of a coincidence.

Screech.

The red brake lights snap on.

Right outside number thirty-nine.

I feel the hairs prickle on the back of my neck. Then again, you do hear of bizarre coincidences. I once read an article about a woman who had three sets of triplets and all three sets shared the same birthday. I mean, what are the odds of that happening?

And yet it happened. This is exactly the same, I tell myself firmly. Well, sort of.

Hurriedly I pull into a space a few cars down, turn off the engine and squint across the street. Damn, I'm too far away. I hesitate. Oh, what the hell, in for a penny, in for a pound. Grabbing my tote bag, I shove on my sunglasses and without even glancing in the Beetle's direction I walk briskly to the little square at the end.

It hasn't changed a jot. Same patch of lawn, same flower beds, same little bench in the middle. I sit down and pull out my book, *Finding Yourself Made Easy*, and pretend to start reading. As I do, I feel a slight thrill. This is like being one of those TV detectives you see on undercover operations.

Either that or a stalker.

Suddenly the sheer absurdity of my situation hits me. Jesus Christ, Charlotte, you're going to get yourself bloody arrested! What on *earth* do you think you're doing? Sitting here, spying on some innocent girl trying to parallel-park and making a complete mess of it. See-sawing in and out of the space, banging bumpers with the cars on either side with reckless abandon.

Honestly, she's the worst parker I've ever seen.

Just like you used to be . . .

Out of nowhere, I suddenly remember the time I tried reversing into a space outside the local pub and mounted the kerb, sending customers scattering and drinks spilling. My parking used to be a family joke. I once kerbed every wheel on my father's new Volvo, and I've lost count of the dings and scratches I put on cars over the years. Thankfully I've got better as I've got older, but when I was twenty-one, I was terrible. In fact, when I lived down this street, I once reversed into a—

I hear the crunch of metal.

—lamp-post.

The engine cuts out and a door swings open. Loud music wafts out into the silent street: (What's the Story) Morning Glory? by Oasis. I feel a rush of nostalgia. Wow, I used to love that album.

My heart starts pounding.

Suddenly the stereo is turned off and a tanned leg appears, then another, revealing the shortest denim miniskirt you've ever seen, followed by a low-cut vest showing off a generous amount of cleavage. *God, what a tart*, instantly flashes through my mind. Her hair is hanging in a dark, curly sheet over the side of her face, and as she gets out of the car, she turns away from me and walks round to the back of the Beetle.

'Fuck,' she curses loudly, as she sees her crumpled bumper. 'Fucking bastard lamp-post.'

And rough too, I decide with disdain. And to *think* for a moment there I thought she somehow bore some resemblance to me. I mean, as if! Feeling somewhat ridiculous, I stuff my book into my bag and stand up. I've seen enough. OK, so she's driving my old car and living in my old street, so what?

She turns.

And I freeze. It's like someone just dropped a ten-ton weight on my stomach.

That can't be.

That can't possibly be —

As I see her face up close, my mind goes into freefall. I'd assumed it was a trick of the light, a combination of not enough sleep and too much stress, but now . . .

Steadying myself on a nearby railing, I squeeze my eyes shut. My mind feels like that symbol on my iBook that whirls round and round when I've opened too many programs and it's confused and overloaded and about to crash at any minute. Because this isn't a case of mistaken identity, a lookalike, a stranger who used to look like I did when I was twenty-one. *I know her* – all five foot six, miniskirted, scrunch-dried, black-eyelinered, suntanned, twenty-one-year-old bit of her.

I snap my eyes wide open.

It's me.

OK, this is scaring the living daylights out of me. This cannot be real. This can't *actually* be happening, I know that, with every single inch of my rational, sensible, thirty-one-year-old self. I know there is only one of me. That's an absolute, a truth not even Dad could argue against. Which means I'm seeing things. I'm hallucinating. *I'm losing my mind.*

As the door to number thirty-nine slams shut and she disappears inside, I come to and set off down the street at a canter, my heels clattering against the pavement as I hurry towards my car. OK, Charlotte, just calm down. You're going to go home, take a Valium and put yourself to bed. Sleep this thing off. Maybe tomorrow even take the morning off work, get some rest—

Shit.

I've got another parking ticket! Reaching my car, I see a familiar plastic envelope slapped on my windscreen. Bloody typical. Snatching it up from under the wiper, I glare at it in annoyance. That's just ridiculous. I've only been gone five minutes. Ripping it open, I scan the details.

Car/Make Model: VW Beetle
Offence: parking in a permit-controlled area.
Time: 6.28 p.m.
Date: 21 August 1997

What? My heart pounds as I stare at it, the date swimming before my eyes – 1997, 1997, 1997 . . .

My hands are shaking. No, that just can't be, that just can't be—

Panicked, I drop the ticket. And as it flutters to the pavement, I jump into my car, fire up the engine and screech away from the kerb. I need to get the hell out of here. And fast.

Chapter Ten

'Hi, Beatrice. It's me, Charlotte. I'm calling in sick.'

'Oh my gosh, you poor darling. What's wrong?'

'I think I have a brain tumour.'

'Sshhhh!' I hear a loud hiss and I glance across the waiting room to see the receptionist glaring in my direction through a potted fern. 'Can't you read the sign? No mobile phones allowed in the doctor's surgery.'

It's the next morning and I'm sitting on a hard plastic chair, surrounded by dog-eared magazines and lots of ill people, waiting to see my GP. Last night I got home, took a Valium and must have immediately crashed out, as I don't remember anything until six o'clock this morning, when I woke up fully clothed on my bed feeling slightly groggy. For like a second, until – *boom* – what happened yesterday came rushing back to me and suddenly I was wide awake.

And worrying.

People always advise you to sleep on things, the theory being you're going to wake up miraculously clear-headed and full of answers. But I had slept on it and I still didn't have answers – just more questions whirling round and round in my head. So I did the only thing I could do: I cancelled my trainer.

And started Googling . . .

'Hallucinations' threw up 936,000 results, all of them terrifying. Some websites talked about serious mental illness: others were diagnosing brain tumours and showing all these gruesome pictures of a woman having the top of her head cut off. But that wasn't all: there were loads of warnings about headaches and fatigue and irrational behaviour.

Such as turning from a sane thirtysomething professional into a crazy stalker.

Well, something like that, anyway. To tell the truth, I can't remember exactly, as I was in a sort of clicking-mouse frenzy, going from one link to the next, reading one horrifying personal blog after another. Until, convinced I had all the symptoms, I raced round to my local GP's, pleading to be seen without an appointment and explaining it was a life-threatening emergency.

That was forty-five minutes ago, I think agitatedly, checking my watch for the umpteenth time.

'A brain tumour!' Beatrice is exclaiming down my BlackBerry. 'Oh my Lord, are you at the hospital?'

'Not yet,' I whisper, trying to hide my BlackBerry in the collar of my jacket, away from the eagle-eyed receptionist. 'I'm at the doctor's. But I'm sure he'll want to send me there for tests.' As I say the word 'tests' a bolt of panic rips through me and I have to fight to steady my nerves.

'That's what they did for my cousin Freddy,' she says darkly.

'They did?' I feel myself grip the phone tighter.

'Oh, yes, it was the oddest thing – one day he banged his head and the next he started having all these weird smells. It was really quite alarming. Everywhere he went he thought he could smell chocolate, which sounds rather lovely in *theory*, but poor Freddy was quite frantic as he hates chocolate. In fact he doesn't have a sweet tooth at all. He's much more a cheese-and-biscuits type of person.'

'Miss Merryweather?' I look up sharply to see the receptionist staring at me with a sour expression. 'The doctor is ready for you.'

'Oh, right, thank you.'

'Unless you'd prefer to continue your conversation outside.'

Wedged underneath my ear, I can still hear Beatrice chuntering away: 'So you can tell he's obviously not from my side of the family, as you know me – I can never say no to a pudding.'

'Beatrice, I have to go,' I hiss, and turning my BlackBerry to silent, I smile gratefully at the receptionist and hurry towards the doctor's consulting room.

'Come in.'

As I push open the door, I see Dr Evans, my GP, sitting in his black swivel chair behind a leather-topped desk. A grave-faced man with a white wispy comb-over and tortoiseshell glasses, he's jotting something down on his pad as I enter.

'Please sit down.' He gestures, looking up with an avuncular smile. Which sort of freezes when he sees it's me. 'Ah, Miss Merryweather,' he says evenly. Putting down his pen, he steeples his fingers. 'How nice to see you again.'

Sitting down, I smile shakily.

'And so soon,' he adds brightly, reaching for my notes, which are lying on his desk in a large blue folder. Opening it up, he begins flicking through.

Admittedly the folder is rather thick, bulging in fact, but like I always say, it's better to be safe than sorry.

'So how is the rash?' he asks, referring to my visit last week.

'Oh, fine,' I say quickly. 'You were right – it was just my eczema flaring up again.'

'And the "sharp pain in the left ribs"?' he continues, reading from my notes.

I feel a flash of embarrassment. That was the week before. I went to a yoga class and in the middle of this really big stretch I felt a sharp pain and thought I'd broken a rib. I swear it was really painful. In fact for a moment I thought I might have even punctured a lung and so begged Dr Evans to send me for an X-ray.

'Um . . . actually, it's much better,' I reply, tugging at an invisible thread of cotton on my sleeve.

As it turned out, I'd just overexerted myself. A hot bath and some Tiger Balm and I was as good as new the next day. But of course I wasn't to know that, was I?

'So,' he says slowly, 'what seems to be the problem?'

I swallow hard, wondering how to put it, where to start, what to tell him first.

'I think I have a brain tumour.'

The words come tumbling out before I can stop them, and hearing my worst fear out loud in the doctor's surgery makes it suddenly real and I'm scared. Really scared.

Dr Evans, on the other hand, doesn't flinch. 'I see . . .' Raising his tufty white eyebrows, he scribbles something down on his pad. I crane my neck to try and see what he's writing, but of course it's indecipherable. 'And what makes you think that?' he asks pleasantly, as if he's discussing the weather.

I take a deep breath as my mind flicks back to yesterday. 'I've been having these hallucinations,' I reply, trying to keep my voice steady.

He continues scribbling. 'Can you describe them for me?'

I take a deep breath. 'I saw myself aged twenty-one.'

There, I've said it.

Only instead of the jaw-dropping, gripping-on-to-the-side-of-the-chair astonishment I'd been expecting, Dr Evans's face relaxes and he smiles ruefully. 'Oh, that happens to us all as we get older,' he says blithely.

I look at him in confusion. 'It does?'

'Indeed.' He nods. 'I fool myself into imagining I'm twenty-one again on many an occasion, until I look in the mirror.' He chuckles, flattening down his wisps of white hair.

'No, you don't understand,' I try again. 'This was real,' I tell him urgently. 'Plus I've been having headaches,' I add, clutching at my temples. 'Terrible, agonising headaches.'

OK, they're not *that* bad, but you always need to exaggerate a bit when you see the doctor.

Dr Evans glances up sharply and looks at me, suddenly concerned. 'So you have to lie in a darkened room?'

See.

'Well, no, not exactly—'

'Nausea and vomiting?'

I hesitate. A little bit of exaggeration is one thing; bare-faced lying is another.

'Actually, I'm usually fine after a couple of Anadin Extra.'

His eyes narrow.

'Although sometimes I have to take three,' I add hastily.

'Miss Merryweather, I need to ask you some questions.'

'OK.' I nod, bracing myself.

'Is there any mental illness in the family?'

'Well, Dad's always saying Mum drives him insane.' I smile, despite myself. Which quickly fades at the sight of Dr Evans's stony face. 'But no. Apart from Great-Aunt Mary, who had a talking parrot,' I add as an afterthought.

'Have you ever suffered a seizure?'

Immediately I have a flashback to last week when I opened my credit-card bill, but I'm pretty sure that doesn't count. 'No.' I shake my head. 'Never.'

'Memory loss?'

'Well, I forgot my dad's birthday,' I confess, glancing down at my hands in my lap, which are twisting up a tissue. 'But I've been really busy at work and it just slipped my mind.'

Dr Evans makes another scribble on his pad. 'And how many hours do you spend in the office a day?'

'Um, six. No, eight. No . . .' I try counting up on my fingers. 'A lot.'

He makes yet another scribble. 'Do you get eight hours of sleep a night?'

'Does anyone?' I quip wearily. Despite twelve hours of drug-induced sleep, I'm still exhausted.

'Do you eat three square meals a day?'

I think about the breakfasts I skip and my lunches, which I eat al-desk-o, not alfresco, and usually only have time to pick at. 'Well, I wouldn't call them square exactly . . .'

There's a pause, and then, putting down his pen, Dr Evans stands up and reaches for his stethoscope, which he proceeds to press against my chest. He makes a little sound – 'Uh-hum' – then takes my blood pressure – 'Uh-hum' – before taking a small torch and shining it into each of my retinas – 'Uh-hum.' Wordlessly he sits back down behind his desk.

I wait, bracing myself for his diagnosis. 'Well, Doctor?'

'It's as I thought.' He nods.

'It is?' I repeat, my voice wobbling fearfully.

'You're suffering from stress.'

'That's it?' I look at him in astonishment. 'But I read on the Internet—' I break off as he shoots me a stern look.

'Stress is a very serious complaint,' he says gravely. 'My advice to you would be to get more rest, try to relax, start eating a healthy diet and cut down on caffeine and alcohol.' Closing my file, he stands up. 'Oh, and one other thing.'

'Yes?' I ask, all ears.

'Do you know what cyberchondria is?'

I feel a clutch of panic. 'No, but is it dangerous?' I ask fearfully. Shit, what if I've got that?

'It's when someone self-diagnoses from the Internet,' he says, raising an eyebrow and shooting me a look.

I feel my cheeks flush hotly. 'Oh, I see.'

'Stay off the Internet and I think you'll find your health will improve tremendously,' he continues, fixing me with a beady eye. Opening the door, he holds out his hand. 'Good day, Miss Merryweather.'

Having raced round to the doctor's still wearing yesterday's clothes, I go home to shower and change before driving to work. Thankfully this time the journey is pretty uneventful. No weird sightings of Beetles. No hallucinations. No inexplicable events.

In fact as I pull into the little mews where our office is tucked away and walk across the cobblestones, I'm starting to think that maybe the GP is right, maybe I am just stressed. After all, stress can do funny things to you. I know, because I've read about it in my self-help books, cases where people have lost their minds because of stress. People who one day are living these perfectly normal lives and then the next day – boom – they're found wandering around naked on Brighton Pier talking about aliens.

But bumping into yourself, aged twenty-one? I mean, honestly, how ridiculous.

So that's it. I've decided. No more Googling, no more getting carried away and no more ludicrous thoughts about me when I was twenty-one. Reaching the door to the office, I push it open. From now on I'm really going to try to relax and take it easy. Doctor's orders.

'Oh my gosh, thank goodness you're alive!'

As I enter, Beatrice scrambles from her chair and rushes over.

'I was so worried . . . I haven't been able to stop thinking about you . . . and poor cousin Freddy. Because of course it dragged it all back up again, you know – the hospital visits, the tests, the alarming smells . . .' She clutches her pearls and stares at me, showing the whites of her eyes. 'Have you noticed any strange . . .' she pauses and swallows hard '. . . *odours?*'

'Actually, I'm fine,' I say, trying to brush it off. 'It was an . . . um . . . misdiagnosis.'

'You mean . . . you're not . . .' Involuntarily she grasps both my hands in hers, then quickly drops them with embarrassment. 'Well, you just sit down and I'll make you a nice cup of coffee,' she says, recovering and darting over to the coffee machine.

'Thanks, but I think I might skip coffee this morning and just have some water. Oh, and do we have anything to eat?'

Beatrice looks taken aback. 'Are you sure you're OK?'

'Yes, fine.' I smile gratefully. Shrugging off my jacket, I sit down at my desk and flick on my computer.

'So what did the doctor say exactly?' She starts busying herself in the small kitchen area we have in the corner of the office.

'Oh, you know . . .' I say vaguely, opening my inbox. My heart sinks. I have fifty-seven unread emails. 'I just need to take it easy.'

'Well, all we have scheduled for this afternoon is the launch party for Exhale, that new spa round the corner. I spoke with the manager earlier and they might be interested in some PR.' She smiles conspiratorially. 'Plus I'm sure there'll be lots of yummy canapés and champagne. That's what you need, a glass of champers,' she advises sagely. 'That always makes me feel heaps better.'

'Well, I'm not sure if I should be drinking alcohol . . .'

'Nonsense. Best medicine ever, Mummy always says.' She passes me a bottle of Evian and a bran muffin.

'Thanks.' I turn back to my inbox. Sipping my water, I start reading an email from a magazine editor about some press for one of our clients.

'Everything fine?'

I glance up to see Beatrice still hovering around my desk.

'Yes, fine. Thanks.' I smile.

'Super.' She smiles back and begins fiddling with the photo frames on my desk. 'So,' she says, trying to sound casual and failing horribly, 'is there anything else you want to tell me?'

'Um . . . no, I think that's everything,' I say, shaking my head and turning back to my emails.

She doesn't budge. 'About what happened yesterday,' she says pointedly.

Apprehension prickles. 'Yesterday?' I repeat, a little nervously.

'Your meeting with Larry Goldstein!' she gasps finally, unable to keep her cool any longer.

'Oh, of course . . . right,' I fluster, my mind rapidly changing gear. With everything that's been going on the meeting had totally slipped my mind, which is ridiculous as it's the only thing that's been *on* my mind for weeks.

'I've been on tenterhooks ever since, but I didn't *dare* call, and then I didn't hear from you until this morning, when you were at the doctor's.'

'It went really, really well,' I reassure her quickly. 'In fact,' I smile, then blurt simply, 'we got it.'

Her jaw drops and her eyes goggle at me. 'Oh my gosh, that's just . . .' She trails off, words failing her momentarily, before coming alive again. '*Splendid!*' she gushes finally. 'Simply splendid!' She beams at me, almost trembling with excitement.

Watching her reaction, it suddenly throws my own into contrast. She's absolutely right. It is splendid, though I'd probably choose to describe it as fantastic, I think, bemused by Beatrice's choice of adjective. And yet . . .

A flashback of Larry Goldstein smiling smoothly at me across the restaurant table stirs a sense of unease. I dismiss it. Firmly. Like I said, nothing happened. It's me and my overactive imagination again.

'I know, isn't it?' I enthuse, mirroring her excitement.

'Absolutely. It's amazing,' she whoops, and then fixes me with a stern look. 'I just can't believe you kept this from me,' she clucks scoldingly. 'When I didn't hear from you . . .' She arches an eyebrow and pouts. 'Well, *you can imagine.*'

I swear, Beatrice has this knack of making me feel like a naughty schoolgirl sometimes.

'I know, and I'm sorry,' I apologise swiftly. 'I did pop back to the office later but you'd already left on an appointment, and then last night I didn't feel well—' I stop myself before I even go there. 'And anyway, as you and I both know, until the deal's actually signed and we've made our press announcement . . .'

I'm referring to an incident that happened last year in which we thought we'd won a big contract with a hotel chain, only to discover they'd changed their minds and gone with a rival PR company, just as Beatrice was cracking open a vintage bottle of Bollinger she'd had 'lying around' at home.

As compared to normal people, who have things like coffee cups and loose change lying around.

'Ah, yes, that was rather a waste of good champagne,' she concedes, frowning. 'Well, we'll keep it on ice this time, shall we?' She smiles cheerfully, before adding, 'So when do you want to schedule your next meeting? I'll need to check the diary and make sure you're free.'

The diary is our bible. We don't do anything unless it's in the diary, the keeper of which is Beatrice, who takes her job very seriously. Screwing up her forehead, she returns to her disk and begins jabbing at her keyboard. The calendar opens up on her computer and she peers at it intently. 'What day were you thinking? You've got a window at eleven o'clock next Tuesday.'

'Actually, we need to announce on Tuesday, so we've arranged to meet up on Thursday.'

'Thursday next week? Yes, I think that will be fine if I just juggle a few things . . .' She starts typing.

'No, *this* Thursday. *Tomorrow.*'

She gives a sharp intake of breath.

'Well, it's important to get the ball rolling. We don't have much time.'

'Gosh, yes, absolutely.' She nods, her face serious. 'Well, it's not going to be easy as it's pretty solid, but I'll do it – you can rely on me.' She turns back to the keyboard, a look of determination on her face. 'Now, let me see, you've got a meeting at ten o'clock with Trinny from the *Guardian*, at lunchtime you're seeing the house with Miles, and in the afternoon you've got meetings with some journalists from *Sainsbury's* magazine, but if you'd like, I can rearrange that for—'

'Actually, it's tomorrow evening.'

'*Evening?*' she repeats, her eyebrows shooting up.

'We're having dinner,' I say, trying to sound all casual. 'At his hotel.'

'Oh.' She's nodding, digesting this piece of information. 'How very intimate. Though that's probably what they do in Hollywood,' she muses.

'Yes, probably,' I agree, brushing away my doubts.

Turning back to her keyboard once more, she types, 'Thursday. Evening. Dinner with Larry Goldstein —' 'OK, you're all set.' Grabbing her mouse, she clicks 'save' with a flourish. 'It's in the diary.'

Chapter Eleven

The rest of the day flies by returning calls, talking to journalists, dealing with clients, until before I know it it's late afternoon and Beatrice and I leave the office and walk the few hundred yards to Exhale, the newly opened spa.

Arriving, we discover the party in full swing, *spa-style*: soft, tinkly, harp-like music is wafting from out of the concealed speaker system, a fountain made from a thousand-year-old Indonesian rock is gently trickling water, and dozens of barefoot staff are flitting around in togas, handing out lotus flowers and offering free treatments.

Casting my eye around the large crowd, I take a gulp of ice-cold Moët and savour the sensation of bubbles fizzing on my tongue. I never would have believed it but it seems Beatrice's mother might be right about something. OK, I wouldn't call it the *best* medicine ever, and I wouldn't say I'm *heaps* better, but I've only had half a glass and I have to admit I'm already starting to feel a lot more relaxed about things.

'Canapés?' A waitress walks past with a large silver tray.

'Mmm, yes, please,' I enthuse. 'What are they?'

'Quail's eggs with tomato,' she proffers brightly, passing me one on a napkin.

About to take a bite, I hesitate. 'Are they free-range?'

Well, OK. Not that relaxed.

The waitress's smile fades. 'Um . . . I'm not sure —'

'Ooh, those look yummy,' interrupts Beatrice, helping herself to a couple. She glances at me. 'What? You're not eating yours?' she gasps, staring incredulously at my untouched canapé.

'Actually, I'm not that hungry,' I fib.

'Well, if you don't want it . . .' As the waitress moves away, she swiftly takes it from me. 'Mmm, this is a really good launch party, I have to say.' She nods approvingly. Juggling her pile of canapés, she takes a sip of champagne. 'Are you going to try one of the free treatments?'

I glance at my watch. 'I should get back to the office.'

'Free five-minute facial?' offers a woman in a toga wafting past. She looks at me enquiringly.

'Ooh, Charlotte, go on, you should try one,' elbows Beatrice.

I shake my head. 'I really need to finish up a press release.'

'It will only take five minutes,' she points out insistently.

Honestly, you'd never think I was the boss and she was my assistant. Then again – I hesitate – a relaxing facial might be just what the doctor ordered, and I can always take some work home with me. Saying that, when don't I take work home with me?

'OK, why not? That sounds great.' I smile at the therapist.

She beams back. Her hair's plaited neatly into cornrows and she has the kind of amazing skin that can only be acquired through an exotic heritage, and which is the envy of someone like me, whose entire family tree is made up of freckly skinned, mousey-haired generations from such far-flung places as York-shire, Newcastle and the truly exotic Skegness.

'Wonderful.' Pressing her hands together, she does a little bow. 'My name's Suki, and if you'd just like to come over to one of the chairs . . .'

Dutifully I follow Suki over to one of three large leather recliners, which are tucked away behind a small painted screen featuring a Zen-like landscape. Aromatherapy candles are burn-ing, and there's a large pot of bamboo in the corner. It screams relaxation and inner peace.

Sinking into the soft leather, I close my eyes as Suki removes my make-up and presses a hot towel on my face. It smells of eucalyptus and I take a deep breath.

'Now, we're just going to open your pores,' Suki's voice chants soothingly.

As she begins gently dabbing the towel against my cheeks, then slowly on to my forehead and over to my chin, I can feel the tension slowly trickling out of my body like sand through an egg-timer. The doctor was right: I am really stressed.

'And then we're going to apply a cleanser to draw out impurities and clean pores.'

With Suki's fingertips gently massaging my face in a circular motion I can feel myself drifting off. Gosh, this is rather lovely.

'Followed by a special mask made of clay minerals that will revitalise the skin and help balance out skintone . . .'

Mmm, this is bliss. Sheer, unadulterated bliss.

'. . . because you've got rather a lot of sun-damage.'

'What?' Jolted out of my reverie, my eyes snap open.

Clucking her tongue reprovingly, she continues massaging. 'All over your cheeks and forehead' – I stiffen – 'resulting in quite severe pigmentation and discolouration.'

Severe pigmentation and discolouration?

'But I always use sunscreen,' I cry with alarm.

'Mmm,' she murmurs, and continues massaging.

'SPF forty-five,' I say urgently, trying to sit upright, but she pushes me back down firmly.

'Ssh, relax,' she soothes. 'You're very tense.'

'And I never sunbathe,' I protest, but I'm muffled by a hot flannel as she wipes off the cleanser and begins rubbing on a thick layer of clay. Actually, this facial is getting a bit irritating.

'Eight-five per cent of irreversible sun-damage is caused before the age of twenty-five,' she intones. She stops sweeping clay across my temples and fixes me with a beady eye. 'Did you sunbathe in your youth?'

My memory produces a snapshot of me slathered in Hawaiian Tropic and frying in the midday sun. Actually, there's not just the one snapshot; there are whole albums full of them. From my teenage years right through to my late twenties I would dive into a string bikini at the first ray of sunshine.

'A little,' I fib, under the beady glare of Suki.

'Well, that explains it.' She nods, arching an eyebrow and tutting. 'The sun is the skin's number-one enemy. It causes premature ageing, fine lines, wrinkles, sagging, loss of collagen . . .'

As she reels off a long list of terrible things I've done to my skin, I listen with horror. It's all right for Suki: she has skin the colour of an iced mocha latte. She's never had to suffer the milk-bottle-leg syndrome that haunts every fair-skinned woman when it's time to ditch the trusty opaques at the end of spring. She doesn't know what it's like to have a complexion that, without bronzer, prompts complete strangers to enquire about your health.

'Isn't there anything I can do?' I ask anxiously, clutching my face.

'Well, we do have some specialist laser treatments that could help.' Suki passes me a leaflet.

I glance at the price list. 'Five hundred pounds?' I gasp.

'I'd recommend a course of five or six sessions.'

Five or six? That means . . . Hurriedly I do the calculations. Oh my God, that's a fortune. I glance up at Suki, who's smiling at me brightly.

'Would you like me to book your first session today?'

'Um . . . I think I might wait.'

'Are you sure that's wise? We're giving away complimentary foot rubs as part of a special promotion . . .' she continues with her sales pitch.

I'm beginning to feel quite stressed. I only wanted a relaxing facial.

'. . . and I would also recommend a whole new range of products to treat your damaged skin—'

'Excuse me, but I think the five minutes might be up,' I interrupt as she draws breath.

'Oh, yes, so they are.' She smiles, taking two cotton-wool pads and wiping my face clean. 'Well, if you change your mind . . .' She hands me a card and a bag. 'Here are some free samples for you to try.'

'Great. Thank you,' I say, standing up with relief. Five more minutes and my credit card and I would have caved under the pressure.

Beaming widely, she puts her hands together and gives a little bow. '*Namaste.*'

After hastily reapplying my make-up in the loos, I find Beatrice on her third glass of champagne and chatting animatedly to a journalist. As with most launches, it's largely press and industry people here, though as always there's the odd C-list celebrity with prerequisite fake boobs and blonde hair extensions posing for photos in a white spa robe.

'Oh, hi, Charlotte.' Beatrice breaks off from her conversation as I approach. 'This is Patrick.' Throwing out her hand as if to say, 'Ta-dah,' like a magician, she looks at me, her eyes sparkling.

I know that look. She fancies him, and she's drunk.

Or, as Beatrice likes to put it, 'a little squiffy.'

Patrick and I exchange pleasantries. He's wearing a blazer and checked shirt, under which I can see the outline of a white vest.

'He works for *Golfing Weekly.*' She beams, playing with her pearls like some people play with their hair. She smiles eagerly at Patrick. 'Isn't that exciting?'

Patrick chuckles in an attempt at modesty.

'So you're a keen golfer?' I ask, making conversation.

'I play off seven,' he says knowledgeably.

'Wow, that's amazing,' coos Beatrice, leaning closer with what is supposed to be a surreptitious move and is instead a clunking great big sideways shuffle. Subtlety is not Beatrice's strong point. She hangs at his elbow, looking up towards his shiny, pink face.

'And my wife plays off five, so we like to make a lot of golfing trips. The Algarve's our particular favourite.'

'Wife?' repeats Beatrice, her mouth hanging open like a carp's.

'Yes. She's semi-professional,' he adds proudly.

There's a beat.

'I'm sorry, will you ladies excuse me?' Patrick smiles politely. 'I've just spotted a colleague.' He disappears into the crowd.

I glance at Beatrice. She looks crestfallen.

'Oh, well,' she says, forcing a smile, 'never mind.'

I can tell she's upset, but she'll never admit it. Stiff upper lip and all that. In fact Beatrice could probably plunge thirty thousand feet in an aeroplane, crash into the ocean and find herself surrounded by man-eating sharks and she'd still say, 'Oh, well, never mind.'

Polishing off the rest of her champagne, she plucks another flute from a passing tray. 'So, tell me, how was the facial?' she asks, swiftly changing the subject and trying to be all cheery.

Deeply disturbing, I want to reply, but instead I settle for, 'Very educational,' and pass her the bag Suki gave me. 'I got you some free samples,' I say, trying to perk her up.

'For me?' Pressing her hand to her chest, she looks at me as if I've just given her diamonds. 'Ooh, Charlotte, you shouldn't have!'

'Beatrice, they were free,' I point out. 'Free samples usually are.'

'Well, I know, but still . . .' Putting down her champagne glass, she dives on the bag and starts pulling out products. 'A body lotion . . . foot scrub . . . a moisturiser. Oh, goodee, I need some new moisturiser. I've totally run out of the Pond's Cold Cream Granny gave me.' She starts reading off the back label, ' "Turn back the clock with this luxury moisturiser, which erases fine lines with our specially patented formula, leaving your face looking and feeling ten years younger." ' She gives a little snort. 'Well, that's nonsense.'

'Mmm, yes, I know,' I murmur absently. I'm still feeling perturbed about my facial.

'No moisturiser can make you look ten years younger. It's impossible.'

'Mmm, yes.' Digging out my compact, I peer at my skin. It doesn't look that bad, but still.

'I don't care whether it's made of crushed pearls from the Adriatic or not . . .'

Hurriedly I start powdering my cheeks and forehead.

'. . . there's only one thing that's going to make me look twenty-one again and that's time travel.'

Out of the blue I get the weirdest feeling. 'What did you just say?' I ask, abruptly zoning back in and snapping my compact shut.

'I said, "I don't care if it's made of crushed pearls from the Adriatic—"'

'No, not that bit,' I say quickly.

Beatrice frowns. 'Gosh, I can't remember.'

'You said something about being twenty-one again,' I prompt, my stomach fluttering.

'Oh, yes, I was talking about time travel.' She nods matter-of-factly. Putting the products back in the bag, she takes a swig of champagne. 'Though strictly speaking if you *were* to travel back through the frontiers of time, you wouldn't *look* like you were twenty-one; you'd *meet* yourself when you were twenty-one.'

I suddenly feel really light-headed, dizzy almost.

'But you know Stephen Hawking says time travel isn't possible,' she continues, and then laughs. 'Otherwise we'd all be run over from tourists from the future.'

'Well, of course it's not possible,' I scoff, quickly recovering. It must be the champagne, I tell myself, using a pamphlet to fan myself. And it is really stuffy in here.

'However, the theory of general relativity does suggest scientific grounds for thinking time travel could be possible in certain unusual scenarios,' she adds as an afterthought.

I stare at her in disbelief. 'What? You're saying you *believe* in time travel?' I always knew Beatrice was a bit ditzy, but totally goo-goo-ga-ga? 'Come on, you're joking, right?'

'Actually no, I'm not joking,' she refutes stiffly, pursing her lips. 'According to the rules of physics, there are several ways it could be theoretically feasible. For example, there are some quantum physicists who believe every historical event spawns a new universe for every possible outcome, resulting in a number of alternate histories.' She pauses to take a swig of champagne. 'This is rooted in the many-worlds interpretation of quantum mechanics formulated by the physicist Hugh Everett in 1957, an alternative to the Copenhagen interpretation originally formulated by Niels Bohr and Werner Heisenberg around 1927.'

Er, hello?

'Can you say that again, but in English this time?' I ask, completely lost.

'Think of it like this.' Putting down her champagne glass, she reaches over to a passing waitress. 'Excuse me.' She smiles, grabbing a handful of mini-quiches, before turning back to me and spreading out her napkin on a nearby table. 'Rather than a universe,' she explains, placing a mini-quiche in the middle, 'it's a multiverse.' She continues dotting several more mini-quiches around it. 'And together these multiverses comprise all of physical reality. The different universes within a multiverse are called parallel universes.' She picks up a mini-quiche and waves it at me. 'Imagine this is a parallel universe,' she suggests, her face serious.

'Um . . . OK.' I nod dubiously.

'It's existing at the same time as all these other parallel universes.' She gestures to all the other mini-quiches. 'And you can travel between them, see?'

I stare, bewildered, at the mini-quiches, trying to grapple with the information. For someone who dropped physics in favour of creative writing it's all rather confusing. Actually, make that *very* confusing.

'But then of course there's the other theories that include travelling faster than the speed of light, moving large amounts of physical matter, which releases energy and can cause a crack in time, or the use of cosmic strings or traversable wormholes,' she says nonchalantly, helping herself to a parallel universe. Sorry, I mean a mini-quiche.

'A wormhole?' I repeat, my mouth twitching.

Well, I'm sorry, but I can't take this seriously. What next? Dr Who's Tardis?

'You know, like a portal.' She shrugs. 'Or some kind of tunnel that allows you to travel from one time' – with her finger she traces a line across the napkin – 'to another.'

Suddenly I get that weird fluttering feeling again in my stomach and a cog in my brain turns. No, but that's just crazy, I tell myself firmly, dismissing the thought before it's even fully formed. In fact it's more than crazy. It's totally ludicrous.

'I know. Even I don't understand it properly,' she soothes, misinterpreting my silence and patting my arm in consolation. 'And if I try to explain it in more detail, I'm afraid your head will explode, or implode, depending on what universe we are currently in and the particular wave-funtion collapse laws,' she adds, frowning. 'Saying that, I loved *Back to the Future*, didn't you?' Draining her glass, she smiles brightly. 'Another glass of bubbly?'

Chapter Twelve

M aking my excuses, I leave Beatrice drinking champagne and sneak out of the launch party early. I drive home feeling unsettled, like on a hot summer's day, just before a storm, when the air gets all charged and seems to prickle with electricity and anticipation, and you're filled with a strange mixture of excitement and apprehension, knowing something is going to happen. Waiting. Watching. Wondering.

Which is ridiculous, as nothing is going to happen, I think sharply. Nothing at all.

It's another warm evening and as usual the rush-hour is in full swing. Motorists with their windows wound down and elbows sticking out jostle for every inch of tarmac, while on the pavements pedestrians hurry and scurry like worker ants towards the tube. Following the signs for the diversion, I turn on the radio. A DJ's chirpy banter wafts out of my speakers, filling the space around me with jokes and jingles and call-ins, and I listen, glad of the distraction.

For about thirty seconds.

Then before I know it my mind is wandering back to the launch like a guest reluctant to leave, sidling over to my earlier conversation with Beatrice. Her words start playing in my head: '. . . be possible in certain unusual scenarios . . . parallel universes . . . moving large amounts of physical matter . . . tunnel that allows you to travel from one time to another.'

My mind flicks back to yesterday – driving past the diggers moving all that earth, being diverted, turning down that side street and going under the underpass, which I suppose is sort of like a tunnel . . .

Right, that's enough. I screech my imagination to a halt. Like I said, it's totally ridiculous. OK, so Beatrice did some mind-bogglingly brainy maths and physics degree at Cambridge, but time travel? Honestly, what next? UFOs and little green men?

But what about the date on the parking ticket? interrupts a voice in my head.

Stress, remember? I tell myself firmly. I was flustered and misread the date. If I hadn't dropped the ticket, I could check it now, prove to myself I had made a mistake, and that would be the end of it.

And the fact she looked just like you did when you were twenty-one?

Mistaken identity. Happens all the time. In fact I once pinched Miles's bottom when he was queueing to buy popcorn at the cinema. Only it wasn't his bottom. It belonged to someone else's boyfriend, and believe me, that someone else wasn't very happy.

And drove your car?

Coincidence.

Which was scrapped?

No, it wasn't. Dad was wrong.

And lived in your old house?

For God's sake, what is this? An interrogation? Shut up, why don't you?

Right, that's it. I'm not listening to this nonsense any more, I tell myself decisively. Rattled, I reach for the volume button on the stereo, turning it up until the music is blasting out of my speakers. Which is a bit embarrassing, as it's Avril Lavigne and a few people are staring, as I've got the roof down. Oh, bugger it. So what? I'm going to listen to this song and stare straight ahead and not even think about how she reversed into that lamp-post just like I—

Shit. I've done it again.

I tug my mind back firmly, but it's like a restless child and I can't get it to sit still. Before I know it, it's wandering back to play with those questions. I know there's logical, rational explanation for all of it. I know that.

And yet.

Doubt flickers, like lightning on the skyline, momentarily illuminating a qualm lurking deep down inside of me.

What if by some weird, freaky, inexplicable chance I really *did* see myself at the traffic lights? If at that diversion my world collided with that when I was twenty-one, driving to and from work in my old VW Beetle? And what if somehow I managed to follow myself back to 1997?

Honestly, Charlotte, that one glass of champagne really did go to your head, didn't it? I realise, grabbing hold of my over-active imagination by the scruff of its neck. This isn't *Back to the* bloody *Future*. This is real life. My name's not Michael J. Fox; I don't drive a DeLorean. I'm Charlotte; I run a PR company and drive a Beetle. And let's face it, with the traffic in London, I can't have been doing more than thirty.

My attention is distracted by a street up ahead. I recognise that street. It's the one I turned down yesterday when I followed the old Beetle . . .

I look away quickly. OK, enough of that. What was I thinking about? Oh, yes, stupid things. But I'm not going to think about those any more, I tell myself, brushing them away firmly. I'm going to think about something else. Like, for example, how I'm going to take the doctor's advice and run a relaxing bubble bath when I get home. Maybe even listen to that CD Mum sent me. Light an aromatherapy candle.

Shall I turn off? A little voice pops into my head.

No, of course not, I think sharply. I'm going straight home. *It'll only take ten minutes.*

I hesitate, my resolve wavering. Which is stupid as, like I said, this is all nonsense. You don't drive down a street one day and discover yourself back where you were ten years ago, and I hardly think I need to prove that by driving down there again, do I? I feel a flash of amusement at the mere suggestion.

Plus let's imagine for a second that it was somehow magically possible, *which of course it isn't*, the truth is, I don't want to bump into myself when I was twenty-one, thanks very much. I left that girl behind years ago. Why would I want to meet her again today?

Like someone pressing 'play' on a tape-recorder, I suddenly hear Suki: 'Eighty-five per cent of sun-damage is caused before the age of twenty-five.' I get an image of me aged twenty-one sunbathing topless in my back garden, basting myself in Hawaiian Tropic and rotating myself on my towel like a pig on a spit.

OK, I take that back.

Slamming on the brakes, I swerve right across the road and shoot off down the street.

Five minutes later I reach Kilmaine Terrace and I'm already regretting my decision. It's one thing imagining doing something, it's another actually doing it.

And what are you doing exactly, Charlotte? pipes up that annoying little voice again.

I can't answer. Quite frankly I'm too embarrassed. In fact I'm going to have to take this secret with me to the grave. God forbid if anyone were to find out. 'What did you do last night, Charlotte?' 'Oh, I just drove back to the house that I lived in ten years ago, looking for myself when I was twenty-one, as my assistant told me that time travel is possible and I wanted to check.'

Er, yeah, right. Stress or no stress, they'll be carting me off in a straightjacket. Forget Great-Aunt Mary with her talking parrot, I'll go down in the Merryweather family tree as the unmarried career girl who went totally off her rocker. I can hear my mum now: 'Well, it's not surprising – she lived in *Lundun*, you know.'

I head towards number thirty-nine, keeping my eye out for a clapped-out tangerine-orange Beetle. I scan all the parked cars. But no, nothing.

Well, what did you expect, you idiot?

I feel both foolish and relieved at the same time. And something else . . . a twinge of disappointment. Because as unthinkable as the whole fantasy is, there's a secret part of me that's fascinated by tales of the paranormal, that's watched every single episode of *The X-Files* (I had the *hugest* crush on David Duchovny) and loves the idea of it being possible. After all, let's be honest, who didn't adore *The Time Traveler's Wife*?

Abruptly my bladder twinges, interrupting my thoughts, and I realise I need to pee. Damn, it must be the champagne *and* on an empty stomach. I need to find a loo. And fast.

Looping round the garden square at the bottom, I do another quick scan of the parked cars – not because I really think it's going to be there, but because I'm the kind of person who always goes back in the house to check I've turned off the gas – then, satisfied, whiz back down Kilmaine Terrace. There must be a loo around here somewhere . . .

Then I remember – the Wellington. The pub had just opened when I lived here, and Vanessa and I became regulars. It's around here somewhere. I pull up at the give-way sign at the end of the street. I think it's left. Actually no, it might be right. I hesitate for a moment, my bladder nagging me to hurry up and get a move on.

Shit, where is it?

Then I have a flash of inspiration.

I know, I'll type the name into my GPS, I decide, proud of my quick thinking. This thing is brilliant. It will give the precise directions. I just type in the name . . .

That's funny.

I look at the screen of the system sitting on my dashboard. It's totally blank. I randomly punch a few buttons in the hope it's going to suddenly spring back to life, and then give it a little shake, which is my usual scientific approach at fixing electronic gadgets and which, surprisingly enough, generally works.

But nope, not this time. The screen remains resolutely blank.

My bladder twinges hard. Now of course I really want to pee. Bloody thing, I curse, feeling slightly irritated. Oh, well, the pub's around here somewhere. I'll just have to try and go from memory. I take pot luck and turn left and follow the road as it winds round the church. Now, this is looking familiar. It should be on the right . . . I turn another corner. No, it's not there. What about the next corner . . . ?

As I turn right, I feel a rush of happiness as I spot the familiar painted pub sign. Hurrah. There it is, the Wellington Arms. Quickly parking, I dash out of the car and into the pub. God, it hasn't changed a bit, I muse, feeling a rush of nostalgia as I walk inside. Same scuffed floorboards on which are clustered lots of wooden tables and chairs, same large open fire that's all blackened and sooty from winter use, same chalkboards filled with scribbles describing today's specials and a large extensive wine list, which I remember was a totally new thing back in 1997.

Wow. It's like stepping back in time.

Then I catch myself and smile with amusement. No pun intended of course.

Despite still being early evening, it's quite busy with the after-work crowd, and excusing my way through to the back of the pub, I hurry downstairs to the toilets. They're still in the same place, thank goodness, and I dash gratefully inside an empty cubicle.

Good job I've been doing all those pelvic-floor exercises, I tell myself, finally relaxing my muscles. Boy, that's a relief.

I flush the loo and go outside to wash my hands. It's all exactly the same. As I go to dry my hands under the fan, I glance absently in the mirror to check my reflection. I must have looked in this mirror a thousand times when I was twenty-one – checked my hair was OK, my lipstick was just so, reapplied my eyeliner – and now here I am, a whole decade later, back here again. For a moment I pause, lost in thought. It's strange. So much has happened since then. My life is so different now, I feel so different now, look so different now, that it's hard to imagine me back then.

The door swings open and another girl enters. I snap out of my reflections. Catching the door before it swings shut, I scoot out of the ladies' and back up the staircase, fully intending to walk right out of the pub and drive home. But that was before I caught the ponytailed barman's eye.

He cocks an eyebrow. 'So did you find it OK?'

I stop mid-step, like a thief caught in his tracks. Oh God, is he talking to me? 'Um . . . excuse me?' I feign innocence.

'The toilet,' he says pointedly, giving me a look. A look that says, 'I know your type, just waltzing in here to use the loo without buying a drink. What do you think this is, a public toilet?' Trust me. It was that kind of look.

'Oh, yes, thank you.' I smile awkwardly.

'Anything else we can help you with?'

'Just a cranberry juice, please,' I hear myself saying.

Honestly, Charlotte, you don't have to buy a drink if you don't want to. Just turn round and walk out. Who cares what he thinks? He's just a barman.

But it's too late. He's already getting out the Ocean Spray.

'There you go.' He passes me my drink. 'That'll be a pound, please.'

I'm pleasantly surprised. Well, I'm glad to see the prices are still reasonable, I think, digging out my purse. There's nothing worse than those poncy, overpriced bars that charge you £3.50 for a soft drink. But then this pub always was good value for money.

'Thanks, great.' As I hand over the money and take my drink, I look around for a spare seat. It's really busy. I finally spot an empty table and dive on it gratefully. Fab! Pulling up a chair, I am just getting comfy when—

I wrinkle up my nose. Hang on a minute, *can I smell cigarettes?*

As a blast of smoke wafts in my direction, I glance sideways. Sure enough, there, right next to me, is a couple smoking. *Inside!* Haven't they heard of the smoking ban?

'Erm . . . excuse me . . .' They both look over. 'Would you mind?' I say politely, and gesture to their cigarettes. Well, I hate to be one of those people who complain about smoking, but it's really bad for my sinuses. Saying that, I shouldn't feel that bad as it is illegal to smoke in pubs.

'Sure. Go ahead, take one.' He smiles, proffering his packet of Marlboro Lights. 'Do you need a light?'

Oh, no, he's totally misunderstood. 'Um . . . no . . . thank you,' I fluster, shaking my head. 'I didn't mean . . . I meant . . .' Watching him puffing away unfazed, I trail off at a loss. 'My sinuses . . .' I gesture, sniffing a bit for emphasis.

'Right, yeah, summer colds. A bummer.' He nods agreeably and drags hard on his cigarette.

I feel a sting of indignation. I can't believe it. The arrogance of some people! He's just going to sit there and carry on smoking. That's so bloody rude. And when I asked nicely and everything. Right that's it. Picking up my cranberry juice, I stand up huffily.

'You should go sit outside, get some sun,' he advises, slurping his pint.

'Yes, I think I'll do that,' I reply tightly, and throwing my tote bag over my shoulder, I turn and stalk across the scuffed wooden floorboards.

Outside, the beer garden is already jostling with people crowding the few wrought-iron tables and chairs. This is just how I remember it: jammed-packed and buzzing with chatter, I think, weaving my way through. It's also still just as pretty. Vibrantly coloured hanging baskets dangle from the walls scenting the air, and there's a lovely sycamore tree just round that corner. Gosh, I can remember when they planted that tree, I reflect, casting my mind back. It was nothing more than a skinny little sapling, but just look at it now!

Oh.

As it comes into view, I feel a pang of disappointment. Gosh, it hasn't grown very much in ten years, has it? I thought it was going to be this great big spreading tree and I was going to sit underneath its shady boughs. I peer at the weedy little branches. If I didn't know better, I'd think it was still a sapling.

But then, that shows you how much I know about gardening, I muse, spotting a free spot and plonking myself down with my back to the sun. Well, better not get any more sun-damage . . .

I look around me. The crowd looks pretty much the same – lots of cool, trendy people in low-slung jeans and floaty dresses, showing off summer tans and those Celtic armband tattoos that were so fashionable in the nineties. Gosh, am I glad I never got one of those – you're stuck with them for ever. And I used to think they were so cool! How funny.

Resting my drink on the table, I start rooting around in my bag for my mobile. I need to call Miles back. He left a message earlier today when I was at the doctor's saying, 'Nothing important, just checking in,' which is what he always says whenever he calls. When we first started going out, I thought that was really sweet – and I still do. Only, it might be nice if it *was* something important sometimes. Not scary important. Just interesting important.

Dialling his number, I press the mobile to my ear and wait to hear his phone ringing.

Except it doesn't.

Frowning, I look closely at the screen and notice all the bars have disappeared and I don't have a signal. *Again.* Irritation stabs. I called T-Mobile yesterday, but they said there wasn't a problem with reception in the area. I don't understand it. I dig out my BlackBerry, but it's the same. No signal. I stare at in confusion. What was Beatrice talking about the other day? Oh, right, yes. Something about too many people using their mobile phones, I remember, glancing around me. Maybe she's right.

Except . . .

Wait a minute. That's odd. My eyes flick from person to person. Usually everyone is chattering away, handsets pressed to their ears, earpieces dangling, Bluetooth headsets flashing lights as they seemingly jabber away to no one. But now, looking around me, I can't actually see anyone using their phone.

Maybe they don't allow mobiles here, I decide, feeling a little bewildered, though I can't see any signs. Oh, no, look, there's a couple of people on their phones. A few tables away, I spot a guy chatting into his phone. As he finishes his call, I jump up and walk over to him.

'Excuse me.' He looks up. 'Are you with T-Mobile?'

He looks at me blankly. 'Sorry?'

'I saw you on your phone,' I explain, 'but I don't have any reception.'

'Um . . . no, I'm with Vodafone and it seems fine.' He shrugs, putting his mobile down on the table in front of him. I glance at it. God, he must have had that phone for years – it looks really old-fashioned. Still, it has five big black bars showing. Unlike either of my phones.

'Gosh, that's weird.' Confused, I peer at the bars on my BlackBerry again. Nope. They've all disappeared.

'What's that?' He looks at me quizzically.

I pause from performing my usual scientific approach of pressing every button and jabbing the screen. 'Excuse me?'

'Is that a phone?'

'Oh, you mean my BlackBerry?'

'BlackBerry?' he repeats, as if it's a foreign-sounding word. 'I've never seen one of those.'

'Really?' I look at him in surprise. I assumed everyone knew what one was, even my mother. Then again, she does still call it 'that thingamajig'. 'Oh, well, they're not that great, trust me,' I say ruefully. 'Though they're useful for getting your emails.'

'Emails?' he repeats. 'On a phone?' He laughs and shakes his head. 'Yeah, right. Since when? You need dial-up and a computer for those.'

Suddenly I get this really odd feeling.

OK, so now he's definitely pulling my leg, right?

A shiver runs up my spine and despite the beery warmth I can feel goosebumps prickling. There is something very weird going on here.

'Oops, sorry.'

A voice cuts into my consciousness as someone from behind bangs into me, spilling what's left of my cranberry juice down my shirt. Oh, shit. I look down to see it covered in red, seeping splodges.

'Oh God, I'm really, really sorry. It was an accident.'

Digging out a tissue, I start dabbing at my shirt. Damn. It's white linen. I'm never going to get the stain out.

'Can I buy you another drink?'

'No, thank you.'

Except in the split second it takes for me to answer something registers as not quite right; something about her voice sounds familiar. I stiffen. Hang on minute. I twirl round, my heart thudding loudly in my chest, my breath caught tight in the back of my throat. Because I already know exactly who's standing behind me. Even before I see her, I know who she is.

Just like I know that voice.

Our eyes lock. And in that instant every single rational thought I've ever had flies right out of the window.

Because it's me.

Chapter Thirteen

For a moment nothing happens. Time freezes. As if someone just pressed 'pause' on the DVD that is my life and said, 'OK, so what do you think about that, then?'

Except I can't answer.

In books I'm always reading about people being rendered speechless, and I've often thought it an interesting concept, but one that was more literal than realistic. After all, no one's ever *really* speechless, are they? You can always think of *something* to say. Even when I was dumped by Colin Pickles at middle school with a blunt 'I don't like you any more' I found my tongue fast enough to reply with a 'Well, I don't like you either, Spotty.' OK, so it wasn't going to win any awards for the most witty riposte, but at least I said *something*.

Unlike now.

Now I really *am* speechless. Lost for words. Struck dumb. And every other saying that means my earlier irritation has drained completely away as my mind makes that leap from disbelief to belief. This isn't a hallucination. This is real. And all I can do is stand here in stunned silence as I stare at myself. My twenty-one-year-old self. In the flesh. Right here. In front of me.

Oh, fuck.

I feel a thrust of panic and my mind starts whirling like a merry-go-round.

Fuck-oh-fuck-oh —

'Are you OK?'

A strong Yorkshire voice stops me spiralling further and I

snap back to see my younger self looking at me with concern. God, I'd forgotten how broad my accent used to be.

'Um . . . yes,' I fluster. 'I'm fine.'

Which is a pretty crap fib as if there's one word to describe my situation right now it certainly isn't fine. Panicked? Maybe. Freaked out? Definitely. This close to losing it any second? Yup, that as well.

Frantically I try gathering myself together, but it's not that easy. Bewildered, I glance down at my shirt with dismay. It's my favourite Nicole Farhi shirt and it's now splattered with cranberry juice. God, just look at it! I only bought it a couple of weeks ago and it's totally ruined. Maybe if I take it to a dry-cleaner's, they can—

Oh, who am I kidding? I don't give a bloody stuff about my goddamn shirt. I'm just trying really hard not to think about the small fact that I'm having a conversation with a girl in a skimpy top and silver eyeshadow who just so happens to be me a decade ago.

As I look back at her, I wobble and nearly lose it. God, this brings a whole new meaning to talking to yourself.

'It was just a bit of a shock,' I say, trying to appear casual, but it's as if the world has tipped on its axis and I'm teetering on the edge, clinging on for dear life, while having to pretend everything is perfectly normal. 'But no big deal.' I shrug and laugh lightly.

But there's no reaction. My younger self is still staring at me, her smooth, wrinkle-free brow furrowed in concentration. As if she's thinking about something very, very hard. As if something's troubling her. As if—

Suddenly it registers.

Of course! Why didn't I think of this before?

She recognises me.

As it hits me, I know I have to pull myself together. No doubt she's going to be as freaked out as I am, if not more. In fact I'll probably have to calm her down, being the older self. Act like a big sister. Tell her not to worry. That it will be OK, to stay calm and not panic, that we'll figure this out.

She opens her mouth to speak, and despite my own feelings, it's all I can do to stop myself from flinging my arm protectively round her shoulder and saying, 'There, there, dear.'

'Salt.'

Or perhaps she's going to burst into tears, or faint, or have some kind of panic attack, or—

Hang on, rewind. Did she just say . . . ?

'*Salt?*' I repeat, taken aback.

'Yes, that's right. And white wine.' She nods, gesturing at my shirt. 'I'm sure that will get the stain out, though you'll probably need to soak it in hot water.' She smiles apologetically.

What? She doesn't recognise me? *She doesn't know who I am?* I stare at her in shocked disbelief. But surely she has to. I'm her. I mean, she's me. I mean, we're the same person. Fuck, this is confusing.

'I think we've met before,' I try prompting.

Maybe she's in denial. Just like I was.

'We have?' Tilting her head on one side, she peers at me and I can see she's racking her brain. 'Nope, I don't think so.' She grins.

I swallow hard and take a deep breath. 'It's me, Charlotte,' I whisper, leaning closer.

Her jaw drops open with surprise and she clutches her chest. I knew it. At last.

I brace myself, ready to do all the explaining. She's going to want lots of answers, lots of why, how, when, why, whats. Which will be quite tricky, as I don't have answers. But never mind, I'm sure I'll think of something. Just as Vanessa did when Ruby asked her why Daddy had a 'thing' between his legs and she said it was a tail, like George's, their cocker spaniel. Which was pretty inspired, I have to say. Although I don't know what Daddy will do if she asks him to wag it.

'Oh, wow, what a coincidence,' she gasps, her face creasing into a smile. 'That's my name too. But my friends call me Lottie.'

There's not a flicker of recognition. Nothing. It's like I'm a total stranger.

I stare at her in confusion. But how can that be? Unless of course this is all some crazy dream and I'm going to pinch myself and wake up to find Bobby Ewing in the shower. Or something like that.

I pinch myself. Nope, I'm still here. Or should I say both of me are still here?

'Sorry, I'm dreadful with faces, especially once I've had a drink.' She gestures to her empty glass and laughs widely, showing off a mouthful of silver fillings.

God, I'd forgotten about those too. I had them all replaced about five years ago, after reading an article about mercury poisoning and freaking out. I also had my two wonky front teeth straightened with braces. And I had them bleached. In fact my smile's completely different now. Like so many things about me . . .

And then, all at once, it dawns on me. No wonder she doesn't recognise me – not only do we look completely different now, but we are completely different. Of course I'm like a stranger to her; I *am* a stranger to her. She doesn't know me yet. *Me*, the person she's going to become in the future, in ten years' time. The person who no longer goes by her nickname of Lottie, but prefers Charlotte as it's more grown-up and mature. The person without silver fillings, long, brown scrunch-dried hair, bushy eyebrows and an accent that's pure Pennines. We're not the same person at all: I'm not her any more and she's not me yet. We're two completely different people.

I mean, for God's sake, does that look like my cleavage! I stare at it now in astonishment. My younger self is wearing a flimsy top that her boobs appear to be almost spilling out of. Automatically I fasten a button on my shirt. God, I'd forgotten how much heavier I was when I was younger, but then that's not surprising as I didn't do any exercise and used to eat rubbish. Now I work out and watch what I eat and I look and feel so much better.

'Um . . . nice top,' I comment, as she catches me staring.

'Thanks. I made it myself.' She grins proudly.

Yes, I know. From a handkerchief, I reflect, remembering how I thought it was a fab idea at the time. Ten years later it's so revealing I might as well have come to the pub wearing a doily. Seriously, what on earth was I thinking? *I'm practically naked.*

'Aren't you . . . um, a little chilly?' I suggest, resisting the urge to grab someone's jacket from the back of a chair and throw it over her shoulders.

'Chilly?' She laughs. 'Oh, no, not at all. In fact it's really hot out here.' She starts fanning herself with a beer mat to cool down, her wrists covered in bracelets, which chink loudly as they start jiggling up and—

I stiffen. The bracelets aren't the only thing jiggling up and down. The handkerchief is made out of this thin, silky fabric and – oh my God. *Is that a nipple?* Suddenly I realise two things: 1) I'm not wearing a bra and 2) I've magically turned into my mother.

Right, that's it. This is too much. I'm getting out of here. Grabbing my bag, I start to leave.

'Are you sure you don't want another drink?' Lottie asks, following me back inside.

'Er, no . . . thanks. I have to go,' I say hurriedly, shaking my head and gesturing to the door.

'Oh, OK.' She shrugs, and walks over to the bar. I hear her ordering a half of cider.

I feel an unexpected wave of nostalgia. Cider used to be my favourite drink before my tastes became more sophisticated and I started drinking wine, and for a moment I pause and glance back in her direction. Fiddling with her hair, she's waiting for her drink and chit-chatting with the person next to her at the bar, absently playing with her earring, laughing at some joke, chewing her fingernails, pulling faces, making different expressions.

I watch, completely fascinated. It's the weirdest feeling. A bit like when I go home to see Mum and Dad and they get out the old home videos and we all sit on the sofa and hoot with laughter at our funny clothes and hairstyles. Only I'm not laughing. I'm transfixed. This is just so surreal. Did I really used to wear my skirts so short? And what's with all that big, poofy hair? Hang on a minute . . . I watch as the guy next to her offers her a cigarette. *Am I smoking?*

Deep down in my brain I can hear a voice yelling at me to get out of here as fast as my legs can carry me. Quickly! Go on, scram! It's easy – just turn round, get in your car and drive back the way you came. Do not stop until you're safely home and in your pyjamas with a brandy and a box set of *Sex and the City*.

Well, that's always my guaranteed cure-all in any crisis.

I mean, this is insane, Charlotte. It's INSANE.

But it's also exciting, whispers another voice and out of nowhere I suddenly feel a tingle of adventure. Perhaps it wouldn't hurt to stay a little longer, have another drink. After all, it's not as if this kind of thing happens every day, is it?

'Actually, Lottie . . .'

She looks over her shoulder and, seeing me, smiles. 'I thought you already left.'

'No, not yet. I've actually got some time to kill. So I was wondering . . .'

'Cranberry juice, right?'

'Yes, please.' I smile, and hold out a pound coin, but she pushes it away.

'Don't be daft – it's on me,' she protests.

I know she's broke, because I was always broke back then, and as she pays the barman with what little she has, I feel a glow of affection towards my own self. Which is *beyond* weird, but hey. At this point, beyond weird is beginning to feel normal.

'Try not to spill it this time,' she jokes, as she passes me my juice.

'Thanks.' I take it from her. 'Oh, by the way,' I add, before I can help it, 'you get a stain out by soaking it in cold water.'

'Not hot?' She looks at me in surprise.

'No, that sets it.'

'Bloody hell, trust me!' She laughs, pulling a face. 'I guess I've still got a lot to learn.'

I smile.

Actually, it's funny you should say that . . .

Chapter Fourteen

OK, so now what?

Five minutes later Lottie and I have decamped once more to the beer garden. We share a table and for a few moments we both sit there in silence, sipping our drinks, while I grope around for something to talk about. I feel absurdly nervous. As if I'm on a first date.

'So,' I finally say, 'nice . . . um . . . weather we're having.'

No sooner have the words left my mouth than I feel myself cringe. God, Charlotte, *is that it*? You bump into yourself aged twenty-one and of all the millions of things you could say you're chatting about the goddamn weather?

'Mmm, yeah, isn't it?' She nods, closing her eyes and tipping her face to the sun.

Triggering a flashback to Suki's lecture about sun-damage.

'Arggh, no, don't—' I blurt out, then stop myself.

Jerking her head back down, Lottie looks at me, startled. 'Jesus, what's wrong?'

I hesitate. Oh, shit. I really haven't thought this through, have I? I mean, what do I say now? You're going to ruin my skin? I have severe pigmentation and discolouration and it's *all your fault*?

'Um . . . there was a wasp,' I mumble weakly.

'Oh, crap, really?' Waving her hands around, her eyes dart from side to side, looking for the invisible wasp.

'Actually, I think it's gone now,' I add quickly.

'It has? Phew.' Settling back in her chair, she hitches her skirt even shorter and sticks her legs out into the sun. 'God, it's amazing that it's still really hot, isn't it?' she enthuses, basking like a cat in the early evening rays.

'Yes, isn't it?' I nod, watching her helplessly while trying to block out Suki's voice, which is now ringing in my ears. 'Um . . . are you sure you don't want to sit in the shade?'

'*The shade?*' My twenty-one-year-old self turns and looks at me with such horror you'd think I suggested she stick red-hot pokers in her eyeballs. 'Why on earth would I do that? I'm trying to get a suntan.'

Trust me, this girl has a suntan. She's practically mahogany.

'You know, I use this great fake tan—' I confide, but she cuts me off.

'Fake tan? Urgh.' She pulls a face. 'No, thanks. I want a real tan.'

I smile. Tightly.

There's a beat as I watch her turn her face to the sun again and close her eyes. God, this is ridiculous. I can't just sit here and do nothing.

'I have some sunscreen if you want to borrow it,' I suggest, trying to sound nonchalant.

'No, it's OK.' She shakes her head. 'I don't wear sunscreen.'

Now it's my turn to look at her with horror as visions of all the skincare products in my bathroom cabinet swim before my eyes, followed by visions of all my credit-card bills. I've spent enough on miracle creams that promise to reverse the signs of ageing to make a dent in Third World debt.

And no wonder, I realise, watching myself as I sizzle in the sun. In fact, to be quite honest, I'm lucky I don't look like beef jerky.

'Well, it's never too late to start,' I reply, pulling out my sunscreen from my bag while simultaneously fighting the urge to grab hold of her and smother her in it till she looks like a cross-Channel swimmer. 'Sure you don't want some?' I ask, squirting a bit on my hand and rubbing it on my face.

'SPF forty-five?' she says, looking aghast. 'Blimey, no wonder you're so pale.'

'I'm not *that* pale.' I frown, looking at the remnants of my spray-on tan. 'And anyhow, sunbathing is really bad for your skin, you know. In fact a tan is just melanin,' I quote from one of the many skincare articles I've read on this subject, 'which your skin produces to protect itself. So in fact you could say that a suntan is actually a sign that your skin is already damaged,' I finish, feeling rather impressed by how knowledgeable I sound. I hadn't really realised how much you learn as you get older, but by the time a woman hits thirty, she's been exposed to enough magazines, beauty products and mirrors to have become an expert in skincare.

'So what?' She laughs carelessly.

Only she hasn't hit thirty yet, has she? This version of me is still twenty-one, I realise, watching my younger self. I know nothing. I have no idea how much money I'm going to hae-morrhage on this stuff in years to come, how many hours I'm going to spend daubing on creams and massaging in scrubs to achieve what I have right now, and what I'm taking for granted.

Frustration stabs. God, was I really so clueless?

'You say that now,' I persist, trying not to think of all the UVB and UVA rays that are right now attacking that perfect, peachy, freckle-free skin, sowing the future seeds of pigmentation and discolouration, 'but you'll regret it when you're in your thirties.'

'Thirties? Oh God, I won't care by then,' she dismisses, slurping her cider. 'I'll be old.'

I flinch. 'Thirties isn't old,' I say tetchily, and reach for my cranberry juice. I'm not actually a big fan of cranberry juice, but it's chock-full of vitamin C and antioxidants. I take a virtuous sip. So much better for me than cider, which is just full of empty calories.

'Yeah, it is,' she retorts, and gives a little shudder, as if she doesn't even want to think about it. 'It's ancient.'

What? She's saying I'm *ancient*?

I feel a slam of indignation. I've been trying to be patient, but this is too much. I mean, honestly, the cheeky cow! I'm younger than Kylie! I still shop at TopShop! Admittedly only online, but still. *And* I have not just one but *two* pairs of skinny jeans! How on earth can she think I'm ancient?

Because you did, reminds a voice in my head. You did, Charlotte.

And all at once I remember a conversation I had when I was twenty-one. I was with a group of friends and we were talking about the millennium and how old we would all be, and when I realised I was going to turn twenty-five that year, I was appalled. I thought that was *so* old. And as for the few friends who would be in their thirties, well, that was just unthinkable. I didn't know anyone over thirty – apart from my parents – and it wasn't just that: I didn't even *notice* anyone in their thirties. They were invisible to me.

Just like I'm invisible to her, I think, glancing at my twenty-one-year-old self sitting just inches across the table from me, oblivious to who I really am.

She catches me looking and throws a hand over her mouth in horror. 'Oh, sorry, I didn't mean you were . . .' she trails off, pulls a face. 'Me and my big mouth.'

'It's OK, no offence taken,' I reply tetchily. 'I was just saying . . .' Absently I scratch the eczema on my elbow. 'Besides, the sun will really make your eczema flare up,' I can't help adding, moving even further into the shade.

She frowns. 'I don't have eczema.'

I look at her in confusion. 'You don't?'

'No, why did you think I did?'

'Oh, no reason.' I shrug quickly. 'It's just very common.' Puzzled, I try remembering when I got my first flare-up. It feels like I've had it for ever, but actually, thinking back, she's right – I don't remember having it when I was her age. In fact the first time I got it was when I was really stressed out over an important deadline.

'What time is it?' I zone back to see her gesturing to my watch. 'I don't have a watch.' She smiles in explanation.

'You don't have a watch?' I repeat in astonishment. It's unthinkable.

'No, I don't wear one.'

Trying to absorb this shocking piece of information, I glance at my own for the umpteenth time that day. 'Um . . . nearly twenty past six.'

She tuts. 'Typical. She's always late.'

'Who is?' I ask, but I already know. *Vanessa*. It has to be.

'My friend Nessy. She's supposed to be meeting me here for a drink, but she's never on time.'

Well, at least some things don't change, I think, suppressing a rueful smile.

'I'll give her another ten minutes, then I'm going home. I only live round the corner, so I can walk there. Which is lucky, as my car's in the garage being fixed.' She pulls a face. 'I had a bit of an accident.'

Of course. The lamp-post. That's why my old Beetle wasn't parked outside the house.

'Which garage did you take it to?'

'Oh, just some place on the Harrow Road.'

'Barry's Motors?'

'Yes, that's it.' She nods. 'How did you know?'

Because they totally ripped me off, I remember grimly, but instead reply vaguely, 'Oh, I took my car there once.'

The details are fuzzy now, but I'll never forget paying some ridiculously inflated bill because I was young and naïve and didn't know to question it, then having to borrow money off Vanessa as I couldn't afford to pay my rent.

'When's it going to be ready?'

'They said next week sometime.'

'Well, if I were you—' The irony hits me and I catch myself. 'I think you should take a male friend with you when you go back to collect it, just to check they've done a good job,' I suggest. 'If you're anything like me, you won't know the first thing about cars.'

She smiles gratefully. 'Thanks for the advice.'

'My pleasure.' I stifle a yawn that's just appeared from nowhere.

There's a lull in the conversation. Suddenly I feel very tired. It's a been a long day. The strangest, most bizarre, most remarkable day of my entire life, but now I can feel it all catching up with me and I just want it to be over. I want everything to go back to normal.

A wave of tiredness engulfs me, and draining my glass, I reach for my bag. If I leave now, I can get an early night. And then, when I wake up tomorrow, all this will have turned into one of those stories people tell at dinner parties that always goes, 'You're never going to believe this, but . . .' Like that one Vanessa has about how she saw a ghost sitting on the landing when she was eight years old.

Although I have to say, I think bumping into yourself is *slightly* better than just seeing a paltry old ten-a-penny ghost clanking some chains. But like I said, no one's ever going to believe me. *I* don't believe me and I'm seeing it with my own eyes, I muse, taking in my surroundings one last time.

'Hey, Lottie, I think I'm going to —' I break off as my gaze lands on a poster on the wall: '**Shattered Genius, playing at the Wellington, this Saturday, SOLD OUT.**' Hang on a minute, that name rings a bell . . . There's a grainy picture of a band underneath. Scrunching up my eyes, I peer closer.

'Have you heard of them? They're amazing!'

Her voice grabs my attention and I turn to see her gesturing at the poster.

Quite frankly I have no idea, but I nod vaguely and concentrate hard on rummaging around in my memory. I'm so tired that everything's fuzzy, but I know it's going to come back to me any second.

'You know, I've got a spare ticket if you want to go. My friend Nessy was going to come with me, but now she's seeing Julian instead.' She rolls her eyes and smiles. 'He's her new boyfriend and they're totally in love.'

It suddenly strikes me how friendly I used to be. I'd just moved down to London from Yorkshire and the city hadn't rubbed itself off on me yet. Now, after being here over ten years, I tend to keep myself to myself and am wary of talking to strangers. London does that to you.

'Thanks, but I think I'm busy that night,' I reply, shaking my head. Seeing myself once is freaky enough, but twice? I don't think my sanity can handle a repeat performance.

'Oh, what a shame,' she tuts in commiseration. 'I can't wait. I love the lead singer.'

'The lead singer?'

'Billy Romani,' she hisses excitedly.

As she says the name, her face lights up like Oxford Street at Christmas and I feel myself stiffen. I haven't heard that name for years, I've blocked it from my mind, but now it's all coming flooding back. Billy Romani was someone I had a crush on for months, and when we finally ended up spending the night together, I thought it was the beginning of some great big love affair.

For about two days. Until I found out I'd just been a one-night stand and he'd already moved on to another girl and—

Pain stabs. Well anyway, the details aren't important. Suffice to say, at the time I was heartbroken, but of course I bounced back, I remind myself, and since then I've never given him or what happened a second thought. Well, maybe sometimes, on the odd occasion, I've wondered what would have happened if things had turned out differently between us.

But they didn't, and I'm glad. Still, it's not something I dwell on. It was so long ago. I'm over it.

'He's so talented, don't you think?' she's saying eagerly.

'Um . . . yes, sort of . . .'

Talented at being a total bastard, I think grimly.

A vague memory stirs. Wait a moment. Wasn't it after one of his concerts that I slept with him? I feel a clench of regret. God, if only I hadn't done that, if only someone had stopped me —

An idea strikes and all at once I feel a flurry of possibility.

No, surely not. I can't.

Can I?

It's like a light going off in my brain. Up until a moment ago I wanted everything to go back to normal, for this all to be over, but now . . . I hesitate, my stomach fluttering nervously as I decide what I'm going to do. I knew before all this went through my head.

'Then again, I'm not *that* busy . . .' I hear myself saying loudly.

Because I might not know *why* this is happening to me or *how* this is happening to me, but one thing's for certain: if I go to this concert, I can save myself from a broken heart.

Stirred up, I smile determinedly. 'How much do you want for the spare ticket?'

Chapter Fifteen

That night I go to bed and have the strangest dream. I'm with Christopher Lloyd, the crazy scientist in *Back to the Future*, and we're driving along the freeway in the DeLorean. Only we're not travelling at the speed of light, we're going about five miles per hour because of the diversion and now the car has changed into my old VW Beetle, and being an American, Christopher Lloyd can't drive a car with gears, so we swap seats.

But when I sit back down, I'm not in a car any more, I'm in the Wellington and it's not the crazy scientist sitting next to me, it's Suki and she's tutting and holding up a mirror so I can see my sun-damage. When I look at my reflection, though, my face is super-smooth and blemish-free and suddenly I realise there is no mirror. It's me, aged twenty-one.

And I'm sunbathing. Without any sunscreen.

And my tan is getting darker and darker, deeper and deeper, and I'm trying to stop myself before I turn into an old leather handbag, but I'm not listening. I'm smoking cigarettes and drinking cider and singing along to Billy Romani.

Hang on a minute, are you sure this is a dream, Charlotte?

Snapping open my eyes, I tug off my eye mask and peer at my alarm: 2 a.m. Urgh. It's the middle of the night and I'm wide awake. For a moment I lie there, watching as the clock changes from 02.00 to 02.01, my mind replaying footage from the pub, over and over and over and over . . .

OK, that's enough. I've got to get up for work in less than five hours. I need to go back to sleep, otherwise I'm going to be exhausted. I feel a gnaw of anxiety. There's nothing worse than the pressure of knowing you have to go to sleep to prevent you from falling asleep, is there?

Flopping back on to the pillow, I put my eye mask back on. I just need to relax. Drift away. In the background the sound machine is set to 'Relaxing Ocean Lullaby' and I listen to the waves rushing in, and rushing out, rushing in and—

This pillow is too hot. I turn it over and place my cheek on the cool cotton. Ah, that's better. I squeeze my eyes closed again and try to fall asleep.

Also, it's a bit lumpy. Hitching myself up on one elbow, I bash the pillow with my fist, pummelling the allergy-free feathers into submission, before flopping back down again. Right, OK. Sleepytime. I wriggle down underneath my duvet. The sound machine is still whooshing rhythmically, the humidifier is still puffing steam. Any minute now I'm going to be lulled into a drowsy slumber.

But first I have to get comfy. I toss, then turn, then toss back again. Gosh, is it me or is it really hot in here? I throw off my duvet and lie there relishing the cold air. Mmm, this is better. Much, much better . . .

Though now my feet feel a little cold. And is that a draught? In fact, you know what, I'm actually quite chilly. I tug back the duvet and strike a compromise by splaying my body half in, half out. OK. Perfect.

I lie very still and focus on clearing my mind, emptying it completely of all thoughts. Like, for example, me with bushy eyebrows, big hair and that God-awful silver eyeshadow that I'd forgotten all about. Or me smoking and drinking and sunbathing and basically doing everything that's bad for me. Or me fancying losers like Billy bloody Romani.

Oh God, this is useless. I'm a terrible sleeper at the best of times, but now, with all this stuff spinning round in my head?

Not a flipping chance. I know, I'll read for a bit, I decide. Flicking on the bedside lamp, I sit up and reach for my new self-help book, *Stress Is a Four-Letter Word*. I turn to Chapter Two: Relax Your Mind. 'You're walking through a beautiful forest. The sun is shining. Birds are singing as they fly gracefully overhead. Tilting your face to the sky, you watch them, imagining what it would be like to be a bird.'

A bird? What kind of bird? I know, I'll be an eagle. No, I can't be an eagle – they don't sing. What about a sparrow? No, too boring. A robin? OK, I'll be a robin.

'You imagine what it would be like to be able to fly away, to soar away into the sky, higher and higher.'

How high? I don't like heights. I get vertigo. In fact I'm not that keen on flying either, especially not after that terrible flight I had years ago coming back from Spain. Oh my God, the turbulence was terrible, I remember anxiously. Everyone was screaming, even the air hostesses! I swear, I thought I was going to die —

OK, that's it. Sod it.

I snap the book shut and chuck it down. It's no good, I can't relax, I'm too restless. Only a few days ago I was living my perfectly normal life, my head full of perfectly normal things like deadlines at work, dinner arrangements with Miles, those extra five pounds I've been trying to shift since Christmas, but now everything's been shaken up and turned upside down and I'm not sure what to do about it.

Except stress about it of course.

I clamber out of bed and tug on my dressing gown. Feeling all agitated, I go into the kitchen, flick on the kettle and grab the soya milk from the fridge, but as I reach for the handle, I pause. I have one of those big American types on which are stuck things – like an out-of-date gym timetable, some photographs of Ruby and Sam, a couple of recipes that I've ripped out of magazines and which I keep meaning to try, one day, and magnets that read things like 'The journey is not the destination' and 'Women are like teabags: they don't know how strong they are until they get into hot water – Eleanor Roosevelt.' Vanessa got me that one.

Only I'm not looking at any of that stuff. I'm noticing an old photograph, half hidden underneath a postcard Mum and Dad sent when they went to Turkey. It's one of those big drunken group shots taken years ago at some party. Peeling it off the fridge, I look at it closely. The sunlight's faded it, bleaching out colours and washing out details, but I can still make out people's faces.

I smile nostalgically. There's me, right at the end, wearing that now-familiar terrible silver eyeshadow, and next to me is Vanessa. She's wearing black, as always, and has her arm draped round Julian, who's doing bunny fingers above her head. I smile to myself. Those two were always joking around back then, I muse, turning the photo over and looking at the date scribbled on the back. 'My twenty-second birthday party'. Wow, what a coincidence. I turn thirty-two on Friday, which means this photograph was taken nearly exactly ten years ago. I peer at the photo again, trying to jog my memory for details, but I can't remember any more. It was so long ago I've completely forgotten.

The kettle boils and I pour hot water on to the teabag, absently watching the water turning a deep brown as my mind starts ticking over. What else have I forgotten? Who else has slipped my memory? How many other make-up horrors have I conveniently erased from my internal hard-drive?

On impulse I abandon the tea and, grabbing a torch from one of the kitchen drawers, pad into the hallway. There's a little cubbyhole under the stairs that I use as storage. Crouching down, I pull it open and crawl inside. It's dusty and there are several large cobwebs. Urgh, I'm terrified of spiders. I take a deep breath and try to remember the stuff I read in *Feel the Fear and Do It Anyway* about facing your fears. Even if they're black and have eight very hairy legs.

Trying not to think about spiders dropping on my head or crawling down the collar of my dressing gown (and thinking *only* about spiders dropping on my head or crawling down the collar of my dressing gown), I start rummaging around. I'm sure they're in here somewhere, amongst all this stuff . . . Christmas-tree decorations, an ancient tea set that was my grandmother's, old clothes that I'm keeping in case they come back into fashion. I hold up a pair of faded, ripped Levi 501s with a bandanna for a patch on the knee. Well, that's the idea . . .

Aha, there it is. Behind a couple of dusty suitcases I spot a large, old-fashioned hat box. Dragging it out, I carry it into the living room and plonk it on the rug, then sitting cross-legged beside it, tug off the dusty lid.

It's filled with photos. Now everything's digital no one hardly ever gets prints made any more, do they? They're all kept on the computer – I've got the one of Miles and me at his birthday last year as a screensaver – but in the old days I always used to be getting films developed at Snappy Snaps and putting them in albums. I've got dozens of them.

I start flicking through one randomly, and then another, and another, until I find what I'm looking for: an album containing pictures of me when I was twenty-one. With renewed curiosity, I open it and gaze at the photographs. I'd just moved to London and it's filled with a social whirl of parties, pubs and picnics. Here's one of the many Christmas parties we had at Kilmaine Terrace, when I snogged Simon, who I worked with. I cringe. Boy, did I regret *that* in the morning.

Oh, and there's Vanessa and I drunk and dancing at the Notting Hill Carnival – shortly after this picture was taken I fell into a bush and twisted my ankle because I was so drunk. I couldn't wear high heels for months. It was such a pain. Literally.

I turn a page. And here's me again in some horrendous patterned flares I bought from Camden Market. I shudder. I used to think they were so flattering, but looking at them now with the benefit of hindsight, I realise they made me look like someone's sofa. God, talk about a fashion faux pas. I'd never let myself go out in those now.

I pause, the photo albums scattered around me. A seed of thought takes hold, starts to grow . . . Hang on a minute. If I can prevent myself from sleeping with Billy the wannabe rock star and save myself from getting hurt, why stop there? What about *all* the hundreds of mistakes I'm going to make, *all* the lessons I haven't yet learned, *all* the dumb, stupid stuff I'm going to do because I'm naïve and clueless and don't know any better? Plus let's not forget all these other fashion disasters. I cringe, spotting another photograph. This time I'm wearing PVC trousers that make my legs look like they are encased in bin-liners. Enough said.

All at once everything seems to broaden, like being in the movies when the curtains pull back and the screen widens, and I can see the bigger picture. And it's not just about something specific, like the importance of wearing sun-screen, being warned about a dodgy garage or staying away from a loser like Billy Romani; it's about everything. It's about all the coulda, woulda, shouldas. It's about getting the one-in-a-zillion chance to hang out with my twenty-one-year-old self.

Like Vanessa said, if only you knew then what you know now. *Well, now I can.*

I feel a rush of exhilaration. Excitement. *Potential.* And suddenly it hits me. Oh, wow, just imagine. I'll be like Yoda! A wise master, teaching myself the ways of the world, bestowing sage advice and words of wisdom, giving myself the benefit of my experience and hindsight. I can see myself now. I'll be firm but fair, wise but approachable, like Dumbledore in *Harry Potter*, or Mr Miyagi in the *The Karate Kid*.

But of course I mustn't get too carried away, I think, catching myself hastily. After all, Lottie has no idea who I am, so it's important I don't appear like a know-it-all. I mean, I'm not going to give her a set of instructions or dos and don'ts or anything like that. No, I'll just drop a few subtle hints, gently lead her in the right direction, give her a bit of friendly advice. I won't make a big deal of it all.

Chapter Sixteen

O K, so I've made a list.

Fast-forward to nine the next morning and I've popped into a pharmacy before my meeting with a journalist from the *Guardian*. Armed with a basket, I'm navigating the busy aisles, on the hunt for a pair of eyebrow tweezers.

If I'm going to do this properly, I don't want to forget anything, so I've just scribbled down a few random thoughts on a piece of paper. Nothing major, just some things off the top of my head. So for example, first things first:

1. Do not sleep with Billy Romani.

I don't care how handsome he is. How charming he is. How amazing that thing was that he did with his tongue — OK, Charlotte, enough of the reminiscing. He's also a liar, a cheat and a heart-breaker.

2. Invest in property.

My dad's motto was always 'Buy, don't rent.' Of course I didn't listen to him. Maybe now I'll listen to myself.

3. Better still, invest in any of the following: Starbucks/Google/YouTube.

Admittedly that might be a bit unrealistic. Especially considering I used to have about two fifty pences to rub together at the end of each month. Plus I'm not even sure those things were around back then. But still, it's important to . . .

4. Think big.

And we're not just talking about you-know-what.

Though of course that's important, I reflect dreamily, my mind wandering off in all kinds of directions, until catching myself, I quickly glance back down at my list of instructions. Right, where was I? Oh, yes.

5. Start a pension.

OK, I'm just going to have to get the boring financial stuff out of the way first, so I can get on to the more important stuff on the list.

Spying the tweezers, I pounce on a super-professional-looking pair made from industrial-strength stainless steel with 'precision edges' for a salon finish. Like, for example . . .

6. Pluck your eyebrows.

Look, I've got nothing against thick eyebrows, but it's one thing having sexy beetle brows like Brooke Shields in *Blue Lagoon* and it's another having Noel Gallagher's monobrow. And while we're on the subject of grooming . . .

7. Do your bikini line.

I know for a fact I didn't have my first bikini wax until I was thirty. A fact I remember because it was *that* painful I still bear the emotional scars. Which means down there I'm currently resembling a German tourist. *Nicht gut.*

Grabbing some Nair hair-remover, I throw it in my basket.

8. There is such a thing as too much eye make-up, so throw away the silver eyeshadow.

And while you're at it . . .

9. Throw away the mousse too.

Scrunch-drying is not a good look. Never was. Never will be.

10. Neither is trying to lighten your hair with lemon juice.

A) It doesn't work and b) it attracts wasps.

11. Start doing your pelvic-floor exercises now.

Remember Vanessa's advice? Kegels are like shoes – there's no such thing as too many.

Reminded, I pause in the aisle to do a couple and notice I'm standing right by the sunscreen section. Like I said before . . .

12. Wear A LOT of sunscreen.

I chuck in a couple of family-size bottles of SPF45. Then a couple more. Well, better safe than sun-damaged.

13. Put down those PVC trousers and back away.

Yes, sadly it's true. Last night I found the damning evidence: a photograph of myself vacuum-packed into a pair of skintight, belly-button-skimming, shiny, PVC trousers. The word 'mortified' doesn't even come close.

14. Cancel that trip to Sicily in 1998.

It rained all week and I was forced to comfort-eat pizza and *gelato*.

15. On second thoughts, don't cancel that trip. ☺

Reaching the end of the aisle, I turn into the next one. There are still a few things I haven't found yet, I muse, as I spot that rare creature: a sales assistant.

'Excuse me?'

For a moment I think she's going to pretend she hasn't seen me and dart off into the back – a bit like Vanessa's cocker spaniel if you catch him sitting on the sofa – but at the last minute she seems to change her mind. 'Yes?' she asks, turning. 'Can I help you find something?'

'I'm looking for Nicorette patches.'

Which brings me to . . .

16. Stop smoking.

'Oh, I see.' She nods briskly. 'To help you with stopping smoking?'

'Oh, no, I don't smoke,' I say, quickly putting her right.

Before realising by her confused glance that that might not have been the best answer.

'Um . . . I mean, I don't smoke any more,' I correct myself.

She peers at me in confusion. 'I'm sorry, I'm not sure if I quite understand . . .'

Welcome to my world, I think ruefully, switching my basket on to the other arm. I've thrown in quite a lot of stuff and it's really heavy.

'I wouldn't advise wearing nicotine patches unless you are suffering the withdrawal effects of nicotine,' she continues, rather firmly.

Oh God, she probably thinks I'm one of those people who get high by drinking cough syrup or something.

'Yes, absolutely,' I agree in my most responsible voice. 'Of course I won't. Unless I am. Which I will be.'

Fuck. I'm digging myself a bigger hole here.

She looks at me sharply, then thinking better of it, says, 'We keep the patches in our prescription section, just on the left.'

'Oh, OK, thank you.'

Hurriedly turning away, I'm heading towards the sign that says, 'Prescriptions', when I see a flash of suit and a familiar profile. Gosh, that looked like Julian, but it can't be – what would he be doing in this part of town? His office is miles away. I glance again to get a better look. But no, it's definitely Julian. A smile spreads over my face in readiness to say hello as I make my way towards him.

'Hey, Julian, fancy seeing you here!' I exclaim, tapping him on the shoulder.

He swings round like he's been shot. 'Charlotte!' he gasps, clutching his tie to his chest, his eyes wide.

'Oh, sorry,' I apologise, smiling. 'Did I startle you?'

He quickly composes himself. 'A little bit.' He laughs awkwardly.

'So what are you up to?'

'Excuse me?' He looks at me blankly.

'In this part of town. I thought your office was in Chancery Lane.'

Gosh, he's acting really weird. *Shifty*, almost. Which is ridiculous. It's Julian. What's he got to be shifty about?

'Oh, right, yeah.' He shakes his head distractedly. 'I have a meeting close by.'

'Snap.' I smile, but he doesn't. 'With a journalist . . .' I trail off uncomfortably and absently glance down into Julian's basket. And there, among the shaving foam and Gilette razors, I see them.

Trojans. Extra large. Ribbed for comfort.

Suddenly it dawns on me exactly why Julian is acting so weirdly. He's all self-conscious, as am I, I muse, feeling a flush of embarrassment. Which is silly as we're both adults.

'Look, Charlotte, I'm running late.'

I snap back to see Julian checking his watch.

'Er, yeah, me too.' I smile, blushing beetroot. 'Well, I'll see you tomorrow.'

He looks at me as if he doesn't have a clue what I'm talking about.

'For dinner,' I add to jog his memory. 'It's my birthday. Did Vanessa mention it?'

'Oh Christ, yes, that's right.' He rakes his fingers through his hair and smiles apologetically. 'Sorry, I've got a lot on my mind at the moment.'

'Well, bye.'

'Yeah, bye, Charlotte.'

I watch as he strides away down the aisle, his dark-suited figure causing a few turned heads among some girls by the make-up counter. Gosh, Vanessa is such a dark horse. Haven't had sex for ages, indeed! Just wait till I see her!

And smiling to myself, I turn back to my list. Now, where was I?

'Morning.'

Arriving at the office after my meeting, I push open the frosted-glass door expecting to be greeted by Beatrice as usual, but instead find her with her head on her desk, fast asleep, drooling. As the door swings closed behind me, she flips upright like a jack-in-a-box.

'Oh . . . um . . . morning,' she flusters, blinking frantically. Her keyboard is imprinted in her face, giving her this strange pink tattoo across her left cheek. 'I was just . . . er . . . clearing up our database.'

Strangely, 'clearing up our database' is something Beatrice only ever does when she's suffering from a hangover. And even more strangely, it seems to be something she can do with her face on the desk and her eyes closed.

Hastily stifling a yawn, she takes a sip of her Berocca, which is fizzing merrily away on her desk. Lying next to it is her copy of *Vogue*, which she reads on the bus into work. Or at least that's what she wants people to think. And I used to think that too, until I borrowed it one lunchtime and discovered her guilty secret: a copy of *New Scientist* tucked away inside.

'Are you OK? I ask, looking at her with concern. Her usually rosy cheeks have a greyish pallor, and her blue eyes are blood-shot.

'Yes, fine.' She winces, massaging her temples.

'Because I've got plenty of paracetamol,' I offer, reaching for my family-size bottle.

She flinches at the noise. 'No, it's fine, honestly,' she whispers, getting shakily up from her chair and walking unsteadily over to the coffee machine. 'Just a little delicate. I think it might have been those mini-quiches.'

'Or the champagne,' I add teasingly.

She looks at me, chagrined. 'Oh dear, I did get rather sloshed, didn't I? I hope I didn't do or say anything silly.'

Without warning my mind flicks back to yesterday afternoon and her speech about time travel and I'm tempted to share my secret with her. Maybe she can help shed some light on how or why this is happening to me. Either way, it would just be a relief to tell someone who won't think I'm going cuckoo for Coco Pops. The theory being because Bea is already a little bit cuckoo for Coco Pops herself.

'Well, there is one thing—' I begin.

'No, stop, don't tell me.' Putting out her hands to defend herself from what I'm about to say, she squeezes her eyes tightly shut as if she's going to be walloped by some great big embarrassing faux pas. 'It's about Patrick, isn't it?'

'Patrick?' I stop my thoughts mid-track. 'Who's Patrick?'

'The journalist I introduced you to,' she reminds me. 'You know, the super-hot chap who was married.'

Suddenly I realise Beatrice wasn't just sloshed; she was well and truly hammered. Beer-goggles, or in Beatrice's case champagne-goggles, can be the only explanation for turning the slightly chubby, shiny, pink-faced Patrick I met into a 'super-hot chap'.

'No. Why? Should it be?'

She blushes, her neck prickling with bright crimson splodges. Opening one of her large blue eyes, she looks at me woefully. 'I'm afraid after you left I got rather . . .' she swallows hard '. . . *flirtatious.*'

'I see.' Though I don't, not really. Beatrice flirting is not an image that comes easily to mind.

'And then his wife appeared.'

'Ouch.' I wince.

'From nowhere. *Poof.* She was there, right in front of me, in a Pringle sweater.'

'Ah, yes, the semi-professional golfer, I remember now.'

Beatrice hangs her head in shame. 'I know it was terrible of me. I knew he was married. And I wasn't going to *do* anything. It's just . . .' She pauses and lets out a sigh. 'Oh, Charlotte, do you think I'm ever going to meet anyone?'

She looks so utterly crestfallen I really feel for her. 'Of course you will,' I say, giving her shoulder a squeeze. 'You're sweet and kind and super-smart—'

'But that's just it,' she stops me. 'When it comes to a girlfriend, men don't want super-smart. They're looking for beauty, not brains.'

'That's not true,' I argue. 'Look at . . .' I stall. Actually, now I come to think of it, I can't think of anyone.

'See. You can't think of anyone, can you?' she accuses sadly.

'Of course I can,' I protest, racking my brains. Come on, Charlotte, come on. There must be someone . . . 'I know! What about Miranda from *Sex and the City*?' I say triumphantly.

Beatrice gives me a look that could kill. 'What about her?'

'Well, she was a super-smart lawyer and she got Steve,' I point out.

Now Beatrice looks more depressed than ever. 'Exactly,' she says, throwing me a doleful look and turning back to the coffee machine.

I'm about to argue, then think better of it. Actually, Bea does have a point. OK, so Steve was a good guy, but he wasn't exactly hunky Aiden or Mr Big, was he? And he did have that really annoying, high-pitched, nasally voice.

'Men want women who spend money on clothes and make-up and designer shoes, not three thousand pounds on a telescope,' she continues, pouring out a fresh brew into two cups.

'Trust me, men don't care what you spend money on, as long as it's not their money—' I break off. 'You spent three thousand pounds on a telescope?' I ask in astonishment.

'Yes, I won it on eBay. Oh gosh, Charlotte, it's just amazing,' she gushes, coming to life, her eyes shining with excitement. 'It's Meade's all-new LX200R telescope with advanced Ritchey-Chrétien optics.'

'Um . . . is that good?' I ask uncertainly.

Beatrice clutches her pearls and looks at me as if I've just asked if the Red Velvet cupcakes with butter frosting from Sprinkles on the corner are worth trying. 'Nearly every observatory reflector in the world is a Ritchey-Chrétien, including NASA's Hubble space telescope!' she announces grandly, then breaks off, her face flushed with exhilaration. Which quickly fades in the space of time it takes to click your fingers. 'See, that's what always happens,' she accuses.

'What always happens?'

'That expression.'

'What expression?' I reply defensively.

'That blank look on your face.'

Oh, shit, is it that obvious? 'That's just how my face is,' I protest hastily. 'That's just how I look.'

'That's not true,' she pouts sulkily. 'I have that effect on everyone. I start talking and people just switch off. Mummy advised me to go into PR "because no man wants a wife who's a scientist". And she's right. Mummy's always right.' Her large blue eyes start to fill up and she blinks rapidly, trying to fight back the tears. She grabs a coffee filter as a tissue.

'Mummy *isn't* always right,' I argue hotly, then quickly catch myself. 'I mean, your mummy . . . *mum*,' I correct myself, 'isn't always right.'

'You think so?' She looks at me doubtfully, and twists the coffee filter in her hands.

'Absolutely.' I nod firmly, then throw her a reassuring smile. 'You just haven't met the right person yet.'

'Like you met Miles,' she says, looking at me meaningfully.

'Well, yes, like I met Miles,' I say feeling a bit awkward as I suddenly realise that I've barely thought about Miles these past couple of days. What with everything that's been going on, my head's been full of other stuff. But now at the mention of his name I'm reminded that I'm seeing him this lunchtime to look at a house.

Out of nowhere I experience a flutter of nerves. But that's just because I'm excited, I tell myself quickly. After all, who wouldn't be excited to go house-hunting with their boyfriend?

'How did you know he was the right person?'

I zone back in to see Beatrice still looking at me.

'Oh, I don't know, loads of things . . .' I trail off.

'Like what?' she asks eagerly.

Abruptly I get this feeling as if I'm on stage under the spotlight and it's my cue to say my lines. Only it's like I've got stage fright and I can't remember any of them. 'Everything,' I answer simply.

'Golly, that's so romantic.' She sighs and passes me my coffee. 'You're so lucky, you know.'

'Yes, I know.' And it's true. I do know I'm lucky. I tell myself that every day. It's just—

'Ooh! Someone's been on a shopping spree!' interrupts Beatrice. 'Giving yourself a makeover?'

I snap back to see her looking at my bulging carrier bags with curiosity. At exactly the same time as I notice the Nicorette patches and several packets of condoms, which I threw in for good measure, balancing precariously on top.

'Um, yes, I suppose you could say that,' I say, and quickly swooping on them, I stuff them in my desk drawer.

'Oh, what fun!' She beams, and hugging her coffee cup, she totters back to her desk.

Leaving me smiling uncertainly and wondering what exactly I've got myself into. For sure, the next few days are going to be a lot of things, but I'm not entirely convinced fun's going to be one of them.

Chapter Seventeen

'Hello, darling.' At one o'clock I park up outside a large red-brick Victorian house on a leafy West London street and find Miles already waiting for me by the gate, a huge grin on his face. 'Isn't it just perfect?' he enthuses, sliding his arm round my waist so we can stand side by side on the pavement and look up at 43 Andlebury Avenue. 'Well?'

As he turns to me, his eyes shining with excitement, I realise I haven't actually spoken yet. 'Gosh,' is all I manage.

Miles smiles. 'Gosh?' he teases. His mouth twitches with amusement. 'Is that it?'

'Well, no . . . I mean . . .' I trail off to take in the large windows, the black-and-white tiled path leading up to the front door, the shiny brass door knocker. It's a real, proper, grown-up house. The kind of house in which you put down roots, raise a family and live for the next thirty years.

'Are you sure we can afford it?' I blurt.

'Oh, I'm sure we can work something out,' he says, like he always does, kissing my nose affectionately. 'But let's not worry about that just yet – we haven't even looked inside!'

'No . . . Yes. I mean, you're right.' I nod.

God, I've never seen Miles this excited. Normally he's so level-headed and moderate about everything, but today he's buzzing with eager anticipation. I feel oddly left out. Why aren't I buzzing too? After all, I'm sure I'm going to love it; I can tell just from the outside, I decide, looking at the shiny navy blue front door and the two large potted yuccas on either side. And we have been talking about moving in together for ages. It's the next step. It makes total sense.

'Mr Richards?'

A sharp voice causes us both to turn round to see a grey pinstriped figure striding along the pavement. It must be at least eighty degrees today in London, and as the man hurries towards us, his jacket flaps open to reveal damp patches spreading out from under the armpits of his blue shirt.

'Benedict Meyers, Formans Estate Agents.' He shakes hands briskly with Miles. 'And Mrs Richards?' Holding out his hand, he turns to me.

'Oh, no,' I correct quickly, then blush. 'I mean . . .'

'Not yet,' jokes Miles, and we all share a polite chuckle.

'Well, if you'd like to follow me . . .' The estate agent jangles a huge bunch of keys authoritatively and briskly sets about unlocking the front door, deftly disabling the alarm and flicking on lights, all while providing a running commentary: 'Into the main hallway, where, leading off to the left, we have the full-width reception room, which opens into the breakfast room, offering a fantastic living and entertaining space . . .'

I walk slowly behind, trying to take everything in. I've always found house-hunting to be slightly bizarre. It's like stepping into someone else's life. All this history, all these memories belonging to someone else . . . My eyes flit across the photographs lining the shelves and try to imagine them being replaced with photographs of Miles and me.

'. . . and an actual working fireplace.'

Looking up, I turn to see the estate agent standing in front of a large exposed-brick chimney breast. 'Wow, really?' I smile eagerly. Miles once told me that you're supposed to act like you're not that interested when you're looking at property, so you can haggle over the price, but I can't help myself. I've always wanted a real fireplace.

'Hmm, is there a gas supply as well?' interjects Miles, frowning slightly.

'Why do you need a gas supply?' I ask, puzzled.

'Real fires look lovely, darling, but they're a lot of work.'

'But everyone loves a real fire!' I cry with dismay. 'They're so romantic.'

'In hotels maybe,' he says firmly. 'But not when you're shovelling ashes first thing on a morning. I used to have to clear out my housemaster's when I was at boarding school, and trust me, it wasn't fun.'

'Actually, I do believe there is a gas hook-up,' the estate agent is saying, crouching down and pointing at something, 'so if you prefer, you could convert this quite easily.'

'Hmm, right, yes.'

I watch as Miles bobs down next to him, their heads bent together.

'And you can get those very realistic gas fires these days. They almost look like the real thing.'

'But we have the real thing,' I protest loudly.

The estate agent and Miles suddenly both look up at me.

'Darling, I had no idea you loved real fires so much,' Miles says, surprised.

'Well . . . sort of,' I say, blushing slightly.

God, now I feel like a bit of an idiot. I didn't mean to make such a big deal of it.

'My wife and I can never agree about anything,' chips in the estate agent jovially. 'We argue about everything.'

'Oh, I'm sure we'll work it out,' says Miles amiably. Straightening up, he squeezes my shoulder. 'Won't don't do rows, do we, darling?' he says proudly.

'No.' I smile awkwardly.

'See. All sorted,' laughs Miles, turning to the estate agent. 'So, shall we move on to the kitchen?'

We spend the next ten minutes exploring the rest of downstairs and then move into the garden. I only have a tiny balcony at my flat and I've always dreamed of having my own proper garden.

This would be perfect, I think, wandering around the neatly trimmed lawn and looking at all the different flowers and plants that I don't know the names of. Still, I'm sure I could get a book about them, I decide, making a mental note to have a look on Amazon.

'Oh, and look, we could have barbecues,' I say, spotting one by a giant fern. I try imagining Miles in a striped butcher's pinny flipping burgers while I stroll around the garden, handing out glasses of Pimm's. Though to tell the truth, I'm not sure when we'd have time to organise a barbecue as we're both always so busy. I look across at Miles, but he's not paying any attention to the barbecue or the garden. Instead he's staring distractedly up at the roof.

'As you know, it's a two-bedroom property, but there's a possibility of a third and even a fourth if you convert the loft,' the estate agent is saying. 'If you'd like to take a look.'

'A loft conversion?' Miles seems galvanised by this news.

'Yes, a lot of the properties on the street have done that. If you'd like to take a look inside . . .'

'Miles, don't you want to look at the garden?'

But it's no good – he's already gone back inside with the estate agent. I feel a stab of disappointment. I wanted to show him the little fountain, and the barbecue, and all those lovely plants. He didn't seem to notice any of it. Still, I suppose I can do that later, I tell myself, as I follow them back into the house.

Upstairs are two bedrooms and a bathroom, and I'm just taking a peek at the second when Miles joins me.

'Well, what do you think?' he whispers, out of earshot of the estate agent.

'I love it!' I enthuse, as we walk inside the second bedroom.

'You do?' Miles's face breaks into a relieved smile.

'Yes, it's gorgeous.' I nod excitedly. 'There's the lovely fire-place, and the garden.' Pausing to take in the dimensions of the room, I'm suddenly hit by inspiration. 'And this room would be *perfect* for an office.' No sooner has the idea struck than my mind is already working overtime. 'We could put a desk over by the window, and there's plenty of room for a printer and everything.'

'I actually had another idea.'

'Oh, you mean put the desk against the other wall?' I frown, trying to picture it. 'Yes, I suppose that could work.'

'No, silly.' Sliding his arm round my waist, he pulls me close and looks at me meaningfully for a few moments. 'I was thinking this room would be perfect for a nursery.'

'You mean . . . for a baby?' I falter.

'Well, what else do you put in a nursery?' He laughs, stroking my hair.

'Erm . . .' I push my hair behind my ears and try to think of something to say. I suddenly feel a bit panicky. One minute we're talking about moving in together, the next I've *given birth*? What happened to the bit in the middle? We've just leapfrogged right over it. The proposal, me saying yes, the wedding . . .

Not that I think you have to be married to have a baby, and not that I don't want to have a baby – *one day* – it's just that we've never even *talked* about babies, except once when we went to the christening of Miles's nephew (Horatio, which I thought was a bit mean – after all, he was only a little baby). It was on the drive home and we had one of those jokey, hypothetical discussions about what we'd call our children, which went something along the lines of:

Me: 'I like Tallulah for a girl.'

Miles: 'Urgh. She sounds like a stripper. What about Tarquin for a boy?'

Me: 'Yuck. He sounds like an idiot.'

Back and forth, until we got bored and started talking about something else and forgot all about it. At least I did. Well, tried to.

'So are you in a chain?' The estate agent reappears with blundering chirpiness and we break apart.

'Well, we'd be putting our own flats on the market, but I can't see that being a problem – they're both desirable one-bedroom properties,' says Miles confidently.

I glance at him sharply. '*We will?*'

God, this is all moving a bit too fast. I don't remember agreeing to that.

'Well, yes, of course, darling,' says Miles. 'We discussed it, remember? Consolidating our assets, selling our individual properties . . .'

'A wise decision,' butts in the estate agent.

'Um . . . yes, I think so,' I say dazedly.

Selling our individual properties? That must have been the point when my attention wandered.

'It makes perfect financial sense.'

'I know, it's just . . .' I falter, my mind slipping back to the conversation about the fireplace and Miles not understanding the magic of real fires. I don't know how to put it into words. I can't even make sense of it myself, let alone explain it to Miles. Or the estate agent, who's watching me intently for signs of hesitation.

'I have to tell you I've got several other interested parties chomping at the bit on this one,' he warns. 'In fact I've already had a couple of offers over the asking price, so I reckon you'd have to make a really good offer to clinch the deal.'

My stomach tightens. God, it's all suddenly very real. Buying a place together is something Miles and I have talked about over mixed olives and a bottle of wine, and it all sounded lovely in theory, but until now I've never really thought it through. Haven't really grasped what it entails.

'I guess I'm just a bit nervous,' I confess.

'I know, darling.' Miles smiles good-naturedly. 'But don't you love this house? You've always said you want a garden, and there's masses of room . . .'

It's true. I am always saying that. Maybe I'm just worrying about nothing. I look at Miles. He's so handsome and smart, and he's found us this amazing house, and he wants us to buy it and move in together.

And I'm standing here dithering?

I grab a hold of myself. Charlotte, are you *completely* mad? What more do you want? What more could *any* girl want?

'You're right,' I say decisively. Throwing my arms round his neck, I give him a kiss. 'Let's make an offer!'

Chapter Eighteen

Back in the office, I sit at my desk eating a salad and stare at the glossy estate agent's brochure of the house. It looks gorgeous. It's got everything I've ever wanted: shiny wooden floorboards, big shutters, south-facing garden. It's my dream house.

But even so, for the rest of the afternoon I can't turn off that nagging feeling in the pit of my stomach. Every time I start to work on a press release, and even in my meeting with some journalist from *Sainsbury's* magazine, I find my mind wandering back to that moment in the bedroom when we talked about a nursery, or get a flash of Miles's excited face as we walked around the garden and he talked about extensions and planning permission and loft conversions.

As the digital clock on my computer screen flicks from 18.29 to 18.30, I put my computer to sleep. I've got my dinner date with Larry Goldstein in half an hour.

'OK, I'll see you tomorrow,' I say to Beatrice, who's hidden behind a barricade of files that are piled up on her desk. Her decision to reorganise the filing cabinets at four o'clock this afternoon not being one of her wisest.

'You're leaving?' Popping her head up above the A4 parapet, she looks at me with disbelief. '*Already?*'

'I'm having dinner with Larry Goldstein at Claridge's,' I remind her.

She rolls her eyes. 'Of course.' She nods, then shoots me a bright smile. 'Good luck! And don't forget to order the chocolate profiteroles.'

*   *   *

Arriving at Claridge's, I valet the car and hurry up the front steps. A uniformed doorman opens the door for me and I smile appreciatively. Gosh, I love Claridge's. It has to be the nicest hotel in London. I always dream about staying here. Once, after a night-out in the West End, I suggested to Miles that we splurge on a suite and spend the night here, but he looked at me as if I'd gone bananas. Why on earth would we pay a fortune to spend the night in a hotel when we only lived a few miles away? Which wasn't really the point, but anyway . . .

I'm a little bit early, so I cross the grand marbled lobby to where a couple of immaculately groomed receptionists are fielding telephone calls and queries from guests.

'Hi, I'm here to meet Larry Goldstein.'

At the mention of his name a look passes between the two receptionists. 'Ah, yes, Mr Celebrity Smile,' says one, smiling brightly. *Too brightly.* I get the impression he's not the most popular guest at the hotel. 'I'll call his room. May I ask your name?'

'Charlotte Merryweather, from Merryweather PR,' I add out of habit.

'One moment.'

As she dials the room, I take in the elegant lobby and try to steady my nerves. Several well-dressed guests are milling around, while over in the corner there's a blond man wearing sunglasses and muttering into his mobile. He looks a bit like Daniel Craig. Actually, I think it *is* Daniel Craig! Excitement stabs. Oh my God, just wait till I tell Miles! A real, live 007. And he's *gorgeous*. Though of course Miles doesn't like Daniel Craig. He says having a blond James Bond is a travesty . . .

He turns to face me. Oh, it's not him at all.

'Miss Merryweather?'

'Yes?' I snap out of my thoughts and look across at the receptionist.

'Mr Goldstein's running a little late, so he has invited you up to his room for drinks before dinner.'

My heart thuds. '*His room?*'

'On the third floor. Number thirty-five. The lift is to your right.'

Fuck. This is it. There's no escaping now. Gripping the handles of my bag, I walk nervously to the lift. My palms have begun to perspire, and as the lift doors open and I walk inside, anxiety grips me. Now come on, Charlotte, I tell myself firmly. Stop worrying. He's just being polite and hospitable.

The doors ping open and I walk down the dimly lit corridor to his room. Nervously smoothing down my skirt, I tuck my hair behind my ears and knock tentatively on the door. I hear footsteps.

I get a sudden image of Larry Goldstein greeting me in a slinky robe.

Argh, no. Stop it.

The door swings open, and bracing myself, I pin a smile on my face.

'Hi, Dr Goldstein—'

Only it's not Dr Goldstein. It's a woman with peroxide-blonde hair wearing a bright pink velour Juicy tracksuit and clutching a small furry dog. At first glance she looks about twenty-five, but on closer inspection I realise she's older. Although I'm not sure how I know this. It's one of those weird situations when there are no visible signs of ageing – no wrinkles, no eyebags, a perfectly taut neck – and yet somehow it's fairly obvious this is a woman nudging sixty.

'You must be Charlene!' she drawls, flashing an identikit smile to Larry Goldstein's.

'Charlotte,' I manage, trying not to stare.

'Well, come in, come in,' she demands, waggling her fear-some-looking acrylic nails at me.

I follow her inside, my mind racing. What's going on? Where's Larry Goldstein? My eyes sweep across the huge room, filled with antique furniture, a large flower arrangement and dozens of bags littered everywhere embossed with designer names: Gucci, Prada, Diôr . . .

'I'm sorry, we haven't been introduced . . .'

'Oh, I love those English manners – so formal.' She laughs gaily, then, cradling her small furball in the crook of her arm, sticks out a diamond-encrusted hand. 'I'm Cindy, Larry's wife.'

Larry Goldstein's wife? Well, that explains the smile. Two for the price of one, I realise, looking at her in astonishment, not to mention a great deal of relief.

'Twenty-five years.' She smiles proudly.

'Congratulations.'

'I can see you're surprised.' She pats her hair, still smiling. 'Most people are when I tell them.'

'Oh, right, yes, because he doesn't wear a wedding ring.' I smile back.

'No, because I don't look old enough,' she says sharply. 'Larry doesn't wear a ring because he's a cosmetic dentist. His hands are his tools.'

Fortunately, before things get any more awkward, the door opens from the en-suite bathroom and Larry emerges from a cloud of steam, like a super-hero appearing from a swirl of dry ice. Primped and smelling strongly of aftershave, he's talking loudly on the phone. 'Yeah Roger, I received the fax. The designs look awesome . . .' Seeing me, he gives a cheerful wave. 'Yeah, my PR person's here right now, so I'll run those ideas by her and get her take on it. OK, later.' He snaps the phone closed and turns his full attention to me. 'Hey, sorry about that.' He smiles brightly, not looking very sorry at all. 'So, I see the two of you have met.'

He walks up to his wife and puts his arm round her. They both smile as if someone's taking a picture of them: Cindy, Larry and the dog. It reminds me of when you see those official-looking photos of the American President and his First Lady.

'Cindy flew over to join me yesterday. She wanted to take in the sights, do some shopping.'

'Oh, I do love that Bond Street of yours,' she enthuses. 'And that Harrods!'

I'm presuming by her exclamation that's a good thing, but it's hard to tell as her face isn't actually moving because she's had so much Botox.

'It was the best mall I've ever been in! Much better than Macy's.'

'Well, it's not really a mall—' I begin, but she doesn't let me finish.

'And that Egyptian escalator!' She rolls her eyes. 'Who would have thought they'd have had escalators in the Pyramids! I said to Larry, "Isn't that incredible? All those years ago." '

I look at her in astonishment. Surely she doesn't think . . . *does she*?

'Dirty Martini?'

I turn to see Larry gesturing a cocktail-shaker.

'Ooh, my favourite,' cries Cindy, her face lighting up. Which is impressive, underneath all that make-up.

'Charlene?'

'Actually, I better not.'

'Oh, I see. Twelve steps?' Cindy taps her nose conspiratorially.

I look at her blankly.

'AA,' she says, lowering her voice as if people might be listening. 'All our friends are in it. In fact I was saying to Larry just recently that maybe we should join. They have some fabulous benefits.'

'Oh, no.' I shake my head. 'I'm just driving.'

'That's what they all say.' She smiles as Larry passes her a Martini.

'No, I really am—'

But Cindy interrupts again. 'Don't worry. Your secret's safe with us.' Pressing a manicured talon to her collagen-enhanced lips, she says in a low voice, 'Larry and I are the souls of discretion.'

'No wine for Charlene – she's in AA.' Throwing her hand protectively over my glass, Cindy hollers loudly at the wine waiter, who's circumventing the table with a bottle of Cabernet Sauvignon. A few people at neighbouring tables turn to stare. I feel my cheeks burn.

'Actually, I'm not—'

'It's OK, honey. You don't need to explain,' she whispers loudly, patting my hand.

That's it. I give up. My name's Charlene and I'm an alcoholic.

Two rounds of dirty Martinis later and we've decamped to the restaurant downstairs. Cindy insisted on bringing Foo-Foo, her miniature chihuahua, and after a tussle with the maître d' – 'No dogs are allowed, madam.' 'Foo-Foo is not a dog, she's my baby!' – we were allowed to our table, under strict instructions that her 'baby' stays in her Fendi handbag.

'So as I said, I'm really interested in hearing your views on the new space we're thinking of for the flagship Star Smile clinic,' says Larry Goldstein, producing a folder and clearing a space for it on the table.

'Yes, absolutely.' I nod, relieved to be finally getting down to business.

'I've just received a fax from the designers in LA and London, regarding the interior of the clinic. We're thinking organic, a totally new visual concept, very modern, minimalist, space-agey, sexy, but with all the latest high-spec equipment. A sort of *Barbarella* meets *General Hospital.*'

'Right, OK,' I say, hurriedly trying to get my head around that.

'Obviously with the total refurbishment, we're hoping for a launch date of late autumn, though realistically its probably going to be December.'

'But that's great,' I enthuse. 'That means we can really utilise that time to build up excitement and interest, raise your profile here in the UK. To an even higher degree,' I add quickly, seeing his face twitch. 'Launch the Star Smile brand, get a waiting list going, involve some celebrities, really build up the hype . . .'

'Exactly.' He nods, looking pleased.

'And you said that you might want my input on deciding on the exact location . . .'

'Well, we have a couple of spaces we're currently negotiating for, both in Harley Street.' He takes out a piece of paper from his folder and slides it towards me.

'Of course.' I nod, as my eyes scan it. It's the floorplans of two offices, together with photographs and architectural drawings. 'Right, I see. Well, they're both large spaces, and they've got all the amenities you'll need.'

'Hmm, yes, yes.' He's nodding and sipping his wine.

'And of course Harley Street is a prestigious address and renowned across the world for the best in medical services.'

Larry Goldstein gives a smile of satisfaction. 'Exactly, that's what the location scout said, which is why we've been working hard on securing premises there.'

I hesitate. 'But if you don't mind me saying, it's a little . . .' I pause.

'Go on,' says Larry Goldstein.

'Old.'

'*Old?*' Up until this point Cindy has been petting Foo-Foo and drinking wine, but at the word she visibly recoils. Like a vampire that's just caught a whiff of garlic.

Larry Goldstein narrows his eyes and fixes me with a stern look. 'But I was told it was the best,' he says, his voice thick with disapproval.

'Well, it depends what your idea of "best" is,' I say hastily. 'The demographic that you're appealing to wants to know that you're not just the best, you're also cutting edge.'

He seems to perk up a little at the words 'cutting edge'.

'You're not *just* a world-famous cosmetic dentist,' I continue, flattering his ego by dumping compliments left, right and centre. 'Choosing the Star Smile brand is not *just* a medical procedure, it's a lifestyle choice.'

He's nodding now, the corners of his mouth turned upwards.

'And most people don't want to spend thousands at the dentist. The British don't like dentists; we have a phobia of them.'

Larry Goldstein gives a slight shudder. 'I've noticed.'

'Going to the dentist is not something that's at the top of our list, but if you can make it into something appealing, something sought-after . . .'

'Such as?'

'Well, think of having a Star Smile as being like having the latest designer handbag, or a pair of shoes, or a new car. *Then* you're on to a winner.'

'A winner,' repeats Cindy approvingly from across the table. 'We all want to be winners in life, don't we? It's like when you and I were in Vegas, honey—'

'So what are you saying?' asks Larry, ignoring her and fixing me with his steely gaze.

'That I think you should be based in a more fashionable location,' I say truthfully. I'm in danger of offending him by disagreeing with his earlier choices, but hell, this is what he's paying me for. 'That you need a young, hip address. Somewhere celebrities are happy to be seen photographed, rather than to be seen trying to disguise themselves as they scuttle out of doctors' offices in Harley Street.'

'Hmm, yes, I think you might be right,' nods Larry thoughtfully. Suddenly galvanised, he whips out his iPhone and punches something in. 'I'll get on to my locations people right away.'

Brilliant, I think, with a beat of pleasure. I feel like giving myself a pat on the back. This meeting couldn't have gone any better.

'So are you thinking of visiting anywhere else while you're in London?' I ask, turning to Cindy. I feel a bit sorry for her as she's been left out of the conversation. But then again, she seems perfectly happy, I note, watching as she beckons the waiter over to refill her glass. Whoever thinks Americans don't drink has never met Cindy.

'Well, we did talk about Paris . . .' she says brightly.

'Oh, yes, you can go on the Eurostar. Now we've got the high-speed link at St Pancras Station it only takes less than two and a half hours.'

'But then I said to Larry, "Why bother? We saw the Eiffel Tower in Vegas."'

I look at her blankly. 'Sorry, did you just say Vegas?'

'Yes, on the Strip!' She frowns, as if I'm a bit stupid. 'They have heaps of cities there: Paris, New York, Venice . . . We went on a gondola. It was awesome.' She takes a slurp of her champagne. 'You should go.'

'Erm . . . yes, maybe I will,' I reply.

'OK, shall we order?' suggests Larry Goldstein.

'Yes, let's,' I say hastily, and picking up my menu, I dive behind it.

Chapter Nineteen

By the time I get home it's almost gone ten. I dump my bags in the hallway and kick off my stilettos. My feet are killing me. Padding barefoot into the living room, I flop on to the sofa and flick on the TV. I'll just watch a few minutes before making a start on the paperwork I brought home from the office, I tell myself, stretching out across the cushions and letting out a huge yawn.

God, I'm exhausted. I hardly slept at all last night. Or the night before that, for that matter. I was up half the night looking at photos. Speaking of which . . . I glance across at the albums still strewn across the rug and the piles of loose photos lying scattered all around. I didn't have time to tidy them up this morning, as I was in a rush as usual, but I'd better do it now, before the cleaner comes tomorrow.

I love having a cleaner. That's one of the great things about being older, being able to afford the luxury of having a cleaner. Only the irony is, I usually end up cleaning up for my cleaner as I don't want her to think I'm really untidy.

Easing myself up from the sofa, I set about tidying the photographs when my BlackBerry rings. I glance at the screen. It's Beatrice.

'So did you get the profiteroles?' she demands as soon as I pick up.

'Excuse me?'

'For pudding?'

'Um . . . no . . . we just had green tea.'

'Just tea?' she exclaims. 'Oh, what a shame! They're so yummy.'

I check my watch. 'Beatrice, did you just call me to talk about dessert? Because it is rather late . . .'

'Oops, no, sorry,' she says breathlessly. Beatrice is always breathless, even when she's sitting still. 'I wanted to find out how the meeting went with Larry Goldstein and if you need any facts and figures, or anything really, ready for first thing tomorrow morning.'

My impatience turns to gratitude. There are assistants and then there is Beatrice.

'It went really well,' I tell her, wedging my BlackBerry underneath my chin so I can continue stacking photos. 'He seemed really impressed with all my suggestions and my ideas for the location for his new flagship clinic, and so we agreed to touch-base on Monday for a final run-through before the press announcement.'

'Oh, bravo!' she cheers. 'So do you want me to check the diary and see when you're free? I have it right here . . .'

Like I said, Beatrice takes her job of looking after the diary very seriously.

'OK, great.'

I turn back to the photographs. Gosh, there's so many of them, and I still didn't look at all the albums, I think, glancing at the ones left in the box. Idly I pick up a couple. Hang on a minute, what's this? One of them is smaller and leather-bound. Flicking it open, I realise it's not filled with photographs, but with pages of my handwriting. Oh, wow, it's an old diary, I realise. And here's a couple more.

Digging them out of the bottom of the box, I spot one embossed with the date: 1997. My heart does a little leap. I wrote this when I was twenty-one.

'So let's see, you have a nine a.m. conference call with the Cloud Nine people to discuss their new range of flavoured water. Then you've got coffee at ten a.m. with Katie Proctor the journalist, followed by an eleven a.m. appointment . . .'

As Beatrice continues running through my diary, I read my own from ten years ago. Here's the entry I wrote on the first day I moved to London, 23 February 1997. My eyes flick over my description of the office, my boss, meeting Nessy:

Tall and blonde and smoking cigarettes on the wall outside the office, she seems really cool but a bit intimidating. She told me her name was Vanessa, 'which was created by Jonathan Swift for "Gulliver's Travels"'. I hope we'll be friends.

Smiling to myself, I thumb curiously to today's date. I wonder what I did ten years ago today? I glance down the page of swirly handwriting:

So exciting! All day I could barely concentrate.

Huh? I wonder what I was so excited about.

I've been looking forward to seeing the band all week and it was great! Shattered Genius were amazing.

Whoah, just one minute.

Frowning, I look again at the entry. I went to see Shattered Genius? But that can't be right – that's not till Saturday. I glance again at the date. Did I read it wrong? No, sure enough it's today's date: 23 August.

'Huh, that can't be right.' I stare it, puzzled.

'What isn't?'

I zone back in.

On the end of the phone Beatrice sounds alarmed. 'But it must be. I've already confirmed your three o'clock,' she's saying anxiously.

'Oh, no, nothing. I was just looking at an old diary and the dates are different. I must have got mixed up.'

'But they will be different,' she replies, sounding relieved. 'Calendars are different from year to year.'

Oh my God, of course. I'm such a dummy. I never even thought of that.

'The Gregorian solar calendar is an arithmetical calendar,' she continues matter-of-factly. 'It counts days as the basic unit of time, grouping them into years of 365 or 366 days. The solar calendar repeats completely every 146,097 days, which fill 400 years, and which also happens to be 20,871 seven-day weeks.'

'Um, really?' I say distractedly, staring at the diary in my lap. So that totally explains it. Today is a Thursday, but when I was twenty-one, today was a Saturday. Which means . . . All at once it registers: Billy Romani's band is playing tonight. Shit.

'Of these 400 years, 303 – the "common years" – have 365 days, and 97 – the leap years – have 366 days. This gives an average year length of exactly 365.2425 days, or 365 days, 5 hours, 49 minutes and 12 seconds.'

Beatrice is chuntering on, but I'm no longer listening. Instead my eyes are frantically glossing to the bottom of the page. Because there, in bold capitals, underlined twice and with four, no *five* exclamation marks are the words I'm dreading:

SLEPT WITH BILLY ROMANI!!!!!!

I take a deep breath. 'Fuck.'

Actually, we did, the whole night, if I remember rightly.

'Charlotte?' says Beatrice uncertainly. 'Is everything all right?'

No, I'm not all right. I'm not bloody all right! I'm about to make a huge mistake!

'Sure, yeah, I'm fine . . .' My mind is whirring and I glance at my watch. Maybe I'm not too late. Maybe I can still stop this. Dropping the diary on the floor, I jump up from the rug. 'But I have to go.'

'Go?'

'Um . . . yes . . .' I fluster. Music blares from the TV and I glance at the screen. '*Project Runway*'s coming on,' I blurt. 'It's my . . . um . . . favourite show.'

'It is? Oh, well, enjoy. See you tomorrow.'

'You too.' I hang up and look wildly around for my car keys.

There they are! And scooping them up from the coffee table, I grab the remote and flick off the TV.

Forget *Project Runway*.

This is Project Cock-Block.

Though I say I was a huge fan of Shattered Genius, I can't remember any of their songs. Not a single one. Which is odd, considering I can still remember the words to Bucks Fizz's, 'Making Your Mind Up' and I can't have been more than about five years old when they won the Eurovision Song Contest.

But I'm sure it's all going to come flooding back when I hear them tonight on stage, I tell myself, as I drive back through the diversion. Unexpectedly I feel a slight thrill. I can't remember the last time I went to see a live band. Actually, yes, I can. It was to see Licence to Thrill, a tribute band that did all the James Bond theme tunes.

Reluctantly my mind slides back to that night a few months ago. Miles got the tickets. He's a huge James Bond fan. He's read all the Ian Fleming books about a hundred times and can quote the films off by heart. Which might drive me nuts if it wasn't for Daniel Craig and *those* swimming trunks. I could watch him for ever. Though according to Miles, you have to prefer Sean Connery to be a true 007 purist.

Anyway, I like Shirley Bassey singing 'Goldfinger' as much as the next person, but an ageing trio from Manchester on keyboards, with a sequenced light show was a bit much. Their big finale was 'Nobody Does It Better', though quite frankly, I beg to differ: *I* could have done better. In fact Great-Aunt Mary's talking parrot could have done better. But of course I didn't tell Miles that. I didn't want to hurt his feelings, so I raved on about how amazing they were.

Unfortunately that slightly backfired as he went and bought me the CD 'because you love them so much'. So now I always have to pretend to be listening to it whenever he's in my car with me.

Taking the same route as yesterday, I cut down the side street. Luckily it's late and there's hardly any traffic on the roads, so it doesn't take long before I'm pulling up outside the Wellington. As I turn off the ignition, I hear a tuneless din wafting out from inside.

Oh dear. Suddenly that vague excitement I felt earlier is replaced with a resounding thud of trepidation and I have a flashback to me in a dingy club, full of cigarette smoke, while a band thrash the hell out of the speakers. Maybe this wasn't such a good idea. Maybe I've forgotten all of Shattered Genius's songs for a reason.

Feeling my resolve wobble, I force myself to rally. I can't turn back now. I'm here for me, remember. For Lottie, the twenty-one-year-old girl I used to be. And who right now is in that pub on course to get her heart broken by Billy Romani.

Unless I rescue her.

Resolute, I grab the handle and swing open the car door. As I step out on to the pavement, I hear the muffled clash of drums, accompanied by a sort of strange wailing that doesn't sound human. OK, so that doesn't sound great, but at least they can't be worse than Licence to Thrill, I console myself, slamming the door and hurrying towards the pub. Plus I used to be a fan of this band, remember? My musical tastes can't have changed that much. Seriously, how bad can they be?

Bad.

Very bad.

Like bloody awful.

Pushing open the door of the Wellington, I'm greeted by what sounds like an entire drumkit being thrown down the stairs, along with the drummer.

'Thank God – you made it!'

And Lottie, who has spotted me waiting unsurely in the doorway, rushes over. She's carrying a pint of cider and wearing those dreaded PVC trousers. Those need to be at the top of my list of 'what not to wear'. Though, saying that, her figure does look pretty fantastic in them, I think with surprise.

'Hi. Sorry I'm late. I was—'

'You nearly missed the whole gig,' she gasps impatiently, thrusting a ticket into my hand. 'Come on, hurry up, they're about to do their unplugged version.'

As the band falls silent, she grabs my arm and charges back towards the small room at the rear of the pub. Packed with people, it's standing room only. She pushes her way through the crowd towards the makeshift stage. Shattered Genius have disappeared off stage and a roadie is setting up a chair and microphone.

'So you really love this band, huh?' Reaching the front, I turn to Lottie, whose eyes are glued eagerly to the stage.

'Well, I love the lead singer, Billy Romani,' she confesses, sipping her pint.

Suddenly there's movement behind the stage. 'Oh my God, he's coming back on. He's coming back on,' she gasps.

My chest tightens and I brace myself. I feel a mixture of anticipation and apprehension at the thought of seeing him again. After all these years I vaguely remember what he looks like, but to be honest it's all a bit of a lustful blur. Plus of course I tried my hardest to forget him.

In the commotion I get pushed behind Lottie, but she's wearing flats like I always used to so now I'm much taller in my heels and can easily see over her head. My stomach releases a cage of butterflies. Any minute now I'm going to see him again and I have no idea how I'm going to feel.

Then, all at once, there he is, dressed in black and striding on stage with his guitar. Folding his six-foot-something frame into the chair, he pauses for a moment to take a swig from his beer.

And I feel absolutely nothing.

I stare at him in astonishment.

That's him? That's the man I used to be so crazy about? I was expecting to feel some kind of powerful emotion – desire, sadness, anger, *anything* – but instead it's just a huge anticlimax. He used to seem so hip and cool, but now—

'He's wearing leather trousers,' I hiss, feeling an unexpected beat of amusement. The last thing I expected was to find him funny, but he looks like such a complete idiot I actually feel sorry for him! 'And they're skintight!' I snort. Ha! This will definitely put her off.

'I know.' She nods, her eyes like saucers. 'Sexy, huh?'

I look at her in confusion. This was not the reaction I was expecting at all. Why am I not sniggering? Taking the piss? Making some joke about Michael Flatley? Can it be . . . ? I hesitate, trying to get my head round this impossible thought. Can it be true that once upon a time I fancied a man *who wore leather trousers*?

And with a lace-up crisscross fly, I notice with horror. I nudge Lottie quickly. 'Look at his crotch!'

'Oy, hands off, he's mine,' she giggles.

'No, I mean—' but I'm interrupted.

'This is a song I wrote about this crazy rollercoaster called life,' Billy Romani is drawling huskily into the microphone, his eyes downcast as if he's uncomfortable being under the spotlight.

Oh, please. If he's shy, so is Paris Hilton, I think, as he closes his eyes and starts wailing soulfully at the top of his lungs. On and on. Until finally, two encores later, it's all over and gratefully I steer Lottie back into the main pub and to safety.

'Over there.' Spotting a couple of free seats, we sit down.

Phew. I feel a wave of relief. Well, that was easy. All she has to do is finish her drink; then we can leave and put all this behind us.

'Hello, ladies, is this seat taken?'

Dammit. I spoke too soon.

We both look up sharply to see Billy standing next to us, smiling lazily. But, whereas before that smile would have melted me at a hundred paces, now it's like I'm made of super Teflon or something.

'Yes!'

'No.'

We both speak at the same time. Lottie and I. Then we both look at each other. She pulls a face as if to say, 'What are you doing?' and throws me a desperate look. All at once my heart goes out to her. Now he has zero effect on me, but back then I'd had a crush on him for ever.

'No . . . no one's sitting there,' she says hastily.

I watch her smiling tentatively and the longing is palpable. God, I really, really liked him, didn't I? I can see it in my eyes, that hopeful desire to be liked back.

And for a brief moment it all comes rushing back to me. The dizzy high I felt that night we spent together. It was amazing. I seriously thought he was 'the one'. Followed by the crushing low when I discovered he wasn't. But then, I thought a lot of foolish things when I was younger, I reflect, glancing at him and wondering what on earth I ever saw in him. God, if only I knew then what I know now . . .

'Cool.' Turning the chair round, he straddles it and hugs the back.

My eyes sweep across his shirt, open to the navel, and the crucifix round his neck that's resting on his smooth, hairless chest. I look back at Lottie, hoping to see her rolling her eyes sardonically or wanting to share a conspiratorial giggle, but no, her eyes have glazed over dreamily in the way men's do when they see *FHM* magazine.

'I'm Billy, by the way.' He holds out his hand and I see a flash of silver in the dimness of the pub. Oh my God, is that . . . ? I peer closer. Just when I thought the lace-up leather trousers and crucifix were bad, it gets worse. *He's wearing a skull-and-cross-bones ring.*

'I'm Lottie.'

'And I'm Charlotte,' I say, grabbing his hand before Lottie

can. Shaking it, I squeeze his fingers just that little bit harder than necessary.

'Firm handshake you've got there,' he quips as I finally let go. 'You nearly broke my fingers.'

Like you broke my heart, I'm tempted to reply, only I make do with an innocent, 'Gosh, really?'

Stretching out his fingers, he turns to Lottie, who's sitting next to him, staring at him adoringly. 'So how did you like the gig?'

'It was great. You were really great,' she enthuses and then, catching herself, blushes.

Argh. Could I be any *less* cool?

Billy Romani smiles appreciatively and, pushing back a shock of black hair that is hanging lazily over his forehead, leans closer so that his face catches the light. It's just as I remember: the high, angular cheekbones, his dark doe eyes, the sultry mouth with the perfect Cupid's bow. I have to say, despite the man-jewellery and the leather trousers, he's still the sexiest man I've ever laid eyes on.

Which of course, by rights, makes him a total bastard.

'That's good to hear, as we're working in the studio right now on the new album, trying to lay down some tracks. It's going to be really raw. It's a totally fresh sound. A combination of the spiritual meets the physical meets the metaphysical.'

'"Spiritual meets the physical meets the metaphysical"?' I snort. He might be able to charm Lottie with this absolute rubbish, but he won't be able to charm me.

But he's not paying any attention to me. I've suddenly turned into the ugly old friend and instead he's focusing everything on Lottie.

'You know, has anyone ever told you you've got really long eyelashes?' he's saying now, gazing at her intently.

It's called mascara, dummy, I think, but my younger self just giggles flirtily.

'And you smell really good.'

I look at him in disbelief. He did not say that line. He did not.

'Thanks.'

I glance sharply at Lottie. And I can't believe I'm falling for it.

In fact scrap 'falling', I realise, watching myself flicking my hair around like I'm in a shampoo commercial. I've crashed slap, bang, wallop right at his feet.

I feel a stab of alarm. Shit. This is worse than I thought. I mean, just look at me! I'm a total pushover. There's a peal of girlish laughter and I see myself angling my body towards his. I swear, leave it another minute and I'll be nuzzling his chest. That's right. *Nuzzling*.

And I'm not even on a first date! Honestly, Charlotte Merryweather, what were you like? I had no idea you used to be so *easy*.

'So do you have a boyfriend?'

Fuck. I've got to do something. And fast. But what? Panicked, I'm desperately racking my brains when out of the corner of my eye I see him slide his hand on to Lottie's knee and before I can stop myself—

'Hey!'

I'm 'accidentally' kicking the table and Lottie's half-finished pint of cider is toppling over and landing all over his lap. Immediately they break apart and he jumps up from his seat.

'Oops, clumsy me,' I gasp apologetically.

Seriously, I should have been an actress. I'd have won an Oscar.

'Hey, no worries,' he says, smiling tightly.

'I've got a tissue.' Lottie pulls one out of her bag and starts dabbing his crotch eagerly as he frowns at the puddle of cider collecting at his feet.

'Hey, can you clear this up?' he hollers to a barman who's collecting glasses from a table nearby.

''S'cuse me?'

As he turns, I see it's the same barman from the other night.

'Oh gosh, no, I'll do it – it was my fault,' I begin quickly, but Billy Romani stops me.

'That's his job,' he says cheerfully. 'Right, man?'

I notice the barman's jaw clench. 'That's right.' He smiles pleasantly and, grabbing a cloth, mops up the spillage. 'Accident, huh?' He winks, catching me watching.

'Um . . . yeah, absolutely.' I nod, colouring up as he walks away.

'Would you like another drink?'

I turn back to Billy, who's speaking to Lottie. But I'm undeterred. Cock-blocking, I'm fast learning, requires a skin thicker than Graham Norton's.

'Yes, please,' I answer loudly. 'I'll have a vodka tonic.' Not that I'm drinking, I'm driving, but if there's one thing I've learned over the years, it's that men hate nothing more than having to buy 'the friend' a drink. 'And can you make it a large one?' I smile sweetly.

He throws me a smile that's tighter than his leather trousers. 'And for you?' As he turns to Lottie, his smile transforms into one that Larry Goldstein would be proud of.

She blushes bright red. 'Um . . . yeah, a cider, please.'

'Coming right up.' He smiles again and gets up.

As soon as he's gone, she turns to me excitedly. 'So what do you think?'

That he's going to sleep with you, promise you the world, then let you down, I want to cry, but it's like it says in *How to Be a Good Friend* – it's important to be diplomatic when a friend asks for your opinion. Plus I don't want to look like a total fruit-loop.

So instead I go for a more tactful approach with an ambivalent 'Hmm.'

'What?' She frowns in consternation.

'Oh, nothing.' I shrug.

Which of course is the sure-fire way to make her insist I tell her.

'No, go on,' she cajoles.

'Well, I didn't want to say anything . . .'

'No, tell me,' she demands, pressing me for more. Just like I hoped she would.

'It's just he's got a really bad reputation.'

Lottie looks at me with both alarm and disbelief. 'That's probably just people being jealous,' she replies after a moment's pause.

I hesitate. I'm aware I'm treading a fine line here. I want to warn her off, but I don't want her thinking it's because I'm after him for myself.

'Believe me when I say I've known guys exactly like him, and trust me, he's no good.'

She looks crestfallen. 'But he seems really cool.'

'He *thinks* he's really cool,' I correct her. 'There's a difference. You need to go out with someone who's going to love you, not themselves. Who understands you, who really, truly *gets* you.' All at once my mind returns to Miles and our conversation about the fireplace. God, what is it about that stupid fireplace? It's not like it's super-important or anything. 'Someone you can trust not to let you down,' I add quickly. Because for all Miles's faults, I know I can always depend on him and, if there's one thing I've learned, that's really important.

Lottie nods, but I can see she's not thinking about loyalty and trustworthiness, she's thinking about attractiveness and coolness. Because when I was her age, that's all I thought about when it came to potential boyfriends. Speaking of which.

'And who doesn't want to be the next Liam Gallagher,' I say pointedly, remembering Rob, who slept with his Oasis records. I start running through a few of the horrors I dated later on in my twenties. 'You also need someone who isn't an alcoholic,' that was Archie the trainee lawyer. I broke it off with him, but he was so drunk at the time he didn't remember. 'Here's a tip: if a man gets so drunk he passes out on the pavement outside the pub, leave him the number of his local AA and lose him faster than you can say "Taxi!"'

Lottie laughs, oblivious to the fact she's got all this to come.

Though with any luck she'll listen to some of what I'm saying and learn by my mistakes, I think hopefully.

'Oh, and you need someone who has ambition,' I add, remembering Zac, who lived in a tent in someone's back garden. Zac was tortured and deep and angst-ridden, and talked a lot about the agony of life and having integrity and passion. I agreed with everything he said, while secretly wishing that I too could be deep and angst-ridden. Unfortunately I was too shallow and ended up paying for everything. 'Someone with prospects,' I finish emphatically.

'Billy's in a band,' she replies eagerly.

'Exactly. Never date musicians or men with skateboards.'

She throws me a puzzled look and laughs. 'Don't be silly.'

'He's going to hurt you, Lottie,' I warn, my face suddenly falling serious. Painful memories that I've buried deep inside of me begin rising to the surface, and I feel a sense of urgency. 'Please stay away from him.'

'Hey.'

We're interrupted by Billy, who has reappeared empty-handed. 'I thought we could get some booze and go back to a friend's house instead. Have a little after-party. There's a few of us going.' He looks straight at Lottie as if I'm invisible. 'Fancy coming along and joining us?'

My heart thuds. This is it.

'Well?' He waits, hands on hips. 'What do you say?'

No! Say no!

'Erm . . .' Lottie glances at me uncertainly. I can feel her wavering. On one side there's me in her head telling her no, and on the other there's her groin telling her very much yes.

'Actually, I don't feel that well,' I blurt desperately.

Well, I can't risk leaving this up to my twenty-one-year-old groin to decide, now can I?

'In fact I feel really nauseous. I think I need to go to the ladies'.'

Lottie looks at me, alarmed. 'Do you want me to come with you?'

'If you don't mind.' I nod weakly.

OK, so I feel a bit mean fibbing, but like I said, it's for my own good.

'Sorry.' Putting her arm round me, Lottie turns to Billy. 'But no, thanks.'

'No worries. Some other time maybe.' He shrugs and, turning away, lopes out of the pub.

Watching him leave, I stifle a small yet victorious smile.

Chapter Twenty

G reat. That's the first thing crossed off my list.

Sitting at my desk the next morning, I unfold the crumpled piece of paper on which I've scribbled down my tips and advice and, taking a large black marker, draw a line through:

~~1. Do not sleep with Billy Romani.~~

I'm feeling really pleased with myself. Last night was a total success. After Billy Romani left, I made a remarkable recovery; in fact ten minutes later I was feeling well enough to drive and gave Lottie a lift home alone. Which partly explains my good mood. The other reason is because it's my—

'Happy birthday!'

I look up to see the door swing wide open with Beatrice attached to it, a bit like one of those magician's assistants on a knife-throwing board. In her hands is a large cardboard box with 'Sprinkles' written across it in large swirly writing.

'There's only two of us so I didn't buy a cake,' she trills, her cheeks pink with excitement. 'Instead I got the Red Velvet cupcakes with special frosting. Just wait, you're going to become addicted!'

What she really means is 'Help! *I'm* already addicted. My name's Beatrice Spencer and I'm a cupcake-a-holic.'

'You shouldn't have!' I smile with amusement.

'Nonsense,' she says, setting the box down on my desk. 'You missed pudding last night, so you deserve a treat.' Flicking open the lid, she takes a deep, languorous inhale.

'Four?'

'Well, one's never enough,' she says sagely, peeling off the paper case.

Beatrice, it seems, has turned into a cupcake-pusher so she can, quite literally, feed her habit.

'Mmm,' she groans orgasmically, burying her mouth in the frosting.

I look at the cupcakes, sitting there in all their red devilness, oozing dairy, wheat and refined sugars, and probably contaminated with nuts from being near peanut-butter-flavoured ones. With all my allergies, I can't possibly eat them. Plus I'm trying to be healthy.

Then again, I don't want to offend Beatrice, and a little bit probably wouldn't hurt, I tell myself, taking a nibble. And it *is* my birthday.

It's like a sugar overload. Soft, sweet buttery frosting and a rich, moist, chocolatey cupcake. Wow, I can see how Beatrice got hooked. Not that I ever would, I tell myself quickly, thinking about my training session this morning and feeling a stab of guilt. Hastily I put the cupcake down.

'So what are you doing tonight to celebrate?' Surfacing, Beatrice looks at me. The tip of her nose is covered in butter frosting.

'Having dinner with Miles and some friends.' I take a swig of coffee. 'Remember Vanessa and Julian?'

'Golly, no, I don't think so.' She taps her finger on her nose to think, then, discovering the frosting, licks it off hungrily.

'Here, look . . .' Tapping my keyboard, I click on to the photos on my computer until I find one of them together.

'Oh, yes, I remember now.' She nods. 'He's a lawyer.'

'Yes, that's right.'

'Jolly sexy,' she adds.

'You think so?' I look back at the photo. I know Julian's attractive, but it's hard to see your best-friend's husband as sexy. I just can't see him in that way. Especially when I know all about his personal habits, such as using a nose-hair-trimmer and leaving the bits around the sink.

'If he was single, that is,' she adds hastily, obviously remembering her confession about flirting with Patrick, the married guy, at the spa. 'I mean, I'd never find him sexy or anything *now*.' She blushes bright red and makes a start on her second cupcake. 'So where are you going?'

'Back to that gastropub I went to with Miles on Monday.'

'Oh, fabulous! What are you going to wear?'

Beatrice's interest in my wardrobe never ceases to baffle me. She has no interest in her own clothes and recently asked me the name of 'that girl that I always see pictures of'.

It was Kate Moss.

'My Chloe dress, the one with the little capped sleeves that Miles bought me for Christmas.' Well, actually, that's not strictly true, Miles bought me a gift certificate for House of Fraser, but I never have time to shop these days, so instead I treated myself to a beautiful dress from Net-à-Porter online. Miles will never know I bought it from there.

Or how much it cost.

Trust me, I've long since learned to tell Miles that everything costs a fraction of the actual price, thus saving him from a heart attack, and me from another financial lecture.

'Which reminds me, I've got to pick it up from the dry-cleaner's on the way home —' I'm interrupted by the phone ringing and glance at my watch. It's 9 a.m.

'That'll be the Cloud Nine people,' remarks Beatrice, polishing off the rest of her cupcake.

As I go to pick up the phone, I catch her staring at the cupcake that's left with a look of such longing that any moment now she's going to start salivating. 'Go ahead, have it,' I tell her, reaching for the phone.

'Oh, no, I couldn't possibly,' she protests. Then, without even a missing beat, 'Oh, well, all right, if you insist.' And diving on it she gives a little hiccup of pure, unadulterated pleasure.

★   ★   ★

When I was younger, my birthday was a huge deal. In 1997, the year I moved to London, I remember spending the whole day in constant celebration: taking phone calls from friends and family, opening presents from my co-workers, enjoying a boozy lunch at the pub with the rest of the office, before returning to work sometime late in the afternoon to eat cake and sober up ready for the evening's celebrations. God, I used to love my birthday!

Now of course it's business as usual.

After my conference call with Cloud Nine, I dash over to the tearooms at Liberty to meet Katie Proctor, which officially is a meeting about getting promotional features for our clients in the newspapers she writes for, but unofficially is a chance to catch up over iced lattes. Then I snatch five minutes to reply to emails on my BlackBerry – my inbox seems to fill up whenever I'm out of the office – before dashing for another appointment.

And another. And another. Until hours later I find myself sitting round a boardroom table with a lot of men in suits, discussing a campaign to raise awareness of a new range of hair masks by Johnny Bird, while surreptitiously glancing at the clock on the wall. It's my last meeting and it's running late. Like, really, *really* late.

Like the dry-cleaner's is shut late.

Screeching into the kerb half an hour later, I jump out of the car and dash across the road, but the shop's in total darkness.

Bollocks.

I stare in dismay at the 'closed' sign on the door.

What am I going to do now? My dress is in there. Along with everything else, I reflect, thinking about the huge pile of dry-cleaning that I finally got round to dropping off a couple of days ago. That's the problem with expensive designer clothes – they're all dry-clean only. You can't just chuck everything in the washer, like I used to do with my clothes when I was younger.

But of course that's because they're better designed, better cut and made from much better fabrics, I remind myself.

Not that any of that is much good if I can't bloody wear them, I think, feeling a clench of irritation. Turning away from the shop, I climb back in my car. Saying that, even if I had something to wear, I don't have time to go home and change now anyway, I realise, glancing at the time on the dash board. The reservation's at 8 p.m. and it's ten to already.

Hurriedly I pull out my make-up bag and after a quick once-over with some lip gloss, blusher and mascara, I turn the ignition and pull out into the traffic.

'Red or white?'

Entering the pub, I'm greeted by Vanessa, who jumps up from the table and energetically throws her arms round me. 'We can't decide and you're the birthday girl, so you get to choose!'

'Um . . .' Breaking free from her bear hug, I slide into the seat next to Miles, who stops munching on a breadstick to kiss me hello.

'Happy birthday, darling.' He smiles pleasantly, then frowns. 'I thought you were wearing the dress I bought you?'

'It's a long story.' I roll my eyes, then glance at the remaining empty seat. 'Where's Julian?'

'Working late,' says Vanessa, and we exchange looks. 'He says to start without him and he'll be here as soon as he can.' She smiles cheerfully. Anyone else would be fooled by her broad white smile, but I've known her too long: it doesn't reach her eyes. 'So what's it to be?' she enthuses, changing the subject and passing me the wine menu.

'Oh gosh.' I look at the dozens of wines. I don't know much about wine. As I've got older, I've progressed from cider to Liebfraumilch to dry whites and learned that if you pay less than a fiver for a bottle, you're going to wake up with a very bad hangover, but that's about it. 'What about this Sauvignon Blanc from Australia . . .?'

'No, no, no.' Miles clicks his tongue. He likes to think of himself as something of a sommelier. 'If you're going to go for a

Sauvignon Blanc, it has to be from the Marlborough region of New Zealand.'

'Oh, OK, then.' I shrug.

'Though personally I think we should go for a nice full-bodied red.'

'What about a Merlot?' suggests Vanessa, tearing off a chunk of bread.

'A *Merlot*?' repeats Miles, pulling a face.

'Oh, please, what is this? *Sideways*?' quips Vanessa, rolling her eyes.

'There's nothing wrong with trying to develop a palate,' he replies, a little rankled.

'She's only teasing,' I say, rubbing his arm and shooting a glance at Vanessa, who's burying her face in a bread roll.

Actually, I know she's not. Vanessa and Miles have never seen eye to eye. They're like the human equivalent of oil and water.

'Not drinking yet?'

I look up to see Julian striding towards us. Carrying his briefcase and wearing a smart navy blue suit, he looks every inch the suave, successful lawyer.

'Happy birthday, Charlotte.' He leans across the table to give me a kiss.

'We're still figuring it out,' replies Miles, a little tightly.

'Well, as long as it's wet.' He grins, lightly kissing Vanessa on the forehead with a 'Hello, hon', before sitting down. 'Sorry, work was insane.'

'As always,' mutters Vanessa, but if Julian hears her, he doesn't react.

'I know, why don't we ask the waiter?' I suggest as a compromise, and closing the menu, I turn round to attract his attention.

Finishing up at another table, he looks over. 'Yes?'

Oh God. My heart sinks as I realise it's the same barman who served us on Monday night. The one who thought my allergies were just hilarious.

'We'd like to order some wine, please,' smiles Julian.

'What would you like?'

'I was thinking about a Pinot—' Miles begins, but is interrupted by Vanessa.

'But we can't decide,' she finishes, throwing him a look.

'Well, I'd suggest the Rioja if you want a red, or the Sancerre if you'd prefer white.'

I'm skulking down in my chair, trying to hide behind my menu. Hopefully he won't remember me.

'They both sound great,' smiles Julian. 'Why don't we have one of each?'

'Excellent.' He nods, then motions to the empty breadbasket, most of which has been gobbled up by Vanessa. 'More bread?'

'Um, no, not for me,' mutters Vanessa guiltily. 'Charlotte?'

'Charlotte doesn't eat bread,' pipes up Miles before I can answer. 'She has a wheat intolerance.'

'Ah, yes, now I remember. The lady with the food allergies.'

I catch the barman's eyes and see they're twinkling with amusement.

'So, what's new Miles?' asks Julian as the barman leaves. Thankfully.

'Well, Charlotte and I put an offer in on a house yesterday.'

'You did?' Vanessa looks at me agog. 'You never told me, Charlotte!'

'Didn't I? Oh, er . . . I was going to.' Suddenly reminded, I feel an anxious twinge. 'It must have slipped my mind.'

'Wow, that's exciting,' nods Julian, raising his eyebrows as if he's impressed.

'Yes, isn't it?' beams Miles.

'I bet Mrs M. was beside herself,' grins Vanessa, referring to my mum. She's known me long enough to know what my mother's like.

'I haven't told her.'

'*You haven't?*' Miles rounds on me, shocked.

'Well, we don't know if we've got it yet, do we?' I say quickly.

'When do you find out if your offer's been accepted?' asks Julian evenly.

'Soon, I hope,' replies Miles, turning to him. 'It went straight to sealed bids, so we're just waiting to hear.'

'Shall we order?' I suggest, trying to sound nonchalant and to change the subject. All this house talk is making me nervous.

'Not until I've given you your present,' bosses Vanessa, pulling out an envelope from her handbag. She hands it to me across the table. 'And I don't want to hear any excuses about you being too busy.'

I look at her quizzically and open my mouth to say something, but I'm shooed by her hand, so I tear it open instead. Out fall two Eurostar tickets to Paris.

'Oh, wow, you shouldn't have!'

'I know.' She grins teasingly. 'But now you *have* to go away for the weekend and relax, otherwise you'll feel very guilty for wasting my money.'

I smile back. She knows me so well. That's exactly what I would do.

'Well, Julian's money,' she adds tersely. I know Vanessa hates the fact that now she's given up working, she doesn't have her own money to spend any more. 'And anyway, now I can live vicariously through you.' She glances at Julian. 'I can't remember the last time we went away for a weekend.'

'We will,' he says, looking uncomfortable. 'It's just that work's crazy at the moment. In fact that reminds me – I'm going to have to go into the office on Sunday.'

Vanessa's face drops. 'But we were going to take the kids to the aquarium.'

'I know. I'm sorry, darling. We'll have to do it another weekend.'

'OK, now my turn.' Seemingly unaware of the tension across the table, Miles jovially interrupts. Vanessa and Julian fall silent, and all eyes are upon him as he reaches inside his breast pocket and produces a small black velvet box.

A small black velvet *jewellery* box.

My heart starts thudding loudly in my ears. Oh my God, is that what I *think* it is? Is he going to do what I *think* he's going to do? I keep my eyes glued to the box in Miles's hand, too scared to look at his face. What am I going to say, in front of all these people? Well, yes, obviously. I'll say yes, right?

'Charlotte?'

His voice snaps me back as he hands me the box. His expression is serious, yet uncertain.

I swallow hard. This is it.

This is it.

I take a deep breath, my fingers fumbling with the catch. My heart is racing. I suddenly feel light-headed, as if time's slowed right down and the chatter and hum of the pub have gone all muffled, like watching a movie in slow motion with the sound turned down. The catch releases, and with the breath caught in the back of my throat, I slowly open the lid.

Pearl earrings?

I stare blankly at them, nestling white and shiny on the black velvet, and almost want to laugh with giddy relief. Abruptly I feel completely ridiculous. What on earth was I thinking? Of course he wasn't going to propose. Honestly, Charlotte, talk about getting carried away.

'Do you like them?'

I snap my focus back to the earrings.

Um . . . yes . . . they're lovely,' I murmur, looking at them properly for the first time.

'I thought you would,' Miles is saying, his face suffused with pleasure. 'They're just so you.'

'You think so?' I feel a tiny voice of protest. I don't feel like someone who'd wear pearl earrings. Don't you have to be over fifty? Or be the Queen or something?

'Absolutely! Try them on,' he encourages.

Taking them out of the box, I slide them into my ears. I hold back my hair to murmurs of approval round the table. 'Thank you, Miles, they're wonderful.' I smile, ignoring my doubts and give him a kiss.

So what if they're not me? It's the thought that counts, isn't it?

The rest of the evening slips away over plates of delicious food, several bottles of wine and the familiar conversations about careers, the housing market and what current antics Ruby and Sam have got up to.

'I had to buy a new phone because Ruby was worried that he was lonely,' sighs Julian, finishing telling a story about how Ruby decided to drop his mobile into the goldfish bowl so that Boris the goldfish could call his friends.

'I think it was her way of getting you off the phone,' remarks Vanessa dryly, as Miles laughs in consolation. 'And pretty effective too,' she adds, before making her excuses to go to the ladies' as the dessert menus are brought out.

'I'll come with you,' I say, pushing back my chair.

'What is it with women going in pairs to the toilet?' wonders Julian aloud as we leave the table.

'So we can talk about you, sweetie,' jokes Vanessa.

At least, I think she's joking, but when we get into the ladies' and I thank her once again for my present, she instructs, 'Just make sure you eat lots of pastries and have lots of sex in Paris. Someone has to.'

'Oh, come on,' I protest. 'I know what you and Julian are up to.' Nudging her in the ribs, I smile knowingly, thinking of the contents of Julian's shopping basket.

'Up to?' she huffs derisively. 'I don't have the energy to be up to anything. I'm exhausted. The only thing we're up to is arguing over who's going to get up and see to Sam when he wakes up crying for the third time in the middle of the night.'

'But I thought . . .' I trail off as I flash back to yesterday. Now I think about it, Julian did seem kind of jumpy. Nervous, almost. As if he didn't want me to see him. My mind cuts back to Vanessa's comment about him having an affair with his secretary.

'Thought what?' asks Vanessa, and I see her looking at me quizzically.

'Oh . . . um . . . you looked closer, that's all.' Quickly I scrub that image from my mind. I'm being totally ridiculous, just like Vanessa was.

'I don't think so.' She smiles wanly. 'I've barely seen him this week. He's always at work. It's almost like we're two strangers, like we don't know each other any more,' she finishes, her shoulders slumping defeatedly.

God, I hate to see Vanessa looking so sad.

'I know what you need,' I say cheerfully, changing the subject.

'A new husband?' She smiles ruefully.

'No, silly, a new lip gloss,' I chivvy, digging a handful out of my handbag.

Vanessa's eyes light up. Since having Sam, she seems to have stopped wearing make-up. She says it takes too long to apply. It's the same with her hair. Instead of blow-drying it straight, she now ties it up in a knot. 'Ooh, where did you get this?' she says, pulling off the top.

'One of the perks of working in PR.'

'By the way, I meant to say . . .' She pauses to wand her bottom lip. 'Isn't that the barman we saw in the shop?'

At the mention of him all the cells in my body jerk to attention. It catches me by surprise. Why is it that someone so annoying can have this effect on me? 'Unfortunately.' I grimace, quickly brushing the thought away.

'Mmm.' Pressing her lips together, Vanessa smiles wickedly. 'I wonder what he's offering for dessert.'

'Whatever it is, it'll be too many points.' I smile back, and then cower as she punches me playfully on the arm.

Five minutes later and a newly lip-glossed Vanessa and I make our way back to the table.

'Ah! Just in time,' says Julian as we reappear.

'For what?' I ask, glancing around.

'Champagne!' announces Miles as the barman appears with a bottle of Veuve Clicquot and four champagne flutes and sets them down on the table.

'Ooh, is this the bit where we start singing "Happy Birthday" really loudly and embarrass Charlotte in front of everyone?' grins Vanessa.

'No, it's not,' replies Miles, shooting her a look.

'Spoilsport.'

Next to me, the barman is deftly easing the cork from the neck of the bottle, and as he starts pouring the champagne, I notice a small tattoo etched on the underside of his wrist. I stare at it for a moment, trying to make it out.

'It's a frog.'

I snatch my eyes away, only to meet those of the barman staring at me, staring at him. 'Oh, right.' I nod, feeling a hot flash of embarrassment.

'My mother's French,' he explains, a small smile playing on his lips.

Is he making fun of me again? Is that supposed to be a joke?

'Isn't that offensive to French people?' I reply a little stiffly.

'You haven't met my mother,' he responds evenly.

A look flashes between us and I suddenly feel all jittery. 'No . . .' I manage, struggling for a witty comeback, but my mind's a total blank. 'Obviously,' I add lamely.

'I want to propose a toast . . .'

Miles's voice snaps me back and I turn to see him raising his champagne flute.

'. . . to Charlotte on her birthday.'

Julian and Vanessa raise their glasses. 'To Charlotte,' they both chorus.

'And to our new house.'

'Our house?' I swivel round to face him.

'I've been saving the best till last. The estate agent called earlier, but I wanted to keep it as a surprise,' he explains, grinning delightedly. 'They accepted our offer. It's ours!'

'Ours?' I repeat, taken aback. So taken aback, it seems, that I've turned into an echo.

'Here you go,' says a voice close to my ear, and I glance up to see the barman passing me a champagne flute. 'You're not allergic to bubbles, are you?' He throws me a look.

'Um . . . no . . . I'm not . . . thanks,' I mumble, meeting those pale grey eyes of his, before quickly averting my gaze. 'I mean, wow, that's great!' I enthuse, turning back to Miles, who's still grinning from ear to ear.

Raising his champagne flute, he clinks it against mine. 'Here's to us!'

I smile dazedly. 'To us.'

Chapter Twenty-one

We leave early.

'Babysitters,' grumbles Vanessa, pulling a face in apology as we stand outside on the pavement.

'If we're not home by ten, it goes into triple time,' adds Julian, raising a rueful eyebrow.

'Crikey, I'm in the wrong job,' chortles Miles, slightly flushed from too much champagne.

'No worries.' I smile, giving Vanessa a hug. 'I need an early night anyway.'

Which is true. I do. Especially after last night. And it doesn't matter that it's my birthday, does it? I mean, so what? It's just another birthday. It's not like I'm disappointed or anything silly like that, I think, as we all say our goodbyes.

Waving them off in a black cab, Miles and I walk to my car.

'Are you OK to drive?' he asks as I beep the lock and slide into the driver's seat. Miles doesn't own a car. He says having one in London is like throwing money down the drain and is always nagging me to use public transport: 'Just think,' he always says, 'with all cash you save you could invest in an ISA.'

Which is true. I could.

Then again, I could also buy a fabulous new handbag.

'Because the number seventy-two goes straight from here.'

Miles has the bus timetable ingrained on his brain. On our first date he took me out for dinner, but he refused to take a cab to the restaurant – even though it was raining and I was wearing a new pair of shoes. A pair of nude suede strappy sandals.

Well, they *were* nude suede. A ten-minute walk to the bus-stop and one packed bus-ride later and they were more of a sludgy grey and completely ruined.

'I'm fine.' I nod, turning the ignition. 'It's a five-minute drive. Plus I only had a glass of wine.'

'And champagne,' he reminds pointedly, clicking on his seat belt. He begins adjusting his seat with the electronic levers.

'Oh, yeah,' I remember uncomfortably. Indicating, I pull out into the main road.

'Though you left most of yours,' he adds, still fiddling with the levers. His seat starts whirring forwards, then backwards and forwards again.

'Well, I couldn't drink and drive, could I?' I say lightly, as I start negotiating the traffic.

'We could have caught the bus,' he replies stubbornly. His seat reclines too far and he begins trying to hitch it more upright. 'It goes straight from here.'

'Yes, I know,' I reply. I'm starting to feel slightly rankled. 'You said.'

Suddenly there's a loud crunch and his seat jack-knifes backwards.

'Miles, will you stop it?' I gasp impatiently.

'Stop what?' he replies innocently. 'I'm just trying to get comfy.'

'I know, it's just—' I break off and take a deep breath. I don't know what it is, but I feel all nervy and on edge. 'Sorry, I didn't mean to snap,' I apologise quickly.

'I know.' He smiles and touches my hand affectionately.

I feel horribly guiltly. God, what's wrong with me? Miles is being so sweet. Why am I behaving like such a grumpy old cow about everything?

'Don't worry, we won't be doing this for much longer,' he says cheerfully.

'Doing what?' I ask distractedly, indicating right.

'Having to alternate between our flats every weekend,' he says, as if it's obvious. 'Soon we'll be in the new house.'

'Oh, right, yes.' I clear my throat, as my voice has gone a little bit grainy. 'Of course.'

'There'll be none of this back and forth – you in your place during the week, me in mine. Just think! We'll be able to spend every single night together.'

He smiles at me excitedly, and I smile back while thinking of spending every night with Miles. Waking up next to him every morning. Brushing our teeth side by side in the bathroom. Day in, day out.

For ever.

I catch myself. For God's sake, Charlotte, I don't know what you're worrying about, I tell myself firmly. It's going to be fine. You love Miles; he loves you. And it won't be any different to the weekends you spend together, will it? It just means that you won't have to keep some of your clothes at his flat, or have to double up on toiletries, or keep your underwear shoved in one measly little drawer. Plus just remember how annoying it was a few weekends ago when you left your mouthguard at your flat and you woke up the next morning at Miles's with a headache from grinding. This way, you'll have everything in one place.

Feeling more positive, I pull up outside my flat. And just think, poor Miles won't ever have to play squash again in my shorts, I reflect, stifling a giggle at the memory of his rather large thighs squeezed into my tight black Lycra running shorts when he'd forgotten his.

'I know, it will be great,' I agree, cutting the engine.

Then again, on second thoughts, that might be rather a shame . . .

Inside my flat, I pick up the post in the hallway. As usual I left early this morning, before the postman arrived, and amongst the usual credit-card bills and mortgage-related bumf, there's a card from Mum and Dad. Bang on time, as usual. Mum is amazing. She has this knack of knowing exactly when to post a card to ensure that it never arrives a day early, or late, regardless of what the postal service is up to.

From the living room I hear the TV playing, and tearing open the envelope, I walk through to find Miles already ensconced on the sofa with the remote control in his hand.

'Did you record this week's episode of *Location, Location, Location*?' he asks, without looking up.

'Um, no . . .' I say vaguely, looking inside to discover Marks & Spencer's vouchers and a note to 'Buy some proper food.' I smile to myself. It's been the same every year since I was at uni. I glance at my watch – they rang earlier, but I was in a meeting – I wonder if it's too late to call them. Actually, it probably is, I realise, with a pang of disappointment. My parents do everything early: 'dinner' at twelve, 'tea' at five thirty, then it's a double-bill of *Emmerdale* and *Coronation Street*, and bed at nine thirty. I'll have to call them tomorrow.

'You didn't?' Miles frowns with dismay.

I zone back in. 'Oh, sorry, I totally forgot.'

'Oh, well, never mind.' He shrugs, flicking through the channels. 'There's probably a film on.' An old Clint Eastwood movie pops up on the screen.

'Actually, I think I might go to bed,' I say, propping my card up on the mantelpiece.

'I'll be there in a minute,' he murmurs, already totally engrossed.

Leaving him glued to the TV, I go into the bathroom, get undressed and begin my usual night-time routine of cleansing, toning and moisturising. I have about a dozen different types of moisturiser. There's this gel I use for under my eyes, which I have to dab on with my ring finger, a cream for my face that I'm supposed to massage in clockwise (or is it anti-clockwise?) sweeping motions and a lotion for my neck.

Opening my bathroom cabinet, I survey the overflowing shelves. To tell the truth, I feel exhausted just looking at them. I have about a zillion products in here that promise to firm, smooth, brighten and erase wrinkles, and despite the fact that none of them seem to make much difference, I'm always buying more. I can't help it. In fact I just bought this new serum that's being hailed as a 'miracle in a jar'. Apparently, it's made of bits of gold leaf and makes your pores disappear.

Saying that, I've never quite worked out *why* exactly I'm supposed to want my pores to disappear, but the results are meant to be amazing. Quite frankly, for that price, they'd better be.

Slathering a few different things all over my face (well, in for a penny, in for a pound – actually, make that several hundred pounds), I clean my teeth using my electric toothbrush and whitening toothpaste, floss and finally rinse.

Done.

With the drone of the TV still coming from the living room, I look back at my reflection, my thirty-two-year-old reflection. Bare-faced, hair tied up in a scrunchie and wearing my oversized Cath Kidston flowery pyjamas, I look about as sexy as, well, anyone wearing oversized pyjamas with their hair tied up in a scrunchie *can* look.

Suddenly Vanessa's words about having sex with Julian here, there and everywhere before they had children flash up like a neon sign in my mind. It's been over a week since Miles and I spent the night together, and even longer since we had sex. Admittedly, we have both been stressed with work, and I know passion can fade when you're in a committed, long-term relationship, but that's why it's important to make even more of an effort.

Padding into the bedroom, I quickly slip on a satin camisole and shake out my hair. Hopefully this will spice things up a bit, I tell myself, spritzing my pulse points with perfume and dabbing a bit on my décolletage like they always tell you to do in women's magazines.

Turning on my bedside lamp, I climb into bed, then climb out again and flick off the main light. Ambient lighting. It's very important. I plump a pillow and arrange myself just so. Then wait expectantly. I can still hear the TV, but I'm sure he'll be in any minute.

I wait a bit longer.

Maybe I should light a candle.

I light a candle. It's vanilla, musk and jasmine and smells gorgeous. I inhale its aroma and fiddle with the straps of my camisole. I let one slip off my shoulder. Then both. Urgh, God, no, that looks too corny, I decide, shoving them back up again.

I listen out for any sound of movement, but all I can hear is the TV. Restlessly I glance at my watch. It's been twenty minutes. I hesitate, then call in my most husky voice, 'Miles? Are you coming to bed?'

Nothing.

I wait a few more moments, then raise it a notch. 'Miles?' I call out.

Again nothing. Just the sound of a gunshot on the TV and the wail of a police siren.

Oh, sod it. 'Miles!' I yell loudly. 'Can you hear me?'

Obviously he can't, as there's no answer. Giving up in frustration, I clamber out of bed and stomp into the living room, to find him lying flat out on the sofa, head lolled back, mouth open, emitting a faint, rattling snore.

I watch him for a moment, half inclined to wake him up and demand he have sex with me on my birthday, and then immediately think better of it. Miles is useless when he's had a few drinks. As if on cue, he splutters slightly, rolls over and nuzzles, snuffling into a cushion. Plus, quite frankly, what flames of passion I was trying to fan have now abruptly been extinguished.

So instead I turn off the TV, cover him in a spare duvet and go back to bed.

And lie there.

I glance at the digits on the alarm clock. It's only 10.30 p.m. and I'm in bed. On my birthday. God, if someone had told me ten years ago that I'd be in bed before 11 p.m. on my birthday I would never have believed them. Back then birthdays were all about partying and getting drunk and staying up till the crack of dawn. Like I said, though, I really do need to catch up on my sleep.

Flicking on the sound machine and humidifier, I blow out the candle and switch off the light. Pulling on my eye mask, I close my eyes, but my mind has other ideas.

I wonder what Lottie is doing? it whispers in my ear.

I dunno, probably partying, I think, trying to ignore it.

Partying where? it demands, a little louder.

I roll over restlessly. At my old house, I reflect, casting my mind back to the house party I threw to celebrate my twenty-second birthday. My memories of it are vague. In fact I was only reminded of it when Lottie mentioned it last night. Actually, she invited me. Which was slightly weird, to say the least, but of course I couldn't go.

But you can go now, the voice says, putting an idea into my head.

Which of course I dismiss immediately. Honestly, how ridiculous. As if I'm going to get out of my nice, warm, comfy bed and go to a party. I've just had a lovely dinner with my boyfriend, my best friend and her husband to celebrate my birthday. I don't want to go to some silly party.

Then again, I suppose it could be kind of fun.

A lot more fun than lying in bed on your own, unable to sleep, while your boyfriend lies snoring on the sofa, pipes up that little voice.

I feel myself wobble.

But what about Miles?

What about him? He's out cold. You'll be back before he wakes up.
I hesitate, my mind ticking over.
No, I can't. It's just too mad . . . It's insane . . . It's—
Oh, shut up, Charlotte. It's a bit late for all that, isn't it?
And flinging back the covers, I jump out of bed and start getting ready.

Chapter Twenty-two

Less than fifteen minutes later I'm in the car heading over to my old house. It's pretty amazing how quickly you can get ready when all your clothes are at the dry-cleaner's and you don't have any choice about what to wear, I reflect, fiddling with the collar of my jacket, which is all tucked under in my haste to get out of the flat.

Sure enough, Miles didn't wake up. I half thought about leaving a note, or maybe even stuffing pillows in the bed to make it look as if I'm still asleep in there, but a) this is real life, not *Shawshank Redemption* and b) unlike me, Miles is a really heavy sleeper even without all the wine and champagne. One time he even slept through the smoke alarm when I nearly set fire to the flat with an aromatherapy candle, but anyway, that's a whole other story.

London is alive with Friday night-life and it takes a while to cut across town, dodging black cabs that, with no notice, will suddenly stop dead in the middle of the road to drop off or pick up a fare, and getting stuck in the heavy traffic resulting from the diversion. And so, despite it fast becoming a familiar route, it's not until nearly midnight that I finally turn into Kilmaine Terrace.

The street is lined with cars, and squeezing into a parking space without hitting any lamp-posts (see, my parking has got a *lot* better over the years, I think with a sense of satisfaction), I check my hastily applied make-up and climb out of my car. Then realise I don't have a present.

Shit. I can't go to a party empty-handed. Even if it's mine. Well, sort of, I think, scrambling through the glove compartment to see if I've got any of those freebie lip glosses left. Then I have an idea. I know! What about all those bags of goodies that I bought yesterday from Boots? I was wondering how I was going to give them to my younger self without appearing odd, and this is the perfect solution.

Grabbing the bags out of the boot, I smooth down my skirt and walk towards the house. A bunch of brightly coloured party balloons tied to the front door are bobbing in the warm summer night's breeze and I can hear the strains of the Verve's 'Bittersweet Symphony' coming from inside.

Opening the gate, I climb up the front steps and then – for a moment – I hesitate, looking at my front door, my hand paused to rap the familiar brass knocker shaped like a dolphin. It seems like only yesterday since I had a key, since this was my home, where I lived, loved, dreamed—

'Whoo-hooooo!'

Abruptly the door swings open to shrieking laughter and a couple fall out on to the doorstep. Heads rolled back in laughter, a can of Tennant's Extra and a cigarette in each hand, they're draped all over one another in what looks like an attempt to hold each other up. I jump back, before they knock me over.

'Whoops,' they slur, then burst into drunken giggles and start snogging in front of me.

I recoil. Oh dear. I'd forgotten what house parties used to be like in my early twenties. Maybe this wasn't *such* a good idea after all.

I can't get past them as they're blocking my way, so clutching the bulging carrier bags in my hands, I shove myself back against the hedge until they get tired of eating each other and untangle tongues.

'Sorry, we're just leaving,' they apologise, grinning madly.

'Oh, is the party over?' I ask, as another few people spill out of the house and squeeze past them, on to the pavement.

'I hope not,' the boy says, turning to the girl draped over his shoulder and licking her face.

Urgh. Lovely.

'Charlotte!'

I whirl round to see Lottie standing on the doorstep.

She shoots me a huge grin. 'Hey, I didn't think you were coming!'

'I know, but . . . well, my evening got cut short,' I finish in an explanation of sorts. 'Anyway, happy birthday.' I smile, thrusting the carrier bags at her. 'I'm afraid I didn't have a chance to wrap them,' I add quickly, suddenly feeling embarrassed for handing her two plastic carrier bags instead of an expensively wrapped present.

But if she minds, she doesn't show it. Instead her eyes go saucer-wide and a look of delight sweeps over her face. 'Oh fab, is all this for me?'

'Well, it's not that much.'

'All of it?' she repeats, in astonishment.

I had no idea she would be so chuffed. She looks over the moon, and just about some stuff from Boots. God, I wasn't this thrilled when I got my new car, I think, looking at her delighted expression and feeling a curious mix of pleasure and envy.

'Uh-huh.' I nod.

'Wow! I can't believe it. You must have spent a fortune,' she gasps, tugging out an Estée Lauder foundation that's the right skintone, instead of that cheap stuff I know she wears that's bright orange. 'That's so kind of you.'

'Hey, don't mention it.' I smile modestly. I'd forgotten just what a treat getting new stuff used to be, I muse, thinking about my own bathroom cabinet at home, stuffed full with unused products, and feeling a bit guilty. Still, it looks like my list has been a raving success so far, I think, with a sense of satisfaction.

'Anyway, I'd invite you in, but everyone's getting ready to leave.'

'Oh, really?' I feel a beat of disappointment. Damn, after all that, I missed the party. 'I suppose it is pretty late. I guess I should be getting to bed too.'

'Bed?' She stares at me, incredulous, then lets out a peal of laughter. 'Ha-ha, very funny. That was a joke, right?'

'Erm, yes, of course.' I laugh uncertainly. 'So . . . um . . . if you're not going to bed, where are you going?'

'Clubbing!' she whoops.

'*Clubbing?*' My smile sort of freezes. Oh fuck. I'd totally forgotten how I used to love to go clubbing, but now it comes back to me with the blunt force of a sledgehammer. Dry ice. Swirly strobe lights. Deafening music. 'But it's a Sunday, isn't it?' I bleat hopefully.

'Yeah, but it's the August bank holiday tomorrow, so the Canal Club are having a special night.' She beams excitedly. 'You're coming too, aren't you?'

'*I am?*' I squeak in a strangled voice.

Me? Clubbing? I don't do clubbing. Not any more. I do Pilates, and yoga, and acupuncture when my back hurts.

'Of course, silly! You're invited.'

I'm rummaging through my memory, as if it's a sock drawer and I'm feverishly looking for a pair that match. Only this doesn't match any recollection I have of this evening. Then again, it *was* ten years ago and I *was* very drunk. In fact, to be honest, every birthday till the age of about thirty is a bit of a blur.

For a brief moment I think about making up some excuse and going home, but before I have a chance she links arms and, with a battle cry, yells, 'Come on, it's time to *paaaartay!*'

And it's too late.

Help.

The club is only a couple of streets away, so we walk there – well, I walk; Lottie's wearing high heels for the first time since I've met her and sort of half totters along the pavement in the four-inch heels, giggling tipsily. She's wearing a dress covered in tiny blue cornflowers that I bought from a flea market. I remember I had to haggle the stallholder down for ages before I could afford it, even though it was only a few pounds.

Nowadays I can afford to shop for designer clothes. What I can't afford is the time to *go* shopping, so I tend to do a lot of it online, and usually only twice a year – summer and winter. Back then I was always so broke most of my wardrobe came from charity shops or markets and I'd spend weekends trawling through the racks at Camden or Portobello, looking for bargains.

Like that dress, which I ended up getting for half-price because one of the straps was broken, I reflect. Though I never did get round to sewing it on, I realise, glancing at it now and seeing it's still being held on by a safety pin. I feel a flash of embarrassment. Honestly, what was I like going out like that? Absently I glance down at my jacket and pick off a couple of bits of fluff from the lapels. Didn't I care? Obviously not, I decide, looking back at myself puffing away merrily on a cigarette without a trouble in the world. I feel a rankle of disapproval.

Ahead of us I see a long line of people snaking round the corner My first thought is, Wow, look at all those people. I wonder what's happening? My second is, Oh fuck, that's the queue to get in.

Lottie doesn't appear to notice the queue and instead waltzes gaily to the front and beams at the bouncer. A huge, six-foot-something Jamaican man with biceps the size of watermelons and an impenetrable grimace. Horror trickles down my spine like icy-cold water. Oh my God, what am I doing? *What am I doing?* I cringe, hanging back in mortified anticipation of the public humiliation I'm going to suffer when I get sent to the back of the queue in front of all these people.

Correction, *all these kids*, I realise, my eyes sweeping over the parade of baseball caps, Celtic armband tattoos and pierced belly buttons and realising the average age is about twenty. Maybe even less, I decide, glancing at a group of rail-thin girls sporting micro-minis and what looks suspiciously like teenage acne. I glance back at the bouncer, who, at this very moment, is turning his hulking great frame towards Lottie, with the sort of slow-motion movement you get in those old dinosaur films, just before the helpless victim gets gobbled up by the big, scary brontosaurus.

'Hi there,' she trills, puffing on her cigarette and grinning wildly.

Oh God, and now everyone's staring. I wince, hardly daring to look as I wait for the inevitable. Or not, I decide, my protective instinct kicking in. I'm supposed to be giving the benefit of my experience – stopping her from making mistakes. I can't just sit back and let this happen, I resolve, taking a step towards her and the thumping music that's pulsing out from the club.

'Hey, all right there, darlin'?'

And pause. Hang on a minute. Did he just say . . .?

'Nice to see ya. How ya doing?'

I'm staring in amazement at the bouncer, whose whole de- meanour has now changed. Gone is the fearsome grimace. Instead he's grinning warmly at Lottie.

Er, hello, she's friends with the bouncer?

I'm friends with the bouncer?

'I'm great. It's my birthday.' She's smiling as she stands on her tiptoes and plants a kiss on each of his cheeks. 'And I really wanted to celebrate it in the club.'

Oh my God. And I'm *flirting* with him to get in! What a floozy!

'Well, happy birthday!' he booms, letting out a deep rumble of laughter as he stoops down to accept her kisses, before lifting up the rope and standing back to let her pass. 'You have a great evening.'

'I will, thanks.' She waves cheerfully as she sweeps past him and disappears behind the velvet curtain into the club.

Well, OK, perhaps she didn't need my help *that* time, I think, as one by one the rest of us follow. And at least I didn't have to queue, I tell myself, trying to look on the bright side, but still feeling a sense of dread as I move forwards, the music growing louder and louder, the base thumping harder and harder, the strobe lights shooting out from the gap in the curtain, until it's my turn to go in.

Abruptly my way is blocked.

'If you want to just hold it right there.' Reaching in front of me, the bouncer replaces the red rope.

For a moment I look at him in confusion. What? He's not letting me in? Then it registers. Of course. He obviously doesn't realise I'm with Lottie.

'Excuse me.' I smile confidently, as I get his attention. 'I'm with the rest of the party,' I explain, gesturing to those who have just gone in ahead of me. 'I'm with Lottie.'

The bouncer looks me up and down, his brow furrowed. 'Sorry, luv.' He shakes his head. 'Not tonight.'

My smile fades and I look at him uncertainly. 'Lottie,' I repeat, for want of something to say. 'You know, scrunch-dried hair, major tan, safety pin on her dress.'

'I'm sorry,' he repeats, only more firmly this time. 'Not tonight.'

I stare at him, slow realisation dawning upon me. 'Are you telling me you're not letting me in?'

'We're very busy tonight,' he replies dismissively, before gesturing for me to stand to one side to allow more people to pass though into the club.

Blatantly. While I'm just standing here.

I glare at him angrily. 'Excuse me, but you've just let all those people in,' I say, somewhat obviously.

Sliding his gaze back to me, he looks me up and down. 'We also have a dress code,' he grunts, gesturing to my outfit.

'What are you talking about?' I gasp in frustration. 'I'm wearing a suit.'

'Exactly,' he replies, shaking his head sympathetically.

I feel myself blush hotly. Admittedly my dark grey pencil skirt with matching single-breasted jacket is not the *hippest* of outfits, and if I'd known I was going to go clubbing, I would have worn something a bit more funky. Actually, that's a lie. If I'd known I was going to go clubbing, I'd be wearing earplugs. But even so. It's smart. It's classic. For God's sake; it's *Prada*.

Behind me, I can hear people grumbling that I'm holding up the queue. I look at the bouncer in desperation. Oh God, I can't believe this. This is so humiliating. I'm half inclined to turn round and go home. After all, I've got no desire to go into his loud, stinky, sweaty club. In fact, right now, I couldn't think of anywhere I'd rather go less. Afghanistan, maybe. Blackpool in February, perhaps.

But I can't turn back now. Plus, even if I wanted to, my pride wouldn't let me.

Turning back to the bouncer, I take a deep breath. So he thinks I'm not cool enough, does he? He thinks that because I'm not some young twentysomething and flirting with him I can't get into his stupid club? Indignation stabs. Well, we'll see about that.

Reaching into my handbag, I pull out my purse and count out three twenties. OK, so I might not be young and hip enough to pass the scrutiny of the doormen, but you see, that's one of the great things about being older: I don't have to be.

Like magic, the velvet rope disappears.

'Have a great evening,' nods the bouncer, standing back to let me through.

'I'll try.' Smiling triumphantly, I waft right by him.

Because now I can afford to bribe my way in.

Chapter Twenty-three

If you were to ask me to describe the Canal Club, I'd tell you to try this at home:

1. Turn up the thermostat on the central heating so it's about a hundred degrees and you're sweating profusely.

2. Switch on the stereo, choose a hip-hop CD (preferably one where all the tracks sound the same) and play on full volume so that you can't hear yourself speak and your eardrums feel as if they're about to explode.

3. Then turn it up even louder.

4. Put a tray of oil in the oven and turn it up as high as it will go so that everywhere fills with smoke.

5. Block up your toilet with loo roll so that it won't flush.

6. Now squeeze as many people as you can into your front room.

7. Shut all the windows and ask everyone to start smoking.

8. Charge a fiver for water.

9. And turn out the lights so you can't see a frigging thing.

'Oy, watch where you're going,' yells a gruff voice in my ear.

'Oops, sorry,' I reply, hastily removing my stiletto heel from someone's foot.

Trying to adjust my eyes to the smoky, strobe-lit darkness,

I stumble around the club on the hunt for Lottie. I can't see her. But then again, that's not surprising, considering I can't see *anything*. Or hear anything over this thumping baseline. It's as if two of my senses just disappeared.

Resisting the urge to stick my fingers in my ears, I take off my jacket and begin squeezing, squashing and shuffling my way through the droves of clubbers. The air is sticky with perspiration and cloying and I can already feel beads of sweat pricking the nape of my neck as I move further into the sweltering heat. Jesus, it's as hot as hell in here.

Because this is hell, pipes up a desperate voice inside of me, as I'm jostled into a strange man's hairy armpit. At least I think it's a man. Like I said, it's difficult to see.

A fleeting image of my bed flashes across my brain. My warm, comfy bed, with its pillow-top mattress, goose-down duvet and plumped-up pillows. Me gently sinking into it. Just the sound of ocean waves and the faint puff of the humidifier. The scent of my aromatherapy candle, which has overtones of lavender and—

BO.

Getting a really bad whiff of it, I zone back in. OK, that's it. I can't take much more of this. I remember that song 'It's My Party and I'll Cry if I Want To'. Which is kind of apt, as trust me, I might very well be doing that if I don't find Lottie, I think desperately. Where the bloody hell can she have gone?

Hurriedly extricating myself, I move deeper into the club. To the left I can make out a small bar, and to the right are several sofas filled with dozens of smooching couples. But no Lottie. I glance quickly away and squint through the haze of cigarette smoke and dry ice, towards the small dance floor ahead of me. The odd strobe light sweeps back and forth, briefly illuminating the floor, which is covered in cigarette butts and blackened spots of chewing gum. This is one of those places where if they turned the lights on, it would send you running, screaming for the hand sanitiser.

And yet I used to love this place, I reflect, as blurry, long-forgotten memories of weekends spent here begin coming back to me. How could I? I wonder in amazement. What was there to love?

Reaching the edge of the dance floor, I pause for a moment, my eyes flicking over the sea of bodies. There's a group of girls slap, bang in the middle, dancing round a small pile of handbags, a couple in matching leather trousers bumping and grinding over by the speakers, and then there's Lottie.

I feel a snap of surprise.

Me? *Dancing?*

I never dance.

Well, not any more, I think, watching myself in fascination as I bop around near the DJ, shaking my hips to the music without any inhibition. Nowadays I have to be completely drunk to dance. I'm way too self-conscious otherwise. But look, there I am, shaking my thang for all the world to see and I'm not even drinking, I realise, seeing myself swigging from a bottle of water.

Speaking of which . . . Driven by my own thirst, I make my way over to the bar to get a drink. Away from the dance floor, it's a bit quieter, and spotting a spare bar stool, I plonk myself on it gratefully.

'Yes, what can I get you?'

I glance up to see a pair of pale grey eyes looking at me expectantly from behind the bar. For a split second my brain does that thing where you think you know someone and are about to smile and say hi, before realising that you have no idea where you know them from and have to stop yourself before you look like a moron.

'Um . . . yes, I'll have a bottle of water, please.'

'Coming right up,' nods the barman.

He is about to turn away when my curiosity gets the better of me. 'Excuse me?'

He stops what he's doing.

'Have we met?'

He surveys me for a moment, then shakes his head. 'Nope, don't think so.'

I feel a flash of embarrassment. 'My mistake. I just could have sworn I've seen you before.'

'You probably have. I work behind the bar at the Wellington Arms.'

'Oh, that must be it.' My mind flicks back to last night. 'Sorry about last night.'

He raises his eyebrows.

'I spilled a drink; you cleared it up.'

'Oh, yeah.' He nods, registering. 'You were with the guy from the band. Billy Romani.'

'Don't remind me.' I pull a face and he smiles.

'Not a fan, then?'

'You could say that.' I return a rueful smile. 'What about you?'

He sucks in air between his teeth. 'Not really my kind of music,' he says diplomatically, but the way the muscle in his jaw clenches tightly makes me think it might not be a bad idea to change the subject.

'So . . . um . . . you work here too?' I ask, then immediately wish I hadn't, considering it's rather obvious as he's standing behind the bar.

But if he thinks it's a stupid question, he doesn't show it.

'Well, someone has to,' he quips.

'You don't like it here?' I feel a sudden bond. So I'm not the only one suffering.

'Well, I wouldn't call it my dream job,' he continues, 'but I need the money and the experience. Plus the tips come in useful,' he adds, and winks cheekily.

All at once I feel myself blush like a schoolgirl, and as he turns away to get my drink, I sneak a proper look at him. Despite seeing him in the Wellington, I haven't taken much notice of him before. He's got a straggly ponytail and tie-dye T-shirt, but even so he's really quite attractive, I realise, trying not to look at his tanned, muscular arms and looking right at his tanned, muscular arms.

But only on a purely aesthetic level, of course. I mean, it's not as if I *fancy* him or anything like that. I've got a boyfriend. A really lovely boyfriend. And we're buying a house and moving in together.

Plus he's still just a boy. Practically a baby in fact.

As he leans over to pull a bottle of water out of the fridge, his T-shirt rides up and I watch his back muscles ripple. Hastily I look away. Gosh, it really *is* hot in here, isn't it? Feeling a trickle of sweat run down between the cups of my underwired bra, I grab a beer mat and start fanning myself hard.

'There you go.' Smiling, he passes me the bottle of water, his tanned forearm flexing as he reaches towards me.

'Um . . . thanks.' I go to grab the bottle, but our hands collide and somehow my fingers get all tangled up with his. The bottle slips free.

'Nearly.' He laughs as he catches it deftly and hands it to me.

'God, I'm not normally so clumsy.'

As I look up, I catch his gaze and something very peculiar happens in my groin. What the . . .? I feel a flash of horror. Oh, no, I can't believe it.

I've turned into a cougar.

You know, one of those older women who frequent clubs in order to score with much younger men.

With my cheeks burning like a furnace, I quickly pay him. Honestly, what am I like, lusting after a barman who must be ten years younger than me, at least? I mean, I'm practically old enough to be his mother. Well, OK, not his mother, but his older sister. His *much* older sister.

Still, I shouldn't make a big deal of it, I remind myself quickly. I mean, there's nothing wrong with thinking another man is attractive, is there? And so what if he's ten years younger than me? Men are always looking at younger women. Plus it's only *natural* to look. It doesn't *mean* anything. I'm sure Miles looks at girls all day long.

Well, perhaps not *all* day long, I think, quickly backtracking. But sometimes. Like, for example, at his book-keeper, Helen, who's small and busty and always wears tight Lycra tops. I'm a woman and *I* can't help looking down her cleavage.

Gulping down the ice-cold water, I turn my back on the barman and instead focus on the dance floor, where Lottie is still dancing. But that's easier said than done.

'Amazing, isn't she?'

I turn sideways to find the barman right next to me, leaning against the bar, his chin resting on his elbows. I look around for a moment, just to make sure he's talking to me, before asking, 'Um . . . say again?'

He gestures towards the dance floor, a faraway look in his eyes. 'The girl in the dress.'

I feel a slight twinge of jealousy. Which girl? I think, following his gaze.

'With the little blue flowers.'

I look back at him in astonishment.

'She comes in the pub a lot.'

Me? He's talking about *me*? I look back at myself on the dance floor, through the mass of gyrating bodies, and there I am, doing my impression of the funky chicken. Surely that can't be right. He thinks *I'm* amazing?

'You think she's amazing?' I repeat incredulously. Maybe I didn't hear him right. After all, it is really loud in here.

'Totally,' he sighs.

Nope. I heard him right and that was a genuine sigh.

I turn back to my younger self, boogieing away completely obliviously, while my older self tries absorbing this information. I don't think anyone's ever called me 'amazing' before. I've had compliments like pretty, or sexy, or attractive but never *amazing*. Amazing is for superstars and celebrities like Angelina

Jolie. Not Charlotte Merryweather and certainly not Charlotte Merryweather when she was twenty-one. Sorry, just turned twenty-two.

'Her name's Lottie,' I say, still feeling a bit stunned.

'Oh, right.' He nods. 'Do you know her, then?'

'You could say we're kind of related.' I smile.

He looks at me in disbelief. 'No way!' he snorts. 'You look nothing like her.'

I feel my smile slide off my face. OK, so I know I look a lot different to how I did ten years ago, but there was no need for that snort. Now I'm a lot more groomed and a hundred times more stylish.

And let's not forget about those eyebrows.

'We've got the same noses,' I point out stiffly.

He peers at me for what feels like just a little bit longer than is necessary. 'Hmm, I suppose so,' he concedes, somewhat reluctantly. 'Kinda.'

I feel oddly miffed, and just a little bit jealous. Which is plain ridiculous. How can you be jealous of *yourself*?

'So . . . erm . . . tell me, why do you think she's so amazing?' I ask curiously.

'Oh, I don't know.' He shakes his head. 'She just is.'

'But can't you be more specific?' I persist.

'I can't explain it.' He shrugs. 'It's just the way she is. I wouldn't change a thing about her.'

'You wouldn't?' I look at him in disbelief.

'No,' he says simply. 'She's just . . .' he pauses, as if searching around for the right word, then finally finds it '. . . perfect.'

'*Perfect?*'

'The first time I saw her, it was *boom*.'

'*Boom?*' I'm aware that I'm beginning to sound like my great-aunt Mary's parrot, but I can't help it.

'Yeah, boom. That was it. I'd fallen in love.'

I look at him, bewildered. How did I never know this? How

could it be that there was someone going 'boom' all over me and I was totally unaware?

'Jeez, I sound a total soppy moron, don't I?' he says, mis-interpreting my silence. He smiles self-consciously. 'You must think I'm some kind of idiot.'

'No, not at all,' I protest, shaking my head. Quite the opposite. In fact if it wasn't for Miles, I'd be in danger of falling for him. Ten years younger or not.

'So why don't you speak to her, tell her how you feel?' I suggest.

He pulls a face at the very notion. 'I've spoken to her a couple of times, but I doubt she even remembers me.'

No, I don't, I think, looking at him.

'She probably doesn't even know I exist,' he continues. 'After all, I'm only a barman, and look at her – she could have anyone.'

I feel a tug of regret. Oh God, why didn't I ever notice him all those years ago? He's so sweet and lovely and such a nice guy.

Because you weren't interested in sweet and lovely, Charlotte. You weren't into nice guys. You were into musicians and skateboarders and all the wrong guys, remember? I remind myself. He's right. You wouldn't have noticed a barman with a straggly ponytail who wore tie-dye T-shirts. He wouldn't have been cool enough.

'Well, I think she'd be lucky to have you.' I smile.

He smiles back crookedly and raises one eyebrow. 'You think so?'

'Absolutely.' I nod. 'You're not *that* bad for a barman,' I add jokingly.

He laughs. 'You're not so bad either,' he responds. 'In fact if you were ten years younger, I might go for you myself.'

'Oy!' Affronted, I swat him.

'I'm joking, I'm joking,' he protests, ducking away, chortling. Grinning, he holds out his hand. 'I'm Olly, by the way.'

'I'm Charlotte.'

We shake hands and I notice something on the underside of

his wrist. It's dark in the club, and I only see it briefly, illuminated by the light from the fridge, but there's no mistaking what it is: a tattoo of a frog.

Gosh, what a coincidence. It's just like the one the barman in the gastropub has.

As the thought fires through my brain, it doesn't even have time to register before another one is firing.

My chest tightens. No, it can't be. It just can't.

Can it?

Abruptly my mind divides into a split screen. On one side is Olly with his ponytail, tie-dye T-shirt and hippy bracelets, and on the other is the barman from the gastropub with short curly hair, broken nose and a scar that runs down his upper lip. No, that's impossible. They look completely different.

But so did you ten years ago, whispers a voice inside my head.

And all at once both sides merge and it's like two people suddenly become one. Oh my God, *that's* why he seemed familiar, that's where I've met him before. Sweet, lovely toyboy Olly who I have a bit of a crush on is the barman who thinks my food allergies are funny. Who poured champagne tonight at my birthday and asked me if I was allergic to bubbles. And who bugs the complete hell out of me.

It's him. They're one and the same person. Shit.

Chapter Twenty-four

'There you are!'

Feeling a hand on my shoulder, I twirl round on my bar stool to see Lottie bright-eyed and breathless from dancing. 'I wondered where you'd got to.'

'Oh . . . hi,' I manage dazedly. I feel as if someone just knocked me on the head with a cartoon hammer and I'm seeing stars.

'Propping up the bar, where'd you think?' quips Olly in an attempt to talk to her, but she's busy tying up her hair and isn't paying attention.

'Um . . . Lottie, have you met—' I make a stab at an introduction, but she interrupts me by gushing excitedly,

'Come and dance!'

'No, no . . . I don't think so,' I say, automatically shrinking back.

'Come on,' she encourages, grabbing me by my wrist.

Then again, I don't really want to sit here talking to Olly now I've discovered who he is. It just feels too awkward. I mean, what am I going to say? Why did you turn into someone so obnoxious?

Yeah, right. Exactly.

'Well, OK,' I acquiesce, 'just for one song,'

But she's not listening – she's too busy pulling me off my bar stool. And before I know it I'm being dragged alive and against my will on to the dance floor.

Fuck.

It's like that dream where you're naked and walking through the town centre. Only this isn't a dream. It's a frickin' nightmare,

I curse silently, looking frantically for an escape route and realising I don't have one. I'm stuck frozen like a rabbit in headlights. Or should that be strobe lights? Surrounded by lots of gyrating bodies and with nowhere to hide.

Argh, this is hideous. Feeling as if every single pair of eyes in the club are on me, I take a deep breath and try to move my feet, but it's as if they're encased in heavy lumps of concrete. My arms, on the other hand, are like two ornaments that I don't know what to do with. I wave them about uncertainly and waggle my elbows as if I'm doing the funky chicken. Only I'm not sure what I'm doing. Apart from looking like a total idiot, I think, feeling mortified.

You see, the thing is, I'm a crap dancer. Some people are blessed with natural rhythm, but I'm not one of them. Remember that song by Gloria Estefan 'The Rhythm's Gonna Get You'? Well, it's never got me. I'm still waiting. I'm the only person in the whole of Wembley Stadium who clapped out of time to 'We Will Rock You' at a concert. Try it, it's almost impossible. And yet I managed to.

Saying that, it doesn't seem to be stopping Lottie, I note, glancing across at her. Waving her arms around, she's bopping away, seemingly unconcerned by the fact that she looks like a duck. In fact she's so unconcerned by it, everybody else around her seems unconcerned by it. I'm not sure anyone's even noticed, I realise, glancing around at all the other people on the dance floor.

Reluctantly, I tie my jacket round my waist and attempt to copy her as she gets on down. Only I'm older now and it's a lot harder to get back up again. *Ouch.* Feeling a twinge in my lower back, I grimace. This is torture. Thank God I don't have to endure birthdays like this any more. OK, so dinner tonight ended a touch early, and Miles falling asleep on the sofa was a bit annoying, but a nice low-key evening at a restaurant is a much better way to celebrate than being imprisoned in some hot, sweaty club and forced to dance. Relief rushes over me. Thank

God I'm not twenty-two any more. Thank God my clubbing days are over. Thank God—

I stiffen, my shoulders back, my head up, like a meerkat. Until now, the music's just been a sort of blurred din that's washed over me, but now I hear a couple of familiar chords.

Hang on. Is that . . . ?

It's like an injection of delight.

Oh my God, it is! *Ironic* by Alanis Morissette. I haven't heard it for *years*. Ooh, I love this song.

Feeling a rush of energy, my hips begin wiggling involuntarily. Then it's my waist. And now my shoulders. Gosh, this is *so* great. I start bopping away to the jangling guitar. I can't help it. My body won't stay still. It's impossible. *Oh wow*, I can even remember all the words! Twirling round, my makeshift ponytail comes undone, but I ignore it, and begin singing along. Quiet at first, then louder and louder.

And now it's the chorus and I've got my eyes closed and I'm throwing my arms in the air and belting out the lyrics at the top of my lungs. And in this moment I'm thinking about nothing. Nothing but dancing to this song. Losing myself in the chorus. Leaving behind all my worries and doubts, and totally letting myself go.

This is amazing! I feel great! I feel euphoric! I feel . . .

Someone grinding themselves against my bottom.

Snapping open my eyes, I whirl round and come crotch to crotch with a man wearing a T-shirt that's four sizes too small for him, a goatee and a white man's underbite. He smiles at me lecherously.

Oh, no.

Oh, no, oh, no, oh, no.

Still dancing, I try edging away, but Mr Bump 'n' Grind is having none of it. Putting on all the moves, he follows me around the dance floor like my shadow, until it's all too much. Yelling in Lottie's ear, 'I'm just nipping to the loo,' I leave him and his thrusting crotch behind and make a break for the ladies.

Phew.

Heaving a sigh of relief, I reach the safety of the ladies' and squeeze inside. As usual, there's a long queue, but I really do need to pee after drinking all that water, and so, resigning myself to a long wait, I lean against the wall. My feet are throbbing in their stilettos. They hurt before, but now after so much dancing they're ready to murder me. I wince, tugging off one of the heels and releasing my foot, like a cork from a bottle.

Rubbing my sore toes, my mind slides back to the dance floor. Talk about a lucky escape. Another second longer and I'd have been pinned to the DJ stand by that guy's crotch. I give a little shudder at the thought, which unexpectedly turns into a giggle. Well, I suppose he was rather comical, I muse, replaying a clip of him in my head doing that weird pumping thing with his hips. And at least it was a good excuse to leave the dance floor.

Saying that, I didn't actually *want* to leave the dance floor, I realise. It wasn't *that* bad. In fact I was sort of beginning to enjoy myself.

Oh, who am I kidding? I was having a total blast.

As I have a flashback to myself boogieing on down, I catch myself smiling. It must have released all those endorphins or whatever they are, I decide, feeling in a good mood. I mean, I never would have thought it possible, but I had *fun*. And while sober! What a total shock that was.

And talking about total shocks, what about Olly! I'm still reeling from the discovery that this really lovely barman and that really annoying guy from the gastropub are one and the same person. I just can't wrap my head around it. Or the implications.

I mean, it's perfectly harmless having a crush on someone who's ten years younger than me. It's a bit of a fantasy, like fancying Prince Harry (yes, OK, I admit it, but please don't tell anyone), but what happens when he's not a decade younger? When he's the same age as me. When it's *real*. Does that mean it's no longer harmless? I feel a jolt of panic.

Which of course is completely ridiculous, as I don't even *like* him now, let alone have a crush on him.

''S'cuse me, do you have a light?'

My thoughts are interrupted by a voice and I stop rubbing my feet and look up.

Hang on, that sounds just like —

Vanessa.

Standing next to me with her peroxide hair and bright red lipstick, she waves her unlit cigarette hopefully and smiles her big toothy smile. God, it's good to see her. I feel a rush of affection and have to resist the urge to throw my arms round her and give her a big hug.

'Jesus.'

I suddenly realise she's peering at me, her brow creased up in consternation, as if she's just noticed me for the first time.

'Excuse me?' I try to make my voice sound as normal as possible, but my heart is thumping. She knows it's me.

'Oh, nothing.' She shakes her head dismissively. 'For a moment you reminded me of someone.'

'I do?' I wait in anticipation, caught between fear and excitement.

'No, you did. For, like, a second. But actually you're nothing like her.'

For a fleeting moment I'm struck by a curious flash of disappointment. I know I've changed a lot, and *thank goodness* I've changed a lot, but surely I'm not a *completely* different person now from the best friend she used to have then.

Am I?

'Oh, just ignore me,' she continues. 'I'm all over the place at the moment. That's the problem with being in love.' She tuts loudly, but it's fairly obvious it isn't a problem. Far from it. 'Do you know, someone once told me being in love is a form of madness, and it's true!' Letting out a snort of laughter, she starts digging around in her pink satin-quilted clutch, which is shaped like a strawberry.

I watch her. God, it seems so strange to see Vanessa with such a tiny bag. Now she's had Ruby and Sam, you never see her without one of those giant tote bags, filled to the brim with masses and masses of stuff.

'Damn, I could have sworn I had a lighter in here.'

'Hang on, I think I've got some matches.' Sliding my hand into my jacket pocket, I locate some that I took from the bowl on the bar. Now everywhere's no-smoking, you don't see free matches any more and I always need them for my aromatherapy candles. I pass a packet to her.

'Thanks.' She smiles gratefully and, lighting her cigarette, takes a long drag as we slowly shuffle forward. 'Huh, this is taking for ever,' she complains, blowing smoke down her nostrils. 'My boyfriend's going to think I've run off with another man.' Leaning closer, she confides, 'Well, he's not really my boyfriend *yet*. We've only been out three times, but I've already fallen madly in love with him.' She smiles excitedly. 'His name's Julian and he's training to be a lawyer.'

I listen in fascination as she gushes away to *me*, a total stranger, like girls do when they're all loved up and just want to tell anyone and everyone who will listen about how lucky they are, and how amazing it feels, and how wonderful he is. And yet of course I know all this. I've heard it all before.

And yet . . .

As she keeps chattering away, it suddenly strikes me just how different this Vanessa is to the Vanessa I saw only a few hours ago at my birthday dinner, to the Vanessa who stood next to me in another set of ladies' loos talking about Julian.

She smiles dreamily, then giggles. 'Or maybe *I'm* just crazy.'

Now she's all wide-eyed and excited, bursting with hope and happiness and this shiny new thing called love, but earlier tonight she seemed so resigned and unhappy, almost defeated.

I watch as she pulls out a compact and sets about reapplying what used to be her trademark scarlet lipstick, drawing two perfect arches of colour on her top lip and sweeping across the bottom with one deft flick of her wrist. She hasn't worn red lipstick in a while. In fact tonight she wasn't wearing any make-up at all, until I gave her the lip gloss, I reflect, and her hair was pulled back in a knot as usual. Apparently she didn't have time to take a shower as the babysitter was late.

But it's more than that. It's more than unwashed hair and the lack of lipstick; it's like seeing a photograph that used to be in colour, only now it's in black and white.

'Ooh, look, there's a free one.' She gestures ahead to an empty cubicle I hadn't noticed.

'Oh, yes . . . thanks.'

Leaving her applying a fresh coat of mascara, I disappear inside. I suddenly feel incredibly sad. An awful lot has changed in ten years, and for the first time it hits me that perhaps not all of it is for the better.

Chapter Twenty-five

F ast-forward to 3 a.m.
    If only.

Seeking solace on a sofa in a darkened corner, I check my watch for the umpteenth time. I feel as if I've been here for hours. Days. Weeks, almost. And now I'm bored and tired, I have a headache, my feet hurt, and I want to go home.

But I can't. I have to stay and keep a watchful eye on Lottie, who at some point in the evening switched from water and has proceeded to get completely trollied on free birthday drinks. I'd forgotten just how drunk I used to get. At one point I actually started dancing on the table.

And in those heels. I don't know how I did it.

Rubbing my temples, my eyes do an automatic sweep around the club – like the searchlight from a lighthouse – to check on Lottie's whereabouts and make sure she's not getting into trouble. Or falling off a table. Just then the music stops abruptly and the lights come on.

My heart skips a beat, hardly daring to believe what's happening. Oh my God, does this mean . . .? Hope holds my breath tight as clubbers begin leaving the dance floor and heading for the exit. Yes, it does! I almost feel like dropping to my knees and kissing the floor. The word 'relief' doesn't even come close.

Halle-bloody-lujah. That's it.

It's over.

'Aw, what a bummer,' slurs Lottie, emerging from the crowd, her face sweaty and wearing an expression of utter dismay. 'I can't believe it's finished. *Already!*'

'I know. What a shame,' I fib, hastily grabbing my bag and throwing on my jacket. 'OK, let's go.' I start racing out of the club, my sore feet suddenly coming back to life.

Outside, everyone is milling around on the pavement saying goodnight.

'Hang on, everyone, before you leave I want to take a photo,' Lottie yells. Producing a camera from her bag, she starts herding people together.

'No, you need to be in it, Lottie,' shouts someone.

I'm still standing by her side and she turns to me. 'Charlotte, will you take the photo?'

'Of course.' I take the camera from her with the intention of getting it over with as quickly as possible and then going home, but as I look through the lens, it suddenly hits me: the familiar line-up, the clothes, the smiles.

Oh my God. This is the photograph I have at home on my fridge. The one taken on my birthday.

By me?

My mind whirls in confusion. But how? That can't be. Unless—

'Come on, hurry up,' yells someone.

Quickly I snap to. 'OK, everyone, smile!'

Everyone beams for the camera, and as I press the button, I look at Lottie, at my younger self, eyes wide, smile bright. There's a flash and the shutter clicks, and I capture the moment for ever.

I offer to walk Lottie home. My car is parked outside her house. Plus, more crucially, she's totally legless and needs an escort. I don't think she'll get home without me.

Linking arms, we stroll back to her house. It's a really warm evening. Or should I say early morning? Everything is quiet and slightly magical, as if the whole world is asleep but us.

Arriving at her house, she struggles with her house keys, and after dropping them on the ground three times, I take over. Deftly unlocking the door, I haul her inside.

'I think I should make you a coffee, help you sober up a bit,' I suggest, taking her through into the kitchen, which is in darkness, and plonking her on a chair.

Actually, I *would* plonk her on a chair if each one wasn't heaped with piles of rubbish. Old tea towels, newspapers and, oh God, is that a pair of knickers? I recoil at the sight of what appears to be a discarded G-string. In the dimness I can't tell if it's clean or not. And quite frankly, I'm not getting close enough to find out, I decide, grabbing a wooden spoon with my free hand and looping the thong over the handle. Hastily I drop it on to another pile. Trust me, there are plenty of piles to choose from – it's like a mole's been in here, only instead of mounds of earth, there's just mounds of *stuff* everywhere. Clearing away a mound, I drape Lottie on a chair.

OK, I'll put the kettle on.

Flicking on the light, which is just a bare bulb hanging forlornly from the ceiling, the kitchen is suddenly flooded by a hundred watts of harsh glare.

I freeze.

Sweet Jesus, there's been a robbery! Someone's ransacked the house!

As the thought flashes through my mind, panic ignites. Oh my God, I need to call the police, quick. What if they've stolen lots of stuff? What if – God forbid – the intruder's still in the house? Panic fires up a notch to terror. Shit, where's the phone?

And then suddenly I notice that my younger self isn't jumping up and down yelling, 'We've been burgled!' On the contrary, she's sitting very calmly on the chair as if nothing is out of the ordinary.

Because nothing is out of the ordinary, Charlotte.

All at once it registers. There hasn't been a robbery, and nobody has ransacked the house – *except the people who live here*. I pause to take it in. Did I really used to live like this? My flatmates and I were pigs! Actually, no, pigs are cleaner. And they don't leave dirty knickers lying around . . . My eyes sweep the room – across every surface littered with dirty mugs, half-eaten food, shrivelled-up teabags and bowls with dried-on cereal, which would require a hammer and chisel to remove – and finally land on the pile of dirty dishes. It's almost skyscraper in its proportions. And what about the rubbish? I glance with horror at the plastic swingbin, its top off, the black bin-liner spilling over with empty cans, most of which appear to be Heinz baked beans.

Then there's the smell.

Gagging, I turn away. Unearthing the kettle, which, by the way, has so much limescale there's no need to *ever* take calcium tablets, I fill it up (not an easy task – I have to wedge the spout between the tap and the pile of dishes, in a tricky manoeuvre that reminds me of a game of Jenga) and flick it on.

I think about my own lovely, spotlessly clean flat. Not for the first time am I glad I'm not Lottie any more.

I turn back to Lottie, who's leaning forwards, the side of her face resting on the dining-room table, her eyes closed.

'Coffee won't be a minute,' I encourage, trying not to let out a shriek as I look for a mug that doesn't have mould growing in it.

'Umm,' she moans sleepily.

Somehow in the space of a few minutes she's gone from euphorically life-and-soul-of-the-party drunk to falling-asleep-in-her-clothes-drooling drunk.

'Maybe you should eat something too,' I suggest.

'Mmm.'

Gingerly I tug open a few cupboards. Back at my flat, my shelves are filled with packets of organic wholewheat pasta, jars of sundried tomatoes, a bottle of virgin olive oil . . .

Pot Noodles.

I stare at them blankly. That's it?

I rummage around a bit. There's got to be something else, apart from Pot Noodles. Oh, hang on, there's something else. A bottle of ketchup, which has gone all congealed and manky around the top and probably has the grand total of about one drop of ketchup left in it, and that's only if you stand it upside down for a week.

Still, she needs to eat something, so it's got to be the Pot Noodle or nothing, I decide, grabbing one in desperation and peeling off the tinfoil lid. Mmm, very nutritious, I muse ironically, looking at the freeze-dried dust in disgust. I dread to think how many additives and E-numbers are in there.

The kettle flicks off and I fill it up to the brim with hot water, then turn back to making coffee. Chipping away at the remnants in the bottom of the jar of Nescafé, I turn to the fridge for milk. Quite frankly, I'm scared what I'm going to find in there.

And with good cause.

Bracing myself, I tug it open and come face to face with more ice than is left in the Arctic. Anyone who's worried about the polar ice caps disappearing would be reassured by this fridge. 'Defrosting' is obviously a word I wasn't aware of when I was younger.

Nor was I familiar with the words 'fruit' or 'vegetables'. Instead what lies waiting for me on the top shelf, my shelf in the shared fridge, are two Dairylea triangles, a half-used jar of Ragu and an unidentifiable fossilised object that could be anything, I think, looking at it curiously.

Is this how I used to survive? On Pot Noodles, ketchup, Dairylea triangles and Ragu? I'm surprised I never got scurvy or rickets or something.

I think back to my list and add to it:

17. Eat healthily.

'You know, you really should try and eat a balanced diet,' I advise Lottie, spying a dog-eared carton of milk at the back and pouncing on it. 'You should eat a recommended five servings of fruit and vegetables a day to lower your cholesterol and avoid the risk of colon cancer.' I glance over at Lottie, but she's not listening. Crashed out on the dining-room table, she's emitting a faint snore.

I give up on the dietary tips – for now, anyway – and turn back to making coffee. I take a quick sniff of the milk. Euccchh. It's gone totally sour. In fact it's gone past that and is a sort of solidified lump.

Hastily I put it back in the fridge. (Well, I would put it in the bin, but it's already spilling over.) She'll just have to drink it black. It's better than nothing.

'Here you go.'

I put the coffee and Pot Noodle in front of her, but she doesn't stir. She's out cold. I give her a shake and she wakes up, squinting in the light. For a moment she looks blearily around as if not realising where she is, then pounces on the coffee. 'Mmm, thanks,' she mumbles, perking up and taking a large gulp, followed by a spoonful of the gloop that is the Pot Noodle. 'Yummy.' She grins up at me. 'Want some?' She proffers the pot.

'No, thanks,' I say quickly. 'I'm not hungry.'

'Suit yourself.' She smiles, taking another forkful. 'More for me.'

Whatever, it seems to do the trick, and it's not long before she's revived enough to climb the stairs to her bedroom. I follow, partly out of curiosity, partly to make sure she doesn't slip and fall back down the stairs. I throw out an arm as she wobbles precariously on the top step. Phew, that was a close call.

'Well, here we are, home sweet home.' Pot Noodle in one hand, mug of coffee in the other, she bumps open her bedroom door with her hip. It swings open, revealing she's left the light on. Saving energy was not my thing in those days. Neither, it would appear, was picking my clothes up off the floor.

Following her in, I stare at the scene that greets me. The only way I can describe it is this: imagine emptying your drawers and chucking everything on the floor. Then opening your wardrobe and pulling everything off the hangers and chucking those on the floor too. Add on top a few pairs of shoes. A coat. A couple of wet towels. And bingo, you've got my old bedroom.

'Make yourself at home,' grins Lottie, kicking off her shoes and flopping cross-legged on to the Indian bedspread.

I look around for somewhere to sit. The room is so tiny I can barely turn round. There's a small table and a fold-up plastic chair by the window and I perch uncomfortably on the edge. The table is cluttered with books. An ancient IBM computer takes up most of the space, and there's a pile of pages next to it.

'I'm writing a novel,' she says, seeing me look at them.

'Oh wow, I'd forgotten about that,' I murmur, remembering, then catch myself. Luckily Lottie hasn't heard me; instead she's busily tucking into her Pot Noodle.

'I haven't finished it yet, but I'm going to,' she continues assuredly. 'At the moment I'm working at a puzzle magazine, but I really want to be a writer. Ever since I was a little girl it's been my dream. I couldn't imagine doing anything else.' She smiles and takes another forkful. 'What about you? What do you do?'

'Oh, I . . . um . . . I run my own PR company,' I say, focusing back.

'Wow, really?' Eyes wide, she looks impressed. 'That's amazing. Your own company. You must be mega successful!'

'I wouldn't say "mega",' I say modestly, but inside I feel a swell of pride at how well I've done, at how far I've come, I think, glancing at Lottie, sitting cross-legged on her rickety futon, in the middle of her poky little room, eating a Pot Noodle.

'I bet you live in an amazing flat, don't you? As well as driving that amazing car.'

I smile as I remember giving her a ride home from the concert last night, and her oohing and ahhing about my heated leather seats. 'Well, I like it . . .'

'You're so lucky,' she sighs wistfully. 'I'd love my own place and a new car one day. And some money would be nice.'

I smile, basking in her respect.

'So do you love your job?' she asks eagerly.

'Well, I don't know about *love* it,' I admit, thinking about this last week. 'There's a lot of stress involved—'

'Because it's important to do what you love, don't you think?' she interrupts, before I can finish. 'Like my dad always says, you're at work a long time, so you might as well do something you love, something you're passionate about.'

I feel a jolt of uncertainty. God, Dad always does that say that, doesn't he? To tell the truth, I've never been passionate about PR, not even close, but then how many people are passionate about their jobs? I tell myself in justification.

'True.' I nod. 'But that's also a little idealistic. Sometimes you need to compromise and focus on a career that will allow you to pay the bills and give you financial security,' I reason. 'OK, so it might not be doing something you're truly passionate about, but it can still be challenging and fulfilling.' I can see I've got my younger self's attention and I feel pleased. See. This is the amazing thing about being older: having the experience, the hindsight, the maturity to know what's important.

'Ugh, no, thanks.' Lottie pulls a face. ' "Challenging and fulfilling," ' she repeats, as if the words taste nasty. 'That doesn't sound like fun.'

'Well, life isn't always about having fun,' I reply, feeling a little rankled.

'Then what is it about?' she asks simply.

Her question throws me. I open my mouth to try to respond, only I can't. I don't know how to answer that. Because she's right, I suddenly realise. What *is* it about?

I'm saved from replying by the sound of the front door being slammed.

'Oh, bloody hell, that'll be one of the boys coming in,' she groans. 'Hang on a sec, I'm just going to nip to the bathroom before they do.'

She jumps up and disappears out of the room and I'm suddenly reminded of what it was like sharing a bathroom with six other people. Waiting your turn to take a shower in the morning and finally getting in there only to discover all the hot water has gone. Dashing to the loo in the middle of the night and finding someone already on it. Listening out for the door to unlock so you can go in and have a nice, long, relaxing bath, then one of the boys coming out complaining about last night's curry . . .

'Sorry, what were you saying?' asks Lottie, reappearing.

I look up in surprise. I'd expected her to be ages, brushing her teeth, flossing, rinsing, taking off her make-up, applying creams. I mean, the whole bathroom routine takes me for ever. Then it twigs. 'Oh, was someone in there already?' I pull a face in consolation.

'No.' She smiles, and flops back on to her futon. 'All done.'

All done?

I stare at her in confusion. What does she mean, all done? How can it all be done in about ten seconds? I'm in there forty-five minutes.

Then I realise she hasn't taken her make-up off.

Yet, pipes up a little voice inside my head. Surely she's going to take off her make-up? I mean, every woman knows that your skin regenerates overnight and it has to be squeaky clean to soak up the nutrients from all those creams you've slathered on.

I feel a stab of worry.

Don't they?

'Um, aren't you going to take your make-up off?' I say casually.

'Nah. I can't be bothered.' She yawns, rubbing her eyes with the palm of her hand and smearing black eyeliner across her cheek.

I give a little inward shudder and, trying not to think of my poor skin, mentally add to my list:

18. Always take off your make-up.

Speaking of the list . . .

'You know, instead of renting, you really should think about buying your own place,' I suggest. 'Then you'll have your own bathroom.'

'Yeah, right.' She laughs as if I've just cracked a very funny joke. 'With what?'

'Your savings,' I continue, bending down and picking up a wet towel. It's been bugging me ever since I got in here. Folding it up, I lay it over the back of the chair.

'I don't have any savings,' she tuts. 'Apart from my overdraft. Actually . . .' she pauses, thinking '. . . I've got a three-hundred-quid overdraft and there's sixty quid left, so does that count?'

'No, that doesn't count,' I retort quickly, suddenly feeling a bit like Miles must do when I get confused about investment funds. Saying that, I can see her logic. Sort of. 'But you should start a savings account,' I continue, reaching for another towel. 'You don't have to put much in, just a few pounds a month, but it will all add up.' Finished with the towels, I begin tidying up the rest of the stuff. Well, now I've started . . .

'And if I were you,' I add pointedly, 'I'd start a pension, and maybe invest.' Putting some dresses on hangers, I start running through my list. 'A little bit of an insider tip; if you can, buy shares in something called Google.' Going off into a little fantasy land, I start imagining how I'd spend my millions. Though first of all I'd give a large chunk to my family and friends. My mind jumps to Vanessa, and her advice. 'Oh, and before I forget, you must start doing your pelvic-floor exercises.'

Suddenly I realise Lottie has gone silent and I turn round. 'No, don't worry, they're not difficult.'

My younger self is fast asleep.

I stare in disbelief.

No sound machine. No mouthguards. No aromatherapy mask. No humidifier. No blackout blinds. And with the light on. It's incredible. I obviously didn't suffer from insomnia back then, I reflect, feeling a tug of envy.

Gently I pull the Indian bedspread over her and she mumbles something faintly in her sleep and turns over. I pause, watching her sleeping, then go to leave. My eyes sweep the room for one last look and land on the unfinished novel, sitting on the desk.

And it's never going to be finished, I realise, suddenly feeling a beat of sadness. Because I gave up the dream.

I can't remember how long I stand there, feeling reflective, looking at the girl I used to be. Until finally, switching off the light, I leave her behind and close the door.

Chapter Twenty-six

B *ang, bang, bang, bang.*
    What's going on? It's pitch-black and I'm trapped in a wooden box. I can't see. I can't move. All I can hear is this incessant—

Bang, bang, bang.

Oh my God, I'm being buried alive. That's the sound of the nails being hammered into my coffin.

Bang, bang, bang, bang.

I'm going to suffocate. I won't be able to get out. I'm going to die.

Bang, bang, bang.

Argh, let me out, let me out, LET ME OUTTTTTT!!!!!!

'Darling, wake up, wake up.'

I snap my eyes open and remove my eye mask to find Miles shaking me by the shoulder.

'Wassup . . .? Wha . . .?' I sit bolt upright and look at him, dazedly, trying to get my bearings. I'm in bed, and Miles is lying next to me, his face etched with concern.

'Sshh, don't worry. You were having a nightmare. You were yelling something about "Let me out."'

'Oh . . . right . . . yes,' I murmur, feeling a rush of relief. 'Oh God, it was horrible, Miles, just horrible.' I flop back on to the pillow. 'I was being buried alive.'

He smiles reassuringly. 'Well, don't worry, you're fine now. You're safe here with me.' He strokes my hair, which is stuck to my clammy forehead.

Bang, bang, bang, bang.

I stiffen. It's that noise! 'What was that?' I shriek, sitting bolt upright again. See, I wasn't dreaming. It's real.

'Oh, that? Don't worry, darling, that's nothing.' He laughs at my horrified expression. 'Just the estate agent putting up the sign.'

'*Sign*? What sign?' I gasp, jumping out of bed and dashing to the window. Yanking open the curtain and raising the blackout blinds I stare out into the street. Just in time to see a man with a hammer giving a final thwack to the sign. '"FOR SALE,"' I murmur, reading the large red letters. My heart thuds.

'Well, what did you think it was going to say?' says Miles jovially.

'Um . . . nothing. I dunno . . .' My mind is swirling in uncertain directions. 'It's just . . . isn't it a bit *quick*?'

'Quick?' replies Miles, propping himself up against the headboard. 'You can't be too quick when it comes to the property market, darling,' he advises sagely. 'Now our offer's been accepted, it's important that the buyers see we mean business, and that means selling our own properties, organising a survey, sorting out the joint mortgage and deposit . . .'

As his voice drones on, I feel slightly light-headed. I rub my ears agitatedly. 'I think I'll make us a coffee,' I say, cutting him off as he starts talking about setting up a joint account. I suddenly feel claustrophobic, as though I can't breathe. It's almost as if my nightmare of being buried alive is actually becoming a reality.

'Ooh, yes, good idea,' nods Miles. 'I've got a bit of a hangover after last night. All that celebrating.' He looks at me and I feel a twist of panic. 'I must have crashed out on the sofa as it wasn't till the light woke me up, streaming in through the blinds, that I crawled into bed. Not that you'd remember,' he adds, looking at me pointedly.

The twist of alarm tightens a notch. Oh shit.

After leaving my younger self asleep in bed, I'd driven back from my old house and arrived at my flat when it was just getting light. Assuming Miles was still fast asleep on the sofa, I'd headed straight into the bedroom, which was in complete darkness because of my blackout blinds, and flopped straight into bed. But what if Miles woke up while I was out clubbing? What if he came to bed and discovered I wasn't there? What on earth am I going to say? My mind starts frantically flicking through a Rolodex of excuses. How on earth am I going to explain—

'You were fast asleep. Completely dead to the world,' he continues, and I look at him in astonishment. 'You were obviously exhausted. You're normally such a light sleeper.'

I got away with it. He doesn't know! My body almost sags with relief.

'Must have been all the excitement about the house, hey?' He beams.

'Er, yes, absolutely.' I smile uneasily. 'It totally wiped me out.' I do a show of stretching and throw in a faux yawn. Which turns into a real one. Actually, I am still pretty tired.

'Do you want me to help with the coffee?' Misinterpreting my show of exhaustion, Miles starts to get out of bed.

'No, no,' I say urgently. 'You stay there. I'll get it.'

'Hmm, I think I'm going to like this living together,' he says, and looking pleased, he slides back underneath the duvet.

Leaving him behind in the bedroom, I hurry into the kitchen, grab a bag of coffee beans, pour them into the grinder, switch it on and reach for the espresso pot. Then pause. Hugging it to my chest, I lean against the counter and watch the coffee beans whirling round and round, like all the kinds of strange, unfamiliar thoughts that are whirling round in my head.

I think back to last night. To all of it: my birthday dinner, Miles and the champagne, Vanessa and Julian, Lottie and the club, Olly the barman . . . At the memory of Olly my stomach does a little loop and I feel a flash of something. Excitement, fear, foolishness? I don't know what. A scene from our conversation slides across my mind, down my spine, through my groin and comes to an abrupt full stop as my mind throws up an image of the barman at the gastropub. Annoying, irritating, belligerent and *the same person*. God, it's all got so confusing.

'There you are.'

I twirl round to see Miles standing in the doorway of the kitchen, wearing my bathrobe. It's too small for him and his pale arms and legs are sticking out from the cream waffle towelling, making him look rather comical.

'I wondered what had happened to the coffee.'

I become aware of the noise of the grinder, still buzzing away, and quickly turn it off.

'I thought we could have our coffee and then go take a second look at the house,' he continues, reaching for the Weetabix. He keeps a box at my flat. Apparently he's eaten them since childhood and can't break the habit. Not that he seems to want to. I've never seen anyone get as much pleasure from sprinkling a layer of sugar on top of Weetabix, patting them down with the back of his spoon, carefully pouring milk around them ('like a moat', he once explained), making sure he doesn't pour it on the Weetabix directly, as that would make them soggy, and then eating them with the kind of precision you'd expect from a brain surgeon.

'So we need to hurry up. I've arranged to pick up the keys.'

'Oh, um . . . yes, right.' I nod, feeling a familiar jangle of nerves.

Turning back to the espresso pot, I rub my ears distractedly. They're still itching. In fact they're actually rather painful, I realise, leaning forwards to peer at them in the shiny stainless-steel toaster. I get quite a shock. My ears are red and inflamed, and there's an angry rash beginning to run down the side of my neck. Oh my God, it must be the pearl earrings. I'm allergic to them.

And all at once it's like the earrings are a sign. A sign that this isn't right. Buying this house. Moving in together. *Me and Miles.* I feel a jolt of fear and recognition. It's as if someone just unlocked a door inside me that I've been too afraid to open, because I know what's on the other side.

I'm not in love with Miles.

As soon as the thought pops into my head, I realise it's been there for longer than I care to remember. I've just been avoiding it, ignoring it, pretending it wasn't true, putting a PR spin on my own relationship, trying to convince myself that we are right for each other, that Miles is right for me. And it's only now I've finally admitted it to myself.

Now I just have to admit it to Miles.

Like a drum roll, my heart starts thudding loudly in my chest as I turn to face him. He's sitting on a stool up at the counter, carefully cutting off a slice of Weetabix with his spoon, and still talking.

'There's lots of things we need to start to sort out. For example, are they leaving the curtains and blinds? If not, we'll have to get those ordered and they can take at least four to six weeks.'

I have to tell him. Taking a deep breath, I summon all my courage. 'Miles, I don't know how to say this, but I can't—'

'Oh, don't tell me,' he interrupts, pulling a face. 'You've got yoga.'

I swallow hard. 'No, I haven't got yoga.'

'I mean, surely you can reschedule? This *is* very important,' he continues, turning back to his cereal bowl.

'Miles, you're not listening,' I snap, then immediately feel guilty.

He looks at me in surprise.

I hesitate. It's now or never. I just have to come out with it. 'It's about us.'

There. I've said it.

He looks at me for a moment, confused, searching my eyes for a clue, then nods. 'Oh, I know what this is about.'

I feel a curious leap of optimism. Maybe he feels this way too. Maybe it's not just me.

'It's about last night, isn't it?' he continues, looking uncomfortable. 'Me falling asleep on the sofa.'

I look at him blankly.

'We didn't have sex on your birthday.'

Oh my God, he's got it so wrong. So horribly wrong I don't know what to say.

'Well, we can have it now, if you'd like,' he offers, putting down his spoon and standing up. 'We don't have to pick up the keys and look at the house till ten – we've got time.'

I look at him, standing there, in my towelling bathrobe, his half-finished Weetabix lying soggy in the bowl, and strangely I don't feel very turned on. In fact his offer of sex is so matter-of-fact he might as well be offering to put out the recycling.

'Miles, it's not about last night, and it's not about sex,' I say, quickly glossing over that bit. 'It's about us. Me, this house, *everything* . . .' I flail my arms around.

Miles is looking at me, his face uncomprehending. I'm hoping he's going to butt in, finish my sentence for me, guess what I'm going to say, but after two wrong answers he's not going to, is he?

'I don't want to buy the house,' I finally blurt.

He stares at me, his face a picture of astonishment. 'Why? What's wrong with the house?' he demands.

'Nothing's wrong with the house,' I reply quickly. 'It's perfect. It's a perfect house.'

'Well, then!' His astonishment has disappeared and he's annoyed now. 'Look, Charlotte, I know you're nervous, but you're being ridiculous. What's got into you?'

'Nothing, it's just . . .' I stare fixedly at the floor. 'Miles, I can't do this. I can't move in with you.'

There. Finally I've said it.

There's silence. I drag my eyes upwards. He looks stunned. Then his face sets, harder. 'Can't, or *won't*?'

I swallow hard. 'Miles, I'm not doing this on purpose. You're a wonderful person. It's not you, it's me. I've been having doubts for a while, and I just never realised . . .' God, I'm really making a mess of this, aren't I? I take a deep breath and continue, 'But now everything's sort of come to a head and it wouldn't be fair on either of us to carry on.'

'You've met someone else, haven't you?' he suddenly accuses.

Every nerve in my body seems to jump and I look at him in shock. 'No, of course not!' I protest quickly.

'Yes you have,' he continues. 'I just knew it. You've been acting really strangely these last couple of days. Different. Ever since I got back from Leeds. So come on, who is it?'

'No one.'

Oh God, why is he asking me all these questions? And why am I feeling so guilty? I ask myself, thinking about Olly.

'Tell me who it is and I'll punch him.' Curling up a fist, he shakes it menacingly. Only Miles could never look menacing. Especially not in my terry-towelling bathrobe.

'Miles!' I gasp in exasperation, feeling the conversation veering wildly off course. Fuck, this is not what I planned to happen at all. 'This isn't about anyone else. It's about me.'

His chest deflates, and stuffing his fist in his pocket, he composes himself. 'Look, Charlotte, I'm sure we can work this out. We always do,' he says practically.

He's right. If we ever have a difference of opinion, we don't argue about it, we work things out. But that usually involves a compromise. And this time it's about more than just a fireplace.

'No, Miles, we can't.' I shake my head sadly. 'We can't work this out, not this time.'

'Well, I think you're making a huge mistake,' he snaps.

Guilt stabs. God, I feel like such a bad person.

'We're going to lose out on a real steal with that house,' he continues. 'It's a great investment. How can you do this?'

Slowly it registers. Hang on a minute, he's talking about *the house*?

'Plus I've already organised for the survey. That's at least seven hundred pounds down the drain, unless I can cancel it, but I doubt it, at such short notice.'

Obviously he's upset and just trying to distract himself. It's his way of coping. After all, men aren't like women, are they? I watch as he snatches his mobile off the counter, where it's charging, and starts punching in a number. Then again, maybe he really *is* more bothered about the house.

'I'll call them now, see what I can do . . .'

'Miles, listen, I'll pay for the survey,' I offer. 'I'll pay for all the costs we've incurred so far. It's not important.'

'Of course it's important, Charlotte,' he snaps.

'No it's not, it's really not.' I shake my head. 'It's just a house. We're talking about the rest of our lives.'

'Just a house?' He laughs in disbelief. 'I don't think so, Charlotte. It's in a prime location. It's a hot property.'

'I don't care if it's a hot property!' I yell, before I can stop myself. 'I don't care if it's in a prime location, or if we can get planning permission for a loft conversion, or if it's a great investment. I don't care if we drink Pinot Noir or Cabernet Sauvignon. And I don't care if I never see another episode of *Location, Location, Location*. Or talk about pension plans. Or listen to another James Bond theme tune as long as I live —' I break off, panting.

We both look stunned by my outburst.

'I'm sorry, I didn't mean to shout . . .' I trail off and spread my hands awkwardly. 'It's just that I've been trying to convince myself, going along with things. And I can't any longer. I've got to be true to myself.'

'But you said you loved Licence to Thrill. I bought you the CD.' He looks at me, his face hurt.

'I know, I'm sorry,' I repeat again, only this time more softly.

'Me too,' he replies stiffly, and putting the phone back to his ear, he turns away and stalks out of the kitchen. 'Ah, yes, hello. I'm calling about the survey . . .'

Chapter Twenty-seven

O K, so let's recap. In less than an hour I've gone from having a boyfriend, buying a house and being inches away from being what my mother calls 'settled' to having no boyfriend, no new house and feeling very *un*settled.

Brilliant, Charlotte. Great move. One of your finest.

Feeling a bit stunned, I plop down on the sofa and try to take in this sudden turn of events. I hadn't planned this to happen at all. When I woke up this morning, the first thing on my list of things to do wasn't 'Must break up with Miles.'

It's just that once I faced up to the doubts that have been simmering in the background for so long, it all unravelled at the speed of knots. Like picking at some stitching, the whole thing suddenly fell apart. Right there, in the middle of my kitchen. And now I'm not sure quite what to do next.

Miles leaves, telling me he'll come back for his stuff. I offer to drop it round in my car, as it will be much easier than him lugging it on the bus, but he curtly tells me he doesn't need my help, thank you very much, as the number 47 goes right past his flat. He then pointedly returns my spare keys and slams the door behind him.

He's angry and upset, and I don't blame him. I feel dreadful, responsible, guilty. I also feel a huge sense of release.

I glance across at the coffee table, where the estate agent's brochure of my dream house lies in all its glossiness. As I pick it up, I realise that the nervous twist in the pit of my stomach that I've been trying to persuade myself was just pre-moving-in-together jitters has disappeared, gone. Along with the dream life I always wanted, I reflect, looking at the full-colour photographs.

At least, I *thought* I wanted it, only when I finally got it, it suddenly didn't seem that dreamy. I flop back on the sofa, my head spinning. To tell the truth, I'm beginning to feel a bit disorientated. Like I've been running a marathon this last ten years and now the finishing line has just disappeared. I mean, if I don't want that, what do I want?

God, this is all a bit heavy for a Saturday morning, isn't it?

Scratching my inflamed ears, I give a huge hippo-sized yawn. I haven't even had my coffee yet, I realise, closing my eyes. Saying that, I'm actually really tired. It was getting light when I finally rolled into bed, so I can't have had more than a few hours' sleep last night. I mean this morning, I think sleepily, snuffling into a cushion.

Then stiffen.

Eugh, what's that horrible smell? My nostrils wrinkle up in disgust. Yuck, it smells like stale sweat and cigarettes.

That's because it is stale sweat and cigarettes.

Abruptly I realise I'm smelling my hair. My normally swingy, shiny, glossy hair that smells of elderberry and jojoba and something suitably fragrant now smells like an old ashtray and someone's armpit. I take another cautious sniff. Eugh, that's just gross. I spring up from the sofa.

I might not know what I want, but I definitely know what I need: a shower.

After giving my hair a thorough shampooing, followed by an intensive conditioning, I stay underneath the powerful twin shower heads for the longest time. Eyes closed, face upturned, I relish the hot water blasting my skin. My mind flicks back to Lottie last night, rolling into bed, still wearing her make-up. God, imagine what her skin will look like today, I shudder, squeezing out a blob of special microdermabrasion crystals and vigorously scrubbing my cheeks. There's nothing worse than sleeping in your make-up. She'll look terrible.

And feel terrible, I muse, a vision popping into my mind of her drunkenly stumbling up to bed, a Pot Noodle in one hand, a cup of black coffee in the other. Gosh, poor thing. I might not be having the greatest morning on record, but she's got to be suffering from the hangover from hell.

Wrapped in towels, I make a fresh pot of coffee and then wander aimlessly around my flat for a bit. I check a couple of emails. Pluck my eyebrows. Throw out all the rotting organic vegetables from the bottom of the fridge. Plump cushions.

The whole day stretches ahead of me. Weekends are always spent with Miles, and this weekend was meant to be no different. In fact I purposely kept this weekend free from work stuff and appointments so we could do lots of coupley things as I've been so busy with work recently. *Re-bond*, as it says in my book about how to have a successful relationship. Only that didn't *quite* work out, did it?

Finishing plumping all the cushions on the sofa and putting them all neatly on their corners, I look distractedly around me. I know, I'll call Vanessa, I decide, reaching for the telephone. No, on second thoughts, she'll be busy with the kids and won't be able to talk and we'll have one of those conversations where every third sentence is 'No, Ruby, no. Mummy's on the phone.' Plus, to be honest, she's got enough of her own problems right now without listening to mine, I reflect, thinking about our conversation last night in the ladies' at the gastropub and feeling a beat of worry. I know, maybe I'll go for a run instead, do some exercise. Then again, my muscles are sore from dancing last night. I had no idea dancing was such a workout.

In which case, maybe I'll . . .

I draw a blank. To be honest, what *are* you supposed to do when you've just broken up with someone? I glance over at my bookshelves, bursting with self-help books, guides and manuals. My eyes scan the titles. There's everything there from *Stress Management* to *The Power of Positive Thinking*, but there's nothing on break-ups. Not even in my favourite, *Good Listener*,

Good Lover. But then again, if you're both good listeners and good lovers, you probably won't be breaking up, will you?

Grabbing my laptop, I log on to Amazon and punch in 'break-up'. A whole ream of books appears before my eyes: *Surviving as a Single, When Two Become One, You're Not Alone, Gay Goodbyes* (I skirt over that one), *Getting Over It and Moving On* . . .

Clicking on one of them, I start reading a glossary of what's inside:

It's important to mourn the end of a relationship, as this will allow you to move on. Be kind to yourself. This will take time. You cannot rush this important healing process as you move through the various stages: 1) shock and disbelief, 2) depression and grief, 3) anger and unfairness, 4) acceptance. At this final stage you are ready to move on with your life, feel positive and hopefully begin a new relationship.

Hmm, I suppose I must be at the shock and disbelief stage. I click on the book to order it. Well, I'll need to read it, otherwise I'll forget all the different stages I'm supposed to go through, though I'm not much looking forward to the next stage. I wonder if there's a way you can gloss over that bit.

Out of stock. This product will take 4–6 weeks to ship.

What? I look at the screen in annoyance. I can't wait four to six weeks to start mourning the end of my relationship. Those stages are going to take months and I need to get started right now. Shutting my laptop, I get up from the sofa. I'll have to drive to Borders and buy the book instead.

Quickly I throw on some clothes and towel-dry my hair. I don't need to blow-dry it today: I'm not planning on seeing anyone. I'll just nip to the shops and hole myself up with the book until I finish it. I reach over to my bedside cabinet to put on my watch.

And freeze.

It's not there.

Flummoxed, I stare at the bedside cabinet: alarm clock, eye mask, aromatherapy candle . . . but no watch. How can that be? I take my watch off every night before I go to bed. I'm as regular as clockwork, pardon the pun. It's always there.

But not today.

Fuck, where is it?

I know, maybe I forgot to take it off and it fell off my wrist when I was asleep. Clutching the ray of hope, I fling back the duvet and chuck a few pillows around. But it's nowhere to be found. Panic flickers. It was a present from Mum and Dad on my eighteenth birthday. It's engraved on the back and everything. It's got sentimental value. Plus it's my watch for Christ's sake! I can't survive without my watch. How am I going to know what time it is? There's not always a clock to hand, which means I'll have to look at my BlackBerry every five minutes, and what if I have to turn it off in a meeting? Or it's at the bottom of my bag and I have to keep rummaging for it? Or, God forbid, I forget to charge it?

With spiralling panic I dash around the flat on a desperate hunt. No copy of *Elle Décor*, inflatable exercise ball or packet of organic coffee beans is left unturned, but it's nowhere to be found. I must have lost it somewhere, but where?

OK, Charlotte, just calm down, I tell myself firmly, as I finally exhaust all possible hiding places, and myself. Retrace your steps, isn't that what they always say? Last night I was at my old house, then before that the club and before that the gastropub for dinner . . .

Right, I need to start there. Grabbing my car keys, I dash for the door. I'll drive back to the pub and ask someone.

Like the barman.

My stomach goes up and down like I'm on a swing.

Not that I want to see him or anything. I pause by the mirror. Well, all right, maybe a little, but only out of curiosity. Running my fingers through my hair, I dab on a bit of lip gloss. To be honest, I wouldn't care if he was there or not.

He's not here.

Walking into the pub, my eyes go straight for the bar. I feel a clunk of disappointment.

'Hi, can I help you?' A shaggy, red-headed barman pauses from wiping the bar and looks up.

'I wanted to speak to someone about my watch. I lost it last night and I just wondered if it was handed in.'

'I wasn't working last night – hang on.' He smiles, putting down his dishcloth. 'I'll get someone.'

As he walks towards the kitchen, I glance around the pub. Apart from a couple sitting in a discreet table in the corner, it's practically empty.

'Hey, Oliver,' he calls.

My heart jolts. Olly – Oliver. That must be the same person. Oh my God, he *is* here.

There's a pause, and then, 'Yeah?'

Suddenly I realise I'm very, *very* nervous. It's like my breath's got caught in my lungs and I can't breathe it out. Which is ridiculous. He's just a barman.

Except he's not just a barman, is he? pipes up that little voice inside me. *He's* Olly *from last night.*

As he emerges from the kitchen, I see the red-headed barman saying something to him and pointing at me. He looks over. And for a brief moment I think I've got it wrong. He's not Olly at all: he doesn't look anything like him. He's much older, different, chunkier, I realise, looking at his baggy grey T-shirt. I feel a sense of relief. I'm glad it was a mistake. I'm glad this barman isn't Olly. This way is so much simpler.

And yet . . .

As he walks towards me, my stomach does that weird swingy thing again.

His hair might be cut short, he might have a scar above his lip, and he might now be wearing little round glasses, but behind them the pale grey eyes are the same. I didn't make a mistake. Shit.

'Oh, it's you,' he mutters, not smiling.

I falter. Well, that's a great start.

'Um, hi.' I swallow hard. My throat has suddenly dried up. 'I . . . er, was in here last night.'

'I know. I served you,' he deadpans.

I'm getting the distinct feeling I haven't made as good an impression on him in my thirties as I did when I was in my twenties.

'Um . . . yes, well . . . I lost my watch and so I was wondering—'

'Nope, nothing's been found here,' he says, cutting me off.

I feel a snap of irritation. Has he even looked? 'Are you sure?' I try again. 'I mean, it could be underneath a table or—'

'Nope.' He shakes his head. ' 'Fraid not.'

I have to bite my tongue. 'Right, then,' I say stiffly, hauling back my shoulders and meeting his eyes with my sternest stare. 'Well, thanks for looking and for being *so* helpful. I'll leave you my card in case you do happen to find it.' I take one from my purse and lay it on the bar. 'Sorry to trouble you.'

God, he's *such* an arsehole. Talk about people changing. And not for the better, I fume, scratching my ears in agitation.

'What's wrong with your ears?' he says as I'm about to turn and leave.

'Nothing,' I retort defensively.

'They're all inflamed.'

'I had an allergic reaction to some earrings,' I say, attempting a casual voice.

He tries not to smile, but I catch the corner of his lips curl up in amusement.

Damn, why did I have to say that?

'The ones your boyfriend bought you?' he says evenly.

Triggering two thoughts: 1) that's none of your goddamn business and 2) *he was watching me.*

'He's not my boyfriend,' I snap back, rattled. God, he's such a know-it-all.

'He's not?' He raises an eyebrow.

'I mean, not any more.' I'm beginning to get all flustered. I feel as if I've backed myself into a corner and now I can't get out. 'We just broke up.' I look at the floor, wishing it would open up and swallow me. Usually I think before I speak, but for some reason I seem to have reverted to my younger self and my brain seems to have disconnected from my mouth.

'Hey, I'm sorry.' Dipping his chin, Oliver looks at me from under his heavy brows, his expression one of concern. 'Are you OK?'

I look up and meet his eyes. I don't know why, but somehow I seem to want to pour my heart out to a complete stranger.

Only he's not, is he?

'Sort of.' I shrug.

His mouth twists into a smile. 'You know, I'm a really good listener. Working behind this bar, I get to hear a lot of stories, get to dole out advice, not that it's necessarily any good. I'm a bit of an agony uncle.'

I can't help smiling. 'It's a long story.' I can feel myself softening towards him.

'Well, I've got plenty of time.' I was actually just about to knock off, go for a walk in the park, get some fresh air.' He looks at me questioningly. 'Don't know if you're interested . . .?'

I hesitate, then shake my head. 'Thanks, but I should get going,' I say, feeling awkward.

'Of course. I understand – you've got a better offer.'

'No, it's not that,' I protest, then realise he's fooling around and relax.

At that moment there's a loud scuffling as a door opens at the back and in scampers a big, scruffy black dog. With his tail wagging wildly, and a tongue lolling out of the side of his mouth like a long pink ribbon, the dog rushes up to me and starts trying to lick me all over.

'That's Welly,' says Oliver, smiling.

'Hi, Welly. I'm Charlotte.' I smile, patting Welly's head.

'Looks like you made a friend.' Squatting down, Oliver clips on his lead. 'Leave the lady alone, boy. She doesn't want to come for a walk.'

Watching them both, I think about going back to my empty flat, packing up Miles's things, reading that self-help book. After all, I can't go for a walk with someone I've just met.

Except I haven't just met him, have I?

'Maybe some fresh air would do me good.'

Smiling, he passes me the lead.

Chapter Twenty-eight

We leave the pub and head towards the park, which is only a few streets away. Today, though, those streets suddenly seem to stretch out endlessly in front of me, like those roads you get in America that go on for ever and you always see on the front of album covers. Streets that need filling with conversation, I think, sneaking a look at Oliver, who's silently striding next to me on the narrow pavement, hands tucked deep into his battered jeans.

Anxiously I try to think of something to talk about. He obviously doesn't recognise me as Lottie from ten years ago, otherwise he would have said something by now. So I know, what about: 'Guess what? Last night I went to the Canal Club and met you, only you were ten years younger, and you fancied me when I was ten years younger, but when I was ten years younger, I didn't even notice you, and when I introduced us, I completely ignored you.'

Er, yeah, right, Charlotte. On second thoughts, perhaps not. You're aiming for casual chit-chat, not to get carted off in a straightjacket.

'So, Welly, aren't you a handsome doggy?' I coo, resorting to the much safer option of talking to the dog. Welly ignores me and keeps sniffing the pavement. To tell the truth, I'm not brilliant with dogs. I love them, but I'm not what you call a dog person. I don't know how to do the clicky thing with my tongue and I couldn't tell a Labrador from a golden whatsit.

Saying that, this is rather fun, I think, as Welly trots obediently alongside me. Maybe I could *become* a dog person.

'Yes, you are, you're handsome,' I continue, as if Welly has refuted my claim.

Oliver catches my eye and I rub Welly's head casually, as if I'm a pro at this. Welly stops at a tree and begins sniffing it enthusiastically. 'Does that smell nice?' I coo.

His tail wags excitedly.

'He's like me in the perfume hall at Harrods,' I quip, glancing across at Oliver.

See, I can even make doggy jokes too.

'Is that so?' he says evenly.

'Yes, in fact—' I break off as I glance down at Welly. Hang on a minute, what's he doing now? He's stopped sniffing and is sort of squatting. I bend down to have a look. 'Oh shit,' I gasp, shrinking back.

'Yup,' nods Oliver, his mouth twitching with amusement at my reaction. 'Don't worry, I'll take care of it.' He pulls a plastic bag out of his pocket.

'It's OK, I'll do it,' I protest quickly. I don't want him thinking I'm some kind of stupid girl who's afraid to get her hands dirty. *Figuratively* speaking.

'Hey, don't worry about it.'

'No, seriously,' I insist. 'What's a little bit of dog poo?'

He looks at me uncertainly. 'Well, if you're sure.' Shrugging, he passes me the plastic bag. 'Only Welly's been having a few problems recently. His stomach's a little off . . .'

I glance down just in time to see the last of Welly's—

Oh dear Lord, I can't actually finish that sentence. My stomach lurches like a car with a dodgy clutch. In fact I really don't think I can do this.

But you have to, I tell myself firmly. You can't lose face now.

Holding my breath, I bob down and start trying to scoop it up.

'Let me show you a trick. You see, you put your hand inside the bag . . .' he starts explaining.

Unfortunately he's a bit late for that.

'Ewwuuggh.' He winces. Sucking the air between his teeth, he throws me a sympathetic look.

But I hold firm. Summoning up the same air of forced calm that I need to remove the spiders from my shower, which for some reason is where big hairy spiders like to hang out, I tie the ends of the plastic bag together and dump it in a nearby litterbin.

There, done it.

'First time, huh?' He smiles, looking at my shell-shocked expression.

I nod wordlessly. My heart's racing and I feel all trembly.

He laughs. 'It gets easier, trust me.'

With the ice well and truly broken, the conversation flows easily between us as we enter Holland Park and the inner-city buzz gives way to a sanctuary of tennis courts, grass lawns and flower beds laid out like a colourful patchwork quilt. It's a warm, hazy day, and the park buzzes with the sounds of summer: children's laughter, music wafting from transistor radios, footballs being kicked.

After washing my hands thoroughly in the loos, we meander through the serene Japanese garden, walk over the bridge and watch the orange majestic koi swimming beneath. Welly crouches on his haunches, mesmerised by the fish, his nose almost touching the water.

'Gosh, it's so pretty here, isn't it?' I murmur, gazing around me.

'Yeah.' Oliver nods. 'I come here a lot. It's one of my favourite places. You don't feel like you're in London. You really can imagine you're in Kyoto.'

'Have you been?' I ask with interest.

'Yes, a few years ago I spent a month travelling around Japan.'

'Wow.' I nod, feeling both impressed and envious.

'What about you?'

'The furthest I've been in the last few years is Yorkshire. Too busy with work.' I shrug in explanation.

'No one ever dies wishing they'd spent more time at the office,' he replies. 'Or whatever the saying is.'

'Well, my friend did get me tickets for Paris for my birthday,' I say defensively. 'Then again, I don't suppose I'll be going now,' I add as an afterthought.

He furrows his brow questioningly.

'I was supposed to be going with my boyfriend,' I explain.

'Did you guys have a blazing row or something?'

'No, we don't do rows,' I reply ruefully, quoting Miles.

'So what happened?'

Over in the distance, a peacock is fanning out its tail. I watch it for a moment. 'I'm not sure,' I say, shoving my hands deep into the pockets of my jeans. 'It just wasn't right. We weren't right. It's like everything was perfect, but it wasn't.' I look at him, shielding my eyes from the sunlight. 'Does that make any sense?'

'Emotions don't have to make sense.' He shrugs, and we turn and keep walking.

Squirrels scurry across our path as we zigzag around the flower beds.

'He didn't seem your type,' he says after a moment.

'I know, that's what Vanessa always says,' I begin, then pause. 'Hang on, how would you know what my type is?' I stop walking and turn to him.

'Well, he's nothing like Billy Romani.' He raises his eyebrows.

It takes a second for it to register, and then—

'You do recognise me!' I exclaim.

'People don't change that much,' he says in explanation, and starts walking again.

'I know, but I thought—' I stop myself. Actually, I'm not sure what I thought.

'I recognised you as soon as you walked into the pub on Monday night,' he continues as we make our way towards a stretch of lawn, which is filled with picnickers. 'To tell you the truth, I didn't think you remembered me,' he says quietly, glancing at me sideways.

I didn't, whispers a small voice inside my head. And now I'm wondering how on earth that could have happened.

'I wasn't on your radar in those days.'

'Oh, I wouldn't say that.' I laugh nervously, and then catch his expression. Gosh, he actually looks quite peeved about it. I hope he's not holding some kind of grudge against me. A thought stirs. Hang on a minute. 'Is that why you were so mean to me in the pub? To pay me back for ignoring you ten years ago?' I blurt suddenly.

'I don't know what you're talking about,' he refutes, but I can tell by the flash of colour in his cheeks that I've hit the nail on the head. 'When have *I* ever been mean to *you*?' There's no mistaking the way he says that line. It's abundantly clear he thinks I was mean to him.

'Making fun of my allergies,' I retort, 'ridiculing me.'

'Well, do you blame me? Come on, you've got admit they are a bit ridiculous,' he snorts derisively.

'No they're not,' I snap, bristling. In the space of a few seconds our conversation has jackknifed into an argument.

'So let me get this straight, you can't eat any dairy, refined sugar, wheat or nuts, and you can't eat fish more than once a week.' Counting them off on his fingers, he looks at me, eyebrows raised.

Now it's my turn to blush. Actually, put like that, it does sound pretty ridiculous.

'So that means a ninety-nine ice cream with extra sprinkles and double fudge sauce is out of the question?' he demands, completely straight-faced.

Huh?

He motions to a Mr Whippy ice-cream van and I feel myself weaken. God, I'd love an ice cream.

'Absolutely,' I manage, trying to stay mad.

'So if I get one, you're not going to get one too?'

We move towards the ice-cream van.

As Oliver goes up to the window, I grit my teeth. Boy, this is hard. 'No, definitely not.' I shake my head decisively as he orders one for himself.

'A ninety-nine with extra everything, please.' He grins cheerily.

I shoot him a look. I'm sure he did that on purpose.

'Mmm, this is delicious.' He takes a large lick of the ice cream the vendor has just passed to him. 'Sure you don't want even a lick?' he asks, taking a bite of Flake and doing a very good impression of that woman in the advert.

The bastard.

'No, I can't,' I say stiffly, though I can feel myself salivating. 'A nutritionist told me I'm intolerant, remember?'

'Oh, now, I don't know if I agree with that nutritionist.' He cocks his head and looks at me. 'I think you're pretty tolerant. What do you say, Welly?'

Welly wags his tail as if in agreement and I struggle to stifle a giggle.

'In fact I'd say you were *so* tolerant you'd probably agree to holding this ice cream for a minute while I go to the little boys' room.'

'Oh, you reckon?'

'Uhhuh.' He nods. 'And I think your tolerance levels are so high that even if the ice cream starts melting down the cornet, you'll lick it to stop it going all over your hand.'

'Really?'

'Definitely.' Smiling, he thrusts it at me and walks off.

Leaving me standing there feeling my anger melting away faster than the ice cream, which is already trickling on to my fingers in the hot sunshine. I shoot his retreating figure a smile. 'You know what?' I mutter, curling my tongue round the cornet and tasting the sweet vanilla. 'Sod the nutritionist. I think you might be right.'

Emerging from the park, we wind our way down the skinny side streets that lead into Notting Hill and Portobello, the world-famous market, which is brimming with stalls selling everything from flowers to furniture to fake you name it. Weaving our way through the throngs of tourists, we hit the main road and a row of shops and restaurants. Designer clothes, designer lingerie, designer cappuccinos . . . my eyes skim over the windows, until unexpectedly Oliver stops in front of an antique shop.

'I just need to pop in here for a minute,' he explains, reaching for a well-worn brass knocker. Immediately Welly starts wagging his tail manically.

I suddenly recognise it as the shop I walked past with Vanessa a few days ago, when I saw Oliver through the window. 'Oh, OK.' I nod, following him as he pushes open the door.

Inside, the shop is cluttered with all kinds of treasures in its dimly lit corners, and there's a musty smell of pipe smoke and furniture polish.

'Hello, anyone home?' calls out Oliver as Welly sniffs around, pressing his nose up against the legs of an old leather chair.

'Hmm, it doesn't look like there's anyone around. Maybe I should make off with that rather nice French watercolour,' he says in a low voice, pointing to a painting. 'What do you reckon?'

I look at him in horror, then realise he must be joking. 'Ha, ha, very funny,' I whisper.

'No, seriously,' he says, glancing shiftily around. 'Reckon I could get it under my T-shirt?' He picks it up.

Oh my God, he's not joking! I look at him aghast. Jesus. Oliver the nice barman has turned into a thief!

And I'm his accomplice.

'What are you doing?' I hiss frantically, trying to tug it from him. 'Put it down, put it—'

'Ahem.' Someone coughs loudly and I look up to see an elderly man has appeared from the back and is standing there with a pipe in his mouth, staring at us.

'—*down*,' I finish, throwing a strangulated look at Oliver.

Fuck. Rooted to the spot, my mind spins. How did this happen? I was only looking for my watch and now I'm committing daylight robbery. Literally.

'So what've you got there, son?'

'A rather nice sunset by Claude Derbec.'

I close my eyes. This is all too much. I wait for the inevitable.

'Painted when?'

'Around 1870, I think.'

Wait a second. I open one eye.

'Not bad, not bad at all.'

I look at the old man. He's beaming and stroking Welly, who's lapping up the attention and returning it with giant sloppy licks on his hand.

'So you did learn something,' he's saying, with a hint of pride in his voice.

'Well, I had a good teacher.' Oliver is smiling.

Confused, I watch as they embrace.

'Hello, Granddad. How are you doing?'

'*Granddad!*' I repeat in astonishment.

And anger. I could kill him. I really could.

Oliver throws me a sheepish look. 'Sorry, I couldn't resist. You should have seen your face.'

I shoot him a look of fury. I want to throw something at him, but considering I'm surrounded by antiques, I'd best not.

'And who's your lady friend?'

'Oh, hi. I'm Charlotte,' I say, remembering myself. 'Nice to meet you.' I hold out my hand. He grabs it and hits my knuckles in a hip-hop handshake.

'Granddad's a huge fan of Jay-Z,' smiles Oliver, seeing my expression, then adds in explanation, 'He's got great-grand-children, my sister's kids.'

'So, tell me, what do you see in my grandson?' he's asking, looking at me.

I feel myself colour. 'Um . . .'

'She's not my girlfriend,' jumps in Oliver, his cheeks doing exactly the same as mine are doing. 'We're not . . . you know,' he says awkwardly, gesturing with his thumb back and forth be-tween us.

'Ah, I see,' nods his granddad, puffing on his pipe and surveying us both with interest, before demanding, 'Well, why the hell not?' and letting out a loud, rumbling laugh. 'Time you got yourself a girlfriend. You can't stay single for ever, my boy.'

Oliver looks as if he wants the ground to open up and swallow him and I smile in commiseration, while paying absolutely no attention whatsoever to the little voice in my head, which is gleefully whispering, *He doesn't have a girlfriend. He's single.*

'Charlotte and I just met,' Oliver explains. 'Well, actually, we met a long time ago, but we've just . . .' he searches around for the right word, and I wonder what he's going to say '. . . reconnected,' he finishes.

'I see,' says his granddad, raising his eyebrows, which scuttle up his forehead like two large white caterpillars. 'How marvellous.' He smiles. 'Tea?'

He shuffles into the back to make tea, with Oliver joining him to help, leaving Welly and me exploring. It's like the old curiosity shop. Everything is piled high on top of everything else – an engraved silver pistol, a stuffed peacock, a mahogany table with two large carved claws for feet . . .

'Wow, you've got some amazing things,' I enthuse, as Oliver and his granddad reappear, carrying a tray on which are precariously balanced various mismatched cups and saucers and a teapot shaped like a man in a top hat.

'My Alice in Wonderland teapot,' he says, observing me looking curiously. 'A thirties original, hand-painted, with no chips or cracks on the glazing. It's in perfect condition. One of only fifty sets ever made.' He beams, flourishing it high in the air. A stream of hot tea pours forth from the Mad Hatter's prominent nose. 'A real collector's piece.' He passes me a teacup. 'Milk and sugar?'

'No, I'm fine.'

But it's too late – he's already adding both.

'What was that, dear?'

'Um, nothing . . . thank you.'

He smiles cheerfully and passes Oliver a cup, then rattles a biscuit tin. 'Shortbread finger?'

I hesitate, my eyes flicking over to Oliver, who's watching me with interest. 'Er, yes, thank you.'

Well, he's such a sweet old man, I can't say no, can I? Plus I think the fact that I'd eaten nearly half of Oliver's ice cream by the time he emerged from the toilets disproves the nutritionist's theory that I'm intolerant to wheat, refined sugar and dairy.

'So how are you, Granddad?'

'Oh, you know.' He waves his hand vaguely, a sad expression falling over his face. 'I'll survive.'

'Granddad's got to shut the shop,' explains Oliver, patting his granddad's arm supportively. 'He's been here over sixty years, so he's finding it a bit difficult.'

'Oh, no,' I cry. 'That's awful. Why do you have to leave?'

'Things move on, times change,' shrugs his granddad, taking a sip of tea, his hand trembling slightly.

'It's got nothing to do with time moving on,' gasps Oliver angrily. 'His lease has gone up to something crazy and he can't afford it any more. He's being squeezed out.'

'By who?' I exclaim.

'Probably another overpriced coffee chain,' tuts Oliver, not bothering to hide his disgust. 'Or one of the big designer stores. They're all moving in around here now, taking over the neighbourhood, trying to make it like bloody Knightsbridge.'

'Hey, now, there's no need for swearing,' reprimands his granddad, shooting him a disapproving look.

'Well, I can't help it – it's disgusting. They have no respect for someone who made the area what it is. It's all about money, profits.'

'This shop has certainly seen me through some times. I met my late wife, Betty, here,' remembers his granddad, turning to me. She came in to buy a china teapot. Yes, she did,' he adds as if I don't believe him. 'Ended up with a whole lot more than that,' he quips, and laughs his rumbling laugh. 'After she passed away, I thought about selling up, but to do what?' He shrugs his shoulders. 'Antiques are in my blood, and look at me, I'm a bit of an antique myself now.'

'But what are you going to do with all your antiques?' I ask, then immediately regret it. I don't want to upset him.

'EBay,' he says simply.

'*EBay?*' Trust me, that was not the answer I was expecting.

'I've been having lessons from my great-grandchildren,' he continues, dipping his shortbread finger in his teacup. 'Apparently, it's all the rage. I even have a PayPal account.' He flashes me a smile and I smile back.

'It won't be the same, though,' mutters Oliver angrily.

'Ah, well, what can you do?' sighs his granddad with the calmness of a man who's lived through a lot. 'Everything has to come to an end.' There's a pause as he looks at us both. 'I've spent a lifetime dealing in expensive objects, but do you know what's the most valuable?'

'What?' we both ask with interest.

'Time,' he says simply. 'You can't buy back time, not for any price. There are no second chances. Every second is precious, so don't waste a single one. Time, quite literally, is priceless.'

I look at him, absorbing his words. Is that what I've been given? A second chance?

'More tea?'

I zone back to see his granddad looking at me. 'Um . . . yes, thanks.' And pushing those thoughts to the back of my mind, I hold out my cup. 'That would be lovely.'

Chapter Twenty-nine

Two cups of tea and three shortbread fingers later, Oliver gets roped into helping his granddad pack up some of the heavier items for the imminent move. I offer my assistance, but I'm quickly rebuffed by his granddad.

'Gracious, no, this is man's work,' he puffs from behind a life-sized stuffed grizzly bear. Standing on its hind legs, it has its front paws outstretched and its mouth frozen in a silent snaggle-toothed roar.

'Well, if you're sure.' Normally I'd feel obliged to argue with such a blatantly sexist comment, but in this case perhaps not.

'One, two, three, *hup*.' With a loud grunt the bear is suddenly hoisted into the air and flung over Oliver's shoulder in a fire-man's lift. His legs buckle. 'Jesus, Granddad, this thing weighs a ton.'

'Stop complaining. When I was your age, I could carry one on each shoulder.'

'What? There used to be a *pair*?' He grimaces as a cloud of dust envelops him.

'Aye. I sold Fred to a Japanese man in 1952, but there's only Ginger left now.' He sighs wistfully and strokes the scary-looking bear fondly as if it's a pet.

'She's called Ginger?' I ask doubtfully.

'After the dancer.' He nods proudly. 'Both beauties, don't you think?'

'I think I'm going to collapse, that's what I think,' complains Oliver, still trying to lug the beast across the shop floor.

Quickly stepping out of his way, I take it as my cue to leave.

'OK, well, I better be going. It was nice to meet you.' I go to shake hands with Oliver's granddad, but he's having none of the formality. Grabbing hold of me, he plants a whiskery kiss full of shortbread crumbs on each cheek.

'Are you sure you wouldn't like a nice silver milk jug?' he suggests. 'Or a set of horse-brasses?'

'No, thank you.' I smile as I'm released from his grip. I turn to Oliver, but he's still weighed down by a grizzly balancing precariously on his shoulder. 'Well . . . um, bye.'

I sort of hover awkwardly in the middle of the shop floor, watched by the eagle eyes of his granddad and Wellington, who both seem to stop what they were doing, be it sniffing the leg of a dining-room table or dusting a horse-brass.

Oliver pauses from grappling with the bear and sticks his head out from underneath the wide roar. 'Oh, hey.' He's all red-faced and out of breath. 'You're leaving?'

If I'm not mistaken, he looks a bit dismayed. I feel a tweak of pleasure.

'Yeah, I'm going to walk back.' I nod vigorously, feeling flustered all of a sudden. 'Keep looking for my watch . . .' I trail off, and begin chewing my thumbnail, before realising and snatching my hand out of my mouth. What am I doing? I never chew my nails any more. Not now I have manicures. 'You know, I need to . . .'

'Retrace your steps.'

'. . . retrace my steps.'

We both speak at the same time, then laugh at the coincidence, but the words aren't lost on me. I don't think they're lost on him either, because he gives me a look. Or am I imagining it?

Probably, I decide, grabbing hold of myself. I mean, I'm not exactly at my most lucid right now, am I? I've barely had any sleep, I've just broken up with my boyfriend, I'm probably experiencing a sugar high from the ice cream and shortbread fingers, *and* I'm thinking all sorts about a barman I met ten years ago, and who's about to be suffocated by a giant stuffed bear.

I don't remember this being one of the stages I read about in the glossary for the relationship book.

'Are you OK to walk back?'

'Yeah, fine, fine.' I nod, hastily batting away his concerns with my hand. 'I left my car at the pub.'

'Do you have far to drive?'

'No, I only live five minutes away, by the church, Spencer Avenue,' I gabble. I've come over all hot and jittery, and feel the urgent need to go outside and get some fresh air.

'Well, if you're around, maybe pop in the pub later.'

'Yeah, maybe.'

There's a pause.

'Well, thanks again for the tea.' I turn to his granddad, who immediately colours and pretends to be engrossed in his horse-brasses.

'Oh, you're welcome, my dear,' he says, feigning surprise, as if he's just heard me and not just spent the last five minutes eavesdropping.

'Good luck with Ginger,' I add cheerfully to Oliver, trying to sound all casual. Then, giving Wellington a quick pat on the head, I stride purposefully out of the shop.

Correction: bang into an eighteenth-century cabinet, bruise my knee, wrestle with the door, which appears to have stuck, finally manage to push it open, forget to mind the step and sort of trip outside on to the street. I honestly don't know what's wrong with me. It's like I've suddenly regressed to my clumsy twenty-one-year-old self, I think, as I quickly make my way down the street, my cheeks stinging with embarrassment. No, twenty-two-year-old self, I reflect, thinking of last night's birthday party.

After the dusty darkness inside the antique shop, it's blind-ingly bright outside. In the rush this morning I didn't bring my sunglasses. Squinting in the sunshine, I spot a nearby stall selling cheap sunnies. I know, I'll buy a pair to walk home with, I decide, hurrying over.

There's quite a crowd. Clustered around the racks of glasses, people are jostling to try on all the different styles. For a moment I nearly abandon the mission. This is why I buy my sunglasses at Harvey Nics. That and the fact that they're genuine designer glasses and have proper UV lenses, I think disparagingly, managing to grasp a pair that are copies of the latest style from Chanel.

Then again, these have UV lenses too, I notice with surprise as I pop them on. The stallholder thrusts a mirror at me and I glance at my reflection. Of course when you put them on, they're going to look cheap and plasticky and—

Wow, these look fabulous.

I turn my head from side to side, feeling an old stirring of excitement. It's a feeling I haven't had for years, but I recognise it immediately: the thrill of finding a bargain.

'Do you have any more of those she's wearing?' A woman gestures at me.

'No, that's the last pair.' The stallholder shakes his head.

It's like a shot of adrenalin. I have the last pair! Which of course makes them even *more* of a bargain.

Digging out a tenner, I quickly pay for the sun glasses and start walking back towards the park. Gosh, what an absolute *steal*, I muse, checking out my reflection in every shop window I pass and feeling the bargain-hunter's buzz. I wonder if there's anything else I can buy? Maybe I should have a quick look.

Automatically I go to check the time, but of course my wrist is bare and so I reach for my BlackBerry. I can see what time it is on there, I realise, feeling for it in my pocket. Then I remember. It's in the car. I left it in the little centre well.

As it registers, I feel a knee jerk of annoyance, but it's quickly replaced by something else: a flicker of freedom, release, liberation. As if a window of opportunity is opening before me, and like a schoolgirl, I feel as if I've escaped the confines of time, which are as real to me as any classroom walls, and I have a chance to play truant from my life.

Normally right now I'd be taking the short cut and hurrying home, but all at once I don't feel like hurrying, which is unusual for me, as I hurry everywhere. Even to the loo. But without my watch it's like time becomes this free-flowing thing, not divided into seconds and minutes and hours, to be ticked off, watched, kept to.

And so, taking the long way home through the market, I slow my pace down. It doesn't come naturally. My legs are programmed to trot briskly and my arms to pump up and down like pistons, but I force myself to stroll past the stalls and pavement cafés. To enjoy just *being*, rather than rushing from somewhere to somewhere. Inhaling deep lungfuls of air, instead of my usual shallow breaths, I take a moment to just stop and look around me. I smile to myself.

For the first time in a long time I can, quite literally, smell the coffee.

I have no idea how long I spend meandering down Portobello, but I do know I keep stopping to lust over gold-hammered rings filled with a kaleidoscope of semi-precious stones from Nepal and to marvel at ingenious photograph frames made from the keys of old typewriters.

God, I'd forgotten how much fun flea markets can be, I muse, as I'm distracted by a yellow Indian blouse hanging from a nearby rail. Fluttering in the warm breeze, the tiny sequins sewn round the neck catch the sunlight and twinkle, like a dozen tiny stars, and before I know it I'm haggling with the dreadlocked stallholder and getting it for six pounds. Six pounds! It's incredible. No wonder I always used to buy my clothes from markets when I was younger.

Delighted with my shopping, I'm ready for the next amazing find and I don't have to look far. Next door is a small Chinese lady with dozens of racks filled with vintage clothes, and still on a high from my recent purchases, I rise to the challenge and try nearly everything on in the tiny makeshift changing room. A lot of it's horrible, some of it's worse than horrible, and then just as the buzz is fading and my arms begin aching, I find it: an incredible blue silk dress with a plunging neckline that looks like something you'd see in *Vogue* for a month's salary. It's totally unique. I'll never see anyone wearing another one. I buy it without a second thought.

Now I'm on a roll. Further along is a stall selling second-hand shoes. Almost breathless with excitement, I grab a pair of gold stilettos. Ooh, these look fab, and such a bargain, I tell myself, sticking my feet in. Ouch. The front pinches my toes. I try to wiggle them, only now my foot's slipping forwards. In fact these are actually really uncomfortable. Plus the plastic heel is ugly, I realise, looking at them in the mirror.

I freeze. What am I doing? Snatching my feet out of the shoes, I hastily put them back on the rack. My younger self might have reminded me of the joys of shopping for clothes in flea markets, but there's one thing I *have* learned now I'm older.

I make a mental note to add it to my list:

19. Cheap shoes suck. Save up and buy designer.

Because there are some things in life that are worth spending money on, and Jimmy Choos are one of them.

And happily slipping my feet back into my gorgeous sandals, with their full arch support and hand-stitched leather soles, I set off towards the park.

Chapter Thirty

Only when I reach my car do I finally glance at the clock on the dashboard and realise how much time has passed.

And get the shock of my life.

Bloody hell, it's nearly six o'clock! I stare at the electronic digits in shocked disbelief. I've been *hours*. I didn't just lose track of time, I lost a whole day! It slipped away without me even noticing.

Because you were having fun, chimes that little voice inside my head.

Automatically I feel a sharp stab of guilt. I'm not supposed to be having fun. I'm not supposed to be rediscovering the thrill of flea markets, going on walks with cute barmen or getting whiskery kisses from granddads; I'm supposed to be mourning the loss of my relationship and looking for my watch.

Which is still missing, I remind myself.

I focus back on it. Where was I before I got sidetracked? Ah, yes, retracing my steps . . . My mind spools back. If it's not in my flat or the pub, then I must have lost it in the club – which will be closed now, I tell myself quickly, feeling relieved – or my old house.

Turning the ignition, I stick the car into gear and pull away from the kerb. I'll drive over there now. Maybe it fell off my wrist when I was digging around in the fridge for some milk. I have a flashback to the unidentifiable foodstuffs lurking inside and a shudder runs up my spine. On second thoughts, please God don't let it be in the fridge. I don't think I'm brave enough to stick my hand in there again.

I start heading north towards the flyover and it's not long before I see the now-familiar signs for the diversion. Though of course I don't see any workmen, I muse, filtering into the single lane past the large diggers and cranes that are sitting empty. Typical. In the middle of cursing this peculiar habit of British roadworks appearing overnight in an explosion of orange cones and freshly dug holes and then just sort of sitting there for days on end, causing huge traffic jams, my phone rings.

'Hello?'

'I tried you at home, but you weren't there,' accuses the voice on the other end of the line.

'Oh, hi, Mum,' I say automatically. 'Thanks for the card, and the vouchers. I meant to call you last night when I got in, but it was too late.'

'So did you have a good time on your birthday?'

I think about last night. I'm not sure if 'good' is the right adjective. 'Yeah, it was, um . . .' I try to think of the right one and settle on '. . . interesting.'

'Any surprises?'

'You could say that,' I murmur, remembering me at the club, on the dance floor, talking to Olly, his tattoo . . .

'I knew it!' she gasps victoriously down the line, cutting off my train of thought. 'I said it to your father. Didn't I say it to you, David? Didn't I?' She's hollering at my father, who I can hear grunting in the background. I can picture them now, her on the phone in the hallway, him in the living room trying to read the paper in peace.

'Knew what?' I say in confusion. God, what is my mother going on about now? Holding the phone out from my ear, I pull up at the traffic lights on the diversion.

'Now, now, don't keep us all waiting!' She laughs shrilly. She sounds almost giddy and for a moment I wonder if she's been drinking. She has been known to have a couple of Bianco and lemonades before dinner. Or *tea* I should say.

'Mum, I don't know what you're talking about,' I say, a little impatiently. Oh good, the lights have changed. I put the car into gear.

'The proposal!' she gasps. 'What other kind of surprise do you think I'm talking about?'

Suddenly it registers. When Mum said 'surprise', she thought . . . and I thought . . .

Oh shit.

My heart sinks. I've got to tell her the truth. Only it's going to be like telling a lottery winner there's been a mix-up and actually they don't have the winning ticket.

'So?' Mum's voice nags. 'Are you going to keep your poor old mother in suspense?'

Deep breath. Here we go. 'We broke up.'

There's silence and then—

'What?' She's almost speechless with shock.

I quickly take advantage of the fact. 'Actually, I broke up with him. It wasn't right, Mum,' I try explaining quickly. 'I thought it could work, I really wanted it to work, but it didn't, it couldn't, and when I stopped trying to convince myself and took a moment to look hard at my relationship—'

She cuts me off. 'Have you gone mad?'

Taking the same short cut as always and turning into the side street, I reflect upon the past week's events. Bumping into my twenty-one-year-old self, hanging out together at a concert, going clubbing, turning into a cougar, breaking up with my boyfriend . . .

'Quite possibly,' I admit, whizzing past the parked cars. Maybe Mum's right. Maybe I have flipped my lid and lost the plot. Maybe I'm making a total and utter mess of my life and I'm going to really regret this.

'What on earth has got into you?' she reprimands hotly. 'I'm sure if you call him up now, he'll take you back.'

'I don't want him to take me back!' I exclaim. And if there was any doubt in my mind, there isn't now. 'I'm not in love with him, and I don't think he's in love with me either,' I add, remembering how concerned he was to be losing the house and the survey money, not me.

'But he seemed perfect for you.'

'On paper, yes,' I admit, 'but not in reality. Miles is a great guy, but not for me, Mum. He just never really understood me.'

'Do you think I understand your father?' she butts in. 'Thirty-five years we've been married and that man's still a mystery to me.'

'Mum, that's different. You love Dad.'

'But, Charlotte —'

As I zoom under the bridge, the line suddenly goes dead. I feel a beat of secret relief and, chucking my phone on the passenger seat, I put my foot down.

As I turn into my old street, I spot my vintage VW parked back outside the house. Well, I use the word 'parked' loosely, but it's about three feet away from the kerb and left at a jaunty angle, as if someone was just driving along and got bored and abandoned the car in the middle of the road.

Which, now I come to think of it, I was wont to do, I reflect, pulling up behind the shiny new bumper. Obviously it's just come back from the garage, I note, turning off the engine. Hopefully she followed my advice about taking a male friend with her to pick it up. That way, she won't have got ripped off, like I did.

Feeling cheered up, I climb the steps to my old house and reach for the brass dolphin door knocker. I rap loudly. There's the sound of footsteps and then the door swings open.

'Hi, it's me again.'

I'm expecting my younger self to be hung-over, I'm expecting her to be suffering from the worst headache of her life, and I'm expecting her to look like shit. What I'm not expecting is for her to be crying her eyes out.

'Oh my God, are you OK?'

Tears are streaming down Lottie's face, and her eyes are all red and puffy. In between gasping snorts, she nods vigorously. 'Yes . . . fine . . .'

I was always a crap liar.

'What on earth's happened?' I ask anxiously.

Blowing her nose on a crumpled length of damp toilet roll, she looks at me with total despair. A fist of worry clenches my stomach. Oh my God, what can it be? She looks utterly distraught. Panicked, I start flicking through my stash of memories. I can't ever remember being this upset. What can it be?

'Billy Romani,' she manages to hiccup, before dissolving into more heartfelt sobs.

At the mention of his name, I feel myself stiffen. Of course. *Now* I remember being this upset. It was when I discovered he'd gone off with another girl.

'What about him?' I demand, feeling like the protective big sister.

Her chest is heaving up and down, and she begins stammering between hiccups, 'He's been seen . . . with that posh girl . . . who looks like a rabbit . . .'

'Liberty the trustafarian,' I say grimly.

Her face screws up like a crumpled paper bag and she lets out a pitiful wail. It takes a few moments before she can speak, and then it's more of a stammer. 'Apparently, they are seeing each other. Apparently, he's in . . .' she hesitates, as if unable to say the words '. . . *in love with her*,' she gasps, and then buries her face in her piece of toilet roll.

'He's in love with her trust fund,' I console, putting my arm round her.

I'm rewarded by a brief smile, but then she starts sobbing again.

'Hey, come on, it's not so bad,' I soothe, giving her a squeeze. 'Look on the bright side – at least I warned you about him.' I feel a swell of relief that I managed to do that. 'At least you didn't go home with him after the concert. Now that would be much worse.' I see Lottie's expression. 'Oh my God, you did go home with him, didn't you?'

She nods mutely.

'After everything I said?'

'I know, but I thought . . .'

'You knew better,' I finish.

Her face flushes.

And my heart sinks. I should have known. I've always been crap at taking advice. I've always been stubborn. And when I was younger, I was so headstrong. I always did exactly what I wanted. I never listened to anyone.

Not even myself, I realise, suddenly feeling a burst of anger at Lottie for not taking my advice. I mean, how the hell am I supposed to help myself if I won't listen? But it's not just her I'm angry at; I'm angry at myself. For not stopping her, for not being able to prevent her from making the same stupid mistake as me. After all, isn't that what I'm here for? To protect her? To prevent her from doing all the things I wish I hadn't?

Regret stabs. I've let Lottie down. I've let myself down. I had a chance to put things right and I blew it. Feeling like a complete and utter failure, I glance at Lottie, her face puffy and blotchy with tears, and unexpectedly my anger vanishes as quickly as it appeared. Experience has taught me to stay away from players like Billy Romani, but it's also taught me compassion, I realise, feeling a rush of sympathy. Because if anyone knows how bad she feels right now, it's me, isn't it?

'Do you want to talk about it?' I ask gently.

She glances at me with surprise, then blowing her nose loudly, nods and sits down on the front doorstep. I sit next to her. Hugging her knees to her chest, she stares down at her bare feet. 'After you dropped me off, I went back to the pub to see if he was still there,' she says sheepishly.

'And was he?' I ask, although I already know the answer.

'Uh-huh.' She nods. 'He was still hanging around outside with the rest of the band, so I went with him to the party . . .' She trails off and falls silent for a moment as she thinks back.

As do I.

For me, that night seems like a lifetime ago, and it's hard to think about it without also thinking about everything else that followed. The pain of rejection, the embarrassment, the regret . . . If I really try, though, I can isolate that evening, focus in on my feelings, remember how I felt. Young, happy, *invincible*. God, I felt like a completely different person back then.

'It was amazing,' she sighs, and despite herself, her eyes flash with excitement.

'I know,' I murmur.

'You do?' She glances at me in surprise, her brow furrowed.

'Er, I mean, I know what that feels like,' I say quickly, snapping back and correcting myself. 'To have an amazing night with someone. Anyone,' I add.

She looks at me suspiciously – as if she could never imagine someone like me having a night of amazing sex with anyone, let alone a leather-clad rocker.

'Well, anyway, the next morning when I left, he promised he'd ring me as he was doing a gig in Leeds that night, which is why he couldn't be at my birthday party.' She pulls a face and takes another drag of her cigarette. 'But that was all lies. He wasn't doing a gig. He was with that girl.' Her eyes fill up again and tears spill over her eyelashes and down her cheeks. 'How could he?'

Because he's a selfish, egotistical prick, that's why! I want to cry, but of course she's not going to take too kindly to that. I know, because when Vanessa said the same thing, we had a huge row and I ended up defending him and stomping home in a huff. But if I can't tell her that, what can I tell her? The truth?

I hesitate, contemplating how much I can say, when the phone rings and a voice from inside shouts, 'Lottie, it's your parents,' and someone I don't recognise appears at the door, trailing a phone on a long extension lead.

'Oh, thanks.' She nods, taking the receiver, then glances back at me. 'Sorry, I won't be a minute.'

Now this will be interesting, I muse, watching as she presses the phone to her ear.

'Mum! Hello, how are you?' she exclaims, a wide smile bursting over her face.

I look at her with astonishment. I don't know what I was expecting, but I wasn't expecting this. She seems so pleased to hear from Mum.

'Billy? No, he hasn't called.'

I'm aghast. What? I told Mum about Billy Romani? I can't believe it. I never confide in Mum about anything any more, certainly not anything to do with my love life.

'No, I'm fine,' reassures Lottie, before shooting me a look. 'I'm here with a friend.'

I stop staring and manage a smile.

'OK, well, give my love to Dad, won't you? And remember, I'm coming up next weekend, so I'll see you then . . . Yes, I'm really looking forward to it. We can go shopping together. I'll spend the vouchers you bought me.' She laughs, and I'm sure I can hear Mum laughing on the other end of the line. 'OK, bye, Mum! I'll call you tomorrow. Love you too.' She hangs up and turns to me, her face still suffused with a large smile.

I feel a beat of regret. I never have those conversations with my mum any more. Nowadays ours are so snatched, so abrupt, so much less intimate. Like our relationship, I realise, trying to remember the last time we went shopping together.

'So do you speak to your parents every day?' I ask curiously.

'Oh, yeah, we're really close.' She nods without hesitation. 'I'm lucky. Some people don't get on with their parents, they never go see them or anything, but mine are great. They're really excited about me getting this job in London, and really supportive, but I know they miss me. And I miss them.'

'That's great.' I smile, but inside I can't help feeling saddened at how far my parents and I have drifted apart. I hardly ring them these days, and it's ages since I last saw them. Guilt tugs as I consider how I've neglected them. I think about Mum calling me in the car, asking about Miles. She still worries about me, even now, even if she has a funny way of showing it. That's just Mum.

'Anyway, where were we?' Lottie looks at me expectantly.

'Oh . . . um.' I try quickly gathering my thoughts, remembering our conversation about Billy Romani, about what I wanted to say, all the words of advice. There's so much, and yet part of me can't help thinking it's too late now. The moment's gone and so instead I think of the advice I read earlier from the self-help book on Amazon.

'At first you will experience disbelief and shock about what's just happened,' I opine. 'But that's normal after a break-up. Or encounter,' I add tactfully.

'Says who?' she says, a tad sulkily.

'I read about it in this really good book about break-ups,' I explain. 'In fact I was going to buy it today, but I got side-tracked.'

'Why were you going to buy it?' She frowns.

I hesitate. I don't particularly want to talk about it. But then again, what the hell. 'Because I just broke up with my boyfriend,' I confess. Now I'm the one hugging my knees to my chest and staring at the ground.

'You have a boyfriend?' She sounds shocked.

'Did,' I correct her.

'Wow.' She looks astonished. 'I mean . . . I just thought 'cos you're older you were probably divorced.'

'*Divorced?*' I gasp. Jesus. I thought it was bad enough my mother wanting me to be married, but now my younger self has got me pegged as a divorcee. Then again, I always did have a big mouth and never thought before I opened it.

'Well, you weren't wearing a ring,' she explains, looking remorseful.

'No, I'm not divorced. Or married,' I add, just to make it clear. 'I'm single.'

The irony isn't lost on me. Here we are, sitting side by side, and ten years apart, both single and both talking about men.

Or lack of.

Some things never really change, do they? Except of course now I'm older and more mature and I read self-help books so I know how to deal with these things, I tell myself quickly, relieved I'm not the sobbing wreck I once was.

'God, I'm sorry,' says Lottie. 'So what are you going to do?'

I think back to the blurb on Amazon. 'Well, it's important to mourn the end of a relationship, as this will allow you to move on,' I say, quoting from memory.

Lottie tucks her hair behind her ears and frowns. 'What does that mean?'

'It means you have to get closure,' I explain. I've read a lot about closure. Closure is a big deal in self-help books.

'*Closure*?' she repeats, as if the word's foreign.

And I suppose it is to her, I realise. After all, at twenty-two, I had no idea about any of this stuff. Not like now, I think, feeling proud of how much I've grown. Growing is a big deal in self-help books too.

'You'll need to spend time dealing with what's happened,' I reflect, trying to use the benefit of hindsight. 'But it's going to take time, so you need to be kind to yourself, pamper yourself, spend time with your good friends.' I'm talking about Vanessa. Even now, ten years later, she's always been there for me, whatever's happened. Just as she was back then. My mind flashes back to her sitting next to me on my futon, stroking my hair as I sobbed my heart out. She didn't have to say anything. Just knowing she was there was enough. 'But what's really important to remember is that you can't rush this important healing process,' I add, thinking back to the self-help book. Gosh, I really do sound like Dr Phil, don't I? I feel a beat of satisfaction. See, at least I can be of some help, give some good advice.

'Why not?' she demands, arching an eyebrow.

An eyebrow, I suddenly notice, that has been aggressively plucked to within an inch of its life. She must have used those tweezers I gave her, I realise somewhat regretfully. On second thoughts, it wasn't such a good idea. I was aiming for Jessica Alba arches, not permanently surprised.

'Because it's a process,' I repeat patiently.

'Bollocks,' she admonishes.

I look at her in shock.

'That's just bollocks. Why should I have to go through a frigging process, while he goes out with another girl?' she gasps angrily.

'You're obviously at the angry stage,' I say, trying to calm her down.

'But he told me he was falling in love with me!' she cries.

I raise an eyebrow. If there's one thing I've learned as I've got older, it's never to believe a man who says he's falling in love with you just as he's falling into bed with you.

'God! He's such a liar!' she tuts hotly.

'No, this is good – it's important to get your anger out.' I nod encouragingly. 'All these stages are really crucial in getting over something like this. First you go through shock, then depression, now anger.' I'm trying to remember all the different stages.

'I was just a one-night stand to him, and to think . . .' She lets out an angry howl. 'I could kill him!' She falls silent, and drags on a cigarette, staring off into the middle distance.

'Acceptance is the final stage. Once you reach this, you'll be able to deal with anything life throws at you.' I pause, thinking about my own life, what's happened in the last ten years since I was wearing Lottie's shoes and for a moment it's like I'm talking to myself. 'You'll be able to move on.'

'Actually, I do feel more positive.'

'Really?' I feel a beat of delight.

'In fact I feel a load better.'

'Wow, that's great.' I smile with satisfaction. Though to be honest, I actually thought it would take a bit longer than a few minutes to go through the process, but I've obviously really helped her. 'And in time you'll feel healed enough to begin a new relationship.'

'Mmm, yeah.' She nods distractedly.

'Though don't worry if at first you're a little nervous.'

'Mmm . . .'

Hang on a minute. I suddenly get the impression she's not listening. 'Did you hear what I just said?'

'God, he's really hot.'

'Who is? Billy Romani?' I look at her puzzled.

'Billy who?' she says pointedly, as if to say, 'Keep up, Grandma.' '*Him.*' She gestures with her head, and all at once I realise what's grabbed her attention. Across the road I spot a jogger. Bare-chested, with a body to die for, he's stopped running and is stretching out his muscles. 'Cor, he's gorgeous,' she sighs lustfully.

'Lottie, were you listening to anything I just said?' I feel a snap of annoyance.

'Sorry . . . um.' She turns to me, her eyes flashing and a big grin on her face. Her tears have miraculously vanished and there's two spots of colour high in her cheeks. 'You were saying something about stages?' she says vaguely.

'Yes, and it's really important,' I remind her.

'Well, I'm sorry, but you can keep all that claptrap,' she replies, looking back at the jogger. 'Do you want to know my advice for getting over a man?'

I look at her questioningly, then back at the jogger, just in time to see him smile over, and her smile back flirtatiously. All thoughts of Billy Romani completely forgotten.

'Get underneath another one.'

Chapter Thirty-one

As weekends go, this isn't up there with my best. My search of my old bedroom fails to show up my watch, which I now fear I might have lost in the Canal Club. Leaving Lottie flirting with Mr Bare-Chested, I drive home. It half crosses my mind to pop into the pub and say hi to Oliver, but it quickly crosses back again. What am I thinking? Don't be so silly, Charlotte. He was probably only being polite.

But then so was I, I tell myself defensively.

Instead I stay in that evening and pack up the rest of Miles's things, which plunges me further into gloom. To be honest, even though I know I've done the right thing, it's still quite depressing. I console myself that we can remain friends. After all, we're both reasonable adults; we can be amicable about this. Like when celebrities split up and issue those joint press release statements, I think, remembering the one I did for Melody when she split up from her footballer husband.

I set about concocting one as I clear out Miles's sock drawer:

Charlotte and Miles have made an amicable decision to separate. Their decision was made by best friends with a huge amount of love and respect for one another. Their relationship has ended, but their friendship continues. They would request that the media respect their privacy at this sensitive time.

Gosh, it sounds great, doesn't it? We sound so mature and laid-back about it all, so cool. It makes you almost *want* to split up with your boyfriend.

In fact by Sunday morning I feel cheered up and am imagining Miles and I doing Demi-and-Bruce-type dinners with our future partners. That is until Miles arrives at my flat waving an itemised telephone bill and demanding £7.38 'because it's the principle and everyone has to be financially responsible', bitterly dumps two bin-liners full of my stuff on my doorstep and then informs me in a triumphant voice that he's got tickets to see the James Bond tribute band Licence to Thrill, and he's taking Helen, his bookkeeper, who apparently is a *huge* fan (and has a huge cleavage), and who I know has always had a not-so-secret crush on him.

On second thoughts, perhaps forget the Demi-and-Bruce dinners.

I lie awake on Sunday night, unable to sleep for mulling over recent events in my head. I feel as if I've made a complete mess of things. Miles now hates me, and my younger self hasn't taken any of my advice. And what's worse, I don't blame her. I mean, when it comes to love and relationships, I've hardly got it sussed, have I? What was I doing, thinking I could give advice about men? Maybe she does know better. What was it she said? The conversation starts replaying in my head: 'My advice for getting over a man – get underneath another one.'

Abruptly my mind throws up an image of Oliver. I throw it back again like a hot potato. Honestly, as if. That's just nonsense. You can't go rushing from one man to the next. Even if I did think he was sexy and wanted to sleep with him – *which I don't* – he's not going to be interested in me, not when I ignored him all those years ago. No doubt he's forgotten about me already.

But that's fine. Meeting him again was one of those weird, interesting coincidences, but I don't plan to make a habit of it. After all, it was ten years since I last saw him. Chances are, it's going to be another ten till I see him again.

* * *

I wake up on Monday morning in a much better mood. It's like that saying 'Today's the first day of the rest of your life.' So I've decided. Last week was full of surprises and all kinds of upheaval, but this week I'm determined not to have any more surprises. I can do without it. So I'm going to put everything that's happened behind me. I'm going to forget about relationships and men and giving advice to my younger self and concentrate one hundred per cent on work.

And I'm going to need it. I've got a big week ahead of me. Despite it being a bank holiday today, I still have to go into the office. Tomorrow's the press launch for Star Smile UK and there's masses to organise. Plus I'm supposed to be 'touching base' with Larry Goldstein sometime today, so I need to focus.

In fact it's probably a really good thing I'm not going to have any other distractions, I decide, hurrying into my walk-in wardrobe. The yellow sequinned blouse I bought on Saturday catches my eye, but I brush past and grab a pair of smart cream trousers and a crisp white cotton shirt. A really good thing indeed.

I arrive at the office feeling motivated and positive.

'Morning, Bea.' Throwing her a large smile, I sweep up my coffee and stride over to my desk.

'Gosh, you're in a jolly mood.' She beams, which is impressive considering she's working the bank holiday too. But then, she insisted. She knows how important tomorrow's press launch is. 'Good weekend?'

Briefly I consider telling her about Miles. Then I see her shiny, happy eyes and realise I can't do it. According to Beatrice, we're the perfect couple. I can't face telling her the truth. It would be like telling a child Santa Claus doesn't exist.

'Busy,' I reply, swiftly sidestepping the issue. Well, that's not a fib. It *was* busy. I was up half the night packing Miles's collection of property magazines. He saves all the back issues so he can keep track of house prices. He even drew a graph and stuck it on to his fridge. 'How about you? What did you get up to?'

'Oh, not much.' She shrugs, pushing up her sleeves and folding her arms over her large bosom. 'On Saturday I watched polo – my eldest brother, Toby, was playing. Saturday night I went to the opera with my friend Maddy, who has a box there, and then on Sunday it was Granny's birthday and we all had dinner at the Dorchester.'

'Um, yes, you're right, just a regular weekend, then.' I smile teasingly. I love hearing about Beatrice's weekends. It's like reading the society pages of *Tatler*. She lives in a completely different world to most people, and yet the thing I love about her is that she has absolutely no idea and thinks it's all terribly normal, darling.

'Which reminds me, I saw that friend of yours at the Dorchester.'

Sipping my coffee, I start leafing through the post. 'Who?' I murmur distractedly.

'You know, your friend's husband. The one in the photo.'

I stop what I'm doing and glance up sharply. 'You mean Julian?'

'Yes, that's it. The one I thought could possibly be thought of as sexy, *but only* if he was totally single and definitely not married in any way, shape or form . . .'

'Bea—'

'. . . not even if it was one of those ceremonies that aren't technically legal in England, like a second cousin of mine who got married by some pygmy tribe in the Amazonian rain forest . . .'

'Beatrice —'

'. . . Poor Aunt Fi was so upset, though apparently they brought her back a lovely woven rug for the hallway—'

'BEATRICE!'

She looks at me, startled, as if suddenly remembering I'm here. 'Sorry, you were saying?' She smiles brightly.

'No, *you* were saying. About Julian being at the Dorchester,' I say, fixing her with a hard stare.

'Oh dear, have I said something wrong?' Anxiously she clutches at her pearls as if they can somehow protect her from my wrath.

'No, of course not,' I reassure her quickly. 'But are you sure it was him?'

She eyes me warily.

'Beatrice, this is important.'

'Absolutely,' she says gravely. 'I never forget a face.'

My mind is scrambling around. I think back to Julian's conversation with Vanessa over dinner on my birthday. He said he had to work. That's why he couldn't take the kids to the aquarium. So what was he doing at the hotel?

Business, I tell myself firmly. That's it, he was probably doing business with one of his posh clients. I do it all the time. I'm always in hotels.

'And what time was it?'

'Um, now, let me think . . .' She tips her head on one side. 'Gosh, it was after we'd had the petits fours, which were very good, I have to say. I'm not usually one for petits fours – too fussy, not big enough, I have to eat about a hundred – but these were absolutely deli—' She catches my expression and swiftly stops herself. 'But anyway, yes. It was after the petits fours, because Granny then fancied a brandy and I remember saying I'd have one too, but not before I'd gone to the loo.'

'Bea, is this story leading *anywhere*?' I gasp impatiently.

'Oh, most definitely.' She nods. 'Because you see, it was when I was going to the loo that I went through reception and bumped into him.'

'Julian?'

'The very same. He was coming out of the lift and we sort of collided. He was very apologetic about it all. But there was something else.'

'What?' I feel like a detective in a TV series.

'He dropped his room key on the floor.'

'*Room key?*'

My chest tightens. I can hear Vanessa's voice replaying in my ears: '*I think Julian's having an affair.*'

No, there's got to be a reasonable explanation. Maybe the meeting was in the room. In fact that must be it. I mean, look at me, I met with Larry Goldstein in his room, didn't I?

'Uh-huh.' Beatrice is nodding decisively. 'I know because I picked it up. Actually, it wasn't a room key at all. It was for the' – she lowers her voice to a reverential whisper – 'Oliver Messel Suite.'

I look at her blankly. 'What's that?'

'Only the most romantic suite at the Dorchester!' she exclaims. 'It was Marlene Dietrich's favourite. Granny told me. Apparently, they were good friends.'

OK, so now it's a business meeting in the most romantic suite at the Dorchester. Well, I suppose it's *possible*.

'And what time did you say this was?'

'I didn't. But I would guess it was quite late. Probably after ten.'

But not probable. A business meeting that runs until ten o'clock at night? In the Dorchester's most romantic suite? On a Sunday? When he told Vanessa he had to be at the office?

My stomach churns and flips over. I think about the condoms I spotted in his shopping basket and Vanessa's admission that they haven't slept together for ages. I have to admit, the evidence against him seems overwhelming.

'So come on, tell me.' I zone back in to see Beatrice looking at me, her eyes wide with curiosity. 'Why all the questions? Didn't your friend Vanessa tell you they were staying there?'

'No . . . no, she didn't.' I shake my head and force a smile. 'She must have forgotten – she's terrible like that.' My mind is whirling. I quickly grab hold of it. 'Talking of which, has Larry Goldstein called yet?' I say, swiftly changing the subject.

'First thing,' nods Beatrice. 'You're meeting him at twelve noon at a nail bar in Notting Hill.' I throw her a quizzical look,

'He has a manicure appointment at eleven,' she explains. 'It must be an LA thing.'

'Or maybe because he's a dentist. You know, putting your fingers in other people's mouths,' I suggest. At least I hope so. I hate to think he has manicures just for the hell of it.

'Oh, I didn't think of that.' She beams. 'And there I was wondering what colour polish he'd be choosing – you know, whether he was a pillar-box-red man or more a French manicure.' She starts giggling, then remembers herself. 'Anyway, afterwards he's taking you to see the new space.'

Now she's got my full attention. 'Oh, so he finally made a decision on the location for the clinic?'

'Yes, and he said he was sure you'd approve.'

'Really?' I feel a glow of pleasure. At least something's going right. 'Where is it exactly?'

'He wouldn't say. He said he wanted to keep it as a surprise.' Beatrice hugs herself. 'Gosh, how fab. I love surprises, don't you?'

I feel a flicker of trepidation. What was that about not wanting any more surprises? First it was Julian, and now this?

Still, remember to think positive, I tell myself firmly. Everything's going to be fine. In fact it's going to be more than fine – it's going to be great. And looking at Beatrice, I smile brightly. 'Absolutely!'

Chapter Thirty-two

L arry is having his cuticles trimmed when I arrive.

'Hey, how's it going?' He beams, flashing me his neon smile as I walk into the *über*-trendy nail bar, filled with ladies who do lunch and very little else. He's reclining on a massage chair, being attended to by two pretty therapists in white coats. One is doing his manicure; the other is massaging his bare feet.

'Hi. Great, thanks,' I reply, hovering uncertainly by some shelves, which are filled with different bottles of polish, and looking for a place to sit. This isn't the kind of venue I'm used to for a PR meeting, but then Larry Goldstein isn't my usual kind of client.

'Come on over and meet Andrea and Carla,' he drawls loudly over the hum of small talk and clink of cappuccino cups.

I weave through the massage chairs towards him, carrying my briefcase and handbag, and making sure to hide my nails. I'm in desperate need of a manicure myself.

'This is Charlene, my PR guru,' says Larry Goldstein, gesturing towards me.

The two manicurists glance up briefly and smile. 'Hiya,' they both chirp in unison, before turning back to his cuticles and feet.

'Actually, it's Charlotte,' I correct him, smiling.

'Whatever,' he laughs. 'It's all the same.'

Actually, no, it's not all the same. *How would you like to be called Leslie, or Lenny, or Leo?* I feel like asking, but of course I don't. I remain perfectly calm, a professional smile pinned on to my face. This is an important meeting. Larry Goldstein is a valued client. And this is going to be a good week, remember?

'So, you've decided on the location for the new clinic?' I say brightly, moving straight on to business and the reason I'm here.

'Andrea, honey, can you just press a little harder on my left foot? Yep, that's great.' Satisfied, he glances over at me. 'Sorry about that.'

'It's quite all right.' I smile evenly. 'Now, about the new space . . .'

'Did you know we have these pressure points on the soles of our feet? It's to do with the meridian lines. Like acupuncture. It's a way of rebalancing the *chi*.'

'Actually, yes, I did know that,' I say briskly. 'It's one of the basic principles of reflexology.'

'See, she's not just a pretty face, is she?' he quips to his beauty therapists, who glance at me and laugh politely.

'But anyway, back to the new space . . .' *For the third time.*

'Clear varnish or just buffed?' interrupts Carla.

I curl my fingers into little balls.

'I don't know. What do you think, Charlene?' Larry stops peering at his fingers and looks up at me, eyebrows raised questioningly. 'Clear or buffed?'

OK, that's it – I give up. Trying to conduct a business meeting here is impossible. 'Buffed,' I reply shortly.

He screws up his forehead. 'You think so?' he asks, staring at his nails.

'Clear, then,' I deadpan.

'No, I think you're right. I'll go with buffed,' he says after a moment's deep thought. 'See, I always take my PR guru's advice. She knows best.' He passes his hand to Carla, who's waiting patiently. She reaches for her buffer. 'Actually, before you do that, can we change the setting on this massage chair to "pulse" rather than "vibrate"?'

I watch as Carla starts fiddling with the controls.

'You know, they do great herbal teas here,' he says, casually glancing over at me, as if I'm not actually sitting here waiting for him, but simply passing the time of day. 'You should have one.'

Settling back in his chair, he wriggles a little to get comfortable, then closes his eyes. 'I'll be right with you.'

Right with you.

Now, in my language that means soon, as in a few minutes, as in no more than five. Ten at a push. In Larry Goldstein's language it means just over an hour of having his feet rubbed, his heels pumiced and his hands wrapped in steaming cloths – apparently, it's the special bank-holiday pampering package – while the whole time flirting with Andrea and Carla, offering them discount veneers and tooth-bleaching, and handing out business cards with instructions to give him a call.

It's past one when we finally leave the salon.

'Everything OK?' As we step on to the street, he turns to me, looking very pleased with himself.

'Absolutely.' I smile back breezily, trying not to think about the hour I've just wasted, drinking four cups of herbal tea, because as long as the client's happy, everything is OK. That's the basic rule of PR.

'So are you excited to see the new space?'

'Very.' I nod. *Finally.*

'Awesome. Let's jump in a cab.' He smiles, sticking out his hand.

'Are you sure you don't want me to drive? I've got my car on a meter and—' I begin, but he's already flagging down a passing cab.

'No, this is the only way I travel when I'm in London. They're so cool.' He beams as the cab pulls up at the kerbside. 'I'm thinking about getting one shipped over to the States. I can drive around Beverly Hills in it, instead of the Porsche. What do you reckon?'

I reckon you'll look like a complete prat, I think, while enthusing, 'Wow, yeah, that sounds like a great idea,' as he holds open the door for me. 'So, tell me, where are we going?' I ask, climbing inside.

'Now that would be telling,' he says, looking very pleased with himself as he slides in next to me on the seat. Like really next to me. Like our thighs are pressed up against each other.

All at once I get the same feeling I got in that restaurant the first time we met. I can't be sure, but something feels off. A nagging air of discomfort. Am I imagining it or is he squashing his leg right up against mine?

I go for imagining it. Nevertheless I cross my legs, in a manoeuvre intended to move my thigh as far away from his as possible.

'Just straight ahead, mate,' hollers Larry to the driver, in a faux cockney accent that's even worse than Dick van Dyke's in *Mary Poppins*.

I can see the cabbie grimace in the rear-view mirror. Probably the only thing worse to a black-cab driver than pretending to be a cockney is giving them directions. 'American, are ya?' he asks gruffly.

'Is my accent that bad?' laughs Larry Goldstein jovially.

'Worse,' growls the cabbie.

'Jeez, I love these guys,' confides Larry, flashing a smile.

I nod wordlessly. I'm not sure if Larry even understands the concept of sarcasm. It's as if those teeth of his are a superhero's deflector shield, which no irony can penetrate.

I wonder where we're going. Beatrice mentioned something about how I'd approve, so I wonder if he's taken my advice and gone for a hipper location. Then again, he's really in love with the whole English-tradition thing, so he might have plumped for one of the grand suites in Harley Street, along with all his peers.

'Right here.'

The cab driver suddenly slams on his brakes and we lurch to a juddering halt. I glance sharply out of the window to see we've only gone about a hundred yards.

'How much will that be?' says Larry Goldstein to the driver.

I look at him in puzzlement. I know everyone says people from LA don't like to walk, but this is ridiculous. We've only driven round the corner. I turn to Larry Goldstein, but he's already climbing out of the cab to pay the driver, and totally confused, I climb out after him. 'But I don't understand.'

'It was your idea – it's all credit to you,' he's saying, as the cab drives off and we're left on the pavement. 'You gave me the idea at dinner, telling me I needed to be in a more fashionable area, somewhere a lot more hip, cooler . . .'

I take in my surroundings. We're standing on Westbourne Grove, near the junction with Portobello.

'. . . somewhere that's filled with celebrities, the place to be seen . . .'

How funny. I was just here on Saturday at the market.

Larry starts walking slowly along the pavement, making sweeping movements with his arm, like a pioneer looking at the vista. '. . . and I thought back to our first meeting, and how we met at the Electric at your suggestion, and how cool the location was. So I put in a few calls to my people straight away and they managed to find this place. Of course, it wasn't without its problems – there's someone in there right now – but if you throw money at a problem, it goes away.' He gives me a look that sends a shiver down my spine. 'We just offered the landlord three times the rent. They couldn't refuse.'

'But what about the person who was renting already?'

'Business is business,' he says, his voice steely.

'You mean, they've just had to pack up and move out?'

As I'm speaking, I'm having this really, *really* horrible feeling, it's creeping over me, and my blood is running cold. I'm wrong. I have to be wrong.

'What kind of shop was it?'

We're still walking along, but my legs suddenly feel like dead weights.

'Oh, nothing special, some kind of junk store.' He shrugs dismissively.

I feel myself stiffen in protest. Nothing special! *Junk store!* Because I know what he's talking about. I know before I even look.

'So what do you think?' he says, as he stops outside Oliver's granddad's antique shop and flings his arms out wide in a sort of *ta-dah* motion.

I think I'm going to be sick.

Right here and now on the pavement.

Desperately I muster composure from somewhere. 'Um, it's great,' I manage to stammer.

'Just great?' His face drops with disappointment. Obviously that's not enough enthusiasm for someone like Larry Goldstein.

'No, I mean brilliant,' I gush, mirroring his own celluloid smile. '*Awesome*,' I add, with extra emphasis.

He finally looks satisfied. 'I knew you'd approve.' He beams, running his fingers carefully through his ice-grey hair. 'Just imagine' – he does this sort of rainbow gesture in the air – 'Star Smile.'

Dismay stabs. He's going to replace that lovely old sign with his tacky logo.

'Shall we go in?'

'Excuse me?' I'm still reeling with horror at the thought that I'm responsible for Oliver's granddad losing his beloved shop, which he's been in for sixty years. I'm still trying to register that, and trust me, that's bad enough, *but now I've got to go inside?*

I get a flashback of Oliver's granddad giving me a whiskery kiss on both cheeks.

Oh my God, I can't. I just can't do it.

'Charlene?'

I look at Larry Goldstein and at that moment I know this is it. My career's on the line. Either I go into that shop and get behind this or I can kiss goodbye to my account with Larry Goldstein. And with it my chance of international expansion.

I can see the headlines now, hear the gossip amongst rival PR companies who won't have any scruples about jumping in on this. It will be seen as a huge career mistake. Career suicide, probably. And for what? A rival firm will take over and the deal will still go ahead. Oliver's granddad will still lose his shop. With or without me.

And I can choose to leave here. With or without a career.

I pause. This is what I've been working towards for years, and I only met Oliver's granddad on Saturday. It's business, re-member? Personal feelings don't come into it.

'Sorry.' I smile professionally and throw back my shoulders. 'I was just letting the anticipation build before I went in.'

Now he's pushing open the door and I'm following him inside. And as I step over the threshold, it's like crossing a line. I've made the choice. But the most frightening thing of all is the sudden realisation that Larry Goldstein was right: I am a lot like him after all.

Already waiting for us in the shop is one of Star Smile's design team and I spend the next few minutes trying to hide from Oliver's granddad by skulking behind Larry Goldstein, who's stalking around the shop as if he owns it. Which I suppose he does.

'So we're going to rip out those windows and replace them with a big sheet of top-spec glass . . .' the design-team guy is saying now.

I glance with indignation at the windows. They're the most delightful old bow windows. They've been here for years and add character to the place. They can't rip them out – it would be a travesty.

'. . . And we'll have plasma screens, and concrete floors . . .'

As he continues talking, I feel a rush of protectiveness. It's all very trendy, and *über*-cool, and I know it will look amazing, but not here. Not in this shop.

'. . . We'll pull down that old bookcase and totally renovate so that we create a loft-like space, all open-plan . . .'

Out of the corner of my eye I can see Oliver's granddad listening from the back of the shop. With my hair tied up and still wearing my sunglasses, I look different enough from the girl he met on Saturday that he hasn't recognised me, though I've already been here fifteen minutes. Thank goodness, I reflect, glancing at his face, which looks pinched, and feeling a stab of shame to be part of all this.

'Totally,' nods Larry Goldstein. 'Though at the moment it's hard to imagine. I mean, this place just feels cramped, dark, cluttered . . .'

He's talking as if Oliver's granddad isn't even here. Doesn't he realise how insulting he's being? I think protectively. He's been here sixty years. He loves this shop. It must be like having your heart torn out.

'And yeah, you're so right, those bookcases are just an eye-sore.'

'Those bookcases date back to the turn of the twentieth century,' Oliver's granddad finally says.

'Really?' Larry Goldstein looks unimpressed. 'Well, then, it's time for a facelift, isn't it?' He laughs. 'Get into the new century. Actually, I was thinking acrylic floating shelves that you can suspend from the ceiling.' He turns back to the design guy as if Oliver's grandfather isn't important at all.

I glance at Oliver's granddad. His bright green eyes are flicking over Larry Goldstein, taking him in, weighing him up.

Meanwhile I'm loitering in the back, trying to keep my head down.

'So what do you think . . .'

Please God, don't let him say my name, don't let him say my name.

'. . . Charlene?'

For the first time I'm relieved he's got my name wrong. There is a God.

'Um . . . yeah . . . great.' I nod vaguely, trying to hide behind a large grandfather clock.

'No other suggestions? About décor? Colour? Design?' Larry looks at me, waiting for my input.

I swallow hard. 'Well, obviously I'm brimming with ideas about this place. It's a total blank canvas,' I begin in my best PR spin, 'and I think we're all looking at creating something clean, modern and totally organic' – I glance quickly at Oliver's grand-dad, who's now looking at me suspiciously – 'but naturally your design team will have all the ideas, as they're the experts in this field,' I finish quickly.

Shit, I've got to get out.

'Excuse me, miss.' Oliver's granddad motions towards me.

I try to ignore him, but it's impossible. 'Um, yes?' I say, dipping my head as I turn to him.

'Do I know you from somewhere? Your face seems familiar.'

'No, definitely not,' I say hastily. 'One hundred per cent. Nope. Never been in here before.' I realise I'm blabbering, 'But anyway, I think I just want to pop outside, have a look at the frontage again.' I lunge for the door. It's stuck, but after strug-gling with it for a few moments, I manage to yank it open. 'I'll see you outside, Larry,' I say quickly, and letting the door swing closed behind me, I stumble outside on to the pavement.

Chapter Thirty-three

Afterwards the design guy shoots off in his Mini Cooper and Larry joins me outside to wait for a cab to take him back to his hotel. He offers to drop me at my car, but I make an excuse and tell him I need the exercise – all two hundred yards of it – and I'll walk back.

'Good girl, firm up those glutes,' he says approvingly as he pats me on the bottom.

I flinch. But it's done in that jokey, all-in-good-humour kind of way, so I know I can't say anything, otherwise *I'll* be the one who looks bad.

'So I'll put those finishing touches to the presentation this afternoon,' I say briskly in my most professional voice. 'I've still to finalise one or two things, but then we're all set for the launch tomorrow.'

'Awesome.' He smiles broadly.

'Unless of course there's anything else you'd like to add?'

'Only that it's been incredible working with you on this,' he says, and fixes me with those piercingly blue eyes. I'm sure he's wearing contact lenses. Nobody's eyes can be that blue.

I take a step backwards. 'Er, great, thanks. You too,' I add, hastily returning the compliment.

'Let's hope this is just the beginning of things.' His gaze is still fixed on me. In fact he's not even blinking, I notice, feeling a little unnerved. 'You know, you and I could go a long way together. A long way,' he repeats quietly.

I don't know if it's because he's looking at me so intensely as he says it, or just the *way* he says it, but I get a sense of unease that makes the hairs on my arms stand up and my body stiffen.

'Oh, look, there's a taxi,' I cry, changing the subject. Flinging out my arm, I start waving furiously. It's going in the other direction, but it immediately performs a U-turn and deftly pulls up alongside the kerb. I feel a beat of relief.

'Um, thanks,' says Larry Goldstein, giving me a peculiar look.

'No problem. It's all part of the service,' I quip, slightly breathless.

'Service? Are you sure you don't want that *ride*?' Pulling open the door, Larry Goldstein looks at me, his carefully groomed eyebrows raised questioningly.

'No, I'm fine, thanks.'

'OK, well, we'll speak tomorrow, before the press launch.' Jumping in the cab, he slams the door behind him, then pulls down the window. 'I'm looking forward to it.'

I feel another stab of apprehension, but I ignore it. I always get really anxious before a press launch, especially one done on such short notice. It's totally normal.

'Yes, me too.' I smile brightly, and as the cab pulls away, I hitch my bag over my shoulder, grip my briefcase and stride out energetically on my power walk.

Which lasts about five seconds.

As soon as the cab disappears round the corner, I drop my bag and briefcase on the ground and flop on to a nearby bench. Resting my elbows on my knees, I bury my face in my hands and exhale deeply. It's as if I can literally feel the stress coming out of my pores, oozing all over this bench and trickling on to the pavement in one great big sticky, gloopy, stressful puddle.

Right now I should be the happiest girl in the world. My newest, biggest client loves me, we've found the perfect location for the first UK Star Smile clinic, and the press launch is less than a day away. It can't fail. It's going to be a resounding success. This is going to propel my career into a whole new stratosphere. I'll get my picture in all the trade mags. The business will get tons of publicity, more clients. And then there's Larry Goldstein's talk of Merryweather PR taking on his contract full-time, not just in the UK, but globally. We'll have to expand, take on new staff, get more offices . . . God, it's everything I've dreamed of.

Except . . .

Oliver.

My mind flashes back to Saturday afternoon. Walking through the park with him and Welly. Laughing as he threw sticks and had to fetch them himself. Chatting about anything and everything. Drinking tea and eating shortbread fingers with his granddad.

His granddad.

I feel my heart plummet. I can't do it. I can't take away his shop, his livelihood, his life. I recall his words: 'I met my late wife, Betty, here. She came in to buy a china teapot . . . Antiques are in my blood, and look at me, I'm a bit of an antique myself now.'

But then again, he was probably going to retire soon anyway, I tell myself comfortingly. I mean, he must be over eighty. I'm sure Oliver will understand. Though it's doubtful I'll ever be able to face him again, anyway, or his granddad, I think sadly.

'Beautiful day we're having, isn't it?'

A voice snaps me back and I turn round to see an old woman sitting along from me at the other end of the bench. Resting her swollen ankles, her wrinkled face tilted to the sky, she's like a white-haired cat basking in the sunshine.

If she was there earlier, I didn't notice her, but then it could have been snowing and I probably wouldn't have noticed.

'If you say so,' I manage glumly.

Turning her head sideways, she looks at me. 'Let me guess. It's a man.'

'Excuse me?'

'That sigh. It nearly knocked me over.' She smiles, raising her eyebrows.

Honestly. Why does everyone think a woman's woes are always to do with a man? 'No, not at all,' I say, a little indignantly. 'I've got a problem at work.'

'I see.' She nods, but something in the way she looks at me tells me she doesn't believe a word of it.

'Well, actually, it's not a problem as such,' I add. 'The client's really happy with everything, it's just . . .'

'*You're* not really happy,' she prompts.

I glance at her. She says that so authoritatively it's almost as if she knows exactly how I'm feeling, but of course she can't possibly know. She's an old lady, with snow-white hair, a thick winter coat even though it's summer and a walking stick, I muse, looking at her hand wrapped round it and noticing the sunlight catching her pretty emerald ring, shaped like a flower, next to her gold wedding band. She must be about eighty. What can she know about my life, or how it feels to be me?

'Well, it's not as simple as that,' I try to explain. 'You see, there are other people involved – Oliver and his granddad. And I'm the reason his granddad is going to lose his shop.' It's like now I've started I can't stop and it all comes spilling out. 'Which means Oliver is probably going to hate me, like he no doubt did ten years ago when I ignored him.' For a brief moment I jump back to the moment when I tried to introduce Lottie to him, how she wasn't paying attention, how the whole time her entire head was filled with thoughts of Billy Romani.

'But that's not really my fault, because back then I didn't notice the nice guys. In fact it's only because a few days ago I went to my birthday party from ten years ago, and I was in my thirties, that I met him again, when he was in his twenties, and I got a second chance.' An image of Olly behind the bar in that tight T-shirt releases a butterfly in my stomach. 'And then of course when I found out he was the barman at the gastropub . . .' Suddenly I realise I've got completely carried away. I stop talking.

At the other end of the bench, the old lady is regarding me with a slightly bemused expression.

'Like I said, it's complicated.' I shrug defeatedly.

But she just smiles and, leaning across, pats my arm reassuringly. 'Life isn't complicated. It's very simple, really. It's us who make it complicated.'

I decide not to go back to the office. I just can't face it. Instead I make a quick call to Beatrice to let her know I'll be working from home for the rest of the afternoon and drive back to my flat. Still, at this rate, at least things can't get any worse, I console myself, as I sit in traffic along Holland Park Avenue staring at the parking ticket stuffed underneath my wipers.

The shrill ring of my mobile causes me to hold that thought as I click on my Bluetooth earpiece.

'Hi, Charlotte, it's me.'

Oh fuck, they just did.

It's Vanessa.

A hand grips my stomach. With everything that's been happening today I'd forgotten all about Julian, and my conversation this morning with Beatrice, but now it comes hurtling back.

'Hey, Vanessa, how are you?' I say evenly, forcing myself to sound as normal as possible. That old *Scruples* question is whizzing round in my head: 'If you found out your friend's boyfriend was cheating, would you tell her?' I always used to be the first to reply, 'Yes, absolutely,' with the easy defiance of a twentysomething. Of course you'd tell your friend. It was a no-brainer. But now the stakes are higher. Now you're sharing more than just a cheese plant, Domino's pizzas and a futon. Now it's children, a home, a life together.

'Not great,' she says.

Oh God, she knows. I can tell from her voice. For a split second I feel a flush of relief that I don't have to lie, but it's drowned out by dread.

'Why? What's up?' I try to keep my voice steady.

There's a pause, and then, 'I found a receipt.'

You wouldn't think those four words could have such an effect on me, could make my stomach hurtle into my sling-backs and my hands grip the steering wheel, but they do.

'What kind of receipt?' I'm filled with trepidation. Whatever it is, it's not good. I mean, your best friend doesn't ring you up to tell you she's found a receipt from Tesco, now does she?

'It's from Agent Provocateur.'

First the condoms, then the suite at the hotel and now *this*? My heart sinks, but I quickly rally. OK, let's think damage limitation. I have to put a positive spin on this, and if anyone can do it, I can. A career in PR has to be useful for something.

'Ooh, lucky you,' I gush, with about as much faux enthusiasm as I can muster. 'Julian must have bought you some sexy underwear as a surprise.'

'Yeah, right,' tuts Vanessa. Something tells me she isn't exactly convinced. 'In two sizes smaller than I really am? I called the shop and gave them the barcodes. Trust me, if I can get into a size-ten thong and a B-cup peek-a-boo bra, it'll be more than a surprise, it'll be a bloody miracle.'

Fair point. I love Vanessa dearly and I think she looks great, but there's no way she's a size ten. And as for those boobs of hers – that make anyone like me, who has to make the most of their cleavage with an M&S padded bra, insanely jealous – they have never, and will never, see the inside of anything less than a double-D cup.

'Maybe he got it wrong?' I argue. 'Men are useless about stuff like that. Miles always thought I was a size ten.'

'You are a size ten, Charlotte.'

'Oh, right, yes . . . well, you know what I mean,' I say vaguely. Only I don't think she does, as there's silence.

'Sorry, I know you must be really busy. I'll go.'

'No, it's fine, don't be silly,' I say quickly.

'Really? Are you sure?' She sounds so grateful I feel a twinge of guilt. God, am I always that busy with work that she thinks I won't be able to talk at a time like this?

'Of course. What's more important than my best friend, hey?'

No sooner have those words come out of my mouth than my BlackBerry starts ringing. It's Beatrice, but I ignore it.

'I just don't know what to do,' she sighs. She sounds upset and I'm suddenly reminded of her at the club, queueing at the ladies', gushing happily about how much she was in love with Julian. It makes me wonder how she got to this place, all these years later, where she's on the phone to me, worried he's having an affair.

'Why don't you ask him about it?' I suggest. 'Be honest?'

'I can't. Then he'll know.'

'Know what?'

Now the line on my mobile is beeping to indicate that another call is waiting. It's Beatrice again. I grit my teeth and continue to ignore it. It won't be anything important. It can wait.

'I wasn't snooping,' she protests unprompted. 'I was just doing the laundry and I found the receipt in his trouser pocket and . . . OK, I was snooping,' she confesses. I can hear her puffing furiously on a cigarette on the other end of the line. 'So no, I can't tell him.'

'Look, it's not what you're thinking.' *Or what I'm thinking.* 'Just you watch, there'll be a simple explanation.'

The line stops beeping. I feel relieved. Now I can focus properly.

'Like what?' demands Vanessa. I find a receipt for lingerie that's not my size, but no lingerie. Believe me, I've looked high and low and it's not in the house. So he must have bought it for someone else.'

'Um . . . maybe he was with a colleague who suddenly remembered it was his wedding anniversary . . . and so they popped into Agent Provocateur to buy his wife a gift, but then the colleague realised he'd left his wallet in the office and so Julian stepped in and paid, like the true gent he is.'

Brilliant, Charlotte, though I say it myself. I just managed to turn that round and now Julian looks like a hero instead of a cheating, lying bastard.

Which of course he isn't, I tell myself sharply. Because the more I think about it, the more I refuse to believe that Julian would do such a thing. OK, so I know what it looks like when faced with the evidence, and I know we've all read about footballers who do that kind of thing, and politicians and rock stars and the man next door who's a pillar of the community. But this is Julian, and although I know things between them haven't been that great for a while, he loves Vanessa and he'd never do that.

'Hmm.' Vanessa sounds vaguely convinced. 'I suppose it could happen . . .'

'Of course it could happen. I mean, there's tons of rational explanations.' I stop myself. OK, quit while you're ahead, Charlotte.

'You think so?'

'Absolutely.'

The other line starts beeping again. It's Beatrice. Again. She's nothing if not persistent. Only this time I can't ignore it.

'Look, Vanessa, I'm really sorry, but I'm going to have to go,' I say reluctantly. 'My assistant's calling and I have to get it – it might be something to do with the press launch tomorrow for Larry Goldstein's Star Smile UK.'

'Oh, how is he?' she asks, suddenly perking up. 'Made any more advances?'

'He's married!' I retort.

'Exactly,' she quips dryly.

I ignore her. Though I'm glad to see some of her black sense of humour has returned. 'Look, I'll call you back.'

'I'll probably be divorced by then.'

'Vanessa!'

'It was a joke,' she protests. 'It's fine.'

I know it's not fine. It's far from fine, but I don't know what to do. I've got the office trying to get through with something that could be urgent, my friend's marriage could be in serious trouble, I'm responsible for robbing an old man of his beloved shop, ignoring his grandson when I was a twentysomething, and according to an email received from Miles this morning, a seven-hundred-quid homebuyers' survey from Abbey National. And I *still* haven't called Mum back since we got cut off, I suddenly remember.

It's one thing after another. I feel as if I'm frantically rushing around, like those people you see who try and keep all those plates spinning, dashing from one to another to make sure none of them stops spinning and falls crashing to the ground, smashing into a million little pieces.

Quickly saying goodbye to Vanessa, I switch lines. 'Hi, Beatrice, what's up?'

And I can't let that happen. Because if I do, who's going to pick up the pieces?

Chapter Thirty-four

By the time I pull up outside my flat I'm emotionally spent. After spending twenty minutes calming down Beatrice, who was hysterical because of a mix-up over the caterers for tomorrow's launch, and sorting out the problem, I rang Julian's secretary and left a message telling him to call me at home. I haven't yet worked out what exactly I'm going to say when he does, but I can't just sit back and do nothing.

Though, boy, right now that's all I feel like doing.

Nothing. *Nada.* Zero.

Switching off both my phones, I turn off the engine and, closing my eyes, rest my forehead on the steering wheel. For a moment I just relish the quiet, the sound of my own breath, the rise and fall of my shoulders. I just need to take a moment to calm down. To relax, like the doctor said. What was it they used to tell us to do in yoga? Focus on the breath.

I focus.

Deep breath in . . . and now exhale . . . Deep breath in . . . and now exhale . . . Deep breath in . . .

I concentrate on inhaling through my nostrils, then exhaling through my mouth – I even put my thumb and finger on my nostrils, just like you're supposed to. I feel my chest cavity expand and then slowly collapse. 'As long as the breath can take you,' is what my teacher always says, although usually at this point it's at the end of the class and I've nodded off in *Shavasana.*

Still, it seems to be having the desired effect. I am feeling a lot more calm. In fact, I think I might throw in some *oms* for good measure.

'Ommmm . . . ommmmmm . . . ommmmmmmmmmm—'

'Are you OK?'

A loud rapping on the window nearly causes me to jump out of my skin and I snap upright in shock. 'Argh,' I yelp, cricking my neck in the process. Clutching at it in pain I turn stiffly sideways. 'You stupid idiot! What the bloody hell do you think you're—'

'Charlotte?'

And come face to face with Oliver. Stooped down on the pavement, his hands on his knees, he's peering at me through the side window, a worried expression on his face.

Oh fuck, how long has he been standing there?

'Hey, are you OK?'

No, I'm not OK, I'm mortified. No, scratch that. I'm *beyond* mortified.

'Um, yeah . . . absolutely . . . thanks.' I nod and then wince sharply as a pain shoots up my neck.

'Are you sure?'

The shooting pain has now turned into more of a red-hot-poker stabbing agony.

'It's my neck,' I manage to gasp.

'You probably pulled something.'

'What if I've broken it?' I say, feeling a creeping panic.

'I doubt it.'

'But how do you know?'

'Can you wiggle your toes?'

I wiggle them. 'Yes.'

'Can you wiggle your fingers?'

I wiggle them. 'Yes.'

'Now for the big test . . .'

I brace myself.

'. . . Can you wiggle your ears?'

I try to wiggle them, but nothing. 'Oh my God, no, I can't! What does that mean?' I cry in hysterics, twisting round to look at him.

And see him laughing. Killing himself on the pavement.

I feel my cheeks burn up. I fell right for that, didn't I?

'It means your neck's fine.' He grins mischievously and I can't help but smile back.

Before it hits me again like an icy blow. *The shop.* I've got to tell him.

'So . . .'

'So?' I manage, feeling my body stiffen as I brace myself.

'Well, now you're going to walk again, how do you fancy continuing our conversation without a car window between us?'

'Oh, right, yeah.' I blush again. Nerves are whooshing around in the pit of my stomach. I'm trying to think of the right way to break the news about his granddad's shop, but somehow I can't seem to find one.

Most likely because there isn't one, Charlotte, pipes up that little voice inside, but I disregard it. I'm just going to be honest and tell it like it really is.

'Actually, I wanted to talk to you about something.' Releasing the door catch, I step out of the car and am immediately accosted by Welly.

'Hey, sit down, boy,' instructs Oliver, and Welly immediately sits down. 'Someone's pleased to see you,' he says, and then smiles shyly. 'He's not the only one.'

The nerves that are swimming around in my stomach suddenly turn into butterflies. Maybe I don't have to tell him how it really is *right* this minute.

'So what are you doing around here?' I ask, feeling all jittery, but this time it's in a good way.

'Oh, I was just in the area,' he says vaguely. 'I thought I'd take Welly for a walk . . .' He trails off and stuffs his hands in his pockets.

Those butterflies are going crazy in there.

'Well, now you're here, I suppose I *should* invite you in for a cup of tea,' I say, doing my best to look unenthusiastic.

'Hey, no, I didn't mean—' He begins to protest, then breaks off as he realises I'm teasing. 'I suppose I asked for that.'

'I suppose you did.' I nod. 'Hang on a minute.' Turning back to the car, I reach inside for my bag, folders, briefcase . . .

'Hey, do you want me to give you a hand with all that?'

'Oh, yeah, that would be great,' I reply, leaning over the back seat where I have a big box of files. The top one is Larry Goldstein's and I suddenly notice on the front of it I've scribbled the address of his new clinic. My stomach flips. Shit. I don't want Oliver seeing that. 'If I *needed* you to help,' I finish, re-emerging with all the bags and the files pressed closely to my chest in a Beatrice move. 'But I like to do things for myself . . . um, as a woman . . . You know, *The Female Eunuch* and all that.'

Oh Jesus, what am I talking about? I've never even read *The Female Eunuch*. He's going to think I don't shave my legs and go around burning my bras. But if he does, he doesn't show it.

'Fair enough.' He smiles evenly.

I feel a beat of relief. Phew, that was close. Still, like I said, I've got to tell him.

'OK, well, this way,' I say, puffing under the weight of all my stuff as I walk towards my flat.

I've just got to find the right moment.

I unlock the front door and step into the hallway. Oliver follows and lets Welly off his lead. Immediately he bounds off inside, racing through to the living room, leaving a trail of dirty pawprints all over the pristine cream carpet.

'Oh shit.' Oliver throws me a strangled look. 'Welly! Come here, boy!' he yells, whistling desperately. 'God, I'm so sorry. I'll tie him up outside,' he apologises, looking mortified.

'No, don't be silly, it's fine,' I say quickly.

'But your carpet . . .'

'Is totally impractical,' I finish. 'Don't worry, it's only dirt, it'll come off.'

Er, hello? Have I suddenly been taken over by an alien who is making me act completely out of character? Usually I freak out about the slightest mark on the carpet. I insist everyone takes their shoes off and if anyone drops so much as a *crumb*, I'm there with the Dustbuster.

But for some reason the thought that Welly is scampering all over my cream wool carpet, leaving behind great big dirty pawprints has no effect on me whatsoever. In fact I feel almost *happy* that Welly is scampering all over my cream carpet, leaving behind great big dirty pawprints.

OK, I have been taken over by an alien.

Or I've got a crush.

My insides do a loop-the-loop.

And this time we're not talking a fantasy I-fancy-Olly-the-young-barman crush: we're talking a proper I-fancy-him-now-he's-Oliver-and-all-grown-up crush.

Shit.

'So, um . . . would you like to sit outside?' I say, walking briskly through into the kitchen and opening the French windows that lead out on to the small wrought-iron balcony.

'Wow, it's so pretty out here,' he says approvingly.

'Thanks.' I smile. 'Though I can't take credit – I have a gardener to do the plants.' I gesture to the medley of blue, yellow and pink flowers that I don't know the names of that climb up trellises and spill over the balcony. 'That's my contribution.' I gesture to a string of fairy lights that I've wrapped round a plant pot.

'I think your contribution probably makes it,' he replies, his lips twitching with amusement.

'It does!' I laugh in protest. 'Just you wait till it gets dark!' And then I suddenly realise what I've said and feel my cheeks prickle. That sounds as if I'm going to keep him trapped here until night-time, doesn't it? Like I'm some kind of brazen hussy and I'm going to try and have sex with him or something.

OK, scrap that thought. I can't believe sex just popped into my head like that. I only invited him in for a cup of tea and here I am thinking about sex. Except I'm not thinking about sex. I was thinking—

Oh, who am I kidding? I was thinking about sex.

'So, I didn't see you the other night . . .'

I snap back to see Oliver looking at me expectantly.

'I thought you'd stood me up again,' he says, then smiles. 'Just joking.'

'Oh, no, I had to stay in and . . .' I'm about to say 'pack up all Miles's things', but I quickly change my mind. Then I really *will* look like some brazen floozy, inviting a man back to my flat when it's still warm after my last boyfriend. 'I had to do some stuff,' I finish, wandering back into the kitchen. Flicking on the kettle, I set about making tea.

'Yeah, me too,' he says from the balcony, where he's taken a perch on one of my garden chairs. 'I got back pretty late from my granddad's. There was loads to do. We were packing for ages.'

The kettle quickly boils, and pouring water on to the teabags, my hand trembles and I feel my insides clench with dread.

'Poor guy, he was pretty cut up,' he continues, anger seeping into his voice. 'And then to top it all off, he had some people over at his shop today, talking about how they were going to rip the whole place apart.'

OK, this is it. I've got to let him know about Larry Goldstein, about the shop, about me. My heart thudding loudly in my ears, I grasp the back of my neck, trying to brace myself.

'You know, you should really put some ice on that.' Oliver's voice makes me jump and I turn round to see him standing right behind me. 'Your neck will feel a lot better.'

'Oh, no, it's fine,' I say hastily.

'You won't be saying that when you wake up tomorrow and can't move.' Without further discussion, he tugs open my freezer. I watch wordlessly as he takes out the ice-cube tray, spreads out a tea towel and lays it on the countertop, then deftly cracks out the cubes and ties them up in the tea towel.

'You look as if you've done that a few times,' I say after a pause.

'Yeah, well, I've had a few knocks in my time. I used to like to think of myself as a bit of a boxer, but I wasn't very good. I gave it all up five years ago when this happened.' He gestures to the scar running above his top lip. 'You know, I used to be pretty handsome before.' He smiles ruefully.

'You're handsome now,' I protest, then realise what I've said and blush like a schoolgirl. I hadn't really realised just how sexy he is, but now I have, I can't seem to think of anything else. 'Why? What happened?' I ask, quickly changing the subject.

'A mean left hook, twenty-two stitches and a broken nose.'

'Ouch. Did it hurt?'

'Hurt?' he repeats, and looks at me as if I've affronted his masculinity. 'I cried like a baby,' he confesses.

I laugh, then wince as my neck twinges painfully.

'OK, now go and sit outside,' he orders, picking up the ice-pack.

'But what about the tea?'

'This will only take a minute.'

Without arguing, I dutifully walk outside and sit down on one of my garden chairs. As he moves behind me, I feel a stab of anticipation.

'Right. you need to pull your top down a little,' he instructs firmly.

Dutifully I pull down the collar of my blouse.

'No, more than that.'

My heart beating fast, I undo the top buttons and shrug it down, revealing my bra straps.

It's hot in the late-afternoon sun and I feel a prickle of perspiration on my chest.

'OK, I'm just going to move these . . .' Gently he hooks his fingers underneath my bra straps and lets them slide down my arms.

I can feel my breath quickening, my ribcage rising and falling.

'Where exactly is it sore? Here?' His fingers brush against the nape of my neck.

'Um . . . a little lower . . .' My throat has gone all tight and my voice comes out in a whisper.

His fingers gently trace underneath my hairline, down my vertebrae, circling lower and lower. 'Here?'

I can barely speak. 'Yes, there,' I manage. A tingle rushes down into my groin, all the way down my legs. A tugging, like a thread running between us. I never even came close to this with Miles. It's so erotic. I feel more excited than I've felt in years. If *ever*.

'Now, this is going to be a little cold.'

I let out a gasp as he presses the freezing-cold ice against my neck.

'Sshh,' he murmurs, sliding his arm round my shoulders as my body gives a little shudder. 'Hold still.'

I do as I'm told and breathe in, sucking in the air between my teeth and holding it tight inside me. Every sense seems to be on full alert, every sensation. I can feel the cold ice melting against the heat of my neck, see the dark hairs on his arm, smell his body close to me, hear his breath by my ear . . .

The moment is suddenly broken by the sound of my home phone ringing inside.

'Do you want to get that?' asks Oliver, his voice husky.

'No!' I cry before I can help myself. 'It's, um . . . probably a wrong number,' I add, my mind fumbling around for words, when all I can think is, I don't want this to stop. I don't *ever* want this to stop.

The answering machine clicks on. I hear my voice on the outgoing message – '*Hi, this is Charlotte Merryweather. I'm not here right now, but if you'd like to leave a message . . .*' followed by a beep.

'Hi, it's Beatrice. Sorry to bother you at home, but your mobile and BlackBerry aren't switched on.'

'Oh, it's OK, it's just my assistant,' I dismiss. It's probably about that goddamn press launch again, I curse silently, willing her to hang up. 'It's nothing.'

'Well, if you're sure,' he says quietly, running his fingers across my collarbone.

'I'm sure,' I reply, feeling a tingle down my spine.

'I just wanted to call you and say I'm so sorry for getting into such a frightful panic earlier.'

The icy water is dripping down my back. He moves the ice-pack, sending a trickle down my chest and between my breasts.

'Thank you again for coming to my rescue and sorting everything out with the caterers. You're a total star! But of course you know that already. Oh, and by the way, Larry Goldstein's people called, to say how delighted they are about the new space . . .'

I stiffen. Oh, no. *Oh, no.* I jump up. 'Sorry, actually, I think I do need to get this.' I rush through the French doors.

'. . . and I have to say, Charlotte, what a brilliant idea of yours! Notting Hill is a perfect place for the first Star Smile. Gosh, you are *so* clever. I can't believe you didn't tell me what you had up your sleeve.' She tuts loudly.

I race for the phone, but Welly is in the way, and as I lunge for it, I trip over him.

'Oh, and apparently they're going to try and get the current chap out a bit earlier, so they can start the renovation as soon as this weekend. Apparently, there's loads to do. They mentioned it was a junk shop or something and a frightful old mess.'

My whole body contracts with horror.

'So, just to confirm, the exact address for the press release is . . .'

I scramble for the receiver, but it's too late. Behind me I hear Oliver's voice in stereo with Beatrice's.

'. . . number 114 Portobello, London W11 69P.'

Fuck.

'Anyway, got to run, it's salsa tonight!'

The line goes dead and there's silence. Frozen, I stare at the phone, my mind whirling. Until slowly I turn round. Oliver is standing in the doorway, just looking at me. His face is white with shock.

'I can explain,' I manage finally.

'You?' he says in disbelief. 'It was you.' He's staring at me as if it doesn't make sense, his brow furrowed in confusion. 'Grand-dad said he thought he recognised one of the people who came into his shop. A girl. Blonde. I thought he was getting confused . . .' He trails off, his mind joining up the dots.

'Yes, it was me,' I admit quietly, my whole body suffused with regret.

'You're the reason my granddad's lost his shop?'

His voice may be quiet, but the accusation stings. 'It's not like that,' I say quickly.

'So what is it like?' he replies. There's an edge to his voice now.

'I'm in PR. I represent a client.'

'But it was your idea.'

'I might have made some suggestions about the location, but I wasn't specific.'

'So who's your client?' he demands, his shock fast giving way to anger. 'Don't tell me, it's going to be another coffee shop,' he gasps in disgust, before I can answer.

'No, he's a cosmetic dentist. He's going to open his first UK clinic: Star Smile.' Hearing myself say it, it suddenly sounds ridiculous.

Oliver looks at me incredulously. 'My grandfather's antique shop – sorry, *junk shop*' – he spits angrily and I blush hotly. I've never used that phrase, it was Larry Goldstein, but suddenly by association I'm as guilty as he is – 'is going to be a fucking dentist's?'

'A cosmetic dentist,' I correct, and then by the look on his face wish I hadn't. 'I was going to tell you,' I try again.

'When exactly?'

'I don't know . . .'

'Before or after you spent the afternoon with my granddad?' he says coldly.

A shiver runs down me and I'm suddenly aware that my blouse is still unbuttoned and my bra straps are pulled down. I quickly shove them back up again, feeling vulnerable and foolish.

'I didn't know until today. I just found out too. Look, I'm sorry.' I reach out my hand to touch his arm, but he wrenches it away.

'Yeah, I bet you're sorry,' he retorts, his face set hard. 'Sorry all the way to the bank.'

'That's not fair,' I exclaim. 'You're being unfair!'

'*I'm* being unfair?' he cries acerbically.

'Well, it's not like I killed someone,' I gasp, feeling a snap of impatience.

'You might as well have. It was my granddad's whole life.'

All at once I feel a wave of anger. I feel guilty enough without him going on at me. 'How dare you stand there and judge me? You've got no idea,' I reply hotly. 'You've got no idea the pressure I'm under, or the impossible situation I'm in! I didn't mean for this to happen. I didn't plan it, but when a big client's involved, there's a lot at stake. It's not just about me any more. I have a job to do, a business to run, wages to pay.'

'Please, spare me the sob story,' he tuts scornfully.

That does it. I feel a burst of renewed outrage. 'Oh, silly me!' My voice rises, shrill and angry. 'How could you possibly know what it's like to run a business?'

His eyes flash furiously. 'What's that supposed to mean?'

'Well, how could you?' I gasp, my words tumbling out in a torrent. 'You've never done anything with your life. You're still just a barman!'

As soon as the words leave my mouth, I want to stuff them back in.

But it's too late.

Oliver visibly recoils in shock, a whole range of emotions flitting over his features, before recovering. He looks at me, his jaw set hard. 'And you're a bitch,' he says coldly.

It's like a slap in the face.

For a moment we both stand there in silence, our ribcages rising and falling, the air thick with insults and anger, and in that moment I wonder how we got here, how this happened, how I can turn it all back and start again.

But I can't. What's been said can't be unsaid.

'I think you should go,' I say finally, trying to keep my voice steady.

He nods tightly. 'Trust me, I'm already gone.'

And with Welly following, he turns and strides out of my flat, slamming the door behind him.

Chapter Thirty-five

Grabbing the brass door knocker, I hammer furiously. There's the sound of footsteps and the door is flung open by my younger self, who takes one look at me and gasps, 'Oh my God, are you OK?'

This time there are tears streaming down *my* face. In between gasping snorts, I nod vigorously. 'Yes . . . fine . . .'

Like I said, I've always been a crap liar.

'What on earth's happened?' she asks anxiously.

Blowing my nose on a crumpled tissue, I shake my head. 'We had a huge row,' I manage between sobs. 'He called me a bitch.'

'*He called you a bitch?*' she exclaims. 'Who did, your ex?' Her face flashes with fury. 'Just you wait, I'll sort him out.'

'But I am a bitch,' I sniffle, tears splashing down my cheeks.

'You're not a bitch,' she protests indignantly.

'I am, I am.' I'm wailing now, really quite loudly. In fact I'm making such a scene a couple of people from next door have popped out to see what all the noise is about and are staring at me open-mouthed. Which would usually be more than enough to douse me in self-consciousness and set me alight with shame, but not now. Now I don't care one jot that I'm making a total fool of myself. I don't care if complete strangers are pointing me. All I care about is Oliver.

As the thought hits me, I freeze for a moment, stunned by my admission; then I let out an even louder wail.

'Why? Because you broke up with your boyfriend?' Lottie is saying, trying to calm me down by rubbing my shoulder. 'By the sounds of it, he's a right idiot.'

'I'm not talking about my ex-boyfriend,' I hiccup, looking at her with red, puffy eyes.

'You're not?' She stops rubbing my shoulder. 'Well, who are you talking about, then?'

'Oliver,' I manage to gasp, before bursting into tears again.

Lottie looks at me in confusion. 'I think you need to come in and tell me all about it.'

'So, go on, fire away.'

We're sitting upstairs in my old bedroom, only this time the positions are reversed and now it's Lottie who's perched on the chair surveying me, while I'm curled up on the futon, sipping from a cracked mug containing black coffee, which she made me. My old room's a pigsty, in fact in the daylight it seems worse than ever, but whereas before it bothered me, now I find it comforting.

'I don't know where to start,' I sigh into my instant Nescafé.

'How about at the beginning?' she suggests.

Tucking my hair behind my ears, I shake my head. 'That's just it – I don't exactly know where the beginning is any more. It's like everything's all tangled up together.' I pause, trying to sort through the jumbled reels of my life, trying to put things into some kind of order.

I start with Oliver. Well, it seems as good a place as any. I tell her how our paths crossed ten years ago. 'But nothing happened between us, as I didn't notice him, although now I wish something had,' I add regretfully, pulling at my tissue. 'And then out of the blue we bumped into each other again, and it seemed like something was *going* to happen between us, that maybe I was going to get a second chance.' I pause, reliving that moment just half an hour ago on my balcony, feeling a twist in my stomach. 'But then we had this big row,' I finish miserably.

'Don't tell me. He was a lying arsehole like Billy Romani,' she interjects angrily.

'No, not at all.' I shake my head sadly.

'Then why?' She looks at me in confusion.

I think back to standing outside his granddad's antique shop with Larry Goldstein. 'I let my head rule my heart,' I say quietly. 'I told myself that business was business, that personal feelings don't come into it. I tried to rationalise.'

'You mean you ignored your gut instinct?' she says, translating.

I glance up at her, her words registering. I hadn't thought about it like that, but she's right. 'I guess I've been guilty of ignoring a lot of things,' I hear myself saying. 'I ignored the doubts I had about my relationship with Miles. We were never right for each other from the beginning, but I tried to convince myself we were, because I wanted us to be. Just like I ignore that little voice inside that says I'm not happy. Because I *must* be happy: I've got the life I always dreamed of; I've got the lifestyle, a successful career, size-ten thighs.' Smiling ruefully, I hug my knees to my chest.

'And yet I can't help feeling as if there's something missing in my life.' As I say it out loud, I realise I'm admitting this to myself for the first time. 'But I don't know what it is. And the harder I look, the more I can't find it, because there's just too much pressure and not enough time.'

I've bottled up all this stuff for so long that now it's as if I've lifted off a lid and everything's pouring out.

'It's like I'm always playing catch-up. I'm exhausted and anxious and worried all the time, not to mention hungry.' I roll my eyes and pull a face, remembering I haven't eaten since the power bar I had at breakfast.

'But what's the point?'

'Sorry?' I stop talking and look at my younger self, not understanding.

'I mean, what's the point of worrying all the time?' She shrugs.

I stare at her, perplexed. Is that a trick question?

'Well, it's not about there being a *point* . . .'

'So why do it, then?' she asks simply.

'Because . . .' I open my mouth to explain, only I can't quite think of anything to say.

'It's a total waste of time.' She reaches for a pot of glittery nail varnish and tries it out on her big toe. 'If the worst is going to happen, it'll happen. Worrying can't protect you from that. And if it *doesn't* happen' – she raises her eyebrows – 'then you've missed out on all the time when you could have been having fun.' Smiling brightly, she puts down the pot of glittery nail varnish and picks up a bright purple one instead and starts doing the other foot.

Meanwhile I'm looking at her in astonishment. How did I change from her to me? From this carefree person into someone who spends their whole time with a nervous knot in their stomach. What on earth happened to me?

But before I've even finished asking myself the question, deep down inside I know the answer.

Because you see, I haven't told Lottie the whole story. There's more. A lot more. I've just kept it buried deep inside of me for so long now, I'd almost convinced myself that none of it ever really happened. Almost, until a few days ago when I saw myself again with Billy Romani and all the painful memories came rushing back.

Of course Lottie doesn't know any of this. I haven't told her the real reason why I tried to stop her sleeping with Billy Romani. I haven't explained to her what really broke my heart. And how can I? How can I tell my younger self about the sequence of events that followed? About how I thought I'd bounced back, got over it, only to discover a few weeks after my birthday that something was wrong.

My period was late.

Well, you can guess the rest. Disbelief. Panic. Tears. I can still remember that moment as if it was yesterday, sitting on the toilet, looking at the two little blue lines, feeling my whole world collapsing around me. I was twenty-two years old and had no idea what to do. Emotions threatened to overwhelm me: anger for being so stupid, for letting this happen, for getting myself into this situation. And fear. A cold icy fear that had tightened its grip around my heart leaving me scared and afraid.

The only person I told was Vanessa. She didn't judge me or admonish me, she didn't say anything, just gave me a hug and promised to be there whatever I decided to do. It was Vanessa who lent me the money and came with me to the clinic. If it hadn't been for her, I don't think I'd have got through it, but in a few hours it was all over and I consoled myself with the thought that now I could put it all behind me.

Except I never really did put it behind me. I don't think anyone ever does, do they? From that moment on it was as if something had changed inside of me. I'd crossed a line and I never crossed back. Of course I've changed gradually over the years, people do, it's all part of growing up. But if I look back, it's almost as if that was the moment the old Lottie disappeared.

A lone tear spills from my eyelashes and trickles down my cheek. Because it's only now I realise that I've never really forgiven myself. It was ten years ago but there are still times when I wonder if I did the right thing. Unguarded moments when I see Vanessa with Ruby and Sam, and I see how much she loves them, that I ask myself if I made the right choice. Wondered 'what if'.

But now I know.

Because if spending time with my younger self and seeing Billy Romani again has made me realise one thing, it's that I made completely the right decision. We were so young, so wrong for each other, so not ready, we would have made terrible parents. We weren't even together – to Billy Romani I was just a one-night stand – and I couldn't have brought a child up on my own, I was still practically a child myself. I was silly. I thought I was in love, and it was an accident. It happens to millions of women. It had happened to me. But now I need to finally accept that and stop blaming myself. It's like I said to Lottie, that day as she sat crying on her doorstep: acceptance is the final stage. I need to reach that to be able to move on.

And now I have.

'Hey, are you all right?' Lottie looks up from painting her toenails.

'Yeah.' I brush away the lone tear. 'I think so.'

'You know, you've got to stop worrying about the past, forget about the future and start living for the moment.' Finishing painting her toes, she wiggles them with a satisfied expression.

'I know.' I nod and take a moment to let it all sink in, before smiling ruefully. 'But how?'

She rolls her eyes as if I'm a total moron, then realises I'm completely serious and fixes me with a considered look. 'Loosen up a bit more, be spontaneous, enjoy yourself.'

'Enjoy myself?' I repeat, as if I'm speaking a foreign language.

'Like the other night on the dance floor.' She does a little impression of what I can only assume is me dancing and I feel myself blush. 'You looked like you were having fun.'

'Yes, I was,' I admit. My mind spools back to dancing at the club, walking through the park with Oliver, eating shortbread fingers with his granddad, shopping at the flea market . . . I haven't realised it until now, but I've had more fun in the last few days than I can remember having in the last few years.

'Here, I know what will cheer you . . .' Jumping up from the table, my younger self scrabbles around in a spangly bag hanging on the back of the chair and pulls out a Kit-Kat. 'Chocolate.' She pulls a delighted face and, snapping it in half, holds out a finger.

'Um, no, thanks.' I smile, shaking my head. 'I try not to eat chocolate.'

'Seriously?' She stares at me agog. 'God, no wonder you're depressed.'

And suddenly it hits me. Our roles have completely reversed. It's no longer me giving my younger self advice; it's her giving *me* advice. And I'm fast realising that actually I don't know better at all. About some things, yes – I glance at that terrible silver eyeshadow – but not about everything, far from it.

Age and experience haven't made me this wise old master – they've made me this anxious, strung-out thirtysomething who worries about everything. Whose life is completely out of balance. Who's forgotten how to have fun. And who spends the whole time reading self-help books and trying to find herself when she's been here under her nose all along, I think, glancing at Lottie and seeing this smart, confident, vibrant person.

Honestly, what was I worrying about? She's going to be just fine, I suddenly realise. I can't wrap her up in cotton wool. I can't stop her making mistakes, just like I couldn't stop her and Billy and the inevitable result that came from that. But you know what? I don't want to. There's a saying 'What doesn't kill you makes you stronger.' And yes, she's going to have some rough times ahead of her, but she's gonna be OK.

I'm going to be OK.

Because it's true: there has been something missing in my life. *I* was missing in my life. I lost sight of who I was. I lost myself. And now here, in this bedroom, I've found myself again.

'Actually, pass me some of that Kit-Kat.'

And my sweet tooth.

After polishing off the rest of the Kit-Kat, my appetite reawakens and I suddenly realise I'm starving. Lottie kindly offers me a Pot Noodle, but I decline. While I might have had the right idea about a lot of things when I was younger, this definitely wasn't one of them. Instead I suggest going to eat at the Wellington Arms. My treat.

Which seems like a great idea until we enter the pub and I suddenly see the young Olly. I stiffen. With everything that's been happening, I'd totally forgotten he'd be working here, and seeing him now brings my argument with Oliver whooshing back.

Apprehensively I walk towards the bar.

'Hey, how are you?' As he sees me, he smiles in recognition. 'It's Charlotte, isn't it? We met the other night at the Canal Club.'

'Yeah. Hi, Olly.' I smile awkwardly. It seems weird him being so nice, when only a few hours ago we were standing in my living room, screaming at each other.

'So how are things?' he asks cheerfully, and as I look into his familiar pale grey eyes, my insides tug.

'Great,' I say brightly, forcing myself to sound cheerful. If I felt bad before, now I feel worse. 'And you?'

'Oh, I'm good.' He nods, then pauses and plays with the woven bracelets round his wrist, as if he's got something on his mind. 'Um, actually, I was going to ask you a favour,' he says after a moment, and glances at me nervously.

'Sure, anything.'

Anything to try and make things up to you, I think, looking at him behind the bar and feeling myself almost sag under the weight of regret.

'Well, the thing is' – he swallows hard – 'I'm cooking dinner tomorrow night for a few friends and I wanted to invite Lottie. Do you think she might come?'

He smiles nervously, his face infused with hope. And I know, right here and now, that this is my second chance. I might have messed things up, but it doesn't mean Lottie has to.

'Of course she will,' I reassure him.

'Really?' His face flushes with delight. 'You think so?'

'Leave it to me.' I smile. 'Just give me your address.'

'Oh, OK . . .' He scrambles for a piece of paper, as if hardly daring to believe his luck. 'Hang on, there's a notepad around here somewhere . . .'

'Don't worry, use this.' I dig a crumpled piece of paper out of my bag. It's my list of advice. Nineteen dos and don'ts. Funny, I never got to number twenty. 'I won't be needing this any more.' I glance at it for a moment, thinking how much I got it wrong, before passing it across the bar. 'Just write on the back.'

'Thanks,' he mutters, and scribbles his address. 'Tell her it's at seven thirty, and she doesn't need to bring anything. Just herself,' he adds, with a small smile. He passes it to me.

'Consider it done.' I smile back, slipping it into my bag.

'Now, what can I get you?' he asks. 'Drinks are on the house.'

I order two halves of cider and two packets of salt-and-vinegar crisps as an appetiser – well, if I'm back on the chocolate, it seems only fitting I go the whole hog – and walk back to the table, carrying a couple of menus, where Lottie is waiting.

'Hey, Lottie,' I say casually, handing her the cider and crisps, and sliding into the seat next to her. 'I'm going over to a friend's for dinner tomorrow night and I wondered if you wanted to come along.'

'Oh, yeah, that sounds cool.' She nods, diving delightedly on the crisp packet and ripping it open.

'But I'm going straight from work, so I was hoping you could meet me there,' I continue, trying to sound as nonchalant as possible, hoping she'll take the bait. Because of course at the last minute I'm suddenly not going to be able to make it due to some 'unforeseen problem at work', but by then she'll already be there.

'Sure, what's the address?'

Bingo.

'Here, I wrote it on a piece of paper,' I say, digging it out of my bag and passing it to her. She sticks it in her pocket without even looking at it. Unlike me, who'd be immediately looking it up in my A–Z.

Or at least I would have done in the past, I reflect, taking a sip of my cider. Mmm, that is good.

'So what do you think, Charlotte?'

'About what?' I snap back to see Lottie peering at the menu. 'The fish and chips or the pasta? You've eaten here before. What do you recommend?'

I look at her, in her too-short denim hot pants, drinking cider and playing with a tendril of hair. She hasn't changed, she's still exactly the same as when I first bumped into her, and you know what I'm glad. I don't want her to change. I want her to stay exactly how she is. How I was. How I'm learning to be again.

Well, maybe not the denim hot pants.

Eating a handful of crisps, I take a large slug of cider. 'Oh, I don't think you need any advice from me.'

'OK, well, then in that case I'll have the cheese nachos with refried beans and sour cream.'

I consider the ingredients: dairy, wheat, fat, carbs, deep-fried and not in the slightest bit organic, low fat or remotely healthy.

I throw her a big grin. 'Sounds delicious. I'll have the same.'

Chapter Thirty-six

After what has to be one of the best meals I've had in ages, I drop Lottie at her house and drive home to my flat. Walking back into the living room feels like returning to the scene of a crime. The ice has now melted, leaving a soggy wet tea towel. Two cups of tea, stone cold with a glassy film, sit untouched on the table outside. Welly's muddy pawprints have dried on the carpet.

Everything has moved from the present into the past. Wedging time in between Oliver and me. Pushing us ever further apart.

My chest tightens, but I don't let myself go there. Swallowing hard, I look away, my eyes falling instead on the pile of files sitting on my dining table. I've still got to put the finishing touches to tomorrow's press launch. After all, life must go on, I tell myself firmly, pulling myself together and beginning to clear up. I can't sit around wallowing about what's happened, feeling sorry for myself. I just want to put today behind me and forget about it, pretend it never happened.

I spend the next half an hour tidying up my flat, until every trace has been erased and it's like Oliver was never here. Only then do I sit down to do some work.

Turning my attention to the files, I open my laptop and click on the Word document I've been working on. Everything's been arranged. The press list has been drawn up. The invites have been designed and sent out. The venue's organised. The problem with the caterers is sorted. The speciality cocktails have been decided upon (no champagne – bubbles play havoc with tooth enamel). The goody bags have been put together. All that remains now is to polish the speech I've been working on for the spokesperson.

This was my big idea: getting a celebrity to be the spokesperson for Star Smile. Combined with a goody bag and free teeth-bleaching, it's guaranteed to draw journalists and generate press. It's also an idea that Larry Goldstein fell in love with at our first meeting and which probably swung the account for me. Yet even before I won the contract, I had already spent weeks drawing up a list of appropriate candidates, putting out feelers, approaching celebrities' agents.

Celebrities are renowned for having their teeth fixed. You'd be hard pushed to find a Hollywood A-lister who hasn't had a little help to achieve that perfect smile. Unfortunately you are *really* hard pushed to find one who will admit to it, hence a batch of perfect-toothed, wrinkle-free, bee-stung-lipped celebrities who insist it's all down to Manuka honey and Pilates, not, as everyone in the industry knows, their regular visits to the men in white coats.

Thus, after dozens of rejections, and just when I was about to abandon the idea, Beatrice suggested Melody. Well, we already do the PR on her range of diet books and health foods, she's always on the lookout for more exposure (translated: she's a total media whore), plus she's the nation's sweetheart, with just the right mix of glamour and girl-next-door. And let's not forget, she needs something to counter last week's scandal when she was caught eating a Big Mac.

Sure enough, she's jumped at the opportunity, I muse, reading an email from her that's just popped into my inbox regarding the outfit she's wearing tomorrow. She's also jumped at the new set of promised veneers.

I turn my focus back to the speech. 'Welcome, everyone, to the press launch for Star Smile UK, the brainchild of Larry Goldstein, or, as he's been known in Hollywood, Mr Celebrity Smile. Star Smile promises to offer the latest in teeth-bleaching, the finest veneers, laser-gum contouring—'

'*I really want to be a writer.*'

What? Where did that come from? I ignore it and keep working.

'—state-of-the-art cosmetic dentistry, to cater for all our twenty-first-century smiles—'

'*Ever since I was a little girl it's been my dream.*'

Lottie's voice flashes into my mind again, louder this time. For a split second I pause to listen, to reflect, then hurriedly brush it aside.

'*I couldn't imagine doing anything else.*'

It catches the breath in the back of my throat. It's true. I really couldn't imagine doing anything else, not even slightly. But that was then.

Rubbing my temples, I force myself to sit upright in my chair and focus on the screen. OK, I'll think about that later. Right now I've got to get this finished. Dragging my eyes back to the screen, I begin reading over the rest of the speech.

'You too can have a celebrity smile. You too can dazzle with the stars. A Star Smile is the latest must-have accessory. Forget this season's Fendi, trade in your last-season smile, be it crooked, stained or misaligned.'

Ugh, that's not very sexy, is it? I need to vamp that up. Though God knows how I vamp up 'crooked, stained or misaligned'. I mean, please, I can't believe I'm even writing this kind of crap.

'*Do something you love, something you're passionate about.*'

Oh, be quiet! I think in frustration. That's all well and good, and I'm in total agreement with my younger self on that one, but I can't pull out of this now. It would be insanity. It would be career suicide.

And yet, as I look back at the screen, the words swim in front of my eyes and I realise I'm doing what I did before. It's like Lottie said; I'm not listening to my gut instinct. This isn't writing. This isn't what I wanted to. This wasn't my dream.

'I'm writing a novel. I haven't finished it yet, but I'm going to.'

On impulse I jump up and go into my bedroom, where I get down on all fours and peer under the bed. Underneath is the box of photos I found in the cupboard. Tugging them out, I pull off the lid and rummage through the albums. I didn't even get to look at them all, I reflect, stacking them up on the floor, along with another couple of old diaries and some ancient-looking birthday cards.

And then there it is: a thin pile of faded pages beginning to yellow around the edges.

My novel.

I stare for a moment at the title page, absorbing the feelings whooshing around. I feel suddenly emotional. It's like seeing a part of me that's been buried inside for so long I'd almost forgotten it was there. I swallow hard, tracing my fingers over the typewritten letters. Then slowly I turn the page and begin to read.

When I've finished, I stand up and walk back into the living room. I feel strangely euphoric. It's good. Better than good. Better than I ever remembered. OK, so it's a bit long-winded in parts, and there's some clunky description, but it's got something. Something that excites me. Inspires me. Makes me feel passionate again.

If there were any doubts before, now I'm left with none.

But first there's something I need to do.

I turn back to my laptop, close the Word document and open up the Internet. It's just a hunch, but I'm listening to my gut instinct at last. I hesitate, then type something into Google. Though who knows – I scroll down the page – maybe this time my instincts are wrong.

Then I see it.

I click on the link and suddenly exactly what I suspected pops up on to the screen. My eyes skim through the text as I absorb the information. Then I pick up the phone and dial. Far away across town, I can hear it ringing.

'Um, hello?' mumbles a sleepy voice. It's Katie Proctor, my journalist friend.

'Hi Katie. It's Charlotte Merryweather. Look, I'm sorry to call you so late, but I really need to ask you a huge favour . . .'

Chapter Thirty-seven

**Merryweather PR invites you to the
launch of Star Smile UK!**

Join our guest host, TV-personality Melody, and discover all
about the exciting new London branch of the famous Beverly
Hills clinic. Meet Dr Larry Goldstein, known to all in Hollywood
as Mr Celebrity Smile, and learn how the latest state-of-the-art
techniques can give you that A-list smile.

We look forward to seeing you there.

Tuesday 28 August
Presentation and drinks 5–7 p.m.

The Charlotte Street Hotel
15–17 Charlotte Street, London W1
RSVP: Beatrice@MerryweatherPR.com

OK, so this it.

Standing in the centre of the private room we've hired for the
launch, I sweep my gaze over the dazzling arrangements of white
lilies, rows of sparkling glasses ready to be filled with the Star
Smile cocktail (a delicious blend of vodka, lychees and ver-
mouth) and an elaborate centrepiece of sushi on ice, the snow-
white rice gleaming under the lighting. The theme, as you might
have guessed, is white, to tie in with the idea of bright-white
Hollywood smiles.

OK, I confess, that was my idea.

Although I say it myself, it does look pretty impressive, I muse, taking a moment to admire the empty room. The journalists have already arrived, and after a welcome cocktail are immediately ushered into the private screening room to hear a presentation by Melody and watch a short film about the Beverly Hills clinic. It's good background info. Plus everyone always likes to watch footage of Hollywood celebrities, don't they? Especially when they have the excuse it's for work.

I hear familiar music from the screening room. After having watched the film more than a few times, I know that's the cue that it's nearly over and this room will soon be filled with hungry journalists.

'Mmm, this sushi is delish.'

I turn round to see Beatrice swooning over a piece of sushi she's just stolen from a tray being held by one of the waitresses. I shoot her a look.

'Um . . . I mean, yes, it passed the test.' She nods officiously, straightening up. She smiles at the waitress before turning back to me. 'Well, someone had to make sure it tasted OK,' she protests innocently. 'We don't want to poison the journalists.'

'Only some of them.' I smile ruefully and she giggles back.

For a brief moment I feel the tension that's been holding me hostage all day loosen its grip slightly, but then the screening-room door swings open and out stalks Larry Goldstein. He's deep in conversation with Melody, who's smiling at his flattery, and behind him spill out the journalists, their eyes blinking in the brightness.

Beatrice immediately launches into her meet-and-greet routine. I swear she really should have been a member of the royal family. 'Why hello. How simply wonderful to see you again.'

I glance anxiously at the clock by the door. It's almost six.

'Excuse me,' I say, hurrying into the lobby and over to the front desk. 'Has a Fed-Ex arrived for me, Charlotte Merryweather?'

The receptionist shakes his head and smiles brightly. 'No, sorry.'

My insides clench, but pinning on a smile, I thank him and rejoin the launch.

'Charlotte, this is amazing.' I glance sideways to see a journalist from one of the UK's top beauty magazines. 'And what a coup, getting the Star Smile account. I'd heard a whisper, but until I got the invite . . .' She raises her glass to toast me.

'Oh . . . thanks, yes,' I manage brightly, but my throat has gone dry. I spot Larry Goldstein over by the door, chatting to some journalists, and screw up my courage. It's now or never. 'I'm sorry, but will you excuse me a moment?'

'Oh, sure.' The journalist beams back. 'I think I'm going to help myself to another cocktail.'

As she disappears, I make my way towards Larry. I feel absurdly nervous. The palms of my hands have started to sweat, and I can hear my heart beating loud and fast in my ears over the chattering din. Then suddenly I hear Lottie's voice inside my head: 'What's the point of worrying all the time? If the worst is going to happen, it'll happen.' Drawing reassurance from it, I take a deep breath.

'Hi, Dr Goldstein, could I have word?'

He pauses from narrating some anecdote and turns to me. 'Hey, Charlene, come and join us. I'm just telling these girls about the time I went in Tom Cruise's private Learjet.'

I smile politely and swallow hard. 'Actually, it's really important.'

'What can be more important than Tom Cruise's Learjet?' He cocks his head at the two pretty journalists, who titter into their cocktails.

I clench my fists, digging my fingernails into the palms of my hands. OK, here goes. 'My resignation,' I say evenly.

He looks at me like I've just told him there are little green Martians in the room. Actually, he'd look *less* shocked if I'd told him there were little green Martians in the room.

'Oh, I get it, this is the famous British sense of humour.' He laughs.

I swallow hard. 'No, I'm being serious. I'm afraid Merry-weather PR can no longer represent you.'

The two journalists stop giggling and look at me uncertainly.

Larry Goldstein, on the other hand, looks like he's just been shot. Grabbing me roughly by the elbow, he marches me into the corridor outside. His head tips as if he can't compute what I've just said. 'Say that again?' he demands. 'I'm not quite under-standing here.'

Shaken, I pull my arm free and take a step back to regain my composure. 'It was too late to call off the press launch at such short notice, and it would also have been unprofessional.' I'm struggling to keep my voice steady. 'And so I followed through on that commitment. However, I'm afraid we can no longer represent you or the actual launch of the Star Smile clinic in December and we wish to formally resign from the account.'

There. I've done it.

As my words register, his eyes turn glassy and he pales underneath his tan. '*You. Are. Dropping. Me.*'

'Well, I wouldn't use those words . . .'

His face turns hard and he laughs scornfully. 'I think you're getting a little bit confused, Charlene. I'm the one who drops people, not the other way round.'

'You can call it what you like, Dr Goldstein, but I'm still firm in my decision. Merryweather PR will no longer be responsible for your public relations.'

As the words leave my mouth, his face puckers into a glare and it's suddenly as if the smooth veneer has fallen away and the real Larry Goldstein has been exposed.

'Some poxy little agency is dropping me, Mr Celebrity Smile?' His voice is almost a hiss, and his face is contorted with fury. 'Who do you think you are? I'm offering you the chance to go global. To take on a big-name client. To further your career. To play with the big guys. To take your second-rate agency into the major league.'

'If you thought we were so second-rate, why did you choose us?' I fire back defensively.

'Because I thought I saw something in you. I thought you reminded me of me. That you were hungry for success.'

I shake my head. 'No, I'm not like you. I don't want the kind of success that comes from ruining someone's livelihood.'

He screws up his face. 'Huh?'

'The antique shop.'

Even now he doesn't register. And why should he? Business is business to him. He probably didn't even register what kind of shop it was. He just saw it as an opportunity.

'The space you chose for your new clinic,' I explain, 'the space you threw money at to obtain the lease. The man had been in that shop for over sixty years and suddenly his rent was tripled. He's losing his livelihood.' I'm like Lottie now, the old me, speaking my mind, wearing my heart on my sleeve, putting my personal feelings first, and it feels good.

'Well, let me get out the violin,' he says coldly, and I feel a jolt. Any doubt I may have had that I was doing the wrong thing vanishes in that very moment.

'I didn't expect you to understand,' I reply calmly, then add, 'And as neither of us have signed the final contract, it should be a simple parting of ways.'

'Whoah, just one minute, little lady.'

There's such vitriol in his voice that a shiver of fear runs down my spine.

'We might not have signed anything yet, but I know the law. There's legal binding here. I've got emails outlining your intentions to manage this account, the ideas we've discussed, the plans for the future.' He looks at me and it's like the gloves are finally off. 'I'll haul you through the courts and sue your ass off. I'll take everything you own: your company, your home, your livelihood, every fucking thing.'

My heart thuds. This is what I was afraid of.

'Fine, go ahead,' I reply evenly, trying to stop my voice from trembling.

I turn to leave, but he yells after me, 'You can't just walk away from me like that. You don't know what you're dealing with here, Charlene. *I'm* the one who calls the shots.' He's shouting now and his perfect tan has been replaced by a livid red flush.

'Honey?' There's a high-pitched twang and his wife pops her head round the door.

With everything that's been happening, I'd totally forgotten her.

Holding a cocktail and her beloved chihuahua, she smiles tipsily at him. 'Honey, are you going to come back inside? The shrimp's sensational.'

'Get the hell outta here, Cindy, will ya?' he yells angrily. 'Can't see you I'm talking business?' Her face blanches, and as she scuttles away, he wheels round to face me. 'I'll ruin you. I'll tell everyone in the business that you were unprofessional, incompetent, that you weren't up to the job. I've got friends in high places. I'll go to the press.' He's ranting now, spitting with fury, but I stand firm. I knew this would probably happen, but I was determined to go ahead anyway. I was determined to listen to my instinct.

'Excuse me? Fed-Ex man for Charlotte Merryweather.'

I whirl round to see the Fed-Ex man appear in the corridor. *Just in time*. I feel a rush of relief. My younger self might have helped me rediscover my dream, get my priorities right and speak my mind, but my older self knows it doesn't hurt to take out insurance.

'The person at the front desk said I might find you down here, said it was urgent.'

'Actually, it's for him.' Signing for it, I gesture to Larry Goldstein.

'Huh?' Having stopped yelling, he looks at me, breathless and confused.

The Fed-Ex man shrugs and passes him the envelope. Turning it over in his hands, Larry Goldstein stares at it, a look of bewilderment on his face.

'I think you might want to open that,' I instruct.

'What is this bullshit?' he snaps, finally finding his voice. 'Because I can—'

'Sue me? Go to the press?' I interrupt, trying to keep calm, even though inside my heart is beating very, very fast. 'I wouldn't do that if I were you.'

Impatiently he strips open the envelope, a scornful expression on his face, which immediately disappears when he sees what's inside.

'*Jesus*,' he whispers, turning pale with shock.

Lottie accused me of ignoring my gut instinct, and when it comes to Larry Goldstein, I've been ignoring mine from that first meeting in the restaurant. I was sure I felt his hand grope me under the table, yet I dismissed it, just as I dismissed the intense looks, the flirty innuendo, the uncomfortable feeling I got in the pit of my stomach. It was only later, outside the shop, when he turned to me and said, 'If you throw a lot of money at a problem it goes away,' that I knew for certain. Right then that little voice inside of me knew.

But it wasn't until last night that I finally listened to that voice and, acting on my instinct, decided to do a bit of research.

Because it seems I'm not the first. An entry in the *Santa Barbara Evening Post* in 1992 mentions the case of a sixteen-year-old who accused her then dentist, a Dr Goldstein, of groping her while she was in the dentist's chair. No further details were mentioned.

Which is why I called Katie Proctor. Being a journalist, she's got access to all the international press databases and court transcriptions. I asked her to investigate. My gut told me it was the same person, but I couldn't be sure. There must be hundreds of Goldsteins. And if it was, what had happened? Had he been found guilty? Struck off? Imprisoned?

Her enquiries confirmed my fears, and more. Because there hasn't been just one accusation against Dr Goldstein. Over the years there have been numerous complaints of sexual harassment – from former employees to patients and ex-mistresses – but in every case all the charges were dropped after huge out-of-court settlements.

'And you were right – his first name is Larry,' Katie had said when she'd called me this morning to tell me she was Fed-Exing over all the press cuttings, court transcriptions and documents she'd uncovered.

Otherwise known as Mr Celebrity Smile, I muse, looking at him. Although he suddenly looks nothing like his TV-personality self. His perfectly coiffed hair is now all mussed up, revealing a sizeable bald patch, and he cuts a rather pathetic figure.

'This is blackmail,' he says finally.

'And you'd know all about that, wouldn't you?' I reply evenly.

He swallows hard, still clutching the damning evidence against him. 'So what are you going to do?'

'Nothing,' I say simply. 'Goodbye, Dr Goldstein.' I start to walk away, then stop and turn. 'Oh, and for the record my name's Charlotte.' And turning back, I keep on walking. Somehow I don't think that's a name he's going to forget in a hurry.

Chapter Thirty-eight

By the time I reach the lobby, my legs are wobbly. I've been running on adrenalin since early this morning, but now my face-off is over, I feel limp and drained. Steadying myself against the wall, I take a deep breath. I can't believe I did it. I feel a warm glow of euphoria, mixed with a shot of relief, not to mention disbelief. I did it. *I did it.*

I take a deep breath and close my eyes. For a moment I just stay like that, letting it all sink in, letting my heart rate return to normal.

'There you are!' I open my eyes to see Beatrice bursting through the fire doors. I briefed her on what I was going to do. I thought it only fair – after all, I was putting the company at risk, and with it her job.

But if she'd felt any reservations, she didn't show it. Instead she'd given me a rib-crushing hug and replied rousingly, 'I'm with you. Remember, "We shall fight on the beaches, we shall fight on the landing grounds, we shall fight in the fields and in the streets, we shall fight in the hills; we shall never surrender." ' I'd looked at her in confusion.

'Winston Churchill, Daddy's icon,' she'd explained gravely.

'So how did it go?' she's asking now as she reaches me. 'I just saw Dr Goldstein leaving in a cab with a peroxide blonde and a yappy dog.'

'It went . . . well.' I nod, searching for the right adjective.

She almost crumples with relief. 'Oh, thank goodness,' she cries, before turning pensive. 'So was he terribly angry?' Her voice is hushed and fearful.

'You could say that.'

Beatrice takes a sharp intake of breath. 'Honestly, Charlotte, you're my hero.'

'Oh, I wouldn't say that.' I smile wearily.

'No, you are,' she exclaims loyally. 'You're like a superhero. Like Spiderwoman!'

'Spiderman,' I correct.

'Really? I could have sworn . . .' She frowns, then gives herself a little shake. 'Anyway, chop-chop!' She claps her hands together. 'Let's go have a drink. There are a few cocktails left – we need to hurry up and get them before the journos do.' She reaches out to link arms, but I shake my head.

'No, I think I'm going to go home,' I say quietly, clutching my head, which is beginning to throb. 'I didn't sleep much last night and I'm leaving early tomorrow.'

And that's another thing. After hearing Lottie on the phone to Mum and Dad, it made me realise it's been too long since I saw them, too long since we just sat around watching TV together and chatting about nothing, too long to miss people. Which is why I've decided to drive up tomorrow as a surprise and spend a few days with them.

'Oh, absolutely, of course,' nods Beatrice, who's aware of my plans. 'You run along.' She gives me another hug, then, remembering herself, blushes. 'I'll stay and hold the fort. Finish off the cocktails.' She shoots me a mischievous smile. 'Well, someone has to.' And turning, she stalks quickly away on her sturdy calves.

Leaving me alone in the empty lobby with just my thoughts. I feel slightly numb, dazed almost. Like in the lull after the storm, I realise, wandering over to the cloakroom, where I'd checked in my jacket. Because now it's over, and today is the first day of the rest of my life.

Without Oliver.

Once again I feel that familiar nagging ache, though it's not worry this time. I've been trying to block it out, but I can't, it's impossible. Just when I least expect it, his face pops into my mind. I can be driving in my car and I'll remember something he said, or walking down the street and that erotic moment on the balcony will rush through my head and I'll feel a tugging deep inside.

Ironic, isn't it? Ten years ago I didn't even notice him and now I can't forget him.

Reaching the cloakroom, I zip open my bag and rummage for my ticket. God, there's so much crap in here, I muse absently, while still thinking about Oliver. I'll probably never see him again, never be able to tell him I'm sorry, that I quit the contract, and he's never likely to find out. Well, it's hardly front-page news, is it?

Anyway, so what if he does? It's not as if I will have saved his granddad's shop. No doubt Larry Goldstein will just go ahead and get a different PR firm and it will be business as usual. Ultimately my stand won't make a difference to anyone – not to Larry Goldstein, not to Oliver and certainly not to his granddad.

Except that's not true, I tell myself as I pass my ticket to the attendant. It will always make a difference to me.

'Excuse me, miss?'

I snap back to see the attendant shaking her head. 'This isn't your ticket.'

'It's not? Oh, sorry.' I dive once more into my handbag. Oh, there it is. I hand it to her with an apologetic smile and she passes me back the wrong ticket. Only it's not even a ticket; it's just a scrap of paper. Wow, I really am out of it, I realise, as I glance at it.

At the untidy handwriting, at someone's address.

Olly's address.

My heart suddenly plummets. I must have given Lottie the wrong piece of paper. It's my stupid bag – it's filled with so much rubbish. *The dinner party's tonight.* As a thought strikes, I feel a clutch of panic. Oh my God, if she doesn't get it, she's not going to know where to go. She's not going to turn up. *She's going to stand him up*.

Grabbing my bag from the counter, I make a dash for it.

'Miss, your coat, miss,' cries the attendant, but I don't stop. I just keep on running.

Fifteen minutes later I'm back in my car hurtling through London, zigzagging between other cars, jumping traffic lights, speeding past speed cameras. Come on, come on, come on . . . I get caught up in the diversion again, and as I pull up at the lights, I thump the steering wheel in frustration. I have to get there in time to give her the address. I can't let her stand him up.

But what if you already did?

As the thought fires through my brain, I have a sudden flashback to yesterday in my flat, explaining to Oliver why I didn't pop into the pub: 'I thought you'd stood me up again. Just joking.'

But he wasn't joking, was he? I *did* stand him up. I *didn't* get the address in time, did I?

The shrill burbling of my phone cuts into my thoughts and I glance at the screen: *Julian*. Immediately my mind swings like a pendulum back to Vanessa and her phone call yesterday, the several messages I left with Julian's secretary telling him to call me back. I clip on my earpiece.

'Hello?'

'Hey, Charlotte, it's Julian. I got a message to call you.'

I hesitate for a split second, wondering how I am going to put this, how I am going to broach the subject, then give up. 'The game's up. I know everything.'

'About what?' he replies innocently.

'Julian, don't try this with me!' I cry impatiently. 'This is me you're talking to, remember, your friend. I've known you too long – I can tell when you're hiding something.'

There's a silence, then, 'Oh God, have you told Vanessa?' He sounds stricken.

'No, of course I haven't told Vanessa, but if you don't, I will.'

The lights turn green and I start edging forwards.

'I was just waiting for the right time,' he bleats.

'The right time?' I exclaim in disbelief. 'Of course there's never going to be a right time!' I think about Vanessa and feel a surge of loyalty. 'Julian, I can't believe you could do something like this!'

'Well, I had to do something,' he protests. 'I don't know if Vanessa told you, but we've been having a few problems—'

'*Of course* Vanessa's told me,' I cut him off. Honestly, do men really have no idea that girls tell their friends *everything*?

'And I admit I haven't exactly been the best husband of late. Work's been a nightmare. *I've* been a bit of a nightmare.'

'You're using work as an excuse?'

'Well, no, it's not an excuse, I was trying to explain . . . Look, a colleague of mine just announced his marriage is over, he's getting a divorce, and when he told me, it gave me a wake-up call, which was long overdue —'

'God, I can't believe it!' I gasp furiously, not letting him finish. 'You're all as bad as each other! And to think I always stuck up for you!'

'Well, um, thanks, Charlotte,' he replies, only now he's sounding a little defensive. And no wonder, I think, hotly. 'I'll take that as a compliment.'

'A compliment! You bastard!'

There's silence.

'Charlotte? Are you all right?' he asks after a moment.

'No, I'm not all right,' I gasp. 'Vanessa loves you. She'd do anything for you. And you go and repay her by having a sordid little affair.'

'An affair?'

I'm expecting him to be angry, sad, defensive . . . so I'm more than a little shocked when he suddenly bursts out laughing. 'You think it's funny?'

'I think it's fucking hilarious,' he replies dryly. 'Me, be unfaithful to Vanessa? She'd chop my balls off and eat them for breakfast. With ketchup.'

I feel the stirrings of doubt. 'But . . . I saw you at Boots. You had condoms . . .'

There's a prickle of embarrassment on the other end of the line, then a deep sigh. 'OK, I confess. I'm guilty of planning to have sex with my wife, Your Honour.'

'And my assistant saw you coming out of the Dorchester with a key to a suite.'

'Yup, guilty of booking a suite for a dirty weekend with my wife.'

I can feel the probable fast turning into the possible.

'And then there was the Agent Provocateur receipt.'

'Yup, guilty of finding my wife sexy and buying her naughty lingerie.'

I fall silent, absorbing it all. I'm getting the feeling I might have jumped to the wrong conclusion.

'I love my wife, Charlotte.' Julian's voice turns serious. 'When my colleague at work told me about his marriage falling apart, it brought me up short and made me look at my own marriage. It made me imagine for just a moment what life would be like without Vanessa, made me realise what a bloody idiot I've been, that I've been taking her for granted . . .'

As he continues talking, I realise I've definitely jumped to the wrong conclusion.

'. . . and so I wanted to treat her, spend time together, get to know each other again. I know it's not going to work like magic overnight, but it's a start.'

I feel stupid and delighted all at the same time. 'Oh my God, she's going to love it!' A smile bursts across my face. 'So when are you going to tell her?' I ask, turning off at the diversion and zipping down my usual short cut.

There's silence on the other end of the line.

'Julian?' I glance down at the screen on my phone and see it's blank. We've got cut off. Still, it doesn't matter. At least I know they're going to be OK, I think, feeling a glow of happiness as I glance back up at the road.

And then all of a sudden everything seems to slow right down, as if I'm watching a film in slow motion – frame by frame – only I'm in it. Smiling as I'm lifting my head, catching the blur of colour out of the corner of my eye, turning and seeing the truck heading towards me, hearing the horn blasting out, and pushing hard on the brake pedal. And now I'm opening my mouth to scream, knowing what's going to happen but knowing I can't stop it. I can't do anything.

All this in a split second and then—

Boom!

Everything goes black.

Chapter Thirty-nine

'Urgh.' Groggily I open my eyes. Everything is blurry, kind of foggy. I can make out white shapes. It feels like there are weights on my eyelids.

'Oh thank the Lord! She's awake! She's awake!'

A shrill voice jolts me out of my wooziness. I flop my head sideways and come eyeball to eyeball with Beatrice. White-faced.

'Charlotte, you've come back to us,' she gasps, her voice tremulous with excitement.

Eh? Come back to us? What does she mean, *come back to us*?

'Bea, what's going on?' I open my mouth to ask, but all I hear is a sort of weird croak. Hang on, what was that? 'Where the hell am I?' I try again, but all I hear is a coarse rasp. I feel a jolt of alarm. Oh my God, is that me?

'Nurse! Nurse, come quickly!'

Nurse? Shit, where am I?

I try sit to upright and suddenly I get the most agonising pains shooting through my body. 'Argghhhh,' I yell out. And this time I really do yell out. Trust me, it's not a husky croak.

'Ooh, there, there, be careful now.' I see a figure in white coming towards me. For a moment I think I'm dead and it's an angel, but then I feel a pair of warm, plump hands easing me back down on the pillow and hear a strong Jamaican accent. 'You've had a bit of a nasty accident.'

'Huh?' I look at her blurrily, trying to make sense of what's going on. I feel as if I'm trying to crank my brain into gear, kick-start it like my old car with a flat battery, pushing on the accelerator until finally the engine fires. Only I'm pushing on the accelerator in my brain, pumping it furiously, and my brain's a total flat battery.

'You lie still now,' the nurse is saying, patting my arm gently. 'I'll go see if I can find the doctor,' and she disappears out of my range of vision.

Which is when it registers. I'm in bed. In a hospital. It's hardly toppling dominoes, but it's a start.

'How are you feeling?' whispers a voice.

I glance sideways again to see Beatrice. I'd forgotten she was there. Like I said, I'm a bit out of it.

'Um . . . I've been better,' I manage to quip weakly. My eyes have focused now and I notice she's got dark shadows under her eyes, and her usually neat bob is unkempt. She looks as if she hasn't slept for days.

'You gave us quite a fright,' she reprimands with a small smile.

'What happened?' I manage finally.

'You were in a car accident.'

'*A car accident?*' I repeat in shock.

'A head-on collision with a truck.' She nods gravely. 'The truck driver got away fine. You came off slightly worse – three broken ribs, a fractured left shoulder . . .'

So that explains the pain, I realise, instinctively trying to move my shoulder and experiencing a sharp throbbing.

'. . . a punctured lung,' she continues, counting my injuries off on her fingers, 'and a gash across your left temple, which required twelve stitches.'

Automatically I reach up to touch my left temple and find a bandage. Suddenly I realise how sore it feels.

'You've been in and out of consciousness for the last two days. You're on morphine.'

'Two days?' I look at her in astonishment.

'I've been on a round-the-clock vigil,' she says loyally.

I smile gratefully.

'You've been very, very lucky, Charlotte.'

I lie there in my hospital bed, trying to take it all in: the fact that I've been unconscious for two days, I've been in a head-on collision, I've got broken bones, I could have died . . . My eyes well up and without warning I burst into tears.

'Oh golly, here, take a tissue,' soothes Beatrice. 'It's the shock.'

I nod mutely and blow my nose with my good arm. 'Sorry, I'm being pathetic.'

'Don't be such a silly goose,' Beatrice tuts. 'If it was me, I'd be in floods. I mean, you could be dead, or horribly mangled, or disfigured beyond recognition and you'd have to have one of those face transplants I was reading about in the *New Scientist*.' She stops as she sees my expression. 'Not that you *need* a face transplant of course,' she says quickly.

'I just don't understand . . .' I shake my head, groping my way back through the fog that's clouding my mind. At the press launch, finding the address, racing over to my old house, the diversion, the short cut, Julian.

'According to the police, you were going the wrong way down a one-way street.'

I stop blowing my nose and look at her incredulously. 'What? But that can't be . . .'

'Apparently, the one-way signs were obscured by trees. I've already put in a complaint with the council – it's a complete hazard.'

I feel my certainty wobble. It doesn't make sense, but thinking about it now, the cars were always parked facing one way and I never actually saw any other cars using that side street except . . .

'No, that can't be right,' I say with renewed certainty. 'I saw myself—' I stop myself quickly. 'I mean, I saw a girl driving an old Beetle in that direction.'

Beatrice looks at me sympathetically. 'I think maybe you're confused. That's one of the side effects of morphine, especially in the high levels you've been on.' She gestures to the intravenous drip I'm attached to. 'It can make you imagine all kinds of things.'

She's right about one thing. I am confused.

'It's a really powerful drug. I studied it at Cambridge,' she's saying.

'I thought you did maths and physics,' I say, feeling more befuddled than ever.

'Oh, I did, but I took a chemistry module just for the fun of it.' She smiles brightly.

I look at her in disbelief. Yes, she really did just say that. That's not just the morphine talking.

'Morphine is the principal medical alkaloid of opium,' she continues breezily, 'and like other opiates, it acts directly on the central nervous system to relieve pain. However, one of the side effects can be incredibly vivid dreams. In fact the word "morphine" is derived from Morpheus, one of the Greek gods of dreams.'

'What? You're telling me I dreamed it?' I say disparagingly.

'Most probably.' She nods matter-of-factly. 'You've been murmuring all kinds of things in your sleep. Something about Lottie . . . Olly . . . clubbing.' She gives a little laugh. 'That's when I knew you must be dreaming. I mean, *you*? *Clubbing*? No offence, but when did *any* of us last go clubbing?'

Actually, now I'm thinking about it, it does sound totally implausible.

Wearily I let my eyelids droop. Having just regained consciousness, everything seems a bit too much and I feel as if my brain's about to overload with all these revelations.

'But I wouldn't worry. It's perfectly normal,' she reassures quickly. 'In fact there are many reported cases of people experiencing wonderful dreams when taking morphine, including visions, hallucinations, even lucid dreams.'

My eyelids snap back open. 'What's a lucid dream?' I ask, frowning, then wincing as my temple throbs.

'It's when you feel totally conscious, yet you're really completely asleep,' she explains, helping herself to a mound of grapes next to my bed. 'You're dreaming, but it's as vivid as the "real" waking life. You can go anywhere, meet anyone, do anything. It's a sort of virtual reality.'

I suddenly remember the moment in the pub where I first met Lottie: *Unless of course this is all some crazy dream and I'm going to pinch myself and wake up to find Bobby Ewing in the shower. Or something like that.*

'It's actually incredibly fascinating.' She smiles.

I feel a creeping realisation. What is she saying? What does this mean? That everything I thought was real *isn't*? As the idea strikes, I feel my whole set of beliefs blown apart. Oh my God, does this mean that it really *was* all some crazy morphine-induced dream? That I didn't really meet my younger self? That none of it happened?

'So what about the press launch with Larry Goldstein? Did I dream that too?' My mind is reeling. I'm trying to make sense out of all this, but I feel totally disorientated. It's as if I don't know what's real and isn't real, what to believe and not to believe.

'Oh, no, that *certainly* happened,' says Beatrice firmly.

'And did I . . .?'

'Tell him where he could stuff his bleaching kit?' she finishes, giving me a small smile. 'Metaphorically of course.'

I manage my first smile of the day.

'Speaking of which . . .' She tugs out a trade paper. 'He released a statement saying he's decided not to expand into the UK at this time, due to the economic climate, and he's going to concentrate on his business in the States.'

As she passes me the paper, I look at the short statement. So Oliver's granddad's shop will be saved after all, I realise, feeling a beat of pleasure, followed immediately by a tug of sadness as I think about Oliver. I brush it away quickly. There's no point thinking about it. That's over.

'If you're still feeling a bit confused, I can run through last week's diary. It might make things clearer for you.' I glance up from the newspaper to see Beatrice pulling her laptop out of its case. 'I brought it with me so I could keep in touch with the office.'

'Thanks, that would be really helpful.' I smile appreciatively and make a mental note never to tease Beatrice about the diary again.

Balancing it on her knee, she tucks her hair behind her ears and squints at the screen. 'OK, so on Monday you had a lunch meeting at the Wolseley, followed by dinner with Miles at some new gastropub.'

That was the first day I saw myself at the traffic lights, I think, before I can stop myself.

'Tuesday, you had the lunch meeting with Larry Goldstein.'

And later that evening I followed myself to my old house.

'Wednesday you had a doctor's appointment.'

'Because I thought I was hallucinating,' I say, suddenly galvanised. 'But I wasn't. What I saw was real.'

Beatrice looks at me doubtfully. 'Hmm, well, according to his notes, it just says you came in suffering from stress: the doctors here had access to your medical files after the accident.'

I look at her dazedly. Waking up in hospital and being told you've been in a car accident you *don't* remember happening is bewildering enough, but then being told that the stuff you *do* remember didn't happen is enough to totally freak you out.

'Don't worry,' soothes Beatrice. 'I once dreamed I went to see the doctor and he asked me to get undressed so he could examine me, and when I turned round, he'd morphed into my great-uncle Harold!' She looks at me aghast. 'Though that was probably more of a nightmare than a dream.' Shuddering, she hastily turns back to the on-screen diary. 'Right, where was I? Oh, yes, then in the afternoon we had the spa opening.'

'And we had that conversation about time travel.'

Beatrice looks at me blankly. 'Did we? Golly, I was so drunk we could have been having a conversation with Brad Pitt and I wouldn't remember.'

I feel a beat of disappointment. Maybe she doesn't remember the conversation. Then again, it's more likely it never happened, I admit to myself reluctantly.

'Then on Thursday evening you had dinner with Larry Goldstein at his hotel.'

'And went to see Shattered Genius in concert,' I say almost to myself.

'No, there's nothing in the diary about any concert. Plus I called you afterwards. You were at home, remember?' She looks at me and I realise I'm thinking aloud. 'Then Friday was your birthday dinner.'

'And afterwards I went to Lottie's party,' I murmur.

'No, sorry.' Beatrice looks at me sympathetically. 'Nothing about that either.'

Well, why would there be? I tell myself, but even as I think it, I know I'm clutching at straws. Beatrice is right: I've been mixing fact with fantasy, dreaming about last week's actual events and interspersing them with my own imaginary ones about meeting my younger self, getting everything jumbled up. Unexpectedly I feel a clunk of sadness.

'It just seemed so real,' I sigh. 'I really thought I met my twenty-one-year-old self, that I've been hanging out with her. I could have sworn—'

'Golly, you did get a bang on the head, didn't you?' The doctor walks in and throws me a smile. 'Don't worry, the effects of the drugs wear off in no time.'

I feel my cheeks flush with embarrassment. Well, honestly, what was I thinking? Of course it was just a dream.

'OK, so let's see how the patient's doing.' Walking over to me, he consults my chart and looks pleased. 'Your X-rays are great. Your vitals are great.' He nods, then looking up, glances at my face. 'Brow's healing nicely.' He smiles warmly and I realise he's probably not much older than I am. 'We'll keep you in over-night, just to make sure everything's OK, but you should be out of here tomorrow.'

'And how long before my shoulder heals?' I ask, as he slips my chart back into its holder.

'You should start physio in a couple of weeks, but I'm afraid you won't be able to drive for a while.'

'Thanks,' I say, grateful that I've not done any lasting damage.

'My pleasure.' He nods. 'OK, so I'll check on you later. Bye, Charlotte. Bye, Beatrice.' He smiles, glancing across at her.

'Thank you, Doctor,' she replies, blushing as a look passes between them.

Hang on a minute – I feel something slowly registering.

'Did I just see that look, or was I dreaming that too?' I say, once the doctor's left the room.

Dragging her eyes away from the doorway, she turns to me, her face flushed with delight. 'Isn't he divine?'

I look at her in amazement. 'You're going out with my doctor?'

'His name's Hamish,' she says proudly. 'We met when you were first admitted, and then we kept bumping into each other over the last two days, by the coffee machine, in the canteen. He's been working nights, you know.'

'Now I know why you've been keeping a bedside vigil.' I smile.

She gasps in indignation. 'No, it's not! I've been worried sick.'

'It was a joke, Beatrice,' I say quickly, and her indignation immediately melts away into wistfulness.

'I think I'm in love,' she confides in a whisper. 'He doesn't mind me talking about scientific things at all. In fact yesterday we had a fascinating discussion about X-rays and radiation.'

'But what about Pablo, the salsa teacher?' I tease.

'Oh, didn't I tell you! Oh, well, no, obviously,' she catches herself quickly, then swallows hard, as if bracing herself to tell me some shocking news. 'When I was at the salsa club on Monday night, he introduced me to Julio, his boyfriend!' She looks at me, her eyes wide. 'Apparently he's gay! Would you believe it!'

'A gay salsa teacher? No, never,' I say with irony.

Which Beatrice totally misses. 'I know. Golly, what a turn-up for the books,' she says, shaking her head. 'But I'm so pleased for them, and they danced the fandango together beautifully.'

'Oh my goodness, she's awake!'

Beatrice's reverie is suddenly interrupted by the appearance of Mum and Dad, who, on seeing me propped up in bed, look both shocked and delighted.

'David, she's awake!' repeats Mum, shoving her polystyrene coffee cup at Dad's chest as she rushes over, arms outstretched. 'Charlotte, you're awake!'

'That's right, I'm awake,' I repeat, smiling affectionately. I feel a warm surge of comfort. God, I've never been more pleased to see them.

'Oh, my little baby,' gasps Mum, appearing by my bed, her face etched with concern.

'Your parents and I have been taking it in turns to keep up the vigil,' interjects Beatrice, throwing them both a smile.

'We just popped out for a snack – your father was hungry,' Mum begins explaining apologetically, while Dad waves a half-eaten sandwich sheepishly. 'But we came as soon as we heard about the accident.'

'Well, if the mountain won't come to Mohammed,' smiles Dad, relieving himself of food and beverages on the chair next to the bed and rubbing my cheek affectionately like he used to do when I was little. I feel a glow of pleasure, the months I haven't seen them simply melting away.

'We've all been so worried. Thank goodness you're all right,' continues Mum.

'I'm fine, Mum, don't worry,' I reassure her. 'And about the other day, I'm sorry about not calling you back.'

'Oh, don't be silly,' she gasps, batting away my apology. 'That's not important. All that's important is that you're OK.' She squeezes my hand, and as our eyes meet, I know I don't have to say anything. I don't have to say how much I love her, or how I was going to drive up and surprise them both because I missed them – because that's the thing about parents: you never have to explain, they just know.

'Give her a few weeks and she'll be back to nagging you for grandchildren,' chuckles my dad, as Mum throws him a furious look. 'Only joking, dear.' He smiles, tossing me a wink.

'Well, I better go rally the troops,' announces Beatrice. 'Unless of course you need more time alone.'

'Troops?'

'Your visitors!' she exclaims. 'Everyone's been so worried. They're in the waiting room. Up until now it's only been family allowed – I had to bend the doctor's arm,' she confides smiling. 'But if you're feeling up to it . . .'

'Oh, yes, of course.' I nod, trying to sit a bit more upright. Wow, visitors. As Beatrice disappears, I make an attempt to smooth down my hair and adjust my pyjama top, then give up. Well, I've just been in a head-on collision; I'm hardly going to look my best, am I?

'So, Sleeping Beauty's finally woken up, huh?'

I turn to see Vanessa striding into the room. I try to laugh, then stop myself. Ouch.

'That was some scare you gave us.' She throws me a huge grin. 'Julian was on the phone to you when it happened.'

'And yes, before you ask, she knows about the surprise,' says Julian, appearing next to her.

'Surprise, bloody shock more like,' she tuts, punching him affectionately on the arm. 'Still, he got one of his own when I told him my real bra size, didn't you, darling?'

He smiles sheepishly and wraps his arm round her waist, pulling her close. 'I didn't know what your measurements were, so the assistant asked me which celebrity you looked like, so she could work it out. So I said, "That's easy – Cate Blanchett."'

Vanessa's face breaks into a grin. 'Now I remember why I fell in love with you,' she laughs, and a look passes between them. A look that says things are going to be OK. 'So how are you feeling, honey?' she asks sympathetically, turning to me.

'Like I've got the worst hangover.' I wince, rubbing my temple, which has started to throb again.

She smiles. 'Well, just as long as you're OK. When I think what could have happened . . .' Vanessa breaks off 'It really makes you realise what's important, doesn't it?' she says quietly, and I don't know if she's talking about me or her, or both of us.

'Now I think Charlotte should get some rest,' bosses Beatrice, interrupting, and there's a murmur of agreement and lots of promises to call.

Mum and Dad give me a goodbye kiss. 'Now before we go, do you need anything? I can pop to the shop.' Mum starts fussing, but Dad leads her out, promising to visit first thing tomorrow.

And now it's just me and Beatrice.

'I should be going too,' she says after everyone's filed out of the room. 'I've got a hot date.' She pulls a face and lets out a giggle.

'Thanks, Bea. For everything,' I say gratefully.

'Don't be silly. All part of the service.' She reaches for her coat and bags. 'Oh, and by the way, I picked up your mail for you. Looks mostly like lots of get-well cards.' Popping it on my bedside table, she disappears.

And then the room's completely empty and quiet, and I'm finally alone. Feeling suddenly exhausted, I sweep my eyes around the room, noticing for the first time that it's filled with flowers. I take a deep breath, letting everything sink in.

So that's it. It didn't really happen at all. It seemed so real and yet of course it couldn't *really* happen, could it? I smile to myself. Because although a part of me is sad that it was all just make-believe and I didn't actually meet my twenty-one-year-old self, I feel as if I reconnected with her somehow. Deep down inside.

Plus, let's face it, that was the most fun dream I've ever had. It certainly makes a change from the one about my teeth falling out, I realise, stifling a giggle.

My eyes fall back on the pile of cards, and realising my fingers work OK as long as I don't move my left arm, I start opening them. There's one from Melody, with a big lipstick kiss, a few more from my clients and one from Miles:

Sorry to hear about your accident. Get well soon.
P.S. Did you take out that health-and-sickness insurance policy I told you about? If so, you will be able to claim.

I smile to myself and thank him silently. Trust Miles, I muse fondly, reaching for the next card, then pause as I look at the envelope. It's covered in lots of different addresses and post-marks, as if it's been forwarded loads of times, until finally they got my correct address, I note, realising it's covered in all my old ones. Huh, how funny. I wonder what it is? I start tearing open the envelope and just then I hear a quiet knock on the door.

I glance up. It's probably the nurse, come to check on me.

My heart nearly stops.

It's Oliver.

'Hi.' He smiles bashfully and hovers at the doorway. 'I called your office and your assistant told me you'd had a bit of an accident.'

'Just a bit,' I reply, my heart hammering in my chest now. I feel absurdly nervous.

'I've heard hospital food isn't much good, so I bought you a dish from the pub.' He gestures to a tinfoil-covered plate he's holding. 'Fresh wild salmon, baby new potatoes and grilled asparagus.'

'Oh, um, thanks.' My voice wobbles a bit.

'I hope you haven't had your mercury ration for the week,' he adds, and laughs nervously.

I smile then there's a pause and we both fall silent.

Which is bizarre, as there's just so much I want to say, I realise, desperately constructing elaborate sentences in my head before blurting, 'I'm sorry.'

'I'm sorry.'

We speak at the same time and then laugh with a mixture of relief and self-consciousness.

'Shall I toss a coin to see who can apologise first?' he asks, raising an eyebrow.

'Look, I didn't mean those things I said—' I begin.

'Neither did I,' he interrupts. 'How about we call a truce? Start over?'

I smile, feeling a tiny ray of hope appearing from behind the black clouds that descended when we had our row.

'So you got a lot of get-well cards, huh?' he says, gesturing to the pile in front of me.

'Oh, yeah.' I nod, looking down at the card in my hand and tugging it out of the envelope.

Only it's not a card. It's a parking ticket. I smile ruefully. God, can you believe it? Those pesky bloody parking fines, they even find you in hospital, I think, looking at it. Which is when I notice it seems really old and faded. Hmm, that's odd – I glance at the details.

Car/Make Model: V W Beetle
Offence: parking in a permit-controlled area
Time: 6.28 p.m.

My stomach suddenly goes into freefall.

Date: 21 August 1997

For a split second I just stare at it, my thoughts frozen in shock. Then I jerk back up to speed. So it did happen! It wasn't a dream. This is the parking ticket that I got the first time I followed myself. I dropped it on the ground, but the council always keeps a record. They never let you get away without paying, not even if it was ten years ago. As the realisation hits, I feel a huge smile playing across my face.

'What is it?'

I snap back to see Oliver staring at me, looking puzzled.

'Oh, nothing,' I say quickly, trying to quell the delight that's rushing up inside of me. 'Just a parking ticket.'

'Crikey, I've never seen anyone so happy to get a parking ticket before.' He smiles with amusement.

I laugh, my mind racing, my thoughts tumbling over each other, everything clicking back into place. And that includes me and Oliver, I realise, glancing across at him and noticing he's still standing by the door.

'Do you want to come in and sit down? Stay a while?' I ask shyly. 'But you don't have to, obviously,' I add hastily, realising he's doubtless just come out of politeness. 'You've probably got to get back to work at the pub.'

Oh God, if he says he has to go, I don't know what I'm going to do.

'Actually, I think I'll take the evening off,' he replies. 'Can't leave the patient on her own, now can we?' Smiling, he folds his tall frame on to the plastic chair next to me.

'You can do that?' I say with surprise, feeling a secret beat of pleasure. 'I don't want you to get in trouble with your boss or anything.'

'Well, considering I am the boss, I don't think that will be a problem.' He smiles ruefully.

'The boss?' I repeat, puzzled.

'Yeah, I own the pub, and I've got another couple in London. Didn't I ever mention it?'

I realise I'm staring at him in astonishment.

'But I'd really like to expand abroad one day . . . open someplace in France, or Italy maybe.'

I suddenly blush bright red. And to think I called him 'just a barman'. 'No, I didn't know,' I say, with embarrassment.

'I guess there's a lot we don't know about each other,' he says, his eyes meeting mine. 'Maybe when you get out of here, we can do some catching up . . .' His voice trails off and we gaze at each other as if we're both thinking the same thing. 'Oh, by the way, before I forget . . .' He digs in his pocket. 'I found this.'

'My watch!' I exclaim. As he passes it to me, his fingers brush mine. A spark runs all the way down my spine.

'It had been kicked into a corner. I think someone must have stood on it.'

As I look at it, I realise it's broken. The hands have stopped. Time is literally standing still.

'I can get it fixed for you, if you'd like,' he says quietly, and I realise he hasn't let go of my fingers. I glance at them, and curling my fingers round his, I look up at him, wanting this moment to last for ever.

'Oh, there's no rush.' I smile. 'No rush at all.'

Epilogue

Nine Months later

'*Pardon, monsieur? Combien?*'
The market trader, an old man with a flat cap and Gauloise cigarette welded to his bottom lip, smiles at me as if I'm a native speaker, and just as I'm thinking that perhaps my pidgin French and dodgy accent aren't so bad, he rattles off something in French and leaves me totally lost.

'Um . . .' Digging in my purse, I wave a euro note hopefully. 'It's OK?'

Yes, I'm cheating, and trying to make it sound like French by making my sentences go up at the end isn't fooling anyone, but I've got my eye on that fabulous pair of dangly earrings.

The trader smiles and takes the note, then passes me my change and the earrings. There's lots of smiling and nodding, and I feel a beat of delight. See, we all speak the same language in the end, I think happily as I loop the earrings through my ears and give them a little shake in the mirror. They dance back, the silver strands and pink glass twinkling in the bright June sunshine. *So* much more me than pearl earrings, I think, feeling a burst of pleasure.

Waving goodbye to the vendor and saying *au revoir* (that's one phrase I do know), I continue weaving my way through the maze of stalls – selling everything from ornate jewellery to vintage clothes to handbags of every colour, size and description. Gosh, this is one of the best flea markets I've ever been to, I muse, consulting my guidebook again. 'The most famous flea market in Paris is the one at Porte de Clignancourt, officially called Les

Puces de Saint-Ouen, but known to everyone as Les Puces (The Fleas).'

'Les Puces,' I repeat to myself, breathing the aromas from the food stalls: delicious, sweet, sugary crêpes, savoury croques-monsieurs, freshly brewed *cafe au lait*. My mouth starts watering. Mmm, I wonder if it's nearly lunchtime yet? I think distractedly, wandering from one stall to the next, like a bumble-bee bouncing from flower to flower.

In the old days I would have known exactly what time it was. I would have already checked my watch a hundred times today, but I don't wear a watch any more. Plus I can't look at the clock on my mobile as I've left it back at the hotel. I pick up a raspberry-pink silk dress that's caught my eye. I'm totally out of communication and it feels great. No phones ringing. No BlackBerry buzzing. No emails pinging. I can actually have a conversation that lasts more than a couple of minutes without being interrupted.

Though perhaps not in French, I reflect, resorting to hand gestures and facial expressions to try to explain to the stallholder I want a larger size.

But then, I don't really carry my phone with me a lot these days. I don't have to, not since I made Bea partner and gave her full control of running the company. To tell the truth, I wish I'd done it much sooner. She's a complete natural and has hired staff, rented larger premises, taken on more clients. The business is doing better than ever.

And me? Well, I've taken a sabbatical to finish my novel. In fact I've enjoyed it so much that when I finish it, I might just write another. Or try my hand at a short story. Or even a screenplay. Who knows? I'm not going to look too far into the future. I'm living in the moment, and right at this moment I'm doing something I'm passionate about. Now, if ever that little voice in my head asks whether I'm happy, I answer without missing a beat. Yes. Totally.

The stallholder returns, smiling and with a larger size. Holding the dress against my body, I look at my reflection. Gone is the stressed-out, blow-dried, fully made-up woman I used to be; in her place is someone who leaves her hair to dry naturally, wears just a slick of lip gloss and can't remember the last time she had eczema. I've also gained a bit of weight these past few months due to my more relaxed diet, but I think I look a lot better, younger even, as my face isn't so gaunt. Plus my boobs have got bigger, and you need boobs for this dress, I decide, doing my best to haggle in French, before giving in and buying it for the asking price.

But I don't care – that's all part of the fun of shopping at markets. That's one of the things I rediscovered from my younger self. At least I think I did. To be honest, looking back now, I'm not entirely sure . . .

It's been nine months since my accident. My broken bones have healed, the scar on my brow has faded, and with it my certainty of what exactly happened the week before my car crash. Or didn't happen. Because, you see, with the passage of time the line's been blurred between what's real and imagined, what I believe and what I *want* to believe. Looking back now, I'm not so certain I ever did see my younger self that morning at the traffic lights, that I ever did get to spend a week with her, getting to know her and myself again. After all, let's face it, it does sound crazy. *More* than crazy.

In the weeks that followed there were a few things that made me wonder if Beatrice was right and I did just dream the whole lot. First of all the parking ticket got lost. When I came out of hospital, I looked for it, but it must have got thrown away by accident, so I never got to check the date.

And I was a bit groggy when I woke up. I could have made a mistake, misread the date, got it wrong somehow. And when I was well enough to drive, the diversion was gone and I never saw my younger self or the old Beetle again. Then, when I went back to my old house and knocked at the door, a young couple with a baby answered.

I continue walking through the market, my eyes wandering across the different stalls, on the lookout for a bargain.

But there is one thing that makes me wonder. When the police called me up to investigate the accident, they told me the last time it was a two-way street was in 1997. According to traffic records, it had been made into a one-way street about ten years ago, after a rather nasty car accident. 'The records appear to have been lost, but I seem to remember it involved a truck and a car,' the policeman had informed me over the phone, 'which is something of a coincidence.'

So maybe it did happen. Well, I like to think it did, but who knows? I was tempted to Google 'morphine and dreams', but I remembered what the doctor said. I'm trying to kick my Google habit. I've been clean for nine months now.

So did I meet my twenty-one-year-old self or not? Was it all a figment of my imagination, a desire so deep down in my subconscious to find myself that I ended up *literally* finding myself? I don't think I'll ever know the answer. But one thing is for certain: I've changed. I'm not that strung-out thirtysomething I was before the accident. I've learned how to relax, have fun, take holidays.

'I ordered you a glass of rosé.'

Reaching the little pavement café where we arranged to meet, I find Oliver already waiting for me at a table. Sunglasses on, sleeves rolled up, he's drinking a beer and examining the menu. Wherever we go Oliver examines menus, looking for interesting new combinations of flavours or unusual dishes.

'Thanks.' I smile, giving him a kiss as he curls his tanned arms round me and pulls me on to his knee. I take a sip of the chilled wine. 'Mmm, delicious,' I enthuse, and I'm not just talking about the wine.

We're in Paris for the weekend. I finally got round to using those tickets Vanessa bought me for my birthday last year. We caught the Eurostar over on Friday and checked into this amazing hotel with its own spa and Michelin-starred restaurant.

Though to be honest, we've spent most of our time in the bedroom, if you know what I mean.

'So what did you buy?' He smiles, then rolls his eyes. 'Don't tell me – everything!'

I laugh and start to show him all my goodies. He oohs and ahhs appropriately at my earrings, exclaims at my dress (even commenting on how it will match my new sandals) and doesn't laugh when I show him the vase I bought that's shaped like a guitar. Well, it seemed like a good idea at the time. Best of all, he doesn't tell me I should have invested the money I just spent in an ISA. And for that I truly love him.

But then there's a lot to love about Oliver. He's funny and kind and makes me laugh, and it doesn't hurt that I fancy the pants off him. That's not to say we don't row about things. Boy, can we row. But it's usually over as quickly as it starts, and then of course there's the making-up that comes afterwards.

In fact I used to wonder why we wasted all that time, why it took ten years and a whole strange set of circumstances to bring us together, but I've come to realise it's a good thing we didn't hook up when I was younger, as I wouldn't have appreciated him like I do now. And it wouldn't be as great. Which goes to prove, there *are* some things I've learned as I've got older.

Only now he's acting weird, I realise, as I move to the chair across from him, and he glances at me all shiftily.

'What's wrong?' I ask.

'Nothing,' he says, smiling tightly and taking a big swig of beer.

Oh-oh. Something's definitely up. I observe him for a moment, trying to think what it can be. I draw a blank.

'Shall we order?' I suggest brightly.

'Um . . . sure.' He nods. 'I'll have whatever you're having.'

Right, OK, that's it. Oliver never has what I'm having. He always spends ages deliberating carefully over the menu and then orders all these weird and wonderful combinations. I'm just opening my mouth to tell him so when he suddenly slides off his chair on to his knees.

Correction: one knee.

I feel my breath catching in the back of my throat. Oh my God, is he doing what I think he's doing?

He looks up at me. I don't think I've ever seen him so nervous. 'The first time I met you, I fell in love with you there and then,' he begins, his voice wobbling, 'but you didn't even notice me.'

I try to protest, but he interrupts, 'No, you didn't,' and smiles ruefully.

I blush. 'OK, I didn't.'

'Then you stood me up.'

'I didn't stand you up!' I cry. 'Well, OK, I did,' I admit begrudgingly, 'but only because I didn't get the message.'

'And then I met you again and I hated you.' He grins.

'No, I hated you.' I grin back.

'Well, I tried to hate you, but then when you cleaned up after Welly . . .' He wrinkles up his nose and glances at the ground. When he looks back up, his eyes meet mine and he holds my gaze. 'I fell in love with you all over again.'

Suddenly realising my throat is dry, I swallow nervously.

'Charlotte, it's been ten years, nine months and nineteen days.' Fumbling in his pocket, he pulls out a small antique jewellery box. 'Will you marry me?'

As he says those words, my heart flips right over.

Wordlessly, he passes me the tiny ring box. I open the lid and find nestled inside the most beautiful antique ring. An emerald, shaped like a tiny flower. And I have the weirdest sensation of having seen it before. It catches the sun, glinting, and I suddenly remember. Nine months ago. The old lady, sitting on the bench. She was wearing this ring. But that's impossible, *unless* . . .

My mind reels.

Unless that was me. Years from now. My older self, talking to my younger self. What was it she said? 'Life isn't complicated. It's very simple, really.'

I gaze at the ring, a million different emotions whooshing around inside me, then lift my eyes and look into Oliver's. And it's as if everything else disappears but the love I have for him. Suddenly it all makes sense.

'Yes.' I smile. One word. How much more simple can you get?

Oliver's face splits into a huge smile, and slipping the ring on to my finger, he scoops me up and twirls me round and round, until we're dizzy. Then he pulls me towards him and kisses me. Right here. In front of everyone. In a café in the middle of a Parisian flea market. With everyone staring. But I don't care. I've never been happier.

My mind slides back to Lottie. Just think, she's got all this to come. She's going to love it. And although I've thrown the list away, there's one last thing I want to add, only this time it's a piece of advice she gave me:

20. Hold on to your dreams.

And saying a silent thank-you to her, I smile up at Oliver and wrap my arms tightly round him. I'm sure as hell holding on to mine.

A NOTE FROM THE AUTHOR

If I knew then, what I know now . . .

My top ten list of things I would tell myself:

1. Wear sunscreen
Like my heroine, Charlotte Merryweather, I was a sun-bunny all through my twenties – the first sign of sunshine and I would slather myself in Hawaiian Tropic and baste myself until I turned the deepest mahogany. Fast forward to my thirties and you'll find me on the beach, sitting in the shade under a brolly, wearing a hat and slathered in SPF45.

2. Buy a flat in Notting Hill
When I first moved to London I rented a room in a big house and fell in love with the area. It was long before the movie of the same name, and there were none of the chi-chi restaurants and designer shops that are there now. Back then you could pick up a flat for a tenth of what it would cost today but I still thought they were too expensive! Just imagine, I could now be a zillion-pound property owner, chatting over the garden fence with my rich and famous neighbours, being invited to lots of glamorous parties . . . OK, I'll stop before I get too carried away.

3. Get your legs out
Because at twenty-one they're never going to look this good again. So take off your jeans, put on a mini-skirt, and do not take it off until you reach the age of thirty-five.

4. Do not go blonde
You'll look weird and your eyebrows won't match. Plus, the roots will kill you.

5. Buy that round-the-world ticket
Your career can wait. A year won't make any difference and the memories and experiences will last a lifetime.

6. He's not worth it
Trust me. In ten years' time you'll bump into him again and wonder what all the fuss was about.

7. Back away from those leather trousers
At twenty-one I spent a fortune on a pair of hand-made leather jeans. Not only were they high-waisted (gulp) but they were so skin-tight I had to use talcum powder to get them on. Yes. Really.

8. Start doing yoga
Just think I could be like Madonna! OK, I wouldn't perhaps go *that* far, but it would be nice to actually touch my toes . . .

9. You can achieve anything if you put your mind to it
I used to think that you had to be somehow 'special' or 'different' to be able write a book and get it published. I never thought that could happen to me. I could never be so lucky. It was only when I decided to give it a go and I actually sat down and wrote my first novel that I realised that the only thing that had been stopping me for all those years, was me. *What's New, Pussycat?* was published just over a year later, proving that although luck plays a small part in everything, it's mostly down to enthusiasm, self-belief and a bucket-load of determination. (Oh, and Kettle chips. Bags and bags of Kettle chips.)

10. At 21 you are more powerful than you can ever imagine
When I was younger I didn't have a clue about anything. I was broke, I lacked confidence, and my hair had a funny greenish tinge from dying it with henna. Little did I know that none of it mattered – at that age you have the world at your feet. So any twenty-one-year-olds out there reading this – take note!

Alexandra Potter, 2008

ALEXANDRA POTTER
ME AND MR DARCY

He's every woman's fantasy . . .

After a string of nightmare relationships, Emily Albright has decided she's had it with modern-day men. She'd rather pour herself a glass of wine, curl up with *Pride and Prejudice* and step into a time where men were dashing, devoted and honourable, strode across fields in breeches, their damp shirts clinging to their chests, and *weren't* into internet porn.

So when her best friend invites her to Mexico for a week of margaritas and men, Emily decides to book a guided tour of Jane Austen country instead.

She quickly realises she won't find her dream man here. The coach tour is full of pensioners, apart from one Mr Spike Hargreaves, a foul-tempered journalist sent to write a piece on why Mr Darcy's been voted the man most women would love to date.

Until she walks into a room and finds herself face-to-face with Darcy himself. And every woman's fantasy suddenly becomes one woman's reality.

HODDER

ALEXANDRA POTTER

BE CAREFUL WHAT YOU WISH FOR

'I wish I could get a seat on the tube . . . I hadn't eaten that entire bag of Maltesers . . . I could meet a man whose hobbies include washing up and monogamy . . . '

Heather Hamilton is always wishing for things. Not just big stuff – like world peace or for a date with Brad Pitt – but little, everyday wishes, made without thinking. With her luck, she knows they'll never come true . . .

Until one day she buys some lucky heather from a gypsy. Suddenly the bad hair days stop; a handsome American answers her ad for a housemate; and she starts seeing James – The Perfect Man who sends her flowers, excels in the bedroom, and isn't afraid to say 'I love you' . . .

But are these wishes-come-true a blessing or a curse? And is there such a thing as *too much* foreplay?

HODDER